"JEAN LORRAIN" (1855-1906) was the pseudonym of Paul Duval, adopted at the insistence of his father, a Norman ship-owner, who wanted to protect the family name from the disgrace of employment by a poet. A flamboyant homosexual dandy, when forced to make a living from his pen after his father died ruined, he became one of the most prolific and highest-paid journalists of the *fin-de-siècle*, and the personification, in his lifestyle as well as his writing, of the Decadent Movement. *Monsieur de Phocas. Astarté* (1901; tr. as *Monsieur de Phocas*), compounded out of numerous short stories, is a kind of retrospective summary of the Decadent world-view, written after he was forced to leave Paris because of health problems occasioned by his use of ether as a stimulant, which did not take long to kill him thereafter. English translations of some of his short stories are contained in *Nightmares of an Ether-Drinker* (Tartarus Press, 2002; reprinted by Snuggly Books, 2016), *The Soul-Drinker and Other Decadent Fantasies* (Snuggly Books, 2016) and *Masks in the Tapestry* (Snuggly Books, 2017).

BRIAN STABLEFORD has been publishing fiction and non-fiction for fifty years. His fiction includes an eighteen-volume series of "tales of the biotech revolution" and a series of half a dozen metaphysical fantasies set in Paris in the 1840s, featuring Edgar Poe's Auguste Dupin. His most recent non-fiction projects are *New Atlantis: A Narrative History of British Scientific Romance* (Wildside Press, 2016) and *The Plurality of Imaginary Worlds: The Evolution of French* roman scientifique (Black Coat Press, 2016); in association with the latter he has translated approximately a hundred and fifty volumes of texts not previously available in English, similarly issued by Black Coat Press.

SNUGGLY BOOKS

JEAN LORRAIN

ERRANT VICE

Translated and with an Introduction by

BRIAN STABLEFORD

THIS IS A SNUGGLY BOOK

ISBN: 978-1-943813-71-1

CONTENTS

INTRODUCTION

T HE ITEMS making up *Le Vice errant* by Jean Lorrain were initially published as a series of stories in the daily newspaper *Le Journal* in 1901. The first part of "Propos d'Opium," here translated as "Opium Talk," appeared in the 29 January issue and the first part of "Masques de Londres et d'ailleurs" (tr. as "Masks in London and Elsewhere") in the 24 March issue. The first item in the "Coins de Byzance" sequence, titled "La Baronne Nydorf" in the "Salad Russe" section of the book version, appeared in the 7 May issue, and the 28 chapters of "Les Noronsoff" appeared at slightly irregular intervals thereafter until the final episode, "L'Effondrement" (tr. as "The Collapse") appeared in the 29 November issue. The book version appeared a few weeks thereafter from Albin Michel in 1902.

The book must have sold reasonably well; the copy reproduced on gallica is labeled "eighteenth edition," which probably signified an eighteenth printing of a thousand copies each, although the list of other works by the author advertised therein suggest that it dates from later than 1905. At any rate, "Les Noronsoff" was judged worthy of being reprinted subsequently as a *feuilleton* serial, under that title, in the weekly supplement of another Parisian daily newspaper, *La Lanterne*, in 29 episodes, beginning with a slightly expanded version of the episode separated in the book version as "La Baronne Nydorf," on 22 December 1903 and running through the first half of 1904.

It is worth observing that Lorrain's contributions to *Le Journal* in the first few years of the twentieth century, when he was resident in Nice, were not published in the regular *feuilleton* section of the paper, which was a separate section at the bottom of page two, in which the episodes of a serial novel appeared on a daily basis. Lorrain's contributions appeared on the front page of the paper, with a headline similar to the other articles on that page, often, but not always, as the leading item. This meant that Lorrain was not strictly bound by the narrow word-limit imposed by the volume of space available below the *feuilleton* proper, permitting him slightly greater length and variation of his copy.

That fashion of presentation also blurred the difference between the stories that Lorrain contributed to the paper and other articles that he published there, under the terms of what appears to have been a commitment to deliver copy of some sort every week, or thereabouts. As in the present set of stories, Lorrain routinely inserted himself into the works of fiction he had been producing for various newspapers since the late 1880s, posing as a reporter narrating anecdotes about himself or—more frequently—passing on narrations made by people he encounters: a narrative strategy that seemed considerably more natural in the original context of publication than it tends to do in a book.

As with any ordinary newspaper serial, Lorrain clearly improvised his work for *Le Journal* as he went along, and although he was delivering copy at weekly intervals rather than every day, he still had to cope with the usual problems of producing serial fiction when his work occasionally expanded in the writing to the length of a novella or even a novel. Although each of the shorter items in the 1901 series would probably have been planned out in full in advance, the "Coins de Byzance" sequence cannot have been, and it is therefore not surprising that the storyline tends to wander somewhat, continually subject to *ad hoc* improvisations.

The result of all these aspects of the original publication mean that the finished product of *Le Vice errant*, seen as an ensemble, is more than a trifle odd, and it might be as well to bear these circumstances in mind while reading the work. There are, however, several other aspects of the story told in "Coins de Byzance" that can be more fully appreciated with a more detailed awareness of the precise point in Lorrain's life and career at which he was producing the story.

✳

"Jean Lorrain" had been baptized Paul-Alexandre-Martin Duval in 1855, in Fécamp, a small coastal town in Normandy. His father, Amable Duval, was an apparently prosperous but secretly profligate ship-owner whose vessels were involved in trans-Atlantic trade. Paul Duval appears to have been a somewhat pampered child, indulged by his mother, and he was initially educated at home before completing the initial phase of his education at a seminary, which he hated. He later recalled that he had loved tales of enchantment and dressing up, being particularly fascinated by princesses—interests echoed throughout his life and career, and still evident, albeit muted and deliberately distorted, in "Coins de Byzance."

The Normandy shore was a favorite refuge of English exiles who crossed the channel to avoid scandal. Algernon Swinburne, who had lived near Fécamp for some years, remained the model of notoriety so far as Lorrain's home town was concerned; the lurid decor of Swinburne's house, and the scandalous things that were rumored to have gone on there, remained common knowledge long after the poet's return to England. The legend of his sojourn remained firmly fixed in Paul Duval's memory, again frequently echoed in his life and work. Swinburne provided the forename for the English author Algernon Filde, who plays a minor role in "Coin de Byzance," and the title of some of the works credited to Filde echo those of works by Swinburne. Although Paul Duval never met Swinburne, he did become acquainted with Lord Arthur Somerset, an Englishman of similar tastes and inclinations, who also lived near Fécamp for a while and seems to have had a more direct influence over Jean Lorrain's ideas and attitudes.

Lord Arthur Somerset's influence seems to have been outweighed initially by another summer visitor to the Normandy coast, Judith Gautier, whom Paul Duval met in Fécamp in 1873, and by whom he was fascinated. Judith, who was ten years older than him, was recently separated from her husband, the already-notorious writer Catulle Mendès, who was later to become one of the pillars of the Decadent Movement, producing large quantities of short fiction with narrative strategies and themes closely analogous to those produced by Jean Lorrain.

Judith Gautier does not appear to have attached any importance to Paul Duval's brief infatuation—she made no mention of it in her autobiography—but he was later to comment on the change it had wrought in his life in such terms that Edmond de Goncourt, Lorrain's closest friend and principal mentor within the literary community of Paris, became convinced that it had been the ruination of him. Goncourt came to believe—falsely, one presumes—that Lorrain's homosexuality was some kind of traumatic response to his doomed infatuation with Judith, and that everything he did and became thereafter was a kind of painfully protracted moral and physical suicide. Perhaps that is implausible, but what is certain is that almost all of Lorrain's longer works of prose fiction, including "Coins de Byzance," are indeed graphic accounts of slow and exceedingly painful processes of moral and physical suicide. Edmond de Goncourt did not live long enough to read "Coins de Byzance," but we can be quite sure that he would have appreciated its genius—and also that he would have loathed it.

When he had completed his military service, Paul Duval was sent by his father to study law, but he had no interest in that career, and when he announced his firm determination to follow a literary vocation instead, his father agreed to provide a modest allowance, on condition that the family name was veiled by a pseudonym. In 1880, therefore, Paul Duval became Jean

Lorrain. He found lodgings in Montmartre, and launched himself into the stereotyped lifestyle of a literary Bohemian, hanging out in Le Chat Noir with the members of Émile Goudeau's literary club, the Hydropathes, and the most colorful future subscribers to the Decadent and Symbolist Movements. His first collection of poetry, published entirely under those overlapping influences, *Sang des dieux* (1882), had a frontispiece by Gustave Moreau, and Moreau's art became a very considerable influence on Lorrain's literary imagery. In 1883, he became a regular participant in Charles Buet's salon, where he made his most significant literary acquaintances: Jules Amédée Barbey d'Aurevilly, Joris-Karl Huysmans and "Rachilde" (Marguerite Eymery, who subsequently married Alfred Vallette, the editor of the most successful Symbolist periodical, the *Mercure de France*).

Barbey d'Aurevilly was a leading exponent of the philosophy of "dandyism," whose manifesto he had provided in *Du dandyisme et de G. Brummell* (1845), and although Lorrain had neither the means nor the breeding to compete with such notorious homosexual dandies as Comte Robert de Montesquiou and Pierre Loti, he did what he could to keep up appearances, to the extent that Remy de Gourmont described him, by no means inaptly, as "the sole disciple of Barbey d'Aurevilly," not merely for his attire but for the plangent echoes contained in his work of Barbey's notorious collection of misogynistic *contes cruels*, *Les Diaboliques* (1874; tr. as "The She-Devils").

When Lorrain met Huysmans, the latter author was working on his classic handbook of dandyism, *À rebours* (1884; tr. as *Against the Grain* and *Against Nature*), which became the prose Bible of the Decadent Movement. Lorrain's fourth collection of poetry, *Les Griseries* (1887), consists of material explicitly inspired by *À rebours*, and much of his fiction echoes the same inspiration. "Coins de Byzance" can be seen as one of several modified clones of *À rebours*, similarly providing elaborate character studies of aristocrats afflicted with all the manifestations of ennui and spleen, while dying slowly of various physical afflictions and desperately seeking some kind of psychological remedy for their complex malaise.

Rachilde's literary career was yet to begin in earnest in 1883, although she had already started to cultivate a reputation as an *enfant terrible*, and an article that Lorrain wrote about her, entitled "Madame Salamandre," became the effective springboard of her reputation and public image—a calculatedly scandalous appearance that she cultivated carefully in public, and scrupulously belied in private. She did, however, share Lorrain's passionate fascination for masked balls, which were then in their last period of great fashionability, and he became her regular escort—with the blessing of Alfred Vallette, who knew that he had nothing to fear from Lorrain—competing with her in the outrageousness of their costumes.

While he cultivated these acquaintances, Lorrain was making a name for himself with the outspoken reviews that he wrote for the *Courrier Français*. His negative reviews were vitriolic, while his favorable ones tended to the opposite extreme, and their insistent flamboyance swiftly won him a reputation that attracted at least as much scorn and vituperation as admiration and praise, but which sold papers, and eventually made him one of the highest-paid journalists in Paris—which was why *Le Journal*, the most pretentious of the Parisian dailies, commissioned him in 1901 to produce items on a weekly basis that were proudly displayed on page one: items in which he was naturally expected to live up to his reputation in spectacular style.

In 1885 Lorrain met Edmond de Goncourt, who was thirty-three years older than he was, but who swiftly took the younger writer under his wing, perhaps seeing him as a kind of replacement for his younger brother, who had died young in 1870. Lorrain became a regular at Goncourt's famous salon, the "Grenier." Goncourt's tutelage had its limits, however, and one can only imagine how distraught and disappointed Lorrain must have been in 1896, when he found out that Goncourt had left him out of the list of writers mentioned in his will as the recipients of the bequest that permitted the foundation of the "Goncourt Academy." It probably hurt him almost as much as the discovery he had made ten years earlier, when Amable Duval died in 1886, leaving nothing to his children but debts.

Lorrain's mother had kept control of her own money, and was not reduced to absolute penury by her husband's hidden profligacy, but she could not maintain her son's allowance. His burgeoning career as a journalist thus became a matter of extreme urgency, but if he began to regret the many enemies he had made with his vicious reviews, it was too late for him to change course; his image was already formed, and could only be cultivated—which he did with great success, but not without personal cost. In order to maintain his rate of production, he had recourse to artificial stimulants, including ether. The ether kept him awake when necessary, and also provided him with hallucinations that he eventually mined extensively in his short fiction, but its long-term effects on his health were catastrophic.

When he left Montmartre in 1887 Lorrain installed himself in an apartment in the Rue de Courty, which he furnished in a calculatedly bizarre fashion that took account of the lessons he had learned from Lord Arthur Somerset, Barbey d'Aurevilly and *À rebours*. Under the hallucinogenic influence of ether, however, the apartment came to seem direly discomfiting, and he began to refer to it as his "haunted house". He moved to Auteuil in 1890, telling his friends that he was doing so in the hope of recovering his health and composure. When he invited Oscar Wilde to dinner there in 1891, he thought the occasion sufficiently important to invite Anatole France as well, and the notoriously antisocial writer accepted. Marcel Schwob, who shared with Lorrain an enormous admiration for Edgar Poe, was also present. Schwob is cited in "Masques de Londres et d'ailleurs," and Wilde provided the other half of the compound figure of "Algernon Filde" in "Coins de Byzance."

Lorrain had probably given up ether-drinking by the time he moved to Auteuil, some time before he began producing the definitive series of *contes d'un buveur d'éther* that were reprinted under that subtitle in the collection *Sensations et Souvenirs* (1895). He was, however, already living with consequences that were to plague him permanently, and ultimately to kill him. He had always suffered health problems, often manifest as recurrent fevers, but the ether ulcerated his gut and eventually led to a part of his bowel being surgically resected by the famous surgeon Samuel Pozzi. It was in Pozzi's clinic in Paris that he eventually died, in 1906, from peritonitis consequent on an enema that blew a hole in his rectum, administered during a trip to the capital. Although "Coins de Byzance" certainly cannot be regarded as autobiographical in any straightforward sense, the author was surely capable of sympathizing ardently with the intestinal troubles suffered horribly and ignominiously by Wladimir Noronsoff.

In 1893, Lorrain's mother moved into the house in Auteuil, and lived with her son for the rest of his life, moving to Nice with him in 1900, from which she had to be summoned when he was dying in the hope of catching his last breath. In Lorrain's many stories echoing his childhood in Fécamp, his mother is always represented with the utmost fondness and respect, and he also recalled the pleasure that she took helping him choose his pseudonym. What we do not know, however, is what Madame Duval thought of Jean Lorrain's work and lifestyle, and how the two of them got on while living together, first in Auteuil and then in Nice. We do not know whether Madame Duval even read "Coins de Byzance," or whether, if she did, she detected any echoes of her beloved but afflicted son in the character of Prince Wladimir and his troubled relationship with his mother. One can only hope that she did not.

The *fin-de-siècle* was winding down throughout Lorrain's career, a prisoner of the calendar, and Lorrain, as the most outspokenly fascinated celebrant and most enthusiastic scourge of the mores of the yellow nineties, and the very archetype of its decadence in the eyes of some observers, would have been keenly aware of the countdown even if his health had not been suffering badly enough to motivate a removal to Nice before the century's end, where he installed himself in the Villa Bounin. We do not know whether the physician who treated him there read "Coins de Byzance" either, or what he thought of the depiction of Monsieur Rabastens if he did, but in that instance there would be no cause for retrospective alarm. The citizens and winter visitors of Nice might well have had mixed feelings about the story, although they surely had reason to be proud of the fact that the town plays such an important and prestigious role in setting the scene of the melodrama.

It was not long after settling in Nice that Lorrain produced his most famous and most definitive novel, his first revised clone of *À rebours*: a kind of retrospective summary and analysis of the spleen that was supposedly characteristic of the *fin-de-siècle*, and of an archetypical sufferer from the condition: *Monsieur de Phocas. Astarté* (1901; tr. as *Monsieur de Phocas*). In some ways "Coins de Byzance" is a companion-piece to *Monsieur de Phocas*, similarly offering a type specimen of an individual afflicted with all the typical symptoms of contemporary "decadence" and detailing his attempts to combat his existential malaise. As with any such companion piece, however, it is clearly subject to the pressure of melodramatic inflation, forced to outreach its predecessor in its bizarrerie. Whereas the protagonist of the earlier novel is a French aristocrat and his particular ennui is a very French ennui, Prince Wladimir is Russian; his ennui is far more exotic in its exaggeration and far more Poesque in its alleged origin, although its direct inspiration was surely the history of a similarly cursed family of Russian aristocrats briefly but graphically related in Catulle Mendès' archetypally Decadent novel *Méphistophela* (1890; tr. as *Mephistophela*).

In the two years that separated the two newspaper serializations of "Coins de Byzance," Lorrain's career continued to thrive, even though his health was deteriorating. Early in 1904, however, he suffered a serious setback when the artist Jeanne Jacquemin, recognizing that one of Lorrain's stories for *Le Journal* was based on an episode in her life, sued him for libel. He was not only convicted—on very flimsy grounds—but the court imposed a massive punitive fine, far out of proportion to the offense. Not long thereafter he was summoned to court again to answer a formal charge of corrupting public morals by literary means, brought against *Monsieur de Phocas. Astarté*. Similar charges had been successfully leveled in the past at Charles Baudelaire, Gustave Flaubert, Catulle Mendès, Jean Richepin and Paul Adam, to name but a few, but all of those writers had found defenders to protest the iniquity of the accusation and argue stridently in their favor. Lorrain, much to his chagrin, did not. Hardly anyone came forward to speak in his defense—the most notable exception was Colette—and he seems to have been deeply hurt by the fact that Huysmans remained silent.

Lorrain continued to write for *Le Journal* and *La Vie parisienne* but he soon began signing his articles "Le Cadavre," with prophetic accuracy. We can, of course, be perfectly certain that he was fully aware of the echoes of his own condition that can be identified in the one that he had sketched out in relation to Wladimir Noronsoff in the last few chapters of "Coins de Byzance," and can only hope that he was still able to laugh at their calculated grotesquerie in the months preceding his own final disaster.

It is, in fact, the blackly comic grotesquerie of "Coins de Byzance" that makes it outstanding within Lorrain's oeuvre, and thus a little more difficult to weigh up than *Monsieur de Phocas*. It is a tragicomedy, and many readers might find it difficult now, as they must have done in 1901, to decide exactly when it might be appropriate to laugh and when to mourn, or to be horrified. Many readers would doubtless have found it difficult to find much sympathy for the protagonist of *Monsieur de Phocas*, and might well have found an element of absurdity in his strange plight, but Wladimir is removed by a further order of magnitude from what are conventionally considered to be natural sympathies. He is not merely a monster, but a caricaturish monster—

and yet, his brazen insistence that he is not responsible for his own faults is not entirely unwarranted, and even if his mother can be entirely exculpated, the fact remains that the vengeance inflicted upon him by Comtesse Schoboleska is so far out of proportion to the harm he has done her that he could plausibly claim to be more sinned against than sinning. Even if one leaves out of account, therefore, the intriguing question of the extent to which Lorrain poured his own feelings into his depiction of the character, "Coins de Byzance" is possessed of a fascinating moral and artistic complexity.

It is arguable that "Coins de Byzance" might read better in isolation than in the context of the portmanteau endeavor out of which it grew, as it was subsequently presented in *La Lanterne*. Certainly, if one looks back from "L'Effondrement" at "Propos d'Opium," it is hard to think of them as parts of the same work, or to see how one could possibly have led to the other. Even the introduction of Monsieur Rabastens in "Masques de Londres et d'ailleurs," which then allows an almost continuous flow of the frame narrative through his loquacious mouth, leaves a vast gulf between the initial account of the masked muggers of the London Docklands and the scenes for which Nice forms the backdrop, and the Poesque early chapters of the story of the Noronsoffs clash somewhat with the story's eventual development. Nevertheless, there is a process of organic evolution underlying the whole enterprise, the embryonic phases of which are not without interest. When Lorrain started writing the series he had only been living in Nice for a matter of months, and was only making his first tentative steps in acquainting himself with the society of the town; as the year 1901 wore on, however, he must not only have broadened that acquaintance but also, in quite a profound sense, have been absorbed by the locale and refined his attitude to it— and thus enabled to see within it "corners of Byzantium."

The symbolic invocation of the term "Byzance" in the title of the longest story in the portmanteau is, as several references in the story make clear, a deliberate echo of the title of Jean Lombard's

Byzance (1890), which followed up the same author's account of the emperor Heliogabalus in *L'Agonie* (1888). Although Lombard—a native of the Var—had died in 1891 without having made much of an impact on his contemporaries, in spite of vocal championship from both Lorrain and Rachilde, his two key works were reprinted in 1901 after the enormous success of Pierre Louÿs' *Aphrodite, moeurs antiques* (1888) had started the bandwagon rolling, and achieved much greater sales and fame then than they had the first time around, with the result that Lombard was at the height of his posthumous celebrity while "Coins de Byzance" was being serialized, and had been belatedly credited with having produced archetypal images of imperial decadence—and hence, logically, of the ultimate in decadence.

The Paris of *À rebours* and *Monsieur de Phocas* could play host to a particular kind of sophisticated decadence that could not plausibly be imaged anywhere else, but it was a markedly different kind of decadence from that imagined by Lombard—which was, indeed, intimately bound up with *moeurs antiques*. It was, therefore, necessary to look away from Paris for a purer and more extreme variety of decadence—perhaps to imperial Russia, although the climate had changed drastically there too. Nice was probably not the first location that would have sprung to many minds for the setting of a modern version of quasi-imperial ultimate decadence—with all the absurdity inherent in that notion—but with a little creative imagination, and a certain blackly ironic delight, Jean Lorrain was able to see the Côte d'Azur as an arena where echoes of Byzantium might resound—and the story series contained in *Le Vice errant* is a curious map of the process of that discovery, which would be incomplete without its earlier phases.

That, presumably, is why Lorrain chose to make up the book version of *Le Vice errant* as he did, when it would have been perfectly simple for him to publish "Coins de Byzance" as a novel and put the other items into one of the many short story collections that he compiled in some abundance while living in Nice. Naturally, I have followed the author's example in the present translation.

*

This translation was made from the copy of the Albin Michel edition reproduced on the Bibliothèque Nationale's *gallica* website. There is an error in that text, whereby all but the first few lines of the chapters entitled "Le Complot" and "L'Horoscope" have been transposed, creating a radical discontinuity in the story-line. Having evidently noticed the discontinuity, Albin Michel's copy editor switched the order of the two chapters in the main body of the text, although the original order remains on the contents page. The result of that gross transposition, however, is that the first few lines of text in each chapter are misplaced. (The text of the newspaper version is correct, but the book version is slightly revised, especially with respect to the names of the characters; the book was presumably set from a manuscript rather than the newspaper pages, and two of the pages of the manuscript—the first ones in each of the relevant chapters—must have been accidentally switched.) Neither the author nor Albin Michel's proofreader seem to have noticed the residual disruption of the continuity in the story after the transposition of the chapters. Whether the mistake has been corrected in any subsequent French version of the text, I do not know, but I have amended the continuity of the text in the chapters titled "The Plot" and "The Horoscope" in this translation, in order to conform with the text of the serial version, as consulted in *gallica*.

With regard to the titles of the various characters, I have normally retained the French versions used in the original—not inappropriate for Russian titles at the time, at least in Nice—but I have altered one or two where the narrative places their usage firmly in an English, German or Italian context.

—Brian Stableford

ERRANT VICE

OPIUM TALK

OPIUM TALK

I

"AND they haven't even been able to establish the identity of the victim. From the very beginning of the affair I foresaw that the crime would be classed among the Xs, the unknowns. As the physicians say, the child was wrongly presented."

"Head first!"

"Horrible; even the head was mutilated."

"Monsieur Cochefert has gone there, carrying his three hundred francs."[1]

"The price of blood, fifteen louis! That puts a very low value on denunciation."

"People denounce for less."

"In politics—but that's a vocation."

"And even a pleasure."

"A hope of advancement, the petty joys of rancor."

"Lukewarm rancor, vengeance being a dish best eaten cold. Now, in the criminal world, denunciation is a joy that doesn't pay well and could cost the sensualist who indulges in it a great deal; only women denounce there, obedient, as always, to their nerves. Instinctive, impulsive and passionate, like all creatures that live close to nature—and murder and rapine are primitive gestures—the mistresses of thieves and murderers only deliver

---

1 Armand-Constant Cochefert (1850-1911) was the head of the Sûreté in Paris in the mid 1890s.

their lover out of spite, anger, jealousy or a need for immediate revenge; abandoned, they denounce the man they loved yesterday in order to take him away from a rival; betrayed, they betray blindly, recklessly, risking all for all, for they don't realize what a terrible punishment they are risking by squealing. That special world has severities and rigors unknown to our law for delinquents to its code; from one day to the next the woman who has delivered her man is condemned by the entire army of crime, and that army holds Paris from the plains of Gennevilliers to the quarries of Vanves, from the Route de la Révolte to Les Lilas and the abattoirs of Grenelle.

"Interdiction, the Papacy's formidable weapon against kings and the powerful over the centuries, lives again in the heart of modern Paris against the snitch—the man or woman who informs on an accomplice. Once the guilty party has 'turned rat,' the 'grass' can change residence and stay on the other side of the city in some honest market-gardening suburb, but the word will travel from gang to gang, district to district, and the friends of the victim will set forth on the hunt. Then, one morning, at the corner of a deserted side street, along the wall of a cemetery or in a ditch in the fortifications, a disfigured cadaver will be found, massacred, with multiple stab-wounds, and the police will recognize the daughter of such-and-such, the ex-mistress of such-and-such—the terror arrested two months ago, a year ago, or whatever—police informer. The arrest of Bibi from Montmartre or Charlot from Montrouge is avenged, in accordance with the justice of robbers and pimps."

"My compliments, you know them well."

"Deep down, as a député knows the tax-payers' pockets."

"Yes, you're full of documents."

"Don't you fear trouble someday?"

"Trouble! You're slandering them. They're charming people, much more reliable in relations than the majority of socialites, who have no solidarity between them and, when a back is hardly turned, will abuse and tear into one another with a laxity that only the looseness of their dentures excuses. Oh, the monotony of the gossip heard in the course of the year from the Plaine Monceau to the Faubourg Saint-Honoré! Not the slightest variety, not the slightest unexpected element in the calumnies being hawked. That's why I've made the decision to travel for three months in summer and three months in winter; on my return I find the same faces, a little more wrinkled, and the same talk, a little more faded."

"Which maintains the desire for departures in you."

"You said it. The stupidity of people has revealed the beauty of landscapes to me. There's some good in misfortune."

"And your friends the criminals and malefactors, do you always find them chivalrous, devoted and present at roll-call?"

"I confess that they reserve surprises for me. Some of them are always missing: Julot has been stabbed, Victor is purging a sentence at Fresnes, police raids have done for some, one is in Père-Lachaise and another in the hospital; the ranks are thinned out—poor us! Which permits me to regret them, and I'm grateful to them for the sadness their disappearance causes me. There's no true joy without some melancholy. And finally, there are some who have gone to the bad and joined the police."

"As one becomes a senator among us!"

"You're hard on my friends. In sum, that's a lot of jabber to establish that Monsieur Cochefert is on a false trail with his fifteen-louis reward. The man who talked for that price would barely have enough to get a train ticket to Marseille, and not enough left when he got there to board a ship. What could he do? Live for a week—and then what? Work like a good-for-nothing, mixing plaster for masons or unloading trunks at stations, when one has a crew in Paris, a nice turn, mates and everything? Break his life, his friendships, an entire career and risk the rest for fifteen lousy louis, when one can find that by turning out the pockets of a mark?—no, not so stupid. Oh, if Monsieur Cochefert had gone as far as two thousand, perhaps he'd have learned something; for that price, someone might talk. With two thousand in hand, five hundred for getting kitted out and traveling expenses, one leaves the country with the rest, and in Genoa or Barcelona, or some cheap hole in the sun between Nice and Toulon, one can go to ground with fifteen hundred francs, have oneself forgotten, buy a business under a false name and go straight . . . become an honest man and finally rest easy. Yes, for two thousand, I've often thought, Monsieur Cochefert might perhaps have known something."

"But two thousand is quite a sum!"

"Yes, I know that one works for less in the Chambre, but what those fellows scratch is for gloves and cigars, as they say at the club, they have their twenty-five-franc-a-day député's emoluments for material."

"And messieurs the murderers live from day to day, so they have great needs, and one can't let go of a career for fifteen louis—and that's why no one will ever discover the identity of this mysterious cadaver."

"Assuming that he had been murdered."

Assuming that he had been murdered!

Instinctively, all three of us raised our heads. Nonchalantly slumped amid the cushions of a divan, de Germont smiled the double smile of his bright teeth in his blond beard and his blue Mediterranean eyes. With a weary gesture he finished rolling a cigarette between his fingers, and was now enjoying his effect.

We were in an opium-smoking room that the few continentals exiled to Bastia had installed in the upper city, the old Genoese city in the vicinity of the citadel, in one of those curious houses of seven or eight stories whose Italian terraces overlook the sea: a house of port workers, open day and night, yawning over the street with the false appearance of a tannery. Oh, the steep, narrow, flagstoned streets of old Bastia, and their glacial aspect of corridors strangled between two fortresses, in the eternal shadow of their heights, tall houses overhanging with all their stories the quasi-funeral slabs of their causeway! And when one raises one's eyes, cut out by the advancement of the roofs, that thin—oh, so thin—strip of blue sky!

In that quarter of old corsairs, de Germont had rented a floor in one of the high black houses of the Rue Saint-Jean, had organized a summary installation of drapes and divans, and, twice a week, gathered a few bachelor friends there, companions in exile, retained in Bastia momentarily by their posting or their business affairs, continentals run aground far from France and Paris in that primitive, odorous and somber Corsica, where an unspeakable distress, whatever one does, always grips the heart.

Evening gatherings . . . first one took tea, sometimes one got drunk on raki or myrtle liqueur, got drunk, above all on dreams and memories, talked about the colonies, Paris and France, France above all and always; and sometimes, at about eleven o'clock, when the tramontane was blowing too strongly over the quays of Bastia to attempt a descent to the Rue des Glacis and a visit to the demoiselles, a little opium-smoking party was organized.

Germont had been in Tonkin; Tupier had spent two years in China; Bienvenu, the naval officer, had made all the crossings from the Levant to Constantinople to Smyrna, and the others, out of curiosity, or slackness and the desire to thwart their ennui, had also ended up getting a taste for the green poison of opium.

How, on the first evening of my arrival in Bastia, had I been introduced smoothly into the circle, nevertheless so tight, of that particular smoking-room? A mystery. That is one of the privileges of bad reputations, and one of the great charms of my voyages: all the suspect places are immediately open to the author of *Monsieur de Phocas*, and my name alone defies the most severe prohibitions.

In Bastia, it had sufficed for me to be announced to be invited—an invitation that I had been careful not to decline; winter evenings are long in those little Corsican cities, and all the shops in Bastia close at eight o'clock.

Assuming that he had been murdered! We were still mixing drinks, sufficiently dosed with mastic, chartreuse and kummel, with the addition by some of Benedictine, and by Germont of Spanish anisette; the opium pipes had not yet been taken out of their cases.

Germont's hypothesis revolted everyone's ideas.

"Are you as influenced as that by Madame de Thèbes' horoscope?"[1] hazarded Captain Tupier. "Truly, Germont, I didn't know you were so nervy."

Germont shrugged his shoulders.

Then Bienvenu said: "You don't believe it to be an amphitheater farce? I know that they hesitated momentarily over a macabre prank—interns at the Hôpital Saint-Louis were summoned, an orderly thrown out, but the police had to abandon that trail . . . like all the others."

With a little tap on Bienvenu's hand, Germont made the ash fall from the cigarette that the officer had just allowed to go out.

"Yes, I set aside the hypothesis of anatomical debris removed from a hospital and strewn by joyful interns with the aim of terrorizing; but can't you admit a case of sudden and natural death in circumstances such that the honor and the situation of a woman, or even a young woman, and the respectability of an entire family, necessitated the disappearance, and above all the anonymity, of the corpse? It wouldn't be the first time that such a thing has happened. One doesn't always die in a bad place, and the fairground performer's motto: *Quickly, a plank and salts*, isn't always apt; it's sometimes necessary, above all, that no one knows where the cadaver came from.

"You've all read Barbey d'Aurevilly's 'Le Rideau cramoisi,'[2] and the terrible scene where the lover, barefoot and in his chemise, traverses the bedroom of Alberte's parents with his mistress's corpse on his back, still warm and supple from the supreme embrace, the body of the young woman that a spasm has just killed in his arms, in his bed, that of a guest and an officer! Say that, instead of going to join the officer in his room, Alberte had received him in hers and that it was him the aneurism had bumped off; what

1 "Madame de Thèbes" was the pseudonym of the Parisian clairvoyant Anne Savigny (1845-1916), who published her prophecies every year in an almanac.
2 "Le Rideau cramoisi" (tr. as "The Crimson Curtain") is one of the stories in *Les Diaboliques*.

10

would that ardent daughter of an honest father and mother have done?

"Then again, in d'Aurevilly's story, the lovers live under the same roof, Alberte could have got out of it by throwing herself at the feet of her parents and confessing everything; the worthy folk would have replaced the dead man in his own bed and all scandal would have been avoided. But admit for a moment this hypothesis: your sister, your daughter or your mother—I dare anything, too bad!—arrives in your room, crazed and bewildered by fear, in the middle of the night, and then, stammering, drags you to her room, to her unmade bed, a bed that one cannot doubt, and in that bed, there's a man, a man whose nudity and attitude permit you even less doubt . . . and that man is unknown; worse, he's a rogue. He has a fine figure and dirty feet—don't interrupt me, Messalinas are everywhere; Lust doesn't choose her prey, she finds it . . . An unknown ruffian is lying dead in your sister's, your daughter's or your mother's bed; he's died in such and such conditions. Tomorrow the domestics will be in the know, the whole house informed; tomorrow, it's a scandal, the inevitable, frightful scandal, the police, investigations, your name in the papers, articles in the press, and you're a surgeon or a physician or a butcher. What would you do?"

Germont had emphasized his final words in a frightful silence; we were all silent, dolorously oppressed. Nothing could be heard but the regular plaint, as obsessive as a death-rattle, of the Mediterranean over the blocks of the mole, at the entrance to the old port.

II

There was a rather long silence.

"You definitely have a liking for the macabre, Germont. Another career missed! You'd have been a precious collaborator for Ponson du Terrail."

The charm was broken, the oppressive nightmare charm installed in each of us by Germont's terrifying hypotheses. In his turn, he kept silent, his thick and sensual eyelids half-fallen over his bright eyes, as if lying in ambush behind an enigmatic smile.

One sensed that, withdrawn into himself, the criminal logician he had just revealed was observing, and preparing a new attack. His retreat was only a feint, and, before his silence, more pregnant with threat than his argumentation, each of us, in the instinctive fear of his audacity, tried in vain to break the atmosphere of anguish mysteriously woven in that winter night by Germont's attitude and willpower.

In fact, he broke the truce.

"So be it, you're right. I have the monomania of the macabre, I cultivate the orchid of the rare cadaver, as others do the blue paradox of a mad hortensia. Let's admit that I'm a Robert de Montesquiou of carrion and, to parody a verse of the celebrated Comte:

> *With Goths and Ostrogoths my escutcheon is sown,*
> *Where is one better than the bosom of one's own?*

"I won't try to convince you. A stubborn head has no ears; you're playing Saint Thomas to my judiciary incredulity. Monsieur Macé[1] would have attached me to his cabinet—yes, word of honor; I would have refused anyway; but you, you regard me as some sort of fantastic storyteller, you pass over the windfall of the observer that I am."

"Would you like a censer, Germont?" Bienvenu interjected.

"No, but prepare me a pipe." And, while unbuttoning his waistcoat and loosening his collar to make himself more comfortable: "I'll tell you a story, then—the last . . .

"In ninety-four, or thereabouts . . . yes, it was eight years ago . . . among the wide open salons full of flashy foreigners where

---

1 Jean-François Macé (1815-1894), a famous campaigner for free state-funded secular education.

12

I hung out—it was my debut in society and I had a liking for soirées; it was the happy epoch, which we've all known, when I felt dishonored if I hadn't been in a black frock-coat from six o'clock every evening. Oh, that frock-coat! I even dragged it to the little creamery where my less-than-modest income forced me to dine. I kept my overcoat on, it's true, in order not to see a tip added to my bill, and my carefully folded kerchief hid my white cravat; but from half-past nine to one o'clock in the morning I framed myself in the doorway of at least four or five salons, and my delight was boundless when, as svelte as a wasp in my young man's finery, I threw my overcoat into the hands of the lackey in the antechamber. The innocent and slightly stupid joys of the twentieth year! So, among the slightly flashy salons where I had my entries, American in the Champs-Élysées, Spanish in the Monceau quarter and among Russian princesses and nihilists on the heights of Passy, all the cosmopolitan foam that luxury splashes on the west coast of Paris, Générale V***'s was perhaps the one that attracted me the most.

"The presence of Lina, the daughter of the mistress of the house, an eighteen-year-old creole, a blonde of the reddish blonde of ripe corn, with the arm and flavorsome complexion of a beautiful peach, populated Générale V***'s drawing rooms with a twittering flock of other young women, pretty birds of paradise with brazen gazes and liberal manners, whose amusing carelessness must surely have inspired Marcel Prévost with the first draft of his *Demi-Vierges*.[1]

"Générale V***, the South American widow of a Brazilian or Mexican general killed in some War of Independence or other, was a beautiful woman of about forty, evidently born and created for amour; the strength and health of a generous blood gave her a spectacular maturity. Under the envelope of superb black hair tinted with henna there were large ultramarine eyes, perhaps even

1 Marcel Prévost's *Les Demi-Vierges*, a study of the deleterious effects of Parisian society on young women, described by the *Encyclopedia Britannica* as "exaggerated and revolting," was published in 1894.

more desirable in the générale than her daughter, a camellia-white complexion and the splendor of incomparable shoulders, offered and displayed with a regal magnificence. I've never encountered since, in society, a woman so outrageously naked. Générale V***—Thalasie as she was called in intimacy—must have been, at twenty, one of those admirable creatures who turn the life of a man upside-down, and sometimes that of a nation. Gallant the générale was; it would have required a very poor observer not to yield to the evidence of her open nostrils, incessantly quivering, the eternal vibration of which seemed to be sniffing fresh flesh; then there was the humidity of her large dark eyes, black by dint of being blue, the bruising of bistre eyelids and the indolence of her attitudes, belied by the feverish red of her lips, continually parted by the crimson pepper of the tip of a greedy tongue. Everything in Thalasie, including the immodesty of her proffered nudity, denounced and affirmed an amorous woman.

"The générale lived in the Avenue de Champs-Élysées, a little above the roundabout. She occupied a vast furnished fourth-floor apartment, the garish luxury of which had not been attenuated by her creole taste. She led the life there of a woman who ought to have had an income of eighty thousand francs, although her friends only knew of forty thousand. That two-thousand louis gap between her income and her expenditure was a perpetual puzzle for her entourage, because Générale V*** was not venal.

"The impulses of her head and her heart—and since the death of her husband, the number of her whims could be cited—had burst forth in her life like volcanic eruptions, abrupt, impetuous and unexpected, and always in favor of robust and handsome young men, partners worthy of her; and Thalasie had always abandoned herself to her passions of a day, a month or a year with the fine fervor of her temperament. She had taken no more care to hide her liaisons than to advertise them.

"Sensual and beautiful, no one was more sensible of beauty than she was. With her South American ardor, she had always gone straight for stallions, a choice that must have impoverished rather than enriched her, for she had loved gamblers, swash-bucklers and adventurers; but the cosmopolitan society that she frequented at her home excused her spirited ardors, the men in particular being amused by that whinnying animality of a thor-oughbred mare. It is true that no one charged Générale V*** with either villainy or baseness. She had never been cited, with so many other foreigners, as having credit with some banker who was reputed to be helpful to ladies strapped for cash, nor, like certain authentic duchesses, with being offered to the clients of some house of rendezvous.

"The générale was, therefore, an honest woman, in the ac-cepted sense that the greater part of society accords to that term. In addition, since her daughter had emerged from the convent, Thalasie seemed to have modified her way of life. She adored the delectable Lina, with the kind of savage frenzy that she brought to everything; there was something Spanish in the passionate ardor that that Mexican seemed to have made her unique rule of life. When Lina came home she had dismissed her latest lover, and society, indulgent to all the sentimental manifestations made fashionable by the theater and the novel, had applauded the mother as it had encouraged the lover; and the arrant sluts of Parisian society had felt their souls refreshed by that rupture.

"In addition to Lina, Générale V*** had a son, four years older than her daughter, Antonio V***, who has made his name since as a portrait painter. He was then in Rome, at the Villa Medici, for Thalasie also prided herself on being an artist. With the reliable bad taste of American women, she encouraged art in everything that the industry produces of the most sumptuous and most irremediable in imitation and facsimile; her apartment was overflowing with Italian furniture in the most over-elaborate and various style, and I'll only half-astonish you when I tell you that her antechamber was guarded by two negro standard lamps, painted and gilded, current products of a Venetian furniture fac-tory. Finally, the last detail that completes the woman: Générale V*** spent two months of the winter in Nice, and the banners that she brought back, as many from dance halls as from New Year's Eve parties, were accumulated in her principal drawing room, where the gilded flag-poles intersected in a panoply beneath a full-length portrait of the general.

"Thalasie gave white balls whose luxury went as far as marvelous sprays of narcissi and white carnations from Nice. She received two consignments of them a week. The générale hosted a dance once a fortnight, but she was at home on Tuesday and Sunday evenings; even her intimate gatherings were well attended. The prettiness of the daughter, the beauty of the mother and a choice swarm of young and stirring foreign women made her salon one of the most attractive in Paris.

"An alert observer, however, would eventually have noticed the assiduous presence at all those fêtes of an old gentleman, still sprightly under his white hair, and decorated besides, whose affectionate bonhomie seemed to involve the greatest interest in the two women. Married, and the father of a family himself, that sexagenarian with a rosette happened to be one of the great interior decorators of Paris, one of the princes of contemporary furniture, one of those whose erudition was law. It was said that he had furnished the générale, but it scarcely appeared so, for, if Thalasie dressed divinely, she affirmed in the choice of hangings and furniture the esthetics of a parrot. Monsieur B*** (for I cannot cite names here) nevertheless frequented the générale's salon. He came regularly twice a week, to the Friday hops as well as the fortnightly balls, very happy, one would have thought, to rub his sixty years against all that freshness and all that whiteness . . . and when, one night in December, a night of a reception at Générale V***'s, the police found Monsieur B***, dead of a congestion, sitting on a bench in the Champs-Élysées a few numbers below the house from which he had emerged, no one was astonished either by that sudden death or the location. Monsieur B*** was apoplectic; he had spent that evening, like so many others, in the home of Générale V***; the cold outside had evidently gripped him, he had taken a few steps and had collapsed on a bench, where the congestion had stiffened him."

At that point, de Germont fell silent. A great silence filled the smoking-room, aggravated by the stifled plaint, gasping and monotonous, of the waves against the blocks of the mole. Through the panes of a high window, from which the enervated Tupier had just drawn back the curtains, we could see the nocturnal sky, fleecy with soft clouds, as if tinted with nacre by the light of the moon—the errant, traveling moon—and, spangled with silver at the horizon, the sea.

O nights of Bastia, and opium talk!

III

And Germont, the consummate actor, went on: "The truth about that apoplexy or congestion on a bench in the Champs-Élysées, I only found out later—much later, three years afterwards—and from the very mouth of the scene-setter of that unexpected and quasi-tragic death.

"Laclos-Larive! You all know Laclos-Larive, the indicated arbiter of all affairs of honor, the sportsman and fencer without whose advice an affair cannot be arranged, the judge of all litigations and differences in the matter of duels, the only man in Paris authorized to drag a reluctant champion to the terrain or to aid in avoiding an encounter with a dubious adversary; Laclos-Larive, whose opinion, enunciated between two puffs of cigarette smoke, weighs a gallant man or disqualifies a rogue; in sum, Laclos-Larive, the Laclos of the armory, the grand bars and the night restaurants, the witness of more than twenty-five quasi-celebrated duels, who has perhaps arranged more affairs than he has taken to Villebon or behind the stands at Auteuil.

"Has Laclos-Larive ever been defeated? He is expert with the foil, and follows assiduously all the fights at the clubs or the Grand Hotel; he is on intimate terms with all the provosts in Paris, and his presence brings clients to a fencing school. That presence he displays adroitly in all the places where blades clash, occasionally or frequently; he shoots at Gastinne's, and, without a fortune, he lives in a princely fashion at the club. Laclos-Larive rides in the Bois in the morning and dines at the cabaret in the evening; friends take him to supper after the theater, others for excursions by automobile. Laclos-Larive is in formal dress at premières, his ears pricked for slaps, in quest of an affair to arrange; he is also on the lookout at masked balls, at Larue's or Maxime's; he's a professional with the épée. A somewhat ripe operetta diva whose box he frequents and whose detractors he looks up and down, permits him to show her off; he sometimes takes her back, in the evening, to the Boulevard Maillot, where Laurelle has his little hotel, and comes to collect her officially at the theater; that Manon of the Acacias knows her authors and nourishes her chevalier . . .

"Laclos-Larive is a publicly disreputable man, but we all shake his hand and are all proud to be seen with him. Paris, in any case, shares our laxity. Paris has her baffling indulgences for certain of her adoptive children, as opposed to unmerited severities for others—but bah, that corrects the folly of balances. In any case, Laclos remained spoiled and lithe in spite of being over fifty, and still maintains his illusion; the neck of an athlete and the torso of a groom, Laclos-Larive ought to be, has been and perhaps still is, beloved."

"Our compliments. As a portrait, he's established. It's a painting in the oil of gall; all his enemies would recognize him. I didn't know you had that fine hatred for our national champion, my dear Germont. Might he have forced your hand for a duel?"

And Germont, his bright eyes looking straight into Tupier's, retorted: "He hasn't even killed one of my friends. I hate Laclos for the very story that I'm telling you this evening, which I owe to his loquacity. He ought to have been the first to shut up about that woman, since he had extracted her from a difficult situation and he had been her lover; the braggart completes the swashbuckler in him."

To which Bienvenu, with a vague gesture of the hand, said: "Pooh! He's a man of honor, a known model, and hence devoid of honor, like all professionals of the game."

"You have him exactly."

"We've all known him."

"And recognized him," Tupier underlined. "One word that will finish the man for you; Germont, it's to you that I dedicate that word. One evening, already distant, at the Helder, when there was a Helder, Laclos, recounting his own prowesses with a fine verve, made this sublime confession: 'There's only one man that I've never provoked, and that's my mothers lover; I would have killed him, and she'd never have forgiven me.' There—that's the signature."

Germont inclined, as if for a salutation. "Truly, if he said that, I resent him less for his indiscretion regarding the générale. There's an epic grandeur in unconsciousness, and a stupidity almost of genius. Why render him sympathetic to me?"

"What about your cadaver? He's slipped away, and your story with him."

"That's true. This, then, is very nearly what that imbecile told us. It wasn't at the Helder but at Durand's. Which of us had brought Laclos to supper? No matter—he was there, it was June, the week of the distribution of prizes at the Salon; we were discussing the jury's medals. The first prize of the Champ de Mars had been awarded, justly, to Antonio V***, the générale's son; the générale herself had disappeared, returned to her Brazil or her Mexico once the pretty Lina, today in some legation in Austria or Italy, was married . . . and as, enthused by Antonio V***'s submissions, we were complimenting the painter's composition, his palette and his talent, 'Antonio V***,' declared Laclos, in his insupportable and peremptory tone, his cigarette held between his fingers at eye level, 'I once rendered a famous service to his mother, Générale V***—you all knew her, the good générale? She lived a little high up in the Champs-Élysées. A nature of which B***, the rich furnisher of the Rue Royale maintained the last fires—you know, B***, who was found dead one December night on a bench in the Champs-Élysées? You'll never guess who carried him there!'

"And, mistaking for curiosity the indignation and scorn that was in our eyes he went on: 'I must tell you that story; it's rather amusing. It was five or six years ago. One night, when, by chance, I had come back from the club early—I was living in the Rue de La Trémouille then—I was woken up by a violent ring of the bell. I always sleep alone in the apartment, the valet de chambre lodging in the mansards. *Bah, let him ring*, I grumbled to myself, *when he's had enough he'll go away*. But the trouble is that people don't go away, and the bell kept ringing. I turned on the electricity and looked at the time: two o'clock in the morning, and that damned bell was vibrating throughout the house. Impossible to sleep; I get up, put on pajamas and, determined to throw the accursed ringer down the stairs, I go to open up.

"'Prudence takes hold of me on the threshold. "Who's there?" I say, through the door. Amazement! It's a woman's voice that responds, strangled with emotion. "Is that Monsieur Laclos-Larive?"

"'"Yes. What do you want?"

"'"In the name of God, open up, it's a matter of the honor and life of a woman."

"'"What woman? What honor?" I reply, a little nonplussed. "I don't know your voice."

"'"No, Monsieur, you don't know me, but you know Madame; I'm the chambermaid of Générale V***."

"'I couldn't refuse anything to Générale V***, even though I'd ceased all relations with her five years before; I didn't even encounter her any longer except in rare houses, our existences having bifurcated, but I owed her too many beautiful hours not to remain her friend.' And the lady-killer made a few triumphant gestures, smoothing and caressing his moustaches.

"'So I opened up. It was, indeed, a chambermaid, a poor girl topsy-turvy with emotion, shaken by a nervous tremor, having run from who knows where, without an apron, bare-headed, slippers on her feet, hair undone, and in tears. I invited her in, although she was obstinate in wanting to stay on the landing. My attempts to find out what was wanted of me only extracted supplications from the creature, punctuated by sobs and "Come, Monsieur, come, it's a matter of Madame's salvation." There was some mention of Monsieur B*** but I couldn't understand anything in the girl's jerky babble.

"'I got dressed in haste and put on a pelisse. The girl had a fiacre downstairs. In a carriage, from the Rue de La Trémouille to the number in the Champs-Élysées where the générale lives is a journey of five minutes, at the most. During those five minutes, however, I succeeded in clarifying the situation. When I leapt out of the cab I knew that Monsieur B***, the générale's official lover, who had been sleeping in the Champs-Élysées that night, was dead in Thalasie's own bed, almost next door to her daughter's bedroom, and that the panicked générale didn't know what to do with the cadaver. In her panic she had thought of me; it was on me that she counted to rid her of the dead man, to find a means of getting the accusatory corpse out of her house.

"'Funny work! "Are we keeping the fiacre?" asked the chambermaid, when we arrived.

"'"Let's keep it—we'll see upstairs!" As the concierge was about to pull the cordon, warned by a presentiment, I said: "Tell the lodge it's for the physician." We went up.

"'Générale V***'s bedroom! I'll never forget that spectacle! All the candlesticks and all the chandeliers fully lit up, all the electricity on, in the terror the wretched woman had experienced, in that tête-à-tête with the dead man. On the bed, ravaged like a battlefield, in the disorder of the sheets, puffed-up, pot-bellied and obscene, was the sexagenarian corpse of Monsieur B***; on the carpet, a heap of damp napkins. They'd attempted all the possible reagents, whipped that apoplectic flesh with wet napkins, tried by all means to restore a stalled circulation. The bald head was risible and frightening; the eyes only showed their whites

21

under the eyelid, the irises tipped back; in the swollen and violet face the mouth was gaping, tumefied; in a thread of foam, a thick tongue as black as a parakeet's was dangling.

"'It was the ultimate in the grotesque and the horrific.

"'In the middle of the room, collapsed in an armchair, was Générale V***, Thalasie, but aged by ten years, a face devastated by terror, all the wrinkles showing on the temples and the forehead, and, in the staring eyes, the distraction of madness. She'd put on a peignoir in haste, which veiled her nudity poorly, an entire corner of one shoulder emerging from the lacerated chemise, which her lover must have grasped in his agony, and, careless of the wisps of gray hair that were showing, with the expression of a cornered beast, exhausted by fear, the générale was waiting.

"'As if moved by a spring, everything straightened when I came in. She grabbed my hands, almost throwing herself upon me. "You've come! Thank you. Thank God you were at home. Thank you, my friend, thank you!" And, pointing at the bed: "Look." and, before my silence: "Yes, he was my lover. It's hideous, I know, but life is costly in Paris. Anyway, it's done. Men have cost me dearly, but that's the way it is. That body can't stay here; my daughter's asleep, almost next door, and my daughter mustn't know—and my son's in Rome. It would be frightful—think of it! The police here, the concierge, the scandal in the house, and the newspapers, the reporters, and then, you know, Monsieur B*** is married, he has a wife, children, a family, I can't send *that* back to them." And, with a gesture of terrible simplicity, she designated the heap of flesh collapsed on the bed. "Oh, what to do, what to do?" choked the miserable woman, biting her handkerchief. "Think of something, think, you, you're a man. Think of no matter what, but save me. My head's spinning. I don't know any more. I don't know any more."

"'She had fallen back into her chair now, sobbing, in that bright room, her hands convulsively clasped and her eyes vague, stifling between her lips the same monotonous phrase: "My poor little Lina! My poor little Lina!" It made one queasy to look at her.

""Come on," I interjected, "buck up; there's no time to lose. It's necessary to get the body out of here, isn't it? Are you sure of your chambermaid?" And, at a vague gesture of the pitiful woman: "First, it's necessary to dress him. Oh, no repugnance, no nerves. When he's dressed, we'll take stock. The important thing is that he isn't found naked. Is the fiacre still downstairs?"

""The fiacre!" The générale had a sudden fit of lucidity. "The fiacre? What do you want to do with that fiacre? You're not going to put the dead man in a cab and send him to the Prefecture! The coachman will say where he came from, the subsequent investigation would betray me."

""That's true; it's necessary that no one knows where he's come from." And, turning to the motionless chambermaid: "Go downstairs, send the fiacre away, and tell the lodge again that it's the physician."

""Have you thought of something?" the générale asked me, anxiously.

""Yes, I think so. Come back up quickly," I said to the chambermaid, we can't start without you." The girl went out. Then came the release: Thalasie, standing up, weeping silently, leaning on my shoulder.'"

"This time, Germont has hit the bull's-eye," declared Tupier, in the midst of the silence maintained by the naval officer, desirous of savoring his effect.

IV

"'No, dressing that dead man wasn't an easy matter. First, there were the silk socks, which it was a matter of fitting to those inert feet. We had no purchase on that flaccid flesh, which lent itself too much to the movement we tried to give it, sliding gelatinously between the fabric and our fingers. We had sat the cadaver on the bed. The chambermaid held up the sagging torso as best she could, her arms passed under his armpits, and Thalasie and

I put on his underpants. For that, we almost had to put him upright and thread both legs at the same time, as if in a double sack; the legs, so soft at first, had now become rigid; that stiffness was one difficulty more.

"'The difficulty we had in getting the swollen feet into the shoes! We almost had to break the ankles. On her knees, Thalasie stuck to that task with an obstinate and hard face that was scary, her eyes staring like a somnambulist, and pressing with all her weight on the ball of the foot to get it into the shoe. The trousers of the evening suit, in fine and supple cloth, required less trouble, Monsieur B*** had required forty minutes, watch in hand, to be shod and trousered; the most arduous part still remained to be done. It was a matter of getting the cadaver out of his night-shirt and putting on his day shirt, tying his cravat, and then getting him fully dressed.

"'In order to sleep at his mistress' house, Monsieur B*** had mauve surah chemises embroidered on the side with a gold silk monogram. The hideousness of that inert head in that gallant attire! The unexpected death gave something tragic to that senile coquetry. Bloody foam had run down, staining the whole front of that combat chemise; two red trickles had curdled at the corners of the lips and formed a crust under the chin.

"'We had to get a sponge and clean the cadaver, after which we removed the Parma violet chemise and put on the evening shirt without too much difficulty, although we had some difficulty with the sleeves; the stiffened arms would no longer bend. The waistcoat went on almost of its own accord, but the jacket was harder; there were those terrible arms again, paralyzed at the joints and awfully heavy. Already cold, they now weighed double; and then, that torso slid, deviated and oscillated between our awkward hands; one might have thought that the corpse was refusing that supreme toilette and opposing a muted hostility to our efforts.

"'The enervated générale was manifestly maltreating and brutalizing that macabre doll; an alcoholic gleam was blazing in her eyes and a rictus contracting the malevolent mouth; I divined that she was insulting the dead man subvocally. "We'll never finish," she muttered between her teeth. "We'll never finish."

"'That unique phrase set a rhythm to our work. We reasoned with the recalcitrant corpse, however, but after what alarms and what anguish! We spent five minutes getting his jacket on and then putting his coat on.

"''If he'd only had his pelisse!' Thalasie snapped. She was at the end of the tether; she now hated that cadaver. But we had to renounce buttoning his collar; that apoplectic neck had swelled by half; we'd have broken our fingernails on it. I sketched a knot in the cravat and decided to leave it loose. Monsieur B***, in a choking fit, might have unfastened the collar himself.

"'Thus accommodated, we sat him in an armchair. I demanded his gloves, his cane and his hat, and addressed myself to Thalasie: "You'll have to help me get him downstairs now—yes, down the staircase—and help me get him outside."

"'''Down the stairs! What if we encounter a tenant? You can't think so!"

"'''On the contrary, I have thought so, that's why it's necessary for you and this girl to go down with me. It's three o'clock in the morning, we have every chance of not meeting anyone. If the worst happens, and we do meet someone, the three of us are taking a sick friend home. Monsieur B*** had a fainting fit in your home."

"'''No, I can't, there'd be a scandal. Not that, not that."

"'''Then let's put him back in your bed and go fetch a doctor. He'll certify the death, and my presence with you will attenuate all suspicions. After the soirée, Monsieur B*** felt ill . . ."

"'Thalasie, slumped in an armchair with her head in her hands, didn't reply. The cadaver, bundled up in its clothes, was facing her, and, reminiscent of a grotesque mannequin, that entire body, heaped and collapsed, was widening two vitreous and glaucous eyes.

"The clock chimed quarter to four. I looked at my watch. "Ten to four," I thought, aloud. "In an hour we'll have the street-sweepers. It's necessary to decide. What are we going to do?"

""Let's go!" said the générale, getting up. "What do I have to do?"

""You're strong. The two of us are going to try to get the body downstairs. Your chambermaid can carry the hat and cane, and light the way for us. It'll need both of us. He's heavy, I warn you. You," I said to the chambermaid, "open all the doors as far as the antechamber and go on ahead of us, holding the candle very high. No noise, eh? Are you ready?" And I turned back to the générale.

""Yes. Let me see whether Lina's asleep." But as she was about to go into the other room she stopped and tottered, her hand on her breast, as if she were choking. "Marie," she said to the chambermaid, "go see whether Mademoiselle is asleep. Be careful not to wake her. Quietly, very quietly."

"When the girl came back and made her a sign that yes, the young woman was asleep, Thalasie murmured, in such a changed, extinct voice that it seemed to me that it was her shadow who was speaking: "Let's go, I'm ready. Tell me what I have to do, my friend."

""Cover yourself up first; you might catch cold. And let's go." I put my head under the cadaver's left armpit, holding his arm against my body; I lifted up all his weight like that, and, hanging on to his waist with my right arm, I begged Thalasie to take hold of him solidly under his right armpit and hoist him up with all her strength, so that his feet dragged on the parquet as little as possible. What a weight that dead man had! Thus harnessed to the burden, we made him traverse the apartment. Candle in hand, the chambermaid walked ahead of us.

"Générale V*** lived on the third floor—fortunately, a third floor without an entresol. What a descent that was for Monsieur B***, by that dark and silent stairway, at four o'clock in the morning, by tremulous candlelight, me alongside the banisters, bracing myself with all my might to prevent the body from slipping and falling into the void—that body poorly retained by the fainting Thalasie, whose emotion made her stumble at every step! The entire weight of the cadaver fell on me; his armpit and his rigid arm made a vice for my neck, and at every minute, his feet, slipping into empty space, dragged me forward, and I felt as if I were being projected into the blackness by a mysterious force.

"'Oh, the scraping of his shoes on the wooden steps! And, at intervals, the click of his heels in the silence! They resonated lugubriously through the deserted house and made such a racket, it seemed to us, that we thought that all the doors on the landing were about to open. The chambermaid preceded us, holding the candle high; a brief gleam ran over Monsieur B***'s bald cranium, making it shine like an ivory billiard ball. Générale V***, coming last by virtue of the position of the body, dominated the group by her height, and, spectral in the darkness of that slumbering house, with a truly frightful pallor and a facial expression even more frightful, dolorous and contracted, seemed the instigator of some horrible crime that she was in haste to stifle. We could hear the whistle of her halting respiration. What an atrocious task I had taken on! My forehead and my hands were damp; I could feel my shirt soaked in sweat.

"'At one moment, the chambermaid, who was lighting our way, dropped Monsieur B***'s hat and cane, which she was holding in one hand, and in the shock of the noise they made, she almost dropped the candle. Oh, the tumult of the tumble of that cane and that hat, although they only rolled down ten steps! It seemed to us that the whole house was collapsing. It was a catastrophe. We stopped dead, our hearts beating as if to burst, and all the blood surging in our arteries. The girl got out of it by going down a few steps and picking up the fallen objects. Thalasie and I exchanged a glance then. By what miracle hadn't we let go of the cadaver? Yes, by what miracle? And we continued the descent.

"'How many steps did that stairway have?

"'We kept going down; a moment came when we couldn't go down any further; we were under the coaching entrance, a few paces from the lodge. "Light out," I said to the chambermaid. "And you"—I was taking to Thalasie—"ask for the cordon yourself, so that your voice can be recognized."

"'"I can't! I won't be able to!" And the wretched woman was about to abort that entire escape of a dead man.

"'"Ask for the cordon yourself," I insisted, "or I'll let go of the body." And I said, in a loud and intelligible voice; "and add, in such a fashion that you can be heard: *Come on, general, it's nothing; the fresh air will do you good.*"

"'"But why?"

"'"Do as I tell you: *Cordon, if you please*, and *Come on, general, it's nothing; the fresh air will do you good.*" And she did as I had said.

"'Her extinct voice of a half-unconscious woman murmured the indicated words, and we went past the lodge in complete darkness. "Now the cane, the hat and the gloves. Put the gloves in his pocket." Standing next to the door, which was ajar, I made sure that the avenue was deserted. A heavy market-gardener's cart was going down the Champs-Élysées, but much lower down than the number where we were; the way was clear.

"'It was beginning to snow: a fine, soft snow like eider down falling from a soft and moist sky; the whole avenue was already covered from the Concorde to the Arc-de-Triomphe. "With the snow, we have no time to lose. Are you strong? We're almost saved; we're going to take him as far as the first bench." And, rapidly, to the chambermaid: "Go back upstairs without a light, don't make any noise, and come to look for Madame tomorrow, at nine o'clock, at my apartment. Bring furs and a hat. For Mademoiselle, Madame will be at mass."

"'And, lifting up and putting Monsieur B*** outside, with an abrupt effort, I dragged the générale with me. "Bonsoir, Générale," I said, in a loud voice, and closed the door again rather brutally.

""""What are you doing?" Thalasie asked, nonplussed.

"""I'm saving you. You're not going to go back in now; it's necessary that the concierge doesn't know that you've come out and that he believes you went back upstairs again. You can't go back in. What would he think of these comings and goings—it would awaken his suspicions. Damn! Two *sergents de ville*. Don't budge; let's stay in the shadows. The doorway's deep, they won't see us. We're going to deposit the body on the first bench, and you're going to come and sleep at my place."

""""Your place! What about Lina?"

"""Lina's asleep, and will sleep until nine o'clock. Your chambermaid will come and collect you from my apartment; she has her orders. For your daughter and everyone else you'll be coming back from mass. In any case, you couldn't have gone back to that bedroom up there; that would have ended in a crisis of nerves. There's everything you need in my apartment: ether, bromide, and even morphine. Tomorrow, when you go back, you'll give your chambermaid twenty-five louis. Now, a little courage! Help me take Monsieur B*** as far as that bench."

"And, stiffened by a supreme resolution, galvanized with energy by the very horror of the circumstances, Thalasie, so weak and hesitant a little while before, helped me to drag her lover's body, without flinching, for at least a hundred paces through the snow. It was the most perilous part of the enterprise. If we had encountered a policeman, or even a passer-by . . . ! But we didn't encounter anyone. We sat Monsieur B*** down comfortably on a bench, we adjusted his hat on his head and we left him there, under the fleecy snow, just as he was found the next morning, with his rings on his fingers and his wallet in his pocket, respected and intact, safe from the thieves and prowlers who no longer work on winter nights after three o'clock in the morning, in view of the cold.

"It was two *sergents de ville* who made the lugubrious discovery at about five o'clock in the morning. Monsieur B***, an apoplectic sexagenarian, had died of congestion on a bench; he liked dancing too much. As for the générale, my accomplice, I took her to my apartment to warm up and recover; I lit a big fire, served her burning punch, and, as she was enervated, transfigured and beside herself, beautified by the emotions of the tragic night, and nothing lends itself more to amour than the thought and the presence of death, I resumed our relationship that night and added two more hours of inappreciable intoxication to all the happy hours that I already owed to her.

"'Générale V*** didn't go home until ten o'clock in the morning; she doubtless told her daughter that she had heard two masses, the officiant said them so well!'

"And that was Laclos-Larive's story. Whether he was bragging at the Helder or selling himself at Durand's, am I not right to abominate that man?"

MASCHERE

MASKS IN LONDON AND ELSEWHERE

I

IN the grand hall enchanted by music, on the parquet frosted with rosin, there were the meager steps, the rounding of legs and the sometimes-hopping, sometimes-leaning movements of the eternal amorous couple, the duped Pierrot and the deceptive Columbine. An artistic pleasure offered by an artiste to others of his race and milieu, André Dostonerof was giving us a pantomime matinée, his pantomime of *Columbine Betrayed*, which had already made the tour of all the coastal clubs.

Columbine, Pierrot! A melody, light and seemingly shivering with the appeals of Basque tambourines, underlined their mime, prepared their entrances, escorted their exits and sometimes accompanied with the twittering of a songbird, sometimes with the plaint of a wounded turtle-dove, the alternating gestures of their common passion.

Deceptive surprise of the poem: lunar Pierrot, the candid and pure Pierrot dear to Paul Verlaine and Théodore de Banville; Pierrot the eternally deceived, here deceived the coquette Columbine, and, in chagrin and despair, the Célimène in a short skirt, paragon of all trickeries and all treasons, killed herself: that Bengali soul committed suicide, doubtless more out of chagrin than despair, and her hummingbird death-throes were gracious amid the flowers.

It was over mimosa branches, in the pink flakes of flowering almonds and the sulfurous pallor of vanilla-inebriated carnations, that Columbine was slowly extinguished amid the cushions of the sofa where, two minutes before, Pierrot had solicited her amour.

> *Oh, promises have wings*
> *In infidel hearts!*[1]

And the orchestra, tenderly heart-rending all of a sudden, resumed, without really giving the impression of believing it, the famous song of Ophelia in *Hamlet*.

The women, suddenly interested in the misfortune of one of their own, were all eyes and ears, each egotistically attentive. A large bay glazed with an immense unsilvered mirror framed the scene with a moving and real décor; above the pretty cadaver there was a tangle of palm-trees, Spanish reeds and glaucous agaves, dominated by the writhing crowns of tall cypresses agitated by the mistral; for the mistral was raging during that matinée offered by an artiste to artistes, and through the three giant bays that made the hall into a gigantic ship's cabin, there was, over a porcelain blue sky, a cold, dry, stormy sky, the verdure in emotion, convulsive and contrary, of more than three hectares of olive trees.

Now the resuscitated Columbine and that rogue Pierrot withdrew, saluting the audience. They had been called back several times in order to see them at closer range; approving murmurs underlined mundane applause, the elegant clapping of delicately-gloved hands, with rustling fans in their fingertips, and now, a handsome young man—not too young, but athletically brisk, with a becoming face, seductive eyes and dressed to the nines—allowed himself to be drawn toward a table. Rather ripe women surrounded him, installing him almost by force, encouraging him and assailing him with caresses, and the adulated gentleman,

---

1 The quoted lines are from the opera *Hamlet* (1869) by Michel Carré, with a libretto by Jules Barbier.

his hair so delicately curled and his teeth so white, beneath long blond moustaches, allowed himself to be drawn, thanking the lady-friends and finally leaning his elbows on the table, of which a posed glass of water denounced the peril.

"This is what I feared," my neighbor murmured in my ear. "Why would the disease that afflicts them all, spare this one? Oh, the interminable and indefatigable talker! You know the tap of warm and perfumed water that drips, inexhaustibly from rosy and honeyed lips, of the listener ecstasized by the sound of his own voice whenever someone is listening. And the fingers with opal rings stroking the blond moustaches! And the starry gaze when he pronounces the words *amour* and *fleur*—because he speaks as he writes, in rhyme. But what do you expect? He charms them, he maintains them in their psychic beauty and their state of mind, when it's time to talk to them about their salvation. He leads to Cythera once again that swarm of beauties of Père-Lachaise. Just look at that guard of honor. It's all Sainte-Périne in the breach of Auteuil.[1] It's the flying squadron of Alcibiades Sauvard. They adulate him, congratulate him and stun him with their admiration. He represents for them their past, the errors of the youth and the spirit and mores of an abolished epic, for you know what he's going to lecture about? The kiss."

"The last one, then, that of extreme unction?"

"Oh, the unction is in his words. Shall we take a walk?"

"I was about to propose that to you, all the more so as the mistral has called a truce. Look, the trees are no longer moving."

Installed at his table, Alcibiades Sauvard commenced: "Mesdames, Messieurs . . ."

"Then again, it's beginning to get warm in here. See what an admirable view one has from here."

My interlocutor, an habitué of the house, had led me on to a terrace at one of the extremities of the garden: a terrace with balustrades in the Italian style, leaning over two rockslides bris-

---

1 The Hôpital Sainte-Périne, not far from Auteuil, specializes in geriatric care and the illnesses of the elderly.

tling with agaves and odorous lentisks. A road wound around the foot, as if perceived in the depths of a ravine, and on the edge of the road, with the calm blue of the waves there was the pale and blue-tinted fleece of an olive-grove. The rock of Eze and the summit of La Turbie advanced their spurs into the liquid turquoise of the gulfs, and all the way to the Pointe de l'Italie, delightfully attenuated and luminous, dominated by the enormous crest of the Carnier, there was a heroic curve of capes and promontories. The villas of Beaulieu filled the depths of the bay.

Applause greeted the speech of the lecturer, and the rumor arrived as far as us.

"His holy women grant him a small success. 'I don't feel sorry for Christ; women loved him,'[1] but I feel sorry for Sauvard, for he's loved by old women instead. What need had Dostonerof to serve us up that lecturer? He's like his pantomime: the music is graceful, light with a hint of tender motion, but what a poem! Why always that eternal Pierrot, that eternal Columbine, as if there were no other humankind but the characters of Italian comedy? Oh, who will write us a macabre and true-to-life pantomime, a modern pantomime in the style of Edgar Poe or Mark Twain? The marvelous subjects of poignant pantomimes pullulate in the newspaper articles that we read every day!

"But, in the story that your friend Germont told you the other day, in 'Opium Talk'—for, my God, I have the honor of being one of your assiduous readers—there was a rather fine commencement of a macabre drama. I don't know whether your Laclos-Larive really took Générale V*** to bed in his apartment, but how much greater the horror would have been if, the générale having gone home once the lugubrious deposit had been made on the bench, Laclos had remained on watch to see what would happen, and if a prostitute, one of those lamentable night-workers who rob belated drunks and turn out the pockets of night-owls run aground in the Champs-Élysées had spotted that cadaver and mistaken it for a client!

---

1 The slightly misquoted line is from a poem by the prolific humorist Armand Silvestre (1837-1901).

"Can you see the maneuvers of that girl, circling the dead man, provoking him with a gesture and a *psst! psst!* and closing in, like an osprey swooping on its prey, and finally coming to sit down next to Monsieur B***? Can you imagine the funereal irony of the enticements of that woman to that dead man, her attempts at conversation, her sly feelers, and the slow and discreet possession of the corpse by that ghoul—perhaps the mother of a starving family, for in Paris prostitution doesn't even respect the family—and, encouraged by the fellow's silence and immobility, the whore deciding to go all the way and searching the pockets of the cadaver, which, disturbed, loses equilibrium and collapses, with all his weight, on the thief, whom he drags down with him in his fall into the snow: a fall and a simulacrum of a fall; the frightened cries of the girl; an abominable hand-to-hand struggle that brings the intervention of the police at the double; for two *sergents de ville* run to lift up the delinquents, observe the death of the man and arrest the guilty party! At that point, Laclos-Larive decamps, and runs straight to Générale V***, to narrate to her in detail the sequel to the adventure and reassure that beautiful conscience. They finally have their alibi.

"The following act would show the girl at the tribunal, accused without any means of defending herself, the foolish girl, bewildered by fear, unable to explain to herself how she could have killed that poor fellow, since it appears that it was her who killed him; and, during the advocate's speech, the indicated scene in which the accused falls into dementia. Wouldn't that be a fine opening for a drama?"

"You have a good imagination!" I could not resist replying.

"No better than yours," he riposted, "since the imagination of those horrors came to me from reading you. Confess that the thing might have happened, and in any country in the world. A man dies, or, for some reason, his cadaver is placed, on a bench. It's dark. A prostitute passes by, plying her trade, accosts the dead man and tries, either to shake him or chooses to rob him, until the corpse falls on top of her; with that, the police intervene, or not—it might even be better if they don't intervene. The terror and panic of the girl would be all the more anguishing, alone, at grips in the nocturnal gloom with that cold and inert flesh, which weighs upon her, crushing her, and doesn't fight back. Imagine the state of mind of that whore, struggling under the weight of a corpse, in the distress of a deserted avenue—Fifth Avenue in New York, perhaps, or a path in Hyde Park.

"Yes, Hyde Park, or one of the London squares. It's certainly the décor of an English square that one would like for that scene. London, the crimes, the nights and the masks of London. Has Marcel Schwob ever told you the story of the masked corpses in London's Docklands, on the bank of the Thames? It could have figured with honor in his *Roi au masque d'or*,[1] but he neglected to put it in there: the coquetry of an artist who keeps his finest pearl in his jewel box. He told it marvelously elsewhere, that story, without seeking stylistic effects and terrible words, just as it was, like a newspaper article, and the story gained in flavor for that. That's what I thought of first when I read the last part of your 'Opium Talk' during the grotesque and macabre excursion of Monsieur B***'s body between Laclos-Larive and Générale V***, from the coaching entrance to the bench where they left him seated.

"In a mask, there's almost the same impression of fantastic terror as in reality, but there's even more terror in Schwob's story. Since he never wrote it, I have a yen to tell it to you, for you'll write it."

"Certainly, if it's a windfall!"

"Well, come on, for here come a few masks. The lecture is over, and these gardens will be haunted. A few of these ladies are going to return to the cemetery; they lock them up early there. Let's avoid encounters. I'll take you to dinner in Beaulieu; the Reserve is twenty minutes away, and the road that goes there

---

1 *Le Roi au masque d'or* (1892; selected stories tr. in *The King in the Golden Mask*) by Marcel Schwob was the author's second collection of Poesque stories, most of which had first appeared in the *Écho de Paris*.

via Saint-Jean goes along the bay, a true delight. Yes, I'll enrich you with a tale and repay you with dinner. It's the one who talks who always ought to pay the bill; nothing is dearer than being listened to."

"Let's go."

It was dusk, a dusk that was all violet mist. An attenuated landscape was fading away, a landscape of hyacinth and obscure amethyst, in which only the heights, slightly roseate, still retained any sunlight.

II

"It was twenty years ago, the winter of 1880 or 1881, crimes, always imposing in number in London, were increasing in frightful proportions. Bizarrely enough, the nocturnal murders and attacks were specialized and localized; the criminals seemed to have adopted a neighborhood. It was in the Docklands, along the interminable quays that border the Thames east of the City, further than Whitechapel and the ill-famed districts of the capital, a quarter of sheds and vast hangars, only populated during the day by a swarming army of warehousemen, port employees and stevedores, which changed at seven o'clock in the evening into a bleak and equivocal solitude, all its diurnal population having returned to the suburbs. It was in the Docklands and their sad streets, bordered with tarred planks and palisades, that murders were multiplying that winter in an entirely unprecedented fashion.

"That epidemic of murder initially plagued the workers. People lay in wait for them, on pay day, at the exits from the poor drinking dens, whose lights blinked in the dirty fog of the river, at the corners of hangars and immense construction yards . . . for it was on Sunday morning that the police made an ample harvest of corpses.

"The man was found dead, in some doorway or backed up against a boundary marker, his pockets turned out, robbed, cleaned out of all money and even his meager jewelry: a silver watch or the slender wedding ring of a worker. Curiously enough, however, those cadavers had no wounds, not a single bruise. It was impossible to find on them the slightest evidence of blows; the work was neatly done. It was a neat and careful crime, which bore no signature, and put the police on the back foot. The city was terrorized. At the first discoveries, it was thought that they were congested drunkards, and the police would have liked to accredit that opinion among the population of London, but the press opposed it, and the gin-sellers too, for there really would have been too many deceased drunkards in the capital that year, all the more so as the winter was quite mild, one of those damp winters, all fog and drizzle, colds and flu, but which didn't invoke congestion by freezing.

"And the cadavers continued to mount up. Not a morning passed when some dead man wasn't discovered on the paving stones of a quay or in one of the side streets of the Docklands. The murderers didn't stick to Saturday evening; they worked all week; worse than that, plundered dead men were found on Monday morning; the killers didn't even rest on Sunday. The English gentry were deeply shocked, but public opinion breathed easier; the criminals couldn't be English; even criminals would have rested on the Lord's Day; the assassins were surely foreigners, or they were Irish Catholics, abominable Fenians devoid of faith or law. That was a relief to the public conscience; London congratulated itself.

"However, the killing continued, and the police, run off their feet, couldn't discover anything. Now, as well as workers, the robbers were attacking merchants, and millionaires from the City brought to Docklands by their business affairs. Mr. Thomas Smithson, of Smithson, Burnet & Co., was picked up on the corner of Burde Street; naturally, his wallet, the gold in his fob pocket and all his jewelry had disappeared, but his pelisse had been left. Thomas Smithson, esquire, was found comfortably seated, coiffed in his bowler hat, on a pile of wooden beams, a whole heap of Norwegian wood that had just been disembarked on to the quay. The widow made a big fuss and obtained an audience with the Lord Mayor; the police, severely admonished, redoubled their surveillance. Poor Thomas Smithson, such a fine fellow, the father of seven daughters and three sons, who was a great lover of French wine!

"After Thomas Smithson it was the turn of George Burnett, his associate, and one could believe momentarily in a personal vendetta against the company, but in the meantime, the murder of workers continued. Then it was the turn of Sir Algernon Fisler, Monsieur Staraud, a French merchant established in London, Sir Edward Trostetten, and the worthy Mr. Wellington Clevely, whose widow, a creature so pretty that the Prince of Wales had once eyed her up at Epsom, has since become a peeress. Mr. Clevely left something like sixty millions.

"It was a veritable hecatomb. The Docklands area became impossible after two bigwigs of London commerce had been expedited there. How could one venture there if lives were suppressed there with that impunity and that rascally and admirable celerity? For many people in the clubs and drawing rooms of the aristocracy were beginning to take a veritable interest in those invisible and ungraspable assassins. But business is business, and no business is possible if the head of the company, even if he's a multimillionaire, doesn't go to cast an eye over the population of workers. And as London is, before anything else, a business center, London ended up getting excited.

"The press led the campaign, as ever.

"The chief constable was summoned by the Lord Mayor. There was a bill before parliament, and, following reprimand after reprimand, the police made this observation: although the cadavers picked up in the Docklands bore no trace of wounds or bruises, and no evidence of strangulation, they did exhale—it could not be denied, especially if one sniffed them attentively—a culpable odor of chloroform.

"Among the poor victims of the first murders, the policemen's sense of smell could have been deceived by the reek of dirt and poverty, the odors of sweat and alcohol amassed in the sad garments of those humble folk—men who labor and toil don't smell good anywhere. How could the pharmaceutical odor be discerned in the midst of that composite amalgam, aggravated by the insipidity of the sooty atmosphere of the city's factories and the fog of the river? With the well-dressed and well-groomed corpses or aristocracy and high commerce, however, no error was possible; those dead men had definitely been chloroformed; they were dealing with victims of asphyxiation.

"The rich victims also permitted the police to establish, and even to determine the exact time of the crimes; Smithson, Burnett, Clevely and others, when they came to the Docks, left the construction yards and hangars at seven o'clock, when the workshops closed and the workers left. In their haste to get back to the warmth of their luxurious and comfortable homes, they did not hang about in bars and taverns like the poor port laborers; with them, no idling or lingering could be admitted. The attacks had, therefore, taken place between six and eight o'clock, shortly before or shortly after seven. It was at nightfall that the assassins operated, and with what impunity, great God, since no one had ever seen them at work, let alone caught them!

"They asphyxiated their victims with chloroform, but how? Where? In the middle of the street? That was not admissible. The fog was their accomplice, then, the terrible fuliginous London fog, which fills the streets, especially on the banks of the river, with a fetid and glacial atmosphere, like a russet lining of tinder, through which the water of the Thames and the glow of street-lights blink in such a sinister fashion. It is true that one cannot see five yards ahead in that splenetic and diabolical fog . . . and the police also noticed that one encountered that winter, in the Docklands, more staggering drunkards than the statistics of London intoxication implied, in spite their imposing numbers.

"The policemen suddenly recalled certain groups encountered in recent months at nightfall, along the Thames, always composed of three individuals: a drunkard and two friends, the drunken man in the middle and the two friends sustaining him by the armpits and taking him home fraternally, the man in the middle staggering and the others supporting his steps. They formed a touching group at some street corner, and then fled, rapidly, into the night: the cold, opaque night. Does one follow two workers taking another, somewhat intoxicated, through the fog? In all frankness, however, those encounters, to which the worthy policemen had paid no heed at first, had been repeated with a strange insistence in the last three months, and the police made the decision to keep a lookout henceforth for groups of three who were staggering slackly, at nightfall, amid the russet mists of the bleak deserted quays and somber little side streets bordered with large hangars.

"And the policemen did well, for the first group of three disheveled workers that the policemen attempted to accost in the winter dusk suddenly broke up as they approached; the friend on the right and the one on the left fled precipitately, leaving the drunkard in the middle, who collapsed on the ground. Picked up from the mud, palpated and assisted, the drunkard was found to be a cadaver, a cadaver already robbed, completely despoiled. But the point at which the stupor of the police became almost hallucinatory was when they discovered that the cadaver had a mask: a marvelously modeled wax mask, with nothing excessive or grotesque, a veritable human face with perfectly insignificant features, neutral in coloration: a false face tightly fitted to his own with the aid of a kerchief knotted around the temples.

"The cadaver was masked and, a frightful thing, when the kerchief was unfastened and the mask was removed, it was found to be full of chloroform, like a cup; for the mask, hermetically sealed, had no opening, either in the place of the eyes or that of the mouth. That resistant hood of wax was both a blindfold and a gag; it blinkered and stifled; the chloroform with which it was filled only stupefied the death-throes, it did not even hasten them.

"Once the mask was placed over the face, the man in the hands of the murderers was an inert thing, an automaton, dead flesh. He could neither cry out nor struggle. The thieves walked him round for some time in the fog, like a suffering friend whom they were sustaining and comforting, long enough to collect his jewelry and empty his pockets; then, when the man was cleaned out, his mask was removed and he was deposited gently and neatly in a corner, on a woodpile, or against a hangar.

"What do you think of that little stroll of a dying man, who is being robbed tranquilly, in complete security, whose path you cross and whom you brush almost without suspecting it, between six and seven o'clock when the workshops of the Docks empty, in the humble russet wadding of the fog?"

And sure of his effect, Monsieur Rabastens—we were installed on the veranda of the Reserve, in the process of taking a seven o'clock white port—begged me to choose the dishes myself, and, offering me the menu, relit his cigar from the fire of my London.[1]

III

"And did the murders continue?" I interrogated him, full of interest in the story.

"The assassins attempted to continue, but the fuse had been drawn; the alerted population were suspicious; the masked cadaver had been more than a revelation. When they came out of the dockyards, the workers no longer risked themselves alone; they traversed the Docks in bands and only separated when they

---

1 The manufacture of cigars was a significant industry in the East End of London in the 1890s.

were outside the danger zone. As for aristocrats and businessmen, they only went abroad henceforth flanked by veritable escorts; the very simplicity of the procedure that had guaranteed the murderers' impunity for so long, once it was known, turned against the assassins. Nothing is easier than to apply a mask to the face of an isolated pedestrian who is not suspicious and is walking placidly through the fog, but once an alerted victim is on his guard, try it and see what happens!

"The murderers continued for a while, but purely out of self-esteem, in order not to be vanquished too soon; *noblesse oblige*, and the corporation of assassins has its pride, but the police, severely reprimanded, were on the alert. They intervened now in the middle of operations, and the few cadavers that still illustrated the Docklands were always found with the masks; the police no longer gave them time to remove them.

"It was always the same hermetically sealed wax mask, without openings over the eyes or the lips, and filled with wadding soaked in chloroform, a mask of rare insignificance, the face of a coward or an honest man, which nevertheless contained death; but the authors of those crepuscular attacks remained undiscoverable themselves. The police never laid a hand on any of them, which inspired an anodyne pleasantry in *Punch*, perhaps a trifle macabre but very English. I'll give it to you, for what it's worth; it's necessary not to require humor from our friends beyond the Manche.

"So, *Punch*, as seriously as can be, published this sensational news: *New crime in Docklands. The police have the guilty parties in their hands* . . . And it was the story, in the official-statement style that English papers affect, the story of a fainted man perceived, backed up in the arch of a coaching entrance, in the middle of three workmen who seemed to be helping him; with that, the intervention at the run of the police, scenting, in that care given to a drunkard, the usual maneuver of the local assassins. When they arrived, however, as they were effecting the arrests, it turned out to be an assembly of workers around one of their own, who had just been snatched from the hands of two knights of chloroform. The murderers had fled, but the workers had just removed the unfortunate asphyxiation victim's mask, and were trying to reanimate him; one of those present, in fact, was making the dying man respire smelling salts, and one of them was brandishing triumphantly the wax mask that he had just removed. The policemen, as brutal as they always are in London, pushed the group of rescuers aside and hastened around the unconscious man.

"Immediately, the group of helpful workers took flight in the darkness and the policemen found themselves in the presence of a masked cadaver, the passer-by with the bottle of salts had been holding them out to a mask, the worker whose hand was brandishing a wax mask and had just freed the patient therefrom was only a member of the association with the tools of his trade; the knights of chloroform had bluffed the police once more; the police had had the murders in their hands and had let them escape.

"That was the last story printed with regard to the Docklands crimes. *Se non è vero, è ben trovato.*[1] But try a little of this fish soup. They make it marvelously in this restaurant, one only finds anything similar in Isnart's in Marseille. Delightful, eh? And saffroned to perfection. I almost like it better than the bouillabaisse. And how do you like my story?"

"It would be a good Poe if it weren't a good Schwob."

"And it will be a Lorrain, since I've told it to you.[2] Personally, what enchants me about that macabre story is that it's absolutely English; better than that, it's almost a symbol of life beyond the Manche. Real or invented, those murders could only have taken place in London; it requires the banks of the Thames and the

1 "Even if it's not true, it's a good story" (slightly misquoted in the original, perhaps because the author had only heard it cited, not written down). The remark is general attributed to Giordano Bruno.

2 Actually, Lorrain had used the idea of masks containing ether used for murder before, although he is obviously too modest to mention it here, in "Crime Unconnu" (tr. as "An Uncanny Crime"), one of the etheric tales in *Sensations et Souvenirs* (1895).

supreme indifference of the English passer-by as décor and atmosphere for those anonymous crimes of the street and the fog. In no other country in the world could the suppression of a human being occur with that monstrous security. Those asphyxiations on the public highway also require the complicity of alcohol; it's only in the city of drunkenness—and what drunkenness, that of gin!—that criminals could risk walking a dying man around in a mask without attracting attention. In London individuality is so forceful in everyone, and the passer-by is so absorbed in himself and with himself that he goes straight ahead without seeing anything; he doesn't have the time. In countries of the Latin race, a man staggering between two others, who are sustaining him, would provoke an assembly. Then again, it also required the density of the fog over there to be able to display macabre carnival scenes without provoking a reaction of terror.

"Now, deign to pass over with me the principal characteristics of the crime and see how admirable the invention itself is: the mute death-throes of an anonymous passer-by, who is robbed in the presence of other passers-by who have no suspicion, assassinated under the mask that leaves no trace, impunity established on English egotism, and that under the complicit mantle of the native fog—everything is there, admit it: gin, whisky, chloroform, hypocrisy and all the rest."

"Go on, go on, you can never say enough about the English, their egotism and their hypocrisy; my rancor is magnified in listening to you, and it's rancor more than fifteen years old. They've poisoned the world for me; their presence has been the nightmare of all my voyages. I've encountered them everywhere; they faded the skies of the Orient for me, depoeticized the Bay of Salerno, Amalfi, and even Sicily. I encountered them in Taormina, I found them again at Tripoli in the Oasis. Everywhere, their long teeth, their arrogance and their brutality have spoiled races and landscapes for me. Florence is a suburb of London; they infest all of Venice in autumn; they're the errant wound of the world, and the dishonor of the lagoons.

"But Naples is their triumph, for Naples is an evil place; in any case, the true Englishman is in a brothel everywhere, he takes it with him round the world, with his antiseptic lotions, his Sheffield steel razors and his ennui, for the worst of it is that he is annoyed everywhere, and he annoys all the other people, with the worst mores in the world, and finds the means of rendering them tedious, when they're joyful everywhere else.

"I've seen some of them in the desert who, Bible in hand, compromise camel-drivers, for they only like little girls, and in Venice, the old white-haired lords at the Hotel Danielli are as feared as the bespectacled misses of the Hotel de la Luna by the tribe of gondoliers.

"But it's the ennui that they radiate, above all, for which I reproach them. Their Puritanism saddens the world, as their mania for hygiene has made all hotel cuisine insipid; but that spleen, that foggy humor, they take everywhere. Cannes is an English city where one yawns lamentably after an hour, and they've made a cemetery of Menton. Don't you find that ennui floats over the entire Riviera?"

"Oh, there I must stop you." Monsieur Rabastens interjected. "One can't get bored on the Riviera. The carnival in Nice is November in May, one can only breathe there in August, and if ever there was a society extravagant and eccentric enough to make a dead man laugh, it's surely the one that is encountered here, from Saint-Raphael to Menton, Antibes and Cap Martin included.

"All the madmen and madwomen on Earth, all the unhinged and all the hysterics, meet up here—yes, all of them, in truth. They come from Russia, they come from America, they come from Tibet and southern Africa, and what a choice of princes and princesses, marquises and ducs, the true and the false, the most solidly riveted in public opinion as well as the most notably compromised! And how many Majesties, reigning and fallen, those in exile, the deposed, and those on the eve of being deposed! The kings without a civil list and the ex-queens encumbered by budgets, true budgets, those of the economies of the reign, and what do I know, as well? All the morganatic marriages, all the former mistresses of emperors, the entire stock of ex-favorites! And croupiers married by Yankee millionaires and Tziganes abducted by princesses, and ex-scullions who've become the secretaries of princes, and disconcerting pianists for all the intimate concerts, Lizst, Franck and Chopin, all the consumptive warblings of Schumann, artillerymen loved by great tendernesses, coachmen by Muscovite baronnes and Alpines by nihilist boyars, theosophists and voyagers, and on top of that, what an unspeakable load of old ladies!

"Masks, in truth, *Maschere*, as in Mascagni's opera,[1] and what a noisy and joyful saraband of dollars and millions!"

"A pretty image!" And I inclined toward Monsieur Rabastens. "It will do well as a stage. Are you giving it to me for a novel?"

"You think I'm amusing myself with roulades? No, I said *maschere* and I maintain *maschere*. There are scarcely eight of us on this veranda this evening; people aren't coming to dine here. As the daylight is terribly raw here and the blue of the sea and the blue of the sky emphasize cruelly all the filthiness of consciences and all the physical flaws inscribed in the wrinkles and the fadedness of faces, high society has adopted this restaurant for lunch. Sharp eyes are carbonized here, made-up complexions violet-tinted, raisin smiles blaze with fed lead; there's no costume, whether gauze or linen, that can resist the glare of noon under this sky. Well, they all come here, delighted to look one another up and down and to meet up, to greet one another with the corners of the lips or the corner of the eye; they come to observe their ugliness and the level of their income. The fortunate gamblers bring their mistresses here, the unfortunate ones advertise more, the visiting Majesties listen to their national anthems being mur-

---

1 Pietro Mascagni's opera *Le Maschere* [The Masks] was premièred in six theatres simultaneously on 17 January 1901, including one in Genoa, where Lorrain might have seen it, and he would certainly have heard reports of it from residents of Nice who had popped across the border.

dered by rogues from Naples; it's one of the most elegant places on the coast, and when it's bulging with people, as edifying as a fresco by Orcagna under the justice-administering light of the sky.

"Masks in truth, veritable masks that are attenuating now, softened in the evening lighting. Would you like the history of some of them? You'll see whether I'm exaggerating.

"That smoking-jacket dining tête-à-tête with that pretty, tall and supple young woman—from Milan, I'll wager: those eyes with sinuous eyelids, that bulging forehead and that swollen nape are those of a woman of Luini, that's a face of the Lombard school—that smoking-jacket, then, with the humpbacked buttonhole of yellow carnations, has a great Italian name and one of the largest fortunes in Cannes. Prince Assari, a prince consort, a handsome man married for his physical assets—for that slightly faded fast-liver possessed the strangest eyes in the world, and I believe that he still possesses them, although the rest has melted.

"Such as he is, Prince Assari has, for twenty-five or thirty years, maddened all the sensitive women of Italy with the savant flutter of long-lashed eyelids over the clarity of floral irises. The vivid blue eyes of the handsome prince! They swooned when he opened them; when he came to close them, they languished even more amorously. It was for those palpitating glances that little Vera Wodosof married Assari, encountered one spring in Florence, in spite of her mother, aunts and guardian. Assari let it happen. Vera Wodosof brought him thirty millions.

"Unfortunately, Assari's blue eyes didn't extinguish the lust of his little Cossack. First she deceived him with a few friends, then coachmen, grooms and stable-lads, and, as his wife had granted him a contribution of a million, Assari continued to let it go; but in Cannes, because of the grand dukes, people had virtually stopped seeing them, especially after the adventure of that winter.

"Didn't Princess Assari take it into her head to attach to her person a Neapolitan orchestra heard in I know not what Riviera restaurant? The dozen macaronis were installed in her Villa California; they played by day, they played by night; no one suspected little Wodosof of being a melomaniac, and it ended with the abduction of the orchestra leader. The man with the bow and the princess are in Florence now, where they're playing the tune of perfect amour. The prince stayed in Cannes with the villa and the personnel. He consoles himself by dallying in Beaulieu with the stars of La Scala, engaged for the season at Monte Carlo. Thus the money doesn't leave Italy; these people have the cult of the race in their blood; they're the foremost nationalists in the world.

"Would you like the story of the other couple dining over there, at the back, in that unusual luxury of flowers, at least twenty-five louis of Niel roses? Another two-part household, another chronicle of adultery, but more difficult to relate; it's a ladies-only compartment. The tall blonde, so slender, with a splendid complexion, incomparable in her painted gauzes, one might think her a pastel, so fresh and fluffy is everything in that flower-girl, is Eva Quarante of the Variétés, an actress quoted on the Bourse. The other, that hooked nose and bistre complexion, those hooded eyelids over stormy eyes, is the Comtesse de S***, an authentic Comtesse of the purest faubourg, the daughter of a rich boyar. It's also her who has brought the millions into the household; so, while she flirts delicately with the little actress, her latest infatuation, the Comte punts tranquilly on the red and the black in the casino, and wins what he likes, naturally. He has everything he needs for that.

"I promised you masks."

MADAME AGACHE

"The others are unimportant seigneurs," declared Monsieur Rabastens. "I won't even name them for you. Strictly speaking, there would also be the two fat ladies dining intimately, hidden by a screen, but they're more flotsam from Nice than Riviera masks.

"The woman with the wine-lees capote, however, had a salon in Paris, or, rather, a reflection of a salon. She was a relative of du Sommeraud, the composer, the du Sommeraud of *The Druidess* and *Hero and Leander*, also the du Sommeraud of *The Maccabees*, and people went to her gatherings in order to massage themselves with the glory of the illustrious relative, who naturally failed to appear. Madame Hersaint—she was called Madame Hersaint then, for she's a fanatic for divorce and has also buried two husbands, who preferred dying to continuing—has always been at odds with her family. She has what is known as an independent character: never any duties, only rights.

"She's had lawsuits with her sisters, with her mother, with her sons, she's dismissed two husbands before the tribunal, she'll have lawsuits with her grandchildren. She's a litigious and robust personality: all beak and claws, claws and teeth. She's defended herself, that one, in life, and be sure that she'll defend herself for a long time yet.

"A specimen: I have the greatest admiration for her, but, I admire her as a careful man should, at a distance, as one admires an unleashed force or the dementia of an element. Evil? No, but dangerous, because unconscious. A marvelous vitality, a skill and an energy and an intelligence enslaved by a hellish spirit, inventive in words and images, a comical and sometimes vengeful vision of things and people, and as wily as an old prosecutor, but let down by her moist, eccentric humor, a disconcerting incoherence of conduct, leaps of caprice like gusts of wind, sudden hatreds and infatuations, and such a hunger for malicious gossip that she'll recount her own past rather than shut up. Add to that an absolute scorn for all convention and the most outrageous cynicism."

"A true Saint-Simon portrait," I laughed, under my napkin.[1]

---

1 The Duc de Saint-Simon (1675-1755) became belatedly famous for the catty depictions of his contemporaries in his *Mémoires*, which finally saw print in 1820. They were greatly admired by Barbey d'Aurevilly and Flaubert.

"Indeed, she's of that time; she's a figure such as one finds in memoirs. Here they call her the Brinvilliers of gossip, but truly, they exaggerate. Madame Agache—for she's no longer Madame Hersaint—is afflicted above all with a delirious imagination; her sixty years well chimed have not delivered her from sexual visions. Physical amour has remained the obsession of her old age; ambient society only appears to her as fornicating; the people she sees, receives or encounters are evoked for her in the same implacable attitude; for her, there is neither sex nor age. You can imagine the kind of stories that the malady of vision in question suggests to her, and the scandalous chronicles edited by her imagination.

"'It's the finest case of transport from womb to brain that I've seen in my lifetime,' Doctor Morgan said of her,[1] and the phrase explains Madame Agache while excusing her. The Brinvilliers of gossip? No. Mère Agache is unconscious; at the most, she leaks like a cracked vase, and looses in scabrous narrations the foaming excess of an ardent cerebellum. Apart from that, the most amiable woman, in manners and urbanity.

"She has formed a salon here; she has a semblance of authority there; fools seek her out, the timid fear her, friends fond of their repose avoid her; she's as amusing as a hurricane. The name of du Sommeraud, her illustrious relative, has served her well; she has, in any case, played it with an admirable dexterity. A bust is permanently enthroned in her boudoir, and on reception days the flowers are renewed. Above all, she has a musical salon; it was a political salon in Paris, Orléanist and center-left. Family obligations. Signed scores left on the Pleyel. Everything on the Riviera that sings has filed through Mère Agache's house; her matinées are well attended; the star of the season is always to be heard there, and the second star, the one that only appears on subsidized stages and can never be heard anywhere else. Cost: two one-louis tickets for the concert of the worldly artiste during Lent. Needless to say, the star always sings gratis.

---

1 Presumably the American physician John Morgan, author of *Practical Lessons in the Nature and Treatment of the Affections* (1872) and of a thoroughgoing account of the symptoms of syphilis, considered rather shocking at the time.

"*Gratis* is the motto of the mistress of the house in Nice. *Gratis*, that says everything. Mère Agache has put all her pride into never paying an artiste a fee; she employs all her diplomacy in that, and always succeeds, for she's cunning and tenacious, and then, the name of du Sommeraud is there, a funeral trampoline still solid enough to risk a few gymnastics thereon.

"The portrait would be lacking a touch if I didn't reveal to you that Madame Agache, plebeian in Paris, is Comtesse Agache here, of authentic and very fresh nobility, as are all the women she receives. It's the Nice air that determines that; titles grow hereabouts like peas; it comes to the most innocent in traversing the Var, as the art of *tutu panpan* came to Valmajour on hearing the nightingale sing;[1] it's the Riviera climate, so mild that it develops the coronets of baronnes and the aplomb of flashy foreigners.

"Nice is a unique country.

"If you stay here for some time, it's absolutely necessary to be introduced to the worthy Agache; it's a salon that it's necessary to know. Tender shoots are quite rare there, but old pretentions abound; nowhere else will you encounter such a collection of dressed-up ostriches and clever dogs; all those young centenarians are illuminated like public fêtes; besides which, the food is exquisite and the buffet abundant; the comtesse nourishes her artistes. Nothing of the Baronne du Vitrail—another historic Muse of the literary reception, that one, whom one encounters *chez* Comtesse Agache and who, being rather tight, offers her guests tapioca sorbets, cups of lime tea and tooth-breaking cakes.

"You'll hear the praises of Old Nice sung and declaimed there—not that of the port and Les Ponchettes, but imperial Nice, and even that of the Marchélat, the Nice of Cimiez, Beaumettes and Mont-Boron! Ligie Cruelli, always cruel to hear; Ninon d'Espée, gallantry retired after fortune made; Madame

---

1 Valmajour is a character in Alphonse Daudet's play *Numa Roumestan* (1881) nowadays only remembered because of a cutting remark about his inspiration by the nightingale in Oscar Wilde's "The Decay of Lying."

Estréna; Nachy Robson of Lifts, Robson & Co.; pianists from the Ukraine estranged from their steppe, and poets of Beaulieu, fanatical Lotists, lovers of moonlight and nocturnal fishing on the coast of Saint-Jean. You'll also hear scenes from *Le Misanthrope* there by old Tristamort, ex-doyen of the Comédie-Française.

"It's a unique spectacle: the old actors sing there, the ex-singers warble, and all eyes are tearful and all voices quaver; one always leaves at the peak of emotion. 'Oh, my dear, what a matinée, what an unforgettable hour!'

"'It's great art!'

"'What diction! It's admirable!'

"'And so poignant!'

"'She's never given that at the theater!'

"'Why has she quit the stage?'

"'How simple she is!'

"'And how great she is!'

"'She breaks your heart!'

"'She draws your tears!'

"'Look, I'm weeping.'

"'A little more of this bread and foie gras?'

"'Shall one see you tomorrow at Madame Trotter's?'

"'I haven't been invited.'

"'That doesn't matter, come anyway, there'll be a violinist.'

"'Ah!'

"'Seventeen years old, angelic eyes, still pure, so it's said, and playing the violin!!! The bow-thrust of an archangel.'

"'Oh, you're telling me too much.'

"'Have another of these petit-fours.'

"'No, I'm sticking to the mirlitons.'

"So the society goes; all of Nice is there. Program of the matinée: dry cakes, young artistes, great art and mirlitons."

"You have a precious gift for imitation; you'd make a fortune in Paris," I couldn't help saying to Monsieur Rabastens. "All my congratulations."

The fact is that my host was priceless. He had just mimed and twittered in differentiated and marvelously nuanced intonations the exasperated chatter of worldly parrots with reception fever.

But Madame Agache was leaving. She had just settled the bill and the maître d'hôtel was helping her to wrap herself in a violet mantle in watered silk and satin with a gauzy frill, evidently from a good *maison*. She came toward us. She was an old lady, slightly hunched but solid and robust in her short stature, her nose abrupt and her jaw square, in an extraordinarily fresh face; the smooth and relaxed complexion was astonishing. Madame Agache had a youthful expression: pale eyes of a harsh and cold blue jutting beneath heavy eyelids, and that willful gaze said everything about the woman.

Diademed with wine-lees roses, draped in violet watered silk, Comtesse Agache traversed the restaurant slowly. A tall and stout woman followed her, a sort of giant with large, soft eyes drowned in a face white with fat. As she went past our table Madame Agache blinked at Rabastens and stopped.

"Why, it's you, Rabastens! What are you doing here? One never sees you any more."

And her penetrating gaze looked me up and down.

Rabastens introduced me.

"But it's you that one doesn't see any more, and I lament that, Comtesse," the worthy clown protested. "I no longer encounter you at our friends the de Joussys."

To which Madame Agache retorted: "Your friends, not mine; keep them. That poor de Joussy no longer has a voice and her husband has lost his fortune. They only have their villa and the mortgages; no more money, no more voice! What do you expect me to do with them? Bonsoir, Rabastens."

And she took her leave, with a rather cold bow. "Are you coming, my dear?" And, suddenly relaxing in tenderness, she took the arm of the stout giant with the moist eyes of a good dog.

"'No more money, no more voice. What do you expect me to do with them?' The whole woman is there; that's her cynicism.

Bah! Isn't she right, since society supports her? It's our cowardice, our laziness, and our complicity that lets these characters get away with it. Do you know who's accompanying her? You didn't recognize her? I wanted to leave you the pleasure of recognizing her. Elisa Tavernier, the great Elisa, the café-concert singer acclaimed at the Tuileries as at soirées in Compiègne. Elisa the crowd-stirrer, Sensibility made woman; Elisa, the glory of the Third Empire and the star, the only one, of *Chanson*. You didn't recognize that bountiful mouth, thick and sensual, which cut a phrase like a stamp, that moving mouth made for diction, and the moistness of those tender eyes!

"Oh, that one is emotion itself.

"She no longer sings, she who sang so much, and, retired to Eze, she sees from afar the world and Paris, where an old chronicler sometimes asks what happened to her. She no longer wants to appear in public.

"You can see that one has curious encounters, even in this restaurant, rather empty in the evening. Masks and Riviera flotsam."

THE HOUSE OF HAPPINESS

W E came back from Beaulieu on foot. It was a moist and nacreous night, the moonlight seemingly humid. The coast road from Beaulieu to Nice, in April, is a scene from Theocritus, especially by night, where the modernity of the villas is blurred and attenuated in the shadow of Sicilian olive groves.

To our right and our left, beds of hyacinths, roses and freesias, staged in terraces, embalmed the calm air, filling the night with vegetal souls. At every bend in the road the vaporous spur of a promontory appeared, enclosing the horizon and the sea in a heroic curve: "the sea that weeps in lamenting the Sirens," as a line of Heredia sings;[1] and other verses quivered within me, as many fluttering wings, lines from eclogues and epithalamia, and lines from idylls too, evoked by the poetry of the moon and the night, the night in which Greek paganism wanted to see the nudity of Selene upright amid the clouds, in the august and familiar attitude of a goddess drawing the bow.

> *The arrows of her quiver are moonbeams,*
> *Parents of visions and legendary fables,*
> *Which dance in the mist and reach out a hand;*
> *And, standing naked, she smiles in dream*
> *At shepherds on the hills and fishers on the strand*
> *And gently whitens the myrtles of the road.*[2]

1 The quoted line is the final line of José-Maria de Heredia's sonnet "L'Oubli."

2 These lines are Lorrain's, as are the other snatches of poetry in the text not otherwise noted.

And it was indeed Selene who extended at our feet the shadows of old fig trees, while our footsteps rang clearly on the road. Gods without number seemed to populate the silence, especially on the somber arabesques of the capes, where we would have liked the colonnades of temples; floating mists, doubtless exhaled by the sea, were reminiscent of the soft ascension of pale Oceanides rising toward some invisible punished Titan.

We were silent, Monsieur Rabastens and I, evidently inhibited by confidences exchanged. I was subjected involuntarily to the movement of recoil that every retailer of malicious gossip inspires in his listeners when his sack is empty. It is the chastisement of tellers of scandalous stories and disastrous raconteurs. Human malignity initially takes pleasure in hearing them; then the instinct of conservation awakes and puts us on our guard; we feel threatened in our turn by the irony of the storyteller and withdraw from him, as if from a danger.

Monsieur Rabastens must have sensed the atmosphere of malaise that had been established between us by his portrait of Madame Agache weighing upon us even more heavily than I did, for he had not unclenched his teeth since we left the restaurant, and, hardly encouraged by my mutism, he continued to match strides with me, evidently regretting having said too much.

We had just passed Villefranche, asleep in the depths of its haven. It was like a great vat of shadow hollowed out beneath us by the sheer wall of the mountains. Above our heads were rocky slopes of Mont Alban and its fort, then the pine-forests of Mont Boron—Mont Boron, resounding by day with the blasts of the clarion school and the hesitant thunder of apprentice drummers. We were following the route that was furrowed by day by trams, but in good weather the Masséna-Beaulieu no longer operated at that hour.

Suddenly, on our left, between the glaucous sabers of a cactus hedge, the whiteness of a colonnade loomed up. Built into the rock, above the bay and overlooking the void, it was the peristyle of a little villa. The moonlight bathed it entirely, and in the calm of the pearly night, made it more Greek than it must have been in reality. Silvered and somnolent under the slender shadows cast by its columns, it seemed the very synthesis of the landscape, the little temple that I had demanded a little while ago in the enchanted quietude of the night.

I had never noticed it in broad daylight. One might have thought that it had surged forth in response to the incantation of the hour and the solitude . . . Never noticed . . . and God knows how often I had made that journey from Nice to Beaulieu. One might have thought it a phantom villa. From what Ionia, what fortunate isle or Attica had it come by night, like a shadow? Had its astral image been voyaging in April on the Mediterranean, and had it alighted, like a Halcyon, on the rocky slope on that mountain?

Delight made me pause before the mirage of that villa.

That was the moment Monsieur Rabastens had been waiting for, in order to return to grace.

"The House of Happiness," he said, without wanting to see my gesture requesting silence. "There aren't only sniggers and grimaces on the Riviera; one also finds smiles there and admirable transparencies of souls, but it's necessary to know where to find them; the treasures are hidden. Not all these villas shelter whores or madwomen; girls rented by the lust of males who have subsequently become honest women—well-earned villas of repose—and hysterics of the two worlds come here to exasperate their neuroses in the endemic folly of their peers and the enervation of the mistral.

"Yes, sometimes elite individuals are encountered here, individuals in conformity with the divine beauty of the décor; they don't all come here to bandage old moral wounds or to wash away old stains in the blue of the sea and the blue of the sky. The Riviera also possesses harmonious guests, and creatures of breeding and grace sometimes come here to die in beauty.

"That's the case of Monsieur and Madame Astra, the couple who live in that villa—an old couple, for Madame Astra is sixty-five and Monsieur Astra seventy.

"Monsieur Astra? That name doesn't tell you anything? It was, however, a well-known name that has its resonance in its time . . . between 1855 and 1870. But you're too young and don't know the Empire. Astra was performed at the Français, Lemerre's anthologies cite fragments of his *Niobides*; Gounod ought to have composed the incidental music, but it's Chasserian who wrote it. He was, above all, the man of *Hylas in Mytilene*, a delightful poem that recalls the manner of Chénier, of which Henri de Régnier seems reminiscent, and he wrote the libretto of *Hero and Leander* for du Sommeraud. But who remembers Chasserian, Astra, and even du Sommeraud now?

"So, Astra was a poet, and even quite a good poet, but classical, ponderous, devoid of the mystery or impetuosity that breaks windows, forces admiration and imposes a man on posterity. He was also very handsome, very poor and—something rare then, which has since become undiscoverable—possessed of a high and verily honest morality. He had conscience and character. Needless to say, he was never a success.

"A position as a librarian at Carnavalet, obtained for him by Ponsard one evening at Compiègne, ensured the mediocrity of his existence; in addition, like many artists and men of letters of the epoch, Astra went to the Court; he was even at the Empress's *petite lundis*. The ex-Comtesse de Théba had a sort of mundane and Spanish infatuation for the cold handsome fellow with the profile of a medallion and a warm and musical voice.

"Morny, always attentive to the slightest caprices of the Tuileries, had imposed the *Niobides* on the Comédie; Arsène Houssaye was reigning there at the time, and if Astra had been able to take advantage of the opportunity he would have been in the Académie, like everyone else. But Astra wasn't a man of that time. He had a soul too elevated not to make a mess of his life, and the proof is that, poor, devoid of intrigue and noticed by a sovereign, it was within the entourage of his protectress that he encountered the passion of his entire existence. Among the swarm of elegant and sumptuous young women who then formed the Empress's flying squadron, it was toward the prettiest, the wittiest, the most adulated, the most celebrated and the most in vogue that his amour ingenuously went. Out of all of them, the poet chose Comtesse Litwiska, the most Slavic and the most delicately blonde of blonde Polish comtesses that were then admired at the Court. Comtesse Litwiska!

"You've seen her portraits at the Centennale. The Comtesse was the most painted woman of the century: portrait by Winterhalter, portrait by Delaunay, portrait by Bonnat, portrait by Carolus. The one by Clairin is perhaps the best.

"Astra wrote the most beautiful verses of his oeuvre for her; his *Hylas at Mytilene* is dedicated to Comte Litwiski. How did the comtesse welcome the homage of the poet? Even the memoires of Vieil-Castel don't say. Carried away in the social whirlwind of the epoch, a fanatical waltzer, an accomplished flirt, witty, coquette, feverish for good works in between times—for she chanced to be charitable—Comtesse Litwiska never gave purchase to any suspicion, and then, Litwiski was a husband of the utmost ability with the épée, and one respects the wives of husbands like that.

"Intelligent and literate, the comtesse was doubtless flattered, perhaps touched, but the matter didn't go any further. Astra, devoured by amour, dried up, became thinner, even became slightly ridiculous; he ceased to be invited to the Tuileries, but his post as a librarian remained to him.

"Then, one day, Comtesse Litwiska returned to Warsaw, the comte was in the embassies; Berlin, London and Madrid possessed the couple. Astra, desperate, riveted to Paris, wrote; the beautiful comtesse had her poetic correspondence. Did she reply? Who can tell? Then there was the war with Germany, 1870, the Commune, the disasters, Monsieur Thiers in power; no more mention was heard of the beautiful Pole; Astra was kept on at his library out of pity. Poor, ill and weak, Astra continued to inundate Europe and the powers, at random, with his adoring prose: fervent letters to Vienna, golden sonnets to Constantinople; and then, perhaps by dint of weeping, Astra lost his sight, his eyes darkened, the poet went blind.

"France had her Homer, and then there was embarrassment at first, and soon the misery, the utter destitution, the atrocious distress and the abandonment of the aged man of letters, an infirm and forgotten old age—when one morning, in that hovel, in the poet's furnished room, there was a visitor: a nice little old woman, agreeable and perfumed, elegant and twittering . . . pretty, no, for the lady with white headbands had a face scarred by smallpox. The malady had spared her but had ravaged her face . . .

"And that little old lady, all silk and lace, was Comtesse Litwiska: a Comtesse Litwiska somewhat disfigured, and somewhat ruined too, or at least of diminished fortune, since she still had an income of thirty thousand francs, but a Comtesse Litwiska finally free, a Comtesse Litwiska now a widow, who had come to find her poet, her poet who had remained handsome and loving, but infirm, her poet devoid of eyes, his eyes perhaps worn away by weeping, her blind poet, quit twenty years ago, and who still saw her beautiful, as he had known her twenty-five years before. And that lover from her past, that inebriate of her triumphs who had remained faithful to her memory, Comtesse Litwiska married, bravely and simply, as if she were paying a debt . . .

"He, the old infant, let himself go. He wept recklessly over the two proffered hands, tears of amazement and tears of joy, he who had shed so many bitter ones, slow and warm tears of blindness and vision, for, in him, the adored image had never budged, had always remained the same.

"Monsieur and Madame Astra live here all year round, in that villa constructed by Madame for her old man of letters. They never go to Paris, nor even to Nice. In the summer, when the heat is aggravated, they go to the mountains, Saint-Martin or Savona.

"I promised you two beautiful souls! What do you think of that Philemon and Baucis of Villefranche? That happy Oedipus and that beloved Antigone of the Riviera? Will you forgive me a little for my others stories, the nasty, the embarrassing and the dirty ones?

"Have you noticed how singularly and intensely radiant that house is in the moonlight? One might think that the light were emanating from its walls, like a psychic glory. It's the radiation of happiness.

> *My closed eyes still see you beautiful*
> *As fresh as the very first day,*
> *And our youth will be eternal,*
> *For eternal is my amour."*

And I sensed that the rancor I had nursed against Monsieur Rabastens was mollified.

THE CHIMERAS

NOW there was Nice and the enchantment of the Baie des Anges; the city, as if in a gulf, at our feet in the mist, pearled by the moonlight and the sea; Nice and its staged circle of mountains, the flight of the Esterel in the distance, on the horizon, a mauve arabesque posed at sea level, while in the foreground, at the entrance to the valley, the somber mass of the château, highlighted by the glare of the rounded port, was like a crouching beast in the immense yellow halo of all the city's lights. In the middle distance, hills sank into the shadow, Saint-Barthélemy, Saint Silvestre, Les Baumettes, Cimiez. Escalades of villas, invaded by hotels, they seemed to be making futile attempts to escape toward the summits, toward the haughty unreality of the Alpilles, upright in the sky with, dominating them all, the rocky, snow-covered, jagged grayness of Mont-Chauve and the Var: a dream landscape, in truth, that was no more Nice than Algiers seen from Mustapha, Naples from Posilippo or no matter what city in a painting by Leonardo da Vinci: clouds, mountains, distant frissons of water, and, spread like aerial milk over the nostalgic *elsewhere* of that deceptive panorama, the luminous poison of the moonlight and the sea.

"*You will love everything that I love and which loves me: the water, the clouds, the silence, the night, the immense green sea, the formless and multiform water, the place where you will not be, the lover that you will not know, the monstrous flowers, the perfumes that trouble the will, and the cats that mewl in soft hoarse voices, and swoon like women over pianos.*"[1]

And it was no longer Greek reminiscences but the prose of Baudelaire that haunted me, as if poured forth by the living light of the stars, into the unreality of that enchanted scenery.

To our right, as to our left, there were now trees of rare species, terraces of villas, lawns of parks and flower beds. All the cosmopolitan luxury in refuge on Mont Boron, to the east of the city, descended from garden to garden toward the port.

And as we passed in front of the gate of one of those villas, a wrought iron gate, appropriately decorative, whose two pillars were ornamented by blue faience chimeras—a broad driveway curved away immediately after the gate and was lost in the bushes, dominated by cypress and parasol pines—Monsieur Rabastens, whose footsteps, matching mine, sounded loud in the calm of the night, and who had fallen silent again, attempted to break the truce by designating with a vague gesture the invisible villa of that garden.

"After the tender and touching, would you like the tragic, drama after the smiling melancholy and fear after tenderness? I have all of that in my stock. After the story of the House of Happiness, would you like that of The Chimeras? That's the name of this villa. Just now, in the restaurant—I regret it now—I only showed you masks of vanity and covetousness, forced grins and sniggers. The people that I've silhouetted were stiffened in the arrogant ennui of a false position or the laxity of a sullen vice; exceeded and riveted by the same habits—worse than that, the same manifestations of habits—by the fashions that sustain them, they dined there pretentiously, condemned to advertise their flaws by the same society to which their flaws belong. Two display an adultery that amuses the salons, the clubs and the chronicles; another tries to closet a confident great artiste and replace with a five louis dinner a twenty-five louis fee. All that

---

1 The quotation is from Charles Baudelaire's prose poem "Les Bienfaits de la lune," from the posthumous assembly *Spleen de Paris*.

is nothing but a comedy, in sum, and the lowest kind, the buffoonery of exhausted, grotesque or hilarious masks; but there are sometimes masks that weep real tears, and the Riviera also sees dramas.

"Would you like to hear one of those dramas?"

Monsieur Rabastens was trying to enter into grace again. At his first words I had stopped outside the gate of The Chimeras. That was an acquiescence. Monsieur Rabastens linked arms with me.

"So be it. One of the most poignant and most intense of those dramas unfolded here, behind this gate, in that villa. Oh, it was thirty-five years ago! It doesn't date from yesterday, but it's had enough fine humanity to be eternal; and then again, it has its perfume of the end of Empire. The heroine, a Marguerite Gauthier of the world, as consumptive and adored as the fictional one, would certainly have tempted Feuillet or Dumas." And, in response a movement on my part: "Don't worry, I'm not going to narrate *The Lady of the Camellias.*

"So, it was 1875. In those days, physicians still sent patients afflicted with pulmonary ailments to Nice to be cured; nowadays they send them to Menton to die. The villa that I've designated to you belonged then to one of the biggest movers of money in Paris, Monsieur T***, the director of the Crédit Rouennais, a financial association now disappeared, whose annual profits were then numbered in the millions. Monsieur T*** had turned into a paltry little old man with a narrow chest and the look of a bird of prey.

"Monsieur T***, in spite of his unseductive exterior, his bilious complexion and his sparse hair, was reputed to have had—and, in fact, had had—the prettiest women in Paris, and that for twenty years already, in the epoch when his marvelous flair as a businessman had imposed him on the finance of Vienna, London and Berlin. First there had been women of the theater, women of elevated gallantry—one said 'high-class whores' in those days. The puny T*** was an ogre in amour; he displayed a disconcerting appetite and went after healthy and plump young women like a cannibal after fresh flesh. Then again, vanity was mixed in with it. After having enjoyed their beauty he enjoyed the luxury of his mistresses. Playing to the gallery, he encouraged their caprices, even their prodigality; and this marvelous property of The Chimeras, whose wall we're going along, was created for one of them.

"Thirty-five years ago, Mont Boron wasn't the agglomeration of villas that it has become; the high road that we're following didn't go around its flanks; one went to Monte Carlo by the old Genoa road, and The Chimeras, hollowed out and built of the same rock as the mines, one of the first villas to blossom east of Nice, caused quite a stir among the population of the Riviera and excited the curiosity of those who winter here enormously. People came from Cannes and Menton to see Monsieur T***'s folly!

"Poor Chimeras! Now there are ten properties on Mont Boron worth as much, and at least five that surpass it. The wings of those Chimeras, whose blue bodies then snaked along all the pathways—the majority have disappeared today—Monsieur T*** had spread in honor of Emma Ritz, an actress at the Variétés. Who remembers that name today? But, a rupture having taken place between the financier and the actress before the villa was finished, The Chimeras remained Monsieur T***'s. He came to spend two months alone here in the first winter; in the second, there was a woman of the world, an adorable young woman, married and the mother of two children, who came, accompanied by her husband the Comte de V***, to install herself in the villa built for the courtesan, and afterwards, in subsequent years, came to spend three months here.

"The Comtesse de V***, very delicate in the chest and sent to the Midi by her physicians, came to The Chimeras as a guest. The Comte de V***, fairly good Poitou nobility, played the Bourse, doing business, and old T*** deigned to enlighten him with his advice. In brief, that old roué made the fortune of the husband in order to provide for the wife. Anyone who knew T***'s habits and his experience of law and property, knew that he didn't give his advice or his hospitality for nothing. In any case, it wasn't as an invited guest but as a mistress of the house that the young woman lived at The Chimeras; the luxury of her carriage, her attire and the very way of life she displayed was such that, however profitable the comte's operations might have been, they couldn't have sufficed; the comtesse was maintained.

"After the daughters of the theater, the good feminist T*** had developed a taste for socialites, and as the fruit was choice, the old satyr had bitten into it. The fact is that for me, who knew her, I've rarely seen a prettier face and a more delightful creature than the Comtesse de V***. Slim, not very tall, but so well made that every one of her gestures was a harmony and seemed a motion of grace, she was brunette with hair tinted russet in the sunlight and blue-black under artificial light. That slightly wavy hair made her delicate and pale face, with a slightly pointed but willful chin, seem even thinner under its thick tresses; her slightly hollow eyes—cavernous, one might say today—were astonishingly bright. They burned with an intense ardor in that slightly fragile face, languishing, and even more promising, in an indescribable lassitude. The sculpted mouth, a feverish red, also seemed to be burning. Such as I remember her, she was a woman that one couldn't see without noticing her, and when one had noticed her, one took away a vision of her that set one's blood ablaze. Her beauty left a passionate sadness in the heart.

"Now, misfortune determined that that dying beauty inspired a veritable and savage passion in the old man. That libertine had her in his blood and in his soul, and, for fear of losing her, in order to conserve her and have him all to himself, he imagined an infamy: he ruined her husband.

"He directed his operations on the Bourse; it was an easy thing for him to do. In two or three speculative purchases advised by Monsieur T***, the Comte de V*** was cleaned out, emptied, executed in the market. The Comtesse no longer had anything on which to rely but the generosity of her maintainer. From the magnificent lover, he became her master. This is where the story becomes dramatic and obscure. At what precise moment did the young woman become the old man's mistress? Malicious gossip represented her as a lover from the first year of her installation in The Chimeras, but the trap set by the financier suggests, on the contrary, that he hastened the ruination of the husband in order to break down the resistance of the wife. Madame de V*** was well born; she wouldn't have given herself like a slut. If she accepted the caresses of the sexagenarian that T*** was, it was because she saw herself threatened in her luxury and the future of her children. Perhaps it was the mother who sacrificed herself, the mother and the wife, for the continuation of the story renders difficult the hypothesis that Comte de V*** was a complaisant husband.

"At any rate, after the ruination of the V***s, the situation at The Chimeras changed completely. It was now T*** who commanded as master there, showing off the young woman, exhibiting her in a box at the Opéra, dragging her to all the charity fêtes, the *corsos* and the *vegliones*, proud to show her off and display her publicly as his property, duly bought and paid for, his possession. The Comtesse de V***, more mortally pale and more dolorously beautiful than ever, seemed to run to pleasure with a sort of bitter sensual avidity. For a woman afflicted in the chest, she dared the most disquieting décolletages, and spent whole nights at supper, only returning home at dawn in the chill of first light; one might have thought that she was burning her life, in haste to finish with it.

"That condemned young woman, whom I had known for three years living the most retired existence in the villa on Mont Boron, was now living the life of a reckless girl, and at that pace, naturally, her health deteriorated rapidly. Those late nights, those suppers, and those early-morning returns advanced the consumption; her pallor became green-tinted, her lips violet-tinted, and her thinness emaciation; the death's-head became apparent and obtrusive in the face of the condemned woman; it was a mask of the Beyond.

"Before the ugliness of the tomb, suddenly argued forth, the old man took fright. Monsieur T*** deserted Nice, leaving his victim to agonize alone in the sumptuousness of The Chimeras. But the victim didn't let go of her executioner. It was at this bend in the road that she waited for the man who had broken her life, and her letters were able to force Monsieur T*** to return.

"What did those letters contain? In my opinion, the threat to reveal everything to her husband, which would establish the Comte's non-complicity. Did he even know that he was ruined? At any rate, Monsieur T*** came back. It was just in time. The Comtesse de V*** was dying, and into the consumptive's bedroom, to which the dying woman had summoned him, in the midst of the reek of oxygen, ether and creosote, the financier went tremulously. The young woman, having made him come close to her bed, grabbed hold of that old man, and hung on to him with a strength that no one would ever have suspected of her weakness, and, riveted to him, with his two hands clenched in hers, already a cadaver, with the ardent eyes of the damned and a smile with the long teeth of vengeful death, she forced him to watch her die.

"She obliged that man of pleasure, that egotist and sensualist, that sexagenarian who had a horror of ugliness, malady and death, to witness her spitting and coughing, all the filth and all the misery of spasmodic death-throes and decomposition. Her hands, sealed like two vices around the man's wrists, did not let go of their executioner until the victim was finally inanimate, half dead. And all that in the bedroom of the utmost luxury, all white silk and old Alençon, before the splendid and chimerical horizon that extends before us.

"Three days later, the Comte de V*** blew his brains out.

"I haven't said the real names. The children of the suicide—of the suicides—are still alive."

RUSSIAN SALAD

BATS

MONSIEUR RABASTENS and I became friends.
His two moving stories, the sentimental adventure of
the Astra couple and the real life drama of The Chimeras had
reconciled me with that devil of a man. Where I had dreaded an
ironist and a braggart, I had found a philosopher and a sentimen-
talist. Certainly, his more than fifty-five years had taken some of
the velvet off Monsieur Rabastens's soul, and he did not believe
in anything much, but he had a keen desire to believe, and that
is the best kind of skeptic. It is life that makes us mistrustful; a
human being, of itself, is avid for faith.

Monsieur Rabastens was very well known in the society of the
Riviera. Although April had already emptied many of the villas
and a contented somnolence seemed to reign in the hotels, not
a day went by when Monsieur Rabastens was not summoned
to Beaulieu, Antibes, Cannes or Menton. He was something
of a doctor . . . homeopathic, allopathic or dosimetric, I never
could clarify the matter. I suspected him above all of amusing
and interesting his patients; his consultations must have been
particularly moral, and sometimes immoral, for his memory
was inexhaustible and Monsieur Rabastens recounted his reminiscences without hesitation. Oh no, he didn't draw a veil over
them. In the twenty-five years he'd been living on the Riviera he'd
stuffed himself with anecdotes and he loved to reel them off, with
a so-called insouciance that gave the story he was narrating the
charm and carelessness of shredding a flower with the fingertips.

And I was subject, in my turn, to the kind of empire exercised by the man; Monsieur Rabastens was able to make himself rare. Soon, my joy was truly lacking on the days when I did not see him, but I must confess, to his credit, that he did not put over-much coquetry into weaning me too severely from his presence. He gave me a good three of his evenings a week, and if that man, so sought-after, was invisible by day, he habituated me to seeing him arrive at my hotel, one evening in two, at about nine o'clock, at the precise moment when the young misses of the table d'hôte were filing away in Burne-Jonesesque procession, each holding an orange stolen from the dessert, which, eaten on an empty stomach in the first light of dawn would assure them toward nine o'clock of a good and facile little *alas!* (Albion is rather con-stipated.) Monsieur Rabastens always arrived at the moment of the exodus of the processionary young women, and as I was then lodging on the Promenade des Anglais, we went out to take the air and smoke a cigar outside.

One evening, when we were strolling along the Promenade, the two red dots of our Londons competing with the rotating beams of the lighthouses—it was a spring night, devoid of a moon, but mild, with an impalpable and yet insistent caress, a night soft enough to make you faint—two silhouettes suddenly became confused nearby. Rapid, gangling, unexpected and ec-centric, they surprised us like a sudden gust of wind. Like two cut-outs in the obscure and living weave of the shadow, they went past in a whirlwind, bodies tilted forward, borne by a furious surge as if a blast had lifted them up . . . reminiscent, in truth, of two giant bats in the flying capes of their overcoats.

They were two men in macfarlanes, coiffed with the small flat caps adopted here by winter visitors. They were marching so rapidly that I had not seen them coming, and now they were already far away, dragged by the frantic velocity of their stride. By the glow of our burning cigars, however, I had glimpsed the face of the smaller one, a thin and grimacing Neapolitan visage, punctuated by thick moustaches: rather fine eyes, a mat pallor, black hair and a waxy complexion, the fatal head of the models of the studios of Posilippo. Of the other I had only seen the bristle of long blond moustaches under the abrupt ridge of a Cossack profile, a bulldog muzzle and a thick and heavy torso. Their appearance had been so sudden in the night—the night that was so mild and so calm—that I started violently.

"They're in a hurry," I couldn't help saying. "What a hellish pace! They're in training! One doesn't walk like that for pleasure—and what an appearance of nocturnal birds! I was almost scared. Two bats!"

Monsieur Rabastens had let his cigar go out. He shook the ash off the tip with his little finger, and relit his London from mine.

"One doesn't walk like that for pleasure. Two bats! You don't know how right you are. One of those men is damned, and the second isn't much better, since he's in the other's pay, as good as in a labor camp—but that forced laborer might free himself, while his master . . . and it really is the road to the abyss that they're following at that hectic speed, in the transparency of this beautiful *walpurgisnacht*. As satanic stories go, that's one which it would never have occurred to me to tell you, without that encounter, and the amazement I see you in."

"Go on," I said, touching Monsieur Rabastens's arm lightly. The dear fellow had a habit of lingering somewhat over his preambles.

"All right. I'm not telling you anything in saying that the Riviera, among so many foreigners, pullulates particularly with Russians, males and females and others still. Some are authentic, others subject to caution, liberated for the most part from Holy Russia and all prejudice: millionaires and starvelings, all seductive, eccentric, wheedling, caressing and Slavic to their fingertips, refined, barbaric and Asiatic, some having lost status, others worse than flawed, all devoted subjects of the Tsar, who doesn't want them back and would rather they were in Cannes or Beaulieu than in Saint Petersburg or Livadia: divorced princesses, cashiered officers, comtes too lucky at cards, expelled favorites, bankers who've been requested to cross the frontier, and even ex-chamberlains and ex-policemen who have ceased to please—in a word, an entire violent, poisonous, sumptuous and dangerous bouquet of flowers of the steppes and flowers of the hothouse. To sum up: a spoiled suburb of Byzantium.

"The man we've just passed is one of those good 'caviar and marmalades.' That's the nickname we give here to Russians, Slavs and Poles for their drawling accents, coaxing and slightly equivocal, the feline talk that caresses and is caressed by others while it sings, the honeyed purr of their complimentary and always hyperbolic phrases.

"Well, how did the man who just crossed our path—the blond, the taller of the two—one of the largest fortunes in Russia and one of the most authentic names, come by the monomania that cloisters him by day in one of the finest villas of San Moritz, and only permits him to go out by night, in order to avoid any human face? I don't know—but the facts are there, undeniable and constant.

"Scarcely aged forty, afflicted by an income of nine hundred thousand francs, Comte Sternoskef, who had been married twice and, widowed and divorced, had very pretty mistresses in Saint Petersburg, Paris and London, costly whores and even costlier socialites, has been afflicted for five years with such a misogyny that he can't see a woman's face, or even a woman's dress, without falling into a kind of epileptic crisis.

"The neurosis was first manifest in Paris. First it was a matter of clearing the house. From one day to the next, the laundress, chambermaid, cook and kitchen maids were dismissed from the Rue Bassano. Only the male domestic staff remained. But Paris, with its flux and reflux of crowds avid for pleasure, offered the invalid too many occasions for crisis; to fear women in Paris is to renounce, at a stroke, the restaurant, society, the theater and the Bois, no matter what hour it might be; it's reclusion in the heart of Parisian life.

"Of travel there could be no question. With that morbid repulsion for the attire and presence of women, hotel life became impractical; the promiscuity of railway stations also became a danger. The decision that was made was exile from Paris, the choice of a large property on the Riviera, in a city where the invalid wouldn't be too isolated, could still find compatriots of his society . . . and it's Nice that was selected.

"After two or three attempts at renting, the unfortunate Comte has just bought The Wisterias, the property of Madame Montalbey, the most flavorsome shoulders of 1860 and the richest diamonds too, in an epoch when whores weren't yet draining foreigners. La Montalbey was an actress devoid of talent, but a rancorous woman, who, maltreated in a dramatic *feuilleton* by d'Aurevilly, ruminated her vengeance, and at a première one evening, during an entr'acte when d'Aurevilly was going past the box that she was occupying with her lover d'Estera, gave the old writer a mighty slap on the cheek—an insult to which d'Aurevilly, that great seigneur of letters, responded with a single remark addressed to d'Estera: 'Prince, take that woman back to the laundry.'

"It's The Wisterias, a palace in a park, the palace of the imperial courtesan, where the ceilings are by Baudry and the frescoes by Clairin, that Sternoskef inhabits today. No woman has ever passed through the gate; the suppliers have the strictest orders. One solitary female cook is tolerated in the basement, because of her knowledge of Russian cuisine, but she doesn't live in the villa. The gardener and the concierge are forbidden to have children; a household in the town if they wish. The Wisterias is now a convent. For, more than a skirt, more than a sway of the hips or a meager gesture of a gracious hand, what revulses the heart and convulses the nerves of the invalid is the odor of a woman, the particular perfume of her hair, the nape of her neck and the effluvia of her flesh. The poor fellow is at that extreme.

"He has renounced going out by day because the brush of a dress in the street grips him and stifles him and makes his heart lurch. In the marvelous park planted by la Montalbey, a park twenty-five years old, where there are fifty-meter palm trees, he has suppressed all odorous flowers, irises as well as roses, hyacinths as well as carnations. He rediscovers in their fragrances memories of the abominated being. The Baudry ceilings and the Clairin frescoes have been, if not destroyed, removed; the splendor of painted nudes exasperated his illness and awoke iconoclastic rages in him. Only the statues have been respected; the chill and the pallor of marble reassures his mistrust; the white immobility of Ledas and Dianas satisfies him in the manner of a punishment; in the goddesses, he wants to see dead women; it's the enemy petrified, stiffened and disarmed that his eyes want to see in them. Dead the beast, dead the beastliness.

"In any case, even by day, Comte Sternoskef never goes out in his garden. Profound as the shade is, female eyes might be able to glimpse him from other villas; but to ward off his ennui, to dispense his fever, his nerves and his strength, the comte goes out at night. Every night, he fatigues his malaise in hectic races, running like a hare silently along the shore, along deserted avenues, on the causeway of the surrounding roads.

"Many a time I've crossed his path at dawn, near Antibes or in the mountains, at La Vézubie or Guerro, dragging his unfortunate employee in his wake; for in those excursions of the possessed, in his races to the abyss in which you have just glimpsed him, he always takes one of his secretaries.

"His secretaries?"

"Oh, he never has more than one at a time, for as long as they last. Comte Sternoskef wears them out quickly. Comte Sternoskef's secretaries: what a book to write, and Dante alone could have written it; it's one of the circles of the Inferno. He pays them royally, it's true, but imagine the thorns of the employment: one must never quit the comte, take all one's meals with him, sleep in his bedroom and never abandon him for a minute; never go out; never leave the villa; and all night every night, devour space and the kilometers; going where he goes, doing what he does; and Comte Sternoskef never unclenches his teeth. He's taciturn, like all solitaries. He's a man of Silence and the Night, a kind of Philippe II in a modern Escorial, admitting no other will than his own, not suffering a gesture or a reflection. The unfortunate stipendiary must live in silence, bent to the caprice of his master; during the bail signed for one year or two, he must renounce any amour, any occupation, any adventure, any pleasure; it would be a fine thing for a secretary of Comte Sternoskef to have a family or a mistress!

"No Frenchman has ever been able to do it; his first secretary, a scrubbed-up muzjik, obtained nearly five hundred thousand roubles for a two-year stint. Only Italy or petty Russia produce individuals supple enough to accept and retain the employment; it's necessary to be born on one's knees not to die in the job. The present secretary is from Palermo.

"Are you amply enough informed regarding those nocturnal walkers? Do you find the word 'damned' too strong for those convicts of the march and silence, and is it not 'vampire' rather than 'bat'—yes, vampire—that it's necessary to call that frightening millionaire of cynicism and chastity?"

BARONNE NYDORF

WHILE CHATTING, we had arrived at the Spanish Bar in the Jardin Masséna, a bar of prostitutes and croupiers which forms the corner of the square, the ordinary refuge of English alcoholics and those ruined at baccarat expecting registered letters. We pushed the frosted glass of the door and penetrated into the den.

All the mirrors were ablaze in the bright light of electric lamps; an entire florescence of luminous bulbs slapped with pale tones the worn-out complexions of the men and the violent make-up of the women. A den in truth! A strange nocturnal life agitated there, or, rather, a semblance of life, for the same exhausted lassitude was discovered in all the eyes. Males and females seemed similarly done in, the females even less desirable under the artifice of blue eyelids and rouged lips, while the manifest flabbiness of the customers was sickening.

Surrounded by Americans in flat caps, a young giant in a black coat, plump, bearded and hairy, with the air of a carnival skipjack, was perched on one of the stools at the counter, fidgeting madly, threatening to lose his balance, evidently drunk. On a stage, a troupe of *musicanti*, with white trousers and red belts, were sawing enervating tarantellas with thrusts of their bows.

We took our places at one of the tables near the entrance and ordered sodas. Scarcely had we sat down, however, than a prostitute got up at the back of the bar and came toward us.

With a narrow and mat face, as if recoiling in black astrakhan, her cheeks consumed by the wavy black tresses of the esthetes of Montmartre, there was a haggard exoticism about her, already seen elsewhere. Where had I encountered those heavy bronzed eyelids, that triangular smile of pepper-red lips over the teeth of an ogress, that mouth and those voracious eyes, whose moist enamel was exaggerated by the bistre complexion? Where had I seen that gliding and supple gait of a feline hunter?

She was simultaneously Moorish and Tzigane, badly dressed, wrapped up in last winter's mantlet, manifestly falling apart; but her pallor, the carnivorous gleam of her teeth, her eyes and her rapid and bestial stride lent her the aspect of a malevolent nocturnal ghoul, half-hyena and half-bat. I made my companion party to that impression.

"The obsession continues," joked Monsieur Rabastens.

But the whore was in front of us.

"What, you don't recognize me?" sang her delicately nuanced voice. "No, that's too much. Have I changed so much? Well, I've been ill, and I've had troubles. You don't budge! You're an ace, healthy! What are you doing here? Women? Playing at Monte Carlo? Are you winning? Me, I've lost what I wanted. Ah! you've recognized me . . . you took your time! Meryem Isba, Baronne Nydorf, in Jacques Ymer's studo. Exactly!"

The prostitute had sat down at our table. "Can you imagine that I've left Jacques? Beatings, jealous scenes and no dresses. I'd had enough of it. An Austrian took me to Spa, a Belgian took me to Venice; I was here with a Russian but he had to go back to Paris . . . affairs of money. We lost a large sum. We quit the Hôtel de Paris and I'm here at the London House waiting for him. Are you coming to have supper with us this evening? Introduce Monsieur to me."

"Monsieur Rabastens."

"I'm with friends over there, we're having fun. I'm expecting a check for five thousand Nicolas tomorrow, by registered letter . . . but this evening, I'm in a bad way. There are days like that. At the London I have tick, but no pocket money. Be nice, lend me five louis." And, addressing the barman, half-turning toward the counter: "Henri, two packets of Khédives and a Saint-Marceaux ninety-three!"

With a gesture, I put a halt to the barman's zeal, and took a packet of cigarettes out of my pocket. "Don't mistake me for someone else. Marylands and soda is all I can offer you, and, since you've had bad luck, I'll put the traveler's louis at your disposal." I searched in my waistcoat pocket for a ten-franc coin. "Don't take me for a lemon under the pretext that you're in the land of oranges."

"Ten francs! You're no help! What do you expect me to do with your ten francs?"

"You can leave them with the maître d'hôtel who'll serve you supper. Aren't you having supper at the London House? We're not having supper ourselves. Bonsoir, Meryem."

Baronne Nydorf had snaffled the gold coin and the cigarettes. "I thought you were more chic than that." She stood up. "You pay up front, but not much." And, after a few steps into the room: "You don't know what you're missing. I'd have taken you to supper with a woman who'd have interested you, a lovely Tzigane—a real one, who was mixed up here in a funny story. You know, the murder at the Grand Hotel in Monte Carlo, two years ago. She knew Mourline, the man who did it, and you'd have found copy for your paper. Bonsoir, fellows!"

As she went past the counter she risked a swerve as far as the giant youth in the black coat, and, leaning seductively on the broad torso of the young skipjack: "You'll take me out in your auto tomorrow, Gaston, won't you, baby? In your auto or your motor boat. I love it, your lovely automobile."

And she drew from the tottering drunkard a resounding: "Get lost!"

The entire bar laughed. Baronne Nydorf was having no success this evening.

"The art of treating women as they merit," concluded Monsieur Rabastens. "My compliments on your tact, my dear. You're asked for champagne and Khédives, you offer soda and Marylands; to an attack of five louis, you respond with half a louis. You merit success with women."

"Believe, my dear, that they've done me no favors."

"No more than men. The world is full of ingrates."

"Do you know Meryem?"

"I know her only too well. Poor girl! She's thrown out of the casinos; the principality itself is, I think, off limits to her. She picks up belated chips; they call that 'strangling orphans.'"

"And what does she do here?"

"She continues. Burned in Monte Carlo as she must be burned in Paris, she works the bars and the railway stations, Nice and Menton, Toulon and La Spezzia, Marseille and Genoa. I treated her last winter for a touch of pleurisy; she neglected to pay for my visits, and this evening, neglected to recognize me. She was born in Algiers and is bound to die here of consumption, for she doesn't eat every day."

"Damn! If she sups every night!"

"You're feeling remorse for your ten francs, you've been a trifle miserly. Damn! Give another ten francs to a pauper and put your conscience to sleep."

And, given a thirst by our first plate of fries, we ordered more sodas.

At the back of the room, Meryem, at a table with a man and a woman, was making a terrible racket; there were rebukes, orders cried loudly, scandal and noise.

"Who is she with?" I asked, slightly intrigued by the reticences of her adieu. "Do you know the woman accompanying her and the story of this Mourline?"

Coldly, Monsieur Rabastens plunged a hand into the pocket of his overcoat, pulled out a pair of traveling binoculars and aimed them at the group. The examination lasted a good twenty seconds.

"For once, she wasn't lying." Monsieur Rabastens passed me the binoculars. "The tall brunette tinted with henna who is with Meryem really was Mourline's mistress. It was even partly for her that he tried to murder poor Baron Douratieff one night in September 1898. Mouline—that name doesn't tell you anything? Nor Douratieff either? Come on, collect your memories. The crime made quite a stir on the Riviera and in the Russian colony . . . the news even got the Saint Petersburg police excited, because the victim belonged to high society.

"Boris Iwanof Mourline was the son of General Mourline, governor of Moscow, and Baron Douratieff, the sole heir of old Princess Goroulska, whose steward he had been for twenty-five years, possessed, and still possesses, a bagatelle of thirty-four millions, although his barony is recent. I say *possesses* because Baron Douratieff, although assassinated, is quite well today and still living, at present in Monte Carlo, but avoids lodging on the ground floor of the hotel. You have it, now.

"Three years ago, at the height of the autumn season, which is very busy here with Italians and Russians, Baron Douratieff, who was occupying a large apartment on the ground floor of the Grand Hotel, was found one morning with his head bloody and his jaw fractured, lying on the divan in his drawing room. It was his valet de chambre who found him at dawn, collapsed and voiceless, but not unconscious. The casket in which the baron put his money and his jewels had been stolen, and Douratieff declared that it was Boris Mourline who had struck the blow. He had got in through a poorly closed window in the middle of the night, had only had to step inside, and had then demanded that he hand over his valuables. On his refusal, he had hit him with an American revolver. Seized by terror, Douratieff, seeing that he was in peril, had done as he was asked, and Mourline had left, taking the casket.

"But why hadn't the threatened victim called out, or pressed the electric button and raised the alarm in that hotel—deserted, it's true, in September, but nevertheless filled with service staff? Nobody in the neighboring rooms had heard anything.

"The casket was found, forced open and empty, in the gardens. All morning, Mourline continued to stroll and show himself around Monte Carlo, as if nothing had happened; the thing was all the more mysterious because Mourline and Douratieff were on good terms. The quinquagenarian Douratieff showed a considerable sympathy, and even exhibited a certain protection, for the red-haired, thickset young man of twenty-five, with a rather disagreeable physiognomy, and a sly manner. They often dined at the same table in the restaurant and, fervent gamblers, often sat together at the same gaming table. Douratieff also had in his employ a thought-reader named Terko, a Hungarian or Dalmatian, who informed the baron about the numbers to bet on. Mourline's attack was, therefore, very strange. He left Monte Carlo the same day without being disturbed, but he was picked up at midnight at the railway station in Lyon. The telegraph had been busy all morning between Monte Carlo and Saint Petersburg.

"Arrested and interned at Lyon, Mourline didn't deny it. He was carrying eighty thousand francs in French banknotes. Of the hundred and thirty thousand francs stolen from his friend he had extracted twenty thousand in favor of the woman you see over there; the rest had served to settle debts. Interrogated by the examining magistrate, Boris Mourline only contested the version of entry through a window.

"'I didn't climb into Monsieur Douratieff's apartment,' he declared, 'I went in through the door, at any hour of the day or night. When I came out of the casino I had to go continually to render him an account of my wins and losses; I often played for him. That night I had lost two thousand louis. My mistress was threatening to leave me if it didn't give her a thousand in the morning and I had a few debts besides; backed up in a difficult situation, I lost my head. I went into Douratieff's as into a friend's place, explained my situation to him and asked him to lend me four thousand louis; I would have lent them to him, personally, if I'd had them. Douratieff refused; he claimed that he didn't have them; I knew that he was lying and I also knew where his casket was. In brief, I saw red, and I demanded that he advance me that sum; then I threatened him, and as he cried out, I grabbed his throat and hit him on the head. All that was the fault of that miserly dog, and that's it!'

"A week later, Boris Mourline received a visit from his brother and poisoned himself in his cell. In giving him the farewell kiss, which is given between Russians on the mouth, Nicolas Mourline had slipped a strychnine capsule to Boris.

"The tall red-haired woman drinking with Meryem is Mirka Stirbey, the mistress of the suicide; the man accompanying them is the famous Terko, Douratieff's thought-reader, now sacked. How are they at liberty, since they were more than suspected in the affair? Why do the police tolerate them here? Discretion and mystery. It's rumored that they're paid regularly and richly by the victim. There are silences that cost dear. You've understood me. I believe, my dear monsieur, that you haven't wasted your evening. Shall we get out of this cavern now?"

And, once outside, in the fresh air of the night: "Are you free tomorrow?"

"Yes."

"Well, give me your day. I'll enable you to see another corner of Byzantium—not the wings of the Hippodrome, as this evening, but a corner of the imperial box. Be at the port between half-past one and two."

CORNERS OF BYZANTIUM
THE NORONSOFFS

THE HOUSE OF AUGUSTUS

THE NEXT DAY, on the dot of one o'clock, I was at the port.

Monsieur Rabastens made me wait; a physician is always excused, he belongs to his patients. In order to while away the time I went down on to the yacht quay and passed the pleasure boats in review. There were many beauties: comfortable luxury vessels, spick and span, the mere sight of which rejoiced the eye. Two Americans were astonishing in their gigantic proportions, two veritable ironclads. Steam yachts, neat and elegant, were dormant in the shadow of the big yachts. There was even a torpedo-boat among those millionaires' playthings; minuscule compared to the large tonnage craft, one might have thought that there was a flotilla of seagulls side by side with the mastodons of the sea; and aboard all those boats there was the same triumphant neatness, the same gleam of polished brass, varnished wood and clean canvas, in an odor of fir-wood and tar.

"I've made you wait. Apologies. I could tell you that it was a patient, but no, I was delayed at the telephone; they couldn't obtain a connection with Monte Carlo."

Monsieur Rabastens had interrupted my ecstasy.

"I need authorization from the proprietor for you to visit his domain; I'm taking you to a private park. Not just anyone can get in there, even for a price; the position of concierge there is good, and the guardian who has it knows that far too well for him to lose it by transgressing orders. That Gregory is such an eccentric. I'd already telephoned this morning—no reply. Finally, I got the connection, and Gourkau has alerted the gatekeeper. In the past I've given you brief histories of the properties of Nice without taking you to visit one, this time I'm taking you into the domain of the Prince of the Dormant Wood.[1] You'll see—I have a surprise in store for you. It's to the land of enchantment that I'm taking you."

Monsieur Rabastens continued to husband his effects.

"We could take a tram, but we can take a shortcut between the gardens of villas. Those goat-tracks are delightful at this time of year; one can respire all the flowers of the deserted properties—for chic people are like that; they quit the country at the very moment that it becomes habitable. Would you prefer to take the tram?"

"No, I prefer the shortcut—we'll be in the shade."

We had turned left off the highway and were now climbing a rather steep path, scaling Mont Boron between the gates and walls of villas. Sometimes, the path became a stairway; we went up five or six steps and then the stony soil recommenced, sliding underfoot. Here and there, areas of waste ground were framed between the veritable ramparts of princely properties; they were poorly enclosed by palisades, as grassy as meadows, dotted with irises, the dark violet irises of Florence; olive trees shaded them.

We were walking in an atmosphere of essences and perfumes. From all the properties left behind us, as if from an immense cassolette, other fragrances of flowers and rare trees rose up, scents and aromas that were the very soul of the landscape. From the gutters of walls, avalanches of roses fell into the path; as we went past, clumps of mauve clematis shed starry petals; further away, Judas trees burst forth in rockets, fireworks frozen in the blue of the sky. That became an oppression: the Nice spring was pursuing us, climbing the mountain with us, and, as an intoxication

1 The famous tale by Perrault, "La Belle au bois dormant" [The Beauty in the Dormant Wood], is usually known in English translation as "The Sleeping Beauty," thus making Rabastens's wordplay awkward for English readers.

invaded me, numbing me in that hectic race toward space, in the incense, Monsieur Rabastens consented to keep quiet.

We arrived in front of a gate corroded by rust; a concierge's pavilion flanked it on the left. Monsieur Rabastens gave his name. After negotiations through the gate, we were allowed in. Monsieur de Gourkau had sent notification. A broad driveway curved, climbing, toward a glimpsed perspective, of the blue of the mountain and the blue of the horizon; little paths plunged into the bushes; a tangle of cactus, lianas and carobs announced a domain fallen into abandon.

At the next bend in the driveway, the enchantment commenced. Monsieur Rabastens had not exaggerated; a terrace of a hundred meters overlooked the city and the port, twenty leagues of mountains and twenty leagues of valleys: the amphitheater of Mont Chauve, the Vézubie, Guerro and the Var, and the entire Baie des Anges, with the point of Antibes and the mauve arabesque of Esterel on the horizon. There was the unreality of the admired magical panorama; there was a fortnight under the moon, appearing this time in the precision of day and the vibration of light. The gardens of other villas situated lower down prolonged the enchanted park by as many paths and lawns, all the way to the port; there was no more trace of the highway, the domain extended as far as the eye could see. Between the sharp darts of agaves, the yachts were visible, very small, alongside the quay; one might have thought that they were painted on silk by an infinitely delicate brush.

And not a sound. Roses were fading in the heat, branches scarcely creaking in the silence. There was the impression of a dead city at the foot of a royal property emptied by a plague. A strange park, in truth.

Except for the carefully maintained pathways, everything had returned to a state of nature; tangles of periwinkles and brambles ran over the bank; giant palm trees, coconut palms twenty meters high, rose up there like colonnades of a mosque; in a crazy spray of umbels and palms, banana-trees bent over, heavy with fruit;

everywhere, tobacco plants and acanthus had surged forth in large, dark green clumps, and droplets of blue light were raining through the branches of a grove of camellias.

While the distances of the sea and the mountain were pulverized, one might have thought, evaporated by the heat, there was semi-darkness and shadow there, the shade of a sacred wood; nameless flowers, daughters of the solitude, bloomed high in the branches, enormous petals similar to the most enormous butterflies there are in corners of Africa, corners of America and also corners of India. In the grove of camellias the withered calices had snowed in pink and white putrescence, and their slow decomposition was one charm more in that silence and that torpor; gigantic ferns displayed their serrations over the velvet of implausible mosses, and old frayed cork-oaks sheltered wild orchids and little mushrooms in the hollows of their fissures; a life of helminthes and poisons was fermenting in that park. The somber ardor of a cemetery weighed upon it, and I thought of the books of d'Annunzio, in which the gardens of Sicily are described, sunlit and sad, with that charm of obsessive oppression.

The habitation, a large building in the Italian style, stood squarely a little above the terrace. It was hermetically sealed behind shutters scaled by heat, two stories with a ground floor ornamented with a peristyle. One reached it by means of three six-step stairways; large garden vases ablaze with geraniums escorted the descent. Under the peristyle, two magnificent parrots were dreaming on their perches, mute, as if torpid; they did not even greet our advent with a cry.

> And two melancholy macaws
> Are the two symbolic guardians
> Of the abandoned dwelling.

"I told you that the domain is enchanted. It inspires poets."
I had spoken my impressions aloud, in bad verse.
"Have I deceived you?" Monsieur Rabastens continued.

"No, the place is unique, and its beauty is replete with a surprising melancholy. In these scents and this solitude floats the kind of intimate and delectable distress that grips the heart of sensitive individuals before a battlefield, or even in palaces where things are dramatized . . ."

"The Perfume of the Past. Yes, the place has atmosphere. It's not by chance that I've brought you here, and it's by design that, out of so many villas, I've chosen this domain. It has something of the Palace of Augustus . . . it also has, if you prefer, something of the palace of the Strozzi in Florence and our Valois Louvre. Terrible dramas unfolded here thirty years apart, and in the same family. A superb frame, eh, for the agony of a race, this enchanted park?

"I witnessed one of those dramas . . . the other is legendary, already entered, thanks to the passage of time, into the distance of tradition. A strange story, in truth, that of the Noronsoffs, coming at an interval of thirty years to die here, far from Saint Petersburg and their relatives, before this chimerical horizon of mountains and sea. It's almost the chronicle of a dynasty. The story begins like a tale of enchantment and ends like a chapter of Suetonius, with annotations by Saint-Simon in the margins."

"Get on with it, then," I said, impatiently, to that damned chatterbox Rabastens. "You'll never finish, you're playing me the duet from Tristan there."

"All right, let's sit down on this bench."

And when we had taken our places beneath a mobile mauve fall of wisteria:

"First of all, do you believe in magic, atavism and the power of curses? If you don't believe in them, there's no point in my beginning. The entire story I have to tell you rests on a strange case of atavism, an ancient spell, of which a Princess Noronsoff was once the victim and which, through the ages, fell from time to time upon one of the male or female descendants of the family, annihilating all will, condemning the designated prey to an obscure and atrocious vengeance perpetuated through the centuries."

"A recurrent bewitchment! One can explain by that means hysteria and epilepsy leaping from generation to generation."

"If you're more of a physician than the physicians. Do you accept, yes or no, the hypothesis of the curse?"

"Yes."

"Well, listen: in 1415, a Comte Wladimir Noronsoff—the Noronsoffs only became princes under Catherine the Great . . ."

"Services in the bedroom!"

"It doesn't matter. So, in 1415, a Comte Wladimir Noronsoff, a great hunter before God and a great destroyer of serfs and merchants, in the course of a hunting repast in one of his properties in the Ukraine, offered himself as a pastime—he must have been drunk on warm beer and kummel—the rape of a bohemian girl, a pretty daughter of the steppe required with a troupe of other dancers to come, after the drinking, to amuse the boyars.

"The girl, who chanced to be very beautiful, had tempted the desire of that brute Wladimir. Now the gypsy, if not honest, was at least amorous, and her amour protected her. The dancer had her fiancé among the scrapers of guitars and guzlas accumulated in the hall to accompany the gypsies' dance; the bohemian girl repelled Noronsoff, and as the boor persisted, the fiancé emerged from the ranks and intervened, dagger in hand and threats on his lips. That was too much. The comte had the couple seized by his men; the man and the girl were stripped naked, the man was whipped till he bled and the girl, bound and gagged, was thrown like a prey to the lust of the muzjiks, who took turns to rape her before her lover's eyes. After the orgy, the half-dead girl and the bloody man were untied and left to one another; the comte and the boyars went to distract themselves elsewhere.

"The girl died; the man survived, and the whole tribe allied with the man for the vengeance.

"One night, the bohemian was introduced into the bedroom where Comte and Comtesse Noronsoff—the tender Comtesse Helena, Helena Strowenska, the pure and saintly spouse of that dog Wladimir—were asleep. The bohemian could have stabbed the couple, or worse, tied the comte up—because the gypsy did not come in alone—and rendered him, before his eyes, outrage for outrage. His vengeance was even worse than that.

"A narcotic poured between the comte's lips kept him asleep, and while he slept, the damned bohemian stole the soul of the comtesse by playing her Bohemian tunes all night long on an accursed violin, a violin whose strings were made of the guts of hanged men, with a bow made with the hair of a prostitute.

"That infernal instrument bewitched the noble and chaste woman that the comtesse was. The bohemian played all night. The next day, Helene Strowenska awoke with a criminal soul and the senses of a whore. The charm had worked.

"That same day she gave herself to three of her servants. The next day, like a crazed bitch, she went down to the guard room, the kennels and the stables, soliciting amour from frightened men-at-arms, pack valets and grooms. The consternated servants dared not refuse the caprices of the comtesse, and anyway, Helene was beautiful . . .

"A stupor invaded the dwelling because of the possible reprisals of Noronsoff. He, always between two pitchers of hydromel and sure of his wife's virtue, was the only one not to suspect anything, the last one to see anything. The local priest finally enlightened him; Comtesse Helene had taken the scandal too far, now going to search for lovers in the village.

"Drunk with fury, that brute Wladimir had the head of the bewitched woman crushed between two stones; no one suspected yet that the comtesse was the victim of a spell. After the death of the poor creature, the bohemian, then in prison in Krakow for another misdeed, cynically confessed his crime—gloried in it, in fact—and poisoned himself in the presence of the judges in the torture chamber; but in his death-throes, he predicted, with gasps like laughter, that the horrible charm would recur. His vengeance would be revived over the ages, and the Noronsoffs, through the centuries, would always have bitches and prostitutes in their bed. You understand now; the curse was recurrent, the bohemian hadn't lied."

THE BOHEMIAN'S CHARM

"AND THE charm recurred?"
"It's necessary to believe so."
"Even here?"
"Since I've brought you here."
"And you've been a witness, you've seen it?"
"I was summoned as a physician to one of the victims."
"What a marvelous writer of *feuilleton* serials there is in you, my dear Rabastens. Your reticences are as many masterpieces; you possess the consummate artistry of the *continued in the next number*."

Rabastens sketched a slight bow.

"And this property still belongs to the Noronsoffs?"

"It will revert to them after the decease of the present pro-prietor, Comte Gregory de Gourkau, the man I telephoned this morning. Comte de Gourkau lives in Monte Carlo; he only has a life interest in the domain."

"Then the park is fated to see more dramas, since the Noronsoffs will return to it. The present moment is an intermis-sion for the haunted house."

"The property will be sold the day after its return to the family, and the Noronsoffs will never come back here—although they could come back—because the charm is no longer operative. The bohemian's spell was extinguished with the last Noronsoff of the accursed branch; the last descendant of the famous Wladimir, the Wladimir of legend, died here on the second of May 1899.[1] I witnessed his final moments. It's partly in order to narrate that agony to you in the very frame, so that it might frighten you, that we're both here sitting under these cascades of wisteria, but you're not letting me draw breath; your perpetual questions are disabling my story before I've even begun."

"And I'm cutting through all your effects, the effects that you value so much. Go on—I won't say another word. One question, though, is this Comte Gregory de Gourkau, the usufructuary proprietor of the domain, a relative or a friend?"

"Neither—he was the steward of Prince Wladimir, the last Noronsoff, whom I treated here, and he didn't steal the domain or the millions he enjoys, for it was a hard métier to be the steward of the prince's pleasures. Can you imagine being charged with organizing a fête under Nero, or distracting Heliogabalus, in the middle of the nineteenth century, while respecting the prejudices of society and the police regulations? Poor Gourkau's situation was somewhat akin to that. So he has developed a horror for this enchanted park where he was, for eight years, the stage manager: he swallowed too many snakes. Oh, these Cossacks aren't easy to live with, and it's an arduous task satisfying their whims. But I'll begin.

"This property, one of the oldest in Nice—you only have to look at the height and thickness of its palm trees—wasn't created by the Noronsoffs. It was an Englishman who made it surge from the rock and stone of Mont Boron by means of the force of banknotes. He spent millions on it, hence the name of 'the Englishman's folly' still given to the property in old Nice, a property which, moreover, ruined its creator, and it was when it

1 The author changes his mind about this date subsequently, but did not bother to amend the earlier citation between the serial and book versions. The date of the death is subsequently given as December 1898, but the chronology of the story is vague and somewhat inconsistent, presumably reflective of a certain indecision arising as the story extended, probably much further than Lorrain initially intended.

was put up for sale by court order that Prince Serge Noronsoff bought it.

"In 1862, Prince Serge Noronsoff—and it's here that the tale of the enchantment cast in the first chapter commences—Prince Serge Noronsoff, young, handsome, a colonel of a regiment of Preobrajenski, better than a great lord, an intelligent man and an artist, a poet even, married for love a German princess, Archduchess Sophie de Thuringen-Heilberg, the sixth daughter of old Duke Rudolph of Thuringen, the reigning prince of the house of Stilmar. And that marriage was something of a princely idyll in the style of those of the Romantic chronicles of the Golden Legend, for if Prince Serge had millions and millions, all Archduchess Sophie had for a dowry was her trousseau and her jewels—and what jewels! Before those pearls, one of today's demi-mondaines would shrug her shoulders. But at the time, the marriage impassioned all the courts of Europe, because it was amour espousing youth, and the blood of two races fortuitously united in strength and beauty.

"The Thuringen-Heilbergs are celebrated throughout the Gotha for the superb bearing of the men and the incomparable beauty of the women; the Heilbergs are poor, but have in their favor the inestimable wealth of a blood devoid of misalliance transmitted intact and pure to the present day. The males are courageous, skilled in arms and accomplished cavaliers, the women modest, of an honesty and virtue above suspicion.

"Germany is rich in proverbs about that family: *To marry a Thuringen-Heilberg is to make a lily flower in one's bed . . . A sword buckles, but a Heilberg breaks, the crystal cannot be chipped . . . When a Heilberg goes to mass the cornflowers wake up in the meadows and the angels go to sleep in paradise.* Those are the adages best known beyond the Rhine regarding that strange and patriarchal family; and Prince Serge married a Thuringen-Heilberg: the blondest, the slimmest and the purest of the six daughters of the old Duke, of that family of fairy-tale princesses: Archduchess Sophie, so miraculously pale and beautiful that the Emperor of Hungary had, it is said, thought of her for one of the Archdukes—and that marriage was a marriage of amour.

"Archduchess Sophie was as smitten with her fiancé as Noronsoff was besotted with her, and those two privileged lovers were both musicians, curious about art and literature—what am I saying?—writers themselves, already fervent for the work of Richard Wagner, whose star was beginning to rise. Admit the hypothesis of a marriage between Ludwig II of Bavaria and the subsequent Empress Elisabeth of Austria, and you will have something nearly equivalent to the event that the betrothal of Serge Noronsoff and Archduchess Sophie was then in Europe.

"And that is the couple who came to install themselves here.

"For that princesse in the fine gold of legend, Noronsoff had wanted this enchanted frame. Sicily possessed them first for a month, and then the Bay of Naples and Amalfi. During the voyage, the interior decorators dispatched by the prince furnished the villa he had chosen as the décor for his amour; the princess knew nothing about it. She continued her young bride's tour through the Italy of 1860, then only accessible to reigning Highnesses and millionaire bankers. After the esthetic joys of Florence and the divine melancholies of Venice, this wonder awaited them: the culmination of their honeymoon under the tall coconut palms of the Englishman's Folly, the intoxication of legitimate passion satisfied in an oasis of dream and in the most beautiful county in the world, in a Riviera so similar then to the Sicily she had just quit, a Riviera devoid of the Continental Hotel, devoid of telephones and night restaurants, a Riviera with no carnival, no Cook's tours, no pleasure trains, a Riviera of great luxury and elevated poetry, no more visited than Lake Como or Bellagio is today, amid the tropical flora of a park of three millions, then unique on all of Mont Boron, and before the horizon that you can see.

"Can you imagine two young and beautiful individuals, able to adore one another with all the refinements of comfort and luxury in this solitude; two individuals as romantic as people were in those days, impregnated with the reading of de Musset, Hugo and Lamartine; two romantics sitting under cascades of wisteria before this sea and these mountains, in the oppression of these perfumes?

"It's necessary to believe that it was tempting God.

"The Prince and Princesse Noronsoff had come to Nice to spend three months of their honeymoon here; they stayed for two years, two years without setting foot in Paris or Saint Petersburg. They were isolated in their happiness.

"Prince Serge had an older brother, Alexis Noronsoff, who had barely glimpsed Archduchess Sophie on the day of her wedding. One day, old Prince Ladislas Noronsoff, who lived in Moscow, dispatched his eldest son to ask the couple to return; the lovers had lingered in Europe too long, and the Tsar was demanding the retired colonel at the Court.

"Was it this climate, enervating in its continuous mildness, or the hereditary charm brought with him by the eldest of the family; the mysterious influence of the sky of the Midi on the northern temperament, or the horrible emprise of the spell bequeathed by the gypsy? At any rate, at the sight of her brother-in-law, Princesse Noronsoff was dazzled; there was a sudden dislocation of her entire being. She saw red, gusts of heat rose to her face and, simultaneously suffocating and icy, a frightful desire bit her heart. It was as if she had drunk a philter.

"She did not even try to struggle. Like a beast tracked and caught, she lowered her head to the frightful yoke of desire. On the second night that Prince Alexis spent under her roof, she quit the conjugal bedroom, went to that of her guest and, approaching her brother-in-law's bed like a she-wolf or a woman possessed, went directly toward the incest.

"How can I retrace that scene for you, which no one witnessed but which everyone in the city reconstituted? Prince Alexis woke up, and, propped up on his elbow, watched with alarm the most admirable and also the most execrable of mistresses advancing toward him. He recognized the woman, beside herself, whose gesture implored him and whose eyes were delirious: an extraordinary specter of passion and immodesty.

"His sister-in-law came to offer herself to him; but she had not come into the room alone. Prince Serge had followed her; he had sensed her slip into the shadows outside the bed, had thought at first that she felt ill, and then, gripped by a suspicion, had marched softly and slowly in her footsteps.

"He too was nailed to the threshold by alarm and amazement when he saw where his wife had entered. The candle that the princesse was holding in her hand illuminated his nightshirt directly, and the two men, horribly moved, measured one another with their gaze, interrogating one another's eyes without wanting to understand.

"The princesse approached Alexis's bed and, as if swooning in ecstasy, let herself fall into his arms; she would have fallen from her full height if her brother-in-law had not caught her. The husband had bounded toward the couple, crying: 'Wretch!'

"But the elder brother stopped the younger brother's raised fist. 'She doesn't know what she's doing. Look at her eyes, ardent and staring. She's under the influence of a magnetic trance. Feel her moist, cold flesh, her shoulders soaked with sweat. She's obeying I know not what occult will, her desire is only a suggestion.'

"The semi-naked woman meanwhile was suffocating, cooing spasmodically like a dove. The devastated Serge took stock, and could not deny the somnambulistic state: the burning eyes magnified by hypnosis; the evident proof became manifest of a frightful suggestion. The two brothers fell silent, having understood. They had not spoken the supreme word, but they both had it on their lips: the bohemian's charm had returned.

"Prince Serge took that automaton, delirious with amour, gently and slowly back to the conjugal bedroom. He put the wretched victim of a hereditary hysteria to bed, like a child, and watched over her for the rest of the night.

"The next day, Princesse Sophie woke up as if nothing had happened, and the day went by for the two Noronsoffs in anguish and apprehension. What if the horrible disease were about to return? They could not ignore the legend, having been brought up in the menace and the fear of the spell.

"The princesse, closely watched by the two men, gave no sign of sexual alienation all day, but at nightfall her eyes lit up with a flame; suddenly, that delectable visage took on a harsh expression, all the features fixed in a desirous stupor.

"Throughout the family dinner served on this terrace—it was June—her pupils were insistently fixed on her brother-in-law, all her gestures were unconsciously directed toward him. The two Noronsoffs followed with terror the frightful return of the crisis, and, as Alexis's deflected eyes avoided the wretched woman's solicitation, the princesse's eyes now went toward the servants. Her blazing eyes posed on the waiters, she lay languished weakly against the back of her chair when the service passed behind her, and when they went back into the villa, all her being lingered with frictional movements over the footmen in the antechamber.

"The Noronsoffs did not sleep that night. While Alexis kept watch on the landing, a sentinel for the honor of the name, Serge, drunk with rage and despair, was the lover of the possessed woman, resigned to maintaining in his bed by the force of kisses and caresses that unconscious flesh liberated to amour by the bewitchment of lust. It was an atrocious night of joy, sensual pleasure, dolor and regret. Modesty, chastity, everything that had been the charm of the fiancée and the wife had dissolved and disappeared; the Noronsoffs, in accordance with the Tzigane's prediction, had a bitch and a prostitute in their bed once more.

"The next morning, while Princesse Sophie was reposing, pale and sated, in the heavy sleep of courtesans, the two brothers had a three-hour conversation. Enclosed in Serge's study, they both emerged from it pale, with their eyes dry and bruised. One might have thought them two men condemned to death.

"What decision had they made?

"That same evening, between nine and ten o'clock, Princesse Sophie died suddenly of a ruptured aneurism.

"Do you find that sufficiently tragic?"

PROFILE OF AN EMPEROR

"THE DWELLING remained uninhabited for nearly thirty years. The park, left to itself, invaded the terraces, took possession of the paths, gave this oasis, blooming on the Riviera, the aspect of a virgin forest and an enchanted domain that it has retained ever since. The flowers of solitude blossomed here after the efflorescences of magic" (Monsieur Rabastens continued to cherish his phraseology) "and the Noronsoffs disappeared, plunged into the oblivion of their distant Russia; nothing survived but the name, the name given to the property by the former furnishers and engraved, in addition, in golden letters on a plaque of white marble, which I neglected to point out to you as we came in.

"The emotion of the colony and the population was great when, nine years ago, the news spread that the abandoned dwelling on Mont Boron was reopening its shutters and doors. A Noronsoff was returning to live in it. A legion of Parisian interior decorators and a swarm of Italian workmen, mosaic layers from Turin and sculptors from Genoa, preceded the return of the Master; the memory of the sumptuousness and luxury deployed by the previous guests was about to pale singularly by comparison with the research and refinement of the installation and the furniture of the new proprietor.

"There was no talk in the city of anything but the swimming bath dug out in the former billiard room of the villa, a red porphyry basin framed with pink marble paving stones, where the awaited Noronsoff must intend to take his baths. The vast hexagon was staged in three steps, rounded and polished like a woman's torso; heavily crouched on the edge, six monstrous malachite frogs guarded its six angles. Enormous topazes animated the emptiness of their eyes strangely; pressing a spring cleverly concealed in one of the steps made the six monsters spit out six showers of warm, hot or icy water, simultaneously or alternately.

"On the walls, the high plinth of which was ornamented by an erotic stucco motif of swans assailing Ledas, mythological frescoes evoked scenes of oaristys chosen from among the boldest myths of fable. Against the soft and glaucous background of quivering reeds, among groves of olives and oleanders, there was the immortal adventure of Syrinx tracked by Pan, Daphne almost forced by Apollo, the lascivious audacity of Salmacis attempting to impose on Hermaphroditus, the culpable ecstasy of Narcissus, and even the complaisances of Atalanta, and all the scattered lust of the fauns and nymphs of joyous paganism, filling the woods and valleys with the exploits of he-goats and aegipans, and that in a décor of cypress, rocks and promontories, which one could have rediscovered by opening the door: eclogues of Greece evoked in an identical frame, after nearly two thousand years, by the caprice and for the pleasure of a great cosmopolitan aristocrat, instructed by the museum of Naples, the frescoes of Pompeii and the works of erudite Germans on Tiberius and Nero.

"There was also talk of a cabinet of trellises: gilded trellises garlanded with flowers of old Saxe, such as Chantilly and Versailles never knew, an exquisite and mannered folly in the style of Louis XV, such as is only seen in Munich or Potsdam. Finally, there was talk of the theatrophone installed between the Villa Noronsoff and the Théâtre de Monte Carlo; the new guest wanted to enjoy all the concerts and performances of the principality without leaving his apartments. But there was talk, above all, about Prince Wladimir—Wladimir, like the terrible prince of the legend—the nephew of Prince Serge, the acquirer of the Englishman's Folly, and Princesse Sophie, who had died in Nice so unfortunately, and also the only son of Prince Alexis

Noronsoff, who had remained, in his quality of the eldest son, the head of the family after the death of Prince Ladislas.

"Prince Serge had died childless.

"Already born during the lives of the proprietors of the domain—he had been scarcely three years old at the time of Princesse Sophie's tragic death—Wladimir was the child of the marriage of Alexis and an Italian woman, Contessa Benedetta San Carloni, of an old Florentine family, descended, it was said, from one of Alexander Borgia's bastards. From those two princely bloodlines, Borgia and Noronsoff, some redoubtable scion had doubtless sprung.

"In any case, a terrible reputation preceded Prince Wladimir. The death of his father had rendered him free, the proprietor of Uncle Serge's dwelling and master of all the millions accumulated by the two branches. His mother, Princesse Benedetta Noronsoff, née San Carloni, never quit that overly delicate and excessively cherished son; she accompanied that pampered child everywhere, whose celebrated extravagances and ever-compromised health kept her in perpetual alarm.

"Princesse Benedetta Noronsoff was the very statue of Dolor. She had lived all her life in apprehension, and was to die therein. Personally, she had escaped the horrible charm, the shameful heredity of the bohemian spell; she had remained pure and intact in the midst of a family where it was a tradition to suspect the conduct of wives, but she had not been able to preserve her son from the frightful emprise. It was on the orders of physicians that Prince Wladimir came to nurse in the Midi a neurasthenia acquired by all the nervous expenditure and all the excesses of an existence that was already sadly celebrated. Scarcely aged thirty-four, the Russian appeared to be at least fifty. Worn out by sensations and ruined by debauchery, while still young, he already had the face of an old man: a visage aggravated by tics due to the abuse of anesthetics.

"What fantasy had not been dared by the ardent and baroque imagination of that young millionaire, a barbarian raised in the luxury of an emperor? The Russians have the souls of children. Instinctive and impulsive, with a candid naïvety, no people decay more easily in contact with old civilizations; the Cossack soul, coming to grips with our vices, spoiled with the rapidity of a young fruit, and Prince Wladimir was very much a son of that savage and tender race, hastened in his facile decomposition by the drop of Florentine blood brought into it by the San Carlonis.

"It was both a consumptive and a neurotic that Princesse Benedetta Noronsoff came to install in the familial dwelling; nasty stories had constrained the prince to quit Saint Petersburg; an august parentage had not been able to preserve him from police reports. It was on the demand of the governor that the Tsar himself had begged Wladimir to quit his palace on the Nevsky Prospect. The commander in chief of the army intended the uniform to be respected, and for the costumed or, rather, undressed fêtes that renewed those of the Roman decadence, which might perhaps be explained today by the vogue of *Quo Vadis?* Noronsoff had been unwise to recruit his figurants in the barracks. They were men of the garrison, who had, on three occasions, furnished the Gauls and Celts obligatory in any orgy under Nero.

"The personnel of the theaters recruited by the force of roubles had provided the courtesans of the Palatine, the procurers of Suburra, the Augustas and the centurions; the bohemian girls of the night restaurants, conscripted for the ballets of those sorts of fêtes, had, by their presence as well as their lascivious steps, precipitated the denouement of those gatherings; unspeakable scenes had followed; the soldiers, drunk on champagne and maddened by the proffered nudities, had taken their roles seriously, to the great joy of Noronsoff and his friends, naturally curious about human nature in all its manifestations, but the general Minister of War had not appreciated that annexation by a dilettante prince of the men of the regiments. There were complaints to the palace, confirmed by police reports, and, after preliminary warnings, the despotic and headstrong Wladimir having reoffended, the guilty party was asked officially to take his imperial fantasies elsewhere.

"An emperor in truth, and of the miriest and most dissolute Rome, with the cruelties of the grandson of Augustus and a parvenu arrogance worthy of Trimalchio. I'll cite you two facts. In Paris, where Noronsoff came to establish himself during the first year of his exile—the Parisians of '83 still remember his town house in the Avenue du Bois-de-Boulogne and the parties he threw there—did he not conceive a caprice for Ghislaine de Brême, that fine and delicate statuette of old Saxe, that trinket-woman whom one might have thought had stepped out of a display case?

"Ghislaine de Brême was then playing at the Varietés and had recently made All Paris run to the Châtelet for the reprise of *Cendrillon*. You remember the nacre of her shoulders and that profile of a duchesse. So, Noronsoff, one evening, had the fantasy of kneading and bruising that fragility. Two thousand louis was the agreed sum, and Noronsoff, who did not even have the modesty of the maternal roof, invited the actress for supper one evening, after the theater, in the Avenue du Bois. Noronsoff wanted Ghislaine in her costume of a princess of enchantment, with all her diamonds, the spoils of a career unprecedented in such a young woman.

"Ghislaine arrives; the prince is there in a black coat, waiting for her; the supper is served in the bedroom. Was it the lure of a reputedly difficult conquest or the vintage wines mixed with the supper? Ghislaine is coquettish and animated; the prince remains cold; to the advances of the actress he opposes all the ice of Russia. He remains the great seigneur, but does not sketch a gesture; he gazes curiously at the pretty creature strutting and offering herself. When they leave the table, as the slightly chagrined woman provokes, the prince gets up, rings, and, designating the actress to two muzjiks who appear in a doorway, he says to them in Russian: 'Go!' and the poor girl has to suffer the assault of those two brutes; which puts each Russian at ten thousand francs. Rage made Ghislaine ill.

"Those adventures show you the man.

"Noronsoff had, in fact, the most complete scorn for women. The following year he was publicly maintaining Lola Faroudchi, the most expensive whore of the day, and showing her off in all the restaurants. One evening, when he was dining opposite her at Bignon's, at dessert, did he not casually take out his false teeth and deposit them delicately in a glass in front of Lola, who was red with fury? Lola's disgust? Why should he stand on ceremony with her? Did he not pay her royally?

"That Noronsoff had a taste for servitude and treated human-kind like the serfs of his villages. The omnipotence of his fortune had taught him scorn for souls and people. He saw the world domesticated, at his orders.

"In Paris, in his house in the Avenue du Bois-de-Boulogne, he had installed an entire orchestra of Tziganes, and took them with him in the evening to the cabaret. His musicians took up their positions and played without any regard for the other diners. If clients gave up their places, the prince compensated the tavern-keeper. Some evenings he ended up hiring an entire restaurant.

"His suppers at the Café de Paix remain legendary; he never sat down at table before one o'clock. He brought, pell-mell, ac-tresses, journalists, writers, painters sculptors, grand dames and whores, in the company of acrobats, wrestlers, somnambulists and stable lads, invited at the hazard of encounters. The grand dames sometimes left, and artists occasionally quit the table, but most of the time, people stayed out of curiosity; the suppers given by Noronsoff were the only ones where people really ate Norwegian caviar and Volga sturgeon, and every guest always found an ex-pensive gift under their napkin, a gold cigar-case studded with rubies, a monstrous pearl in a hatpin, an opal bracelet, a sapphire ring or some Lalique ornament; neither sex was forgotten.

"Sometimes, the prince would get up in the middle of the supper and plunge behind the curtains of a window; his valet de chambre would hand him a silver ewer, and in the anxious silence of the audience one heard the sound of a small spring.

Standing behind the curtain, the prince was relieving himself as the dowager Duchesse de Bourgogne used to do in the heart of the court of Versailles; the last Noronsoff was worthy of living in the times of Louis XIV.

"At length, Paris tired of his insolences; men invited to those suppers took offense at that contempt, worthy of a prince of the blood of the end of the seventeenth century; the boulevard no longer admitted the wounding cruelty of his treatment of women. A void formed in the Avenue du Bois-de-Boulogne, newspapers took possession of events, articles appeared, envenomed by implication; Noronsoff sensed the hostile atmosphere and left.

"He set forth across Europe, taking his orchestra of Tziganes with him, astonishing capitals and scandalizing crowds with the audacity of his caprices and the spectacle of his neurasthenia. London, where the police are so indulgent to the ruinous fantasies of whoever can pay for them, possessed him for three months. Nero got bored there; the climate exasperated his rheumatism and the Saxon type wasn't his type. In Naples, where he lived in Posilippo for two years, the vicinity of Capri was deadly to him; he wanted to resuscitate in his villa a few feasts of Tiberius, and was asked to leave on the advice of the Quaestor. It was the same in Florence. In Vienna, Prince Noronsoff displeased the Empress, and in Berlin the Emperor; an officious request from the chamberlain hastened his preparations for departure in both cities. In Venice he was nearly drowned in a gondola, the chill of the lagoons made him ill.

"It was then that he came to Nice, sick and purulent in body and soul.

"I promised you a profile of an emperor."

CHEZ HELIOGABALUS

"NORONSOFF—I remember him now. He's the Russian who had that adventure in Menton four years ago with Liline Ablette, Liline Ablette, whom we obtained from England, Liline, who became, by virtue of the protection of a prince of the blood—and yet whom we saw quite maladroit at the Olympia—the first mime at the Aquarium; but in London there was still an aristocracy. It's only in Paris that a great seigneur can't impose his mistress."

"I believe you're in error, my dear monsieur. Four years ago, my Noronsoff was quite incapable of having any adventure with anyone. The prince died three years ago; that tells you that four years ago, he was almost embarking on his death throes. I cared for him throughout that last year of his life."

"But that adventure in Menton resembles him well enough."

"Yes, I know. I'm informed about the matter. It made enough noise. Liline Abelette, with the brazen effrontery that was characteristic of her, strung along a big gambler in Monte Carlo—who was, indeed, a Russian, I remember now—come to break the bank. The Tartar was then the marvel of the Riviera—prodigality and millions, he had it all. Liline had tracked the serious punter down and, fine as she is, hadn't taken long to enamor the seigneur. No one has a more candid air than Liline, when she wants. A few encounters in the gaming room sufficed to set our man ablaze like tinder; the Russian had himself introduced. Liline, who belongs to the aristocracy of courtesans, refused all invitations to the restaurant, but entertained the new suitor at home in Menton, at the Perle-Rose. That Liline! And it's the amorous fellow who became her guest.

"Dinners were served as they're served at her place: exquisite fare, princely luxury of silverware and flowers; every evening Liline Ablette received that Cossack flirt at home, and there was the anticipated flow of jewels, checks and bills negotiated by Lestouffer, the Dutch financier, to the lady, but Liline doesn't accord anything. She allows herself to be desired by her Russian, warming him up to the point of covetousness, exasperating his frenzy, granting him a shoulder one day, a kiss on the ear another, until the evening when the Cossack, weary of postponements, treats the interested Célimène like a little whore. After one last refusal from the beauty he tucks up her skirts brutally, kneels her on the cushions by force in spite of her cries and prayers, and spanks her ferociously until she bleeds; the soul of the knout is revealed in the Russian. He leaves Liline bruised and weeping without even having abused the situation. Thirty thousand roubles were estimated by him as the price of that correction. Liline, spanked and furious, wanted to bring a lawsuit, but recoiled before the scandal.

"You can see that I know the story; but I can affirm to you that Noronsoff had nothing to do with it. At first glance, the story resembles him, but only at first glance. Noronsoff was too great an aristocrat to raise his hand to a woman; to strike oneself is boorish; Noronsoff would have had Liline whipped by his servants."

"But he interests me, you know, your Russian."

"Yes, he would certainly have interested you. He's a figure such as one scarcely encounters once per century. Morally and physically, he summarizes well the end of two races: the man was a resultant, the supreme flower of a lineage of crime, madness and blood.

"I can still remember the strange sentiment of disappointment and malaise I experienced before that man, so different from what I had imagined, the first time I was called to see him. So many stories had deformed in advance the individual whose reality I was confronting.

"In addition to the legends that Noronsoff dragged after him, the legends of his exile, the legends of his sojourn in Paris and his halts in all the capitals of Europe, there were a few resounding stories in the locality. First there had been the scandal of his arrival and installation in Nice, the forty trunks of a traveling Shah of Persia unpacked in tumult, and the cries of a domesticity of all races and colors: negro cooks, Tartar servants, an English valet de chambre, a Hungarian groom, an Arab masseur, Smyrnan bath-attendants, a Japanese gardener and an entire orchestra, no longer of Tziganes but Neapolitan *musicanti*, to live in the villa. An Austrian pianist was set up over all of it, something of a composer and something of a spiritist, a favorite of the beyond, whose fantastic operas and lucubrations about the afterlife caused the despair of Princesse Benedetta, heartbroken to see her son sinking into occultism.

"The villa resounded from dawn to dusk and from dusk to dawn with tarantellas, German waltzes and evocative conjurations; table-turning and melodies by Schumann, doubling as astral images, and pot-pourris of Gluck and Mozart—such was the everyday routine of the house. The exasperated squawks of parrots dominated the cries of a staff assembled from the four corners of the world, for Noronsoff had a mania for macaws and first-rate parrots, and over that Babel of idioms and that aviary racket, reigned, breathless in advance, extenuated by superfluous gestures and orders, the illusory authority of Comte Gregory de Gourkau, the steward of Prince Wladimir's pleasures and the stage-manager of his fêtes and soirées.

"Noronsoff had not been at Mont Boron for two months before the villa became the rendezvous for all the sharpers and all the shady and flawed individuals of the Riviera: ruffians of the big hotels, procuresses and pimps for rich foreigners; sellers of clothing; dealers in jewels; pawnbrokers, former coachmen turned hirers; operators of gambling dens, high interest usurers—everything that lives on the vices and weaknesses of others descended like a flock of vultures on the indicated prey that was our prince. To that blasé individual, that instinctive being overloaded by pleasures, whose imagination alone survived in a sick and devastated body, that whole rabble of parasites tried to offer opportunities for joy and motives for desire. The princesse, frightened by the rush of that horde, took refuge on the second floor of the villa; she lived there with her chambermaids and a chaplain, Florentine like her, who said mass in her apartments.

"She had abandoned the rest of her dwelling to her son, and Noronsoff lived, in the midst of his cosmopolitan staff, his parrots and his Neapolitan fiddlers, adulated and pampered and flattered, with his court of ruffians and whores helping themselves to the smallest and largest prizes while occupied in beating out the local furred and feathered game for him.

"And it was into that court that I was introduced.

"A few executions had decimated it, and after experiments made, the interventions of the princesse had even eliminated a few of the rogues, but Prince Wladimir's receptions remained no less legendary. He received every day, from four to six, clad in sumptuous plush dressing gowns of all colors, all ordered from Worth's, his official supplier since his sojourn in Paris. Some embroidered with pearls, others with turquoises—there were blue ones laden with sapphires and red ones studded with rubies—his robes were the fable and the joy of the Riviera. In order to admire them at close range and to be able to brag about it afterwards, even serious people had solicited the honor of an audience with Prince Wladimir.

"The prince held his reception either in the red porphyry basin in the bathroom or in the trellis room. Installed in the next room, the Italian orchestra played muted tarantellas or slow waltzes, in accordance with the master's humor that day. And, his fingers laden with rings—for Noronsoff had the most beautiful jewels—clad in one of his sumptuous carnival robes, the prince, with the air of an idol, was enthroned in his little court of shady suppliers and courtiers, a true court of Augustus avid for enjoyment or pain, if one adds to the cited turbulence all the Russians of both sexes, all the flotsam of Saint Petersburg, Moscow and Livadia washed up in the Riviera for fear of the police or by order of the Tsar.

"I say *enthroned*, and I maintain the word, for it was not only by caprice that Noronsoff received clad in long floating robes, his knees enveloped in heavy furs, blue fox or sable. He was, in fact, enthroned, but in the fashion of the Duc de Vendôme receiving the king's envoys. His stomach debilitated, his entrails diseased and functioning poorly, his organism atrophied, worn out by excess, the last of the Noronsoffs received his guests sitting on a commode, and it was by necessity that that nineteenth-century Russian led the cloistered existence of a satrap.

"That rival of the despots of Asia had good reasons for not quitting his palace; he only went out when he could.

"You're looking at me with amazement. These things have existed, however, and our ancestors have seen even stranger things; and yet that madman, that cripple, that invalid had a remarkable, not to say superior, intelligence; there was an artist in him."

"As in Nero." I could not repress a smile.

"As in Nero. Yes, in another century this property would perhaps have seen fêtes as fine as those of which Bacoli and Antium were the theater, but nothing succeeds and everything turns to ridicule in modern ugliness and vulgarity. Remind me to tell you about the fêtes of Adonis."

"Adonis?"

"Yes, Adonis—which were celebrated here under the organization of Gourkau. They were the ultimate in the grotesque in terms of the quality of the minor players; they might have been marvels."

"I'll keep it in mind, but we're a long way from your first visit and your introduction."

"I beg your pardon!" And, getting up from the bench where we were sitting, he went on: "So, I was summoned to the villa one day, to the prince's presence, as a physician; and although delighted by the stroke of luck, and curious, I only rang the bell at the gate with a certain apprehension. What was I about to find in this lair?

"Introduced into the park by the gatekeeper, I was welcomed on the perron by a young muzjik dressed in white, a true theater costume, white woolen cloth and velvet overladen with golden embroideries. I recognized under that disguise a street-sweeper from the Place Masséna whom the prince had recently had the whim of attaching to his person. It was a promising augury. I traversed a long marble vestibule guarded by a whole troop of white-clad muzjiks; I assumed that they were guard of honor of that place of a thousand and one follies, and I walked with a slight oppression through that troop of guardians, evidently consecrated to the Virgin, if not to celibacy.

"A door opened. An entire florescence of porcelain roses and convolvulus, scaling the gilt of large Louis XV trellises, told me where I was. In front of a fine marquetry Louis XVI desk a man was sitting, who rose to his feet as I entered. No robe of crimson or turquoise velvet, but a sea-blue suit—it was June—the jacket open over a white silk shirt, with a yellow silk rope knotted at the neck: an indoor or convalescent outfit. A hand, amicably extended, designated a seat; the armature of pearls and enormous turquoises with which the fingers of the hand were covered announced the prince.

"He was a slender man with high shoulders, already a little stooped. The desk cut him off mid-body and it was only afterwards that I perceived that he had a pot belly, when, in the course of the conversation, he started walking. Prince Noronsoff must have been handsome; in his pallor, in his slightly lazy eyes, dull that day, he had the mixture of arrogance and mildness that is the character of the race. The features were delicate, the nose straight and the chin slightly elongated, as in all degenerates. Graying at the temples, his hair, still blond on the top of his head, wavy and falling forward in curls, partly veiled the forehead, as in statues of Narcissus.

"I had not seen a woman clad in black, whom the prince introduced to me: 'Princesse Noronsoff, my mother.' And, after I had been invited to sit down, the consultation commenced.

MOTHER AND SON

"ALL the diseases, he had had. Everything in him had been attacked, corroded by tuberculosis and also worn away by neurosis; the stomach functioned poorly, the intestines no longer functioned, the kidneys were afflicted, the congested liver secreted with difficulty, respiration was painful; he had lost count of his bouts of bronchitis, and, crippled by pains, diabetic and rheumatic, he took a kind of ferocious joy in detailing all his woes. There was sarcasm and pride in the nomenclature he made of all his afflictions; he cited the technical terms, and, as if proud of summarizing within him so many lesions and defects, he told me about his surgical operations; he had undergone three of the most delicate. He had also abused anesthetics: morphine, ether and cocaine were his familiar friends.

"He had had all the morbid accidents, and all the others too, and he named the most shameful maladies forthrightly, to the distress of the princesse, his mother, who, finally emerging from her reserve, tried in vain to impose silence on him and adjured him in Russian with a volubility that seemed strange in a woman of such calm gestures and such slow gazes. An argument blew up between them, she wanting him to shut up and he wanting to talk freely. I couldn't understand a word, in my complete ignorance of their language, but I noticed that in speaking to him she sometimes called him Sacha, which is the Russian diminutive of Alexander, and that she avoided calling him Wladimir.

"The prince finally sat down again. Out of breath, his cheeks injected with blood, he leaned on the back of his chair. He stayed there, his eyes revulsed behind the lids, unable to do any more, ready to faint.

"'How he agitates, how he agitates!' said the princesse. 'He's like a child, a veritable child!' With her crumpled handkerchief she sponged the invalid's temple; the prince's heavily ringed hand had collected a small bottle waiting on the table. He respired it, and was slowly reanimated; it was as if another man reappeared in the face as it became pale again.

"'Well, Monsieur le docteur,' his voice articulated, simultaneously soft and hoarse, 'what can you do for me? No more than the others, eh? Nothing, absolutely nothing.' A fit of strident coughing stifled his laughter.

"A strange consultation! I was quite nonplussed. 'It's necessary that the prince allows himself to be ausculated,' I hazarded, turning to the princesse. 'I can't make any pronouncement without having examined the patient.'

"'Ausculation, yes, I know, you set great store by that ceremony, you physicians. It's part of the décor. Quite useless, moreover, but as you want it, I'll submit to it. You'll be taken to my bedroom. Excuse me, I have to be carried.'

"He rang a bell. A white-clad muzjik came in, who bowed to me and showed me the way. Two other muzjiks, similarly dressed, had taken possession of the prince's armchair; Noronsoff placed his arms nonchalantly on their shoulders. The princesse had stood up, and with a courtly reverence responded to my bow.

"I found the prince undressed, lying on his bed. 'My apologies, Doctor, there's no elevator; I was obliged to make you take another stairway, to save you waiting. No elevator! This villa is a horror, a veritable horror. Not the slightest comfort. Look, I'm ready. Oh, I'm used to it!'

"In fact, the prince allowed himself to be handled and lent himself to my examination with an unimaginable mildness and flexibility; his slender body had become that of a child again.

The ballooning belly, the stomach dilated by gas, was the sole deformation of that man, still young, who must have been handsome—but what a lamentable anatomy and how wretched that hollow chest and those poor limp arms were!

"The prince had not exaggerated. How did he live with that destroyed stomach, that chronic flow of bile, that obstruction of the lungs, sputtering with gasps? The flesh of the torso was marbled by vesicants and the abdomen marked by scars; the legs, blanched beneath their tawny hair, seemed ripe for edema. Meager and overripe, the naked body of that multimillionaire was that of a hospital rachitic.

"The prince had followed my examination with a singularly sharp gaze. Sitting up, he buttoned his soft silk shirt and passed his arms into the sleeves of an ample blue dressing gown. He went to the windows, which had been closed, and opened them wide. 'Yes, there's no denying it, the landscape is beautiful. Might as well die here.' And, pretending only to notice my presence then: 'Until tomorrow, Doctor, at the same time. I never go out. I know, it's a mistake, I ought to take the air. I'll give you all night to elaborate your lies. For you'll lie like the others; it's your profession. You'll also tell me that I can be cured . . . with care and by depriving myself of everything I love, no? I warn you, Doctor, that I won't follow any prescription and won't take any medicament. I only see physicians to convince myself of their falsity, to give my mother pleasure and, above all, to thwart their ignorance. But yes, that amuses me. Don't take a word of all that for yourself, Doctor, I'd be in despair. Until tomorrow.'

"That was my dismissal. One of the muzjiks had just reappeared on the threshold.

"'We don't believe in these wretched doctors, do we, and we're going to die tranquilly without them, the two of us together?' That was the prince, stroking a little Haitian monkey tenderly, which was nestling against his breast, and while caressing its hairy ears with his lips, he petted it, speaking to it softly.

"Such was my first interview with Prince Noronsoff.

"I was still in the garden when a racket suddenly burst forth from the parrots and the macaws. They had waited for my departure before removing the dust-sheets from the aviaries, veiled since my arrival in order that their deafening cackle wouldn't disturb the consultation. A riot of cries now avenged the damned creatures for their silence; the strains of a waltz also reached me, softly intoned by Italian violins. The domain had become once again the realm of the parrots and the *musicanti*.

"And I became Prince Wladimir Noronsoff's physician. The task was scarcely easy, between that despot with infantile caprices and fits of anger, with a fugitive, multiple and incessantly broken will, and the objurgations and remonstrations of the princesse. The mother was now in my consulting room every morning, overwhelming me with recommendations and elaborating plans of conduct, if not salvation, diets and timetables, for that terrible son.

"The next day, at ten o'clock, the princesse was in my home. She had come unknown to the prince and asked me to keep the secret; she wanted to enlighten me regarding Sacha. The poor child wasn't as black as he wanted to appear; he had the best nature but he'd been spoiled by his entourage. 'What an entourage, Monsieur! If there was a means of getting rid of that band of rogues and dastards, he'd soon recover his health.' Sacha was too handsome, he was a prey for those criminal types, and when he did something foolish, one could be sure that it had been suggested to him by some sharper in the troop. 'They're like legends, the stories people tell. Sometimes there's truth in them, but how exaggerated they are! A remarkable intelligence and a true goodness, Doctor—you'll see that when you know him better.'

"And it was a painful, moving and grave thing, to see that mother, so cruelly humiliated and crucified by that monstrous son, trying to excuse and defend him. She took the task seriously, the poor woman, putting all her intelligence and all her authority into washing away the calumnies, and also the verities, of her misunderstood son, her compromised Sacha.

"One influence above all alarmed Princesse Benedetta Noronsoff: that of a certain Comtesse Vera Schoboleska, a ruined Pole, no longer young but still pretty, a bluestocking and a theosophist, whose subversive doctrines and complete amorality enthused Wladimir's extravagance. Next to the prince, she had replaced the Austrian pianist and vague spiritist who had been in favor at the moment of the installation in the neighborhood. With the difference that Comtesse Scholboleska did not live in the villa, she exercised the same empire over the poor fellow. Noronsoff could not do without her; she flattered his manias and cultivated his coquetry of idolatry by means of quotidian gifts of flowers. She chose perfumes for him, sent him make-up and ointments, unmounted precious stones, true and fake, and ran errands for him in Nice. She had the prince's carriages at her orders, descended, in order to please him, to the role of broker and second-hand dealer, and even worried Comte Gregory de Gourka, the prince's right-hand man, the official steward.

"The adroit creature found her niche there. At the end of every week the flowers and the gifts were generously remunerated by some expensive item of jewelry or even donations of money. It was her who had gratified the prince with the sensitive and shivering little monkey that I had seen in his arms. Noronsoff was besotted with it; it was the caprice, the plaything of the moment. He did not notice the beasts rubbery odor or strong breath, amused by a detail of the animal's sexual parts, two pale lapis-blue balls surmounted by a scarlet pepper-pod.

"That disquieting little beast, that equivocal living trinket, had delighted Wladimir.

"'She's the Enemy,' the princesse had declared, on the very first day. 'That Polish woman is the evil installed in the house. She's rendered my son a nihilist. A nihilist! A Noronsoff, whose grandfather had forty thousand serfs, a nihilist! A landowner who still possesses sixty villages and handles a fortune of thirty-three millions! If that isn't a pity! A nihilist! Anyway, she's a Pole, without a sou, divorced. She's the least of adventuresses, a tramp of the spas, still pretty, the whore, under her make-up, for she makes herself up very nicely. The other day, didn't she make up my son? He came to the table like that! He frightened me, he looked like a girl. He laughed at that. Trivial things amuse him. He's a child, a little boy of ten. Oh, that whore knows what she's doing, she knows Sacha better than I do. I bore him and she amuses him. Can you see me competing, with my old face and my grave and sad expression? Sacha's always reproaching me for my sad expression: *Laugh, Mama, laugh, you make me feel suicidal!*

"'At any rate, Doctor, we can't do anything without getting that damned Schoboleska into the game. In order for Sacha to consent to follow your prescriptions, it's necessary for you to go and see that accursed woman at her hotel; the step will flatter her. Talk to her about the prince's health. It's in her interest that he lives; get her by means of the only thing that interests her: her fortune and that of her children . . . for she has two sons, the older of which is fifteen, two amours as pretty as their mother must have been at twenty, whom she brings here every day at four o'clock. Yes, here, and God knows what horrors there are at the prince's four o'clocks.

"'That Pole! I'm always afraid that she has some abominable intention in bringing her sons here. It's because they're as handsome as gods. And that woman is capable of anything—anything, Doctor; she's so poor. Oh, it's a misfortune that God has brought that Schoboleska to Nice! God ought not to permit these things. I have a presentiment of something horrible, of something utterly vile—irremediable, as you say in France—on the part of that woman. Oh, if it weren't a crime to poison someone, there are creatures that one ought to have the right to suppress. I've often said that to the Father confessor. God isn't just. As if I weren't unfortunate enough! Anyway, Doctor, it's necessary to go and see that evil woman and interest her in your cure. Personally, I detest her. I don't receive her. I don't receive any of my son's friends. But I'd receive her if I only sensed a little pity in her for Sacha. After all, we're both mothers.'

124

THE HARD METIER OF PLEASING

"AND the most extraordinary and complicated life commenced for me.

"What a course of treatment! I brought a patience to it that still astonishes me, but what documents I collected therein on the Russian soul!

"In the beginning, the thing went better than I had dared to hope; Noronsoff consented to follow my prescriptions for a while. Thanks to the employment of certain expertly dosed powders, and thanks also to electric massages, I succeeded in almost regularizing the functions of his atrophied bowels; the wretched invalid was no longer completely enslaved by them. If the mornings were still difficult, he could at least respire from noon onwards, and with his reconquered liberty there was an abandonment of long trailing dressing gowns until nightfall, a suspension of audiences in the bathroom or the trellised boudoir on the equivocal throne on which his infirmities required him to sit; finally, with the faculty of going out, there was an intermission in that idle and cloistered life of a satrap, in which the invalid's last strength was being exhausted.

"Life in the open air! That was what I wanted to bring the prince to adopt. The afflicted lungs would have resumed a semblance of vigor. It was the atmosphere of perfumes and powders, aggravated by animal odors and pharmaceutical reeks, that it was necessary to make the consumptive quit. Oh, the air, the vivifying air of the mountain and the trade winds from the sea in the whistling and obstructed bronchii!

"On that matter, the princesse shared my opinion completely. To extract her Sacha from the poisonous and deleterious ambience of his little court of schemers and toadies, that was what was important above all. To get him away, if only for three hours a day, from that atmosphere of baseness, of complicity and folly, far from the reek of the menagerie, the stink of the aviary and the stifling and musky insipidity of a dwelling encumbered by parrots, monkeys and all the scented waters of a harem.

"I recommended excursions in a carriage; the prince resigned himself to it but he imposed conditions. Every day, unless the mistral was blowing, Noronsoff's horses came to pick me up at quarter to four at my house in the Boulevard Dubouchage. From there I went to collect Comtesse Schoboleska from the Finald Hotel, with one of her sons, Nicolas one day, Boris the next, and we went up Mont Boron to fetch the invalid, who then consented to go out with us.

"The road to Guerro, the one along the Vézubie, the turnings at Beaulieu, the slopes of the coast road and the heights of the old road to Genoa saw us by turns. When he had got up in the morning in a good humor, we went as far as Monte Carlo, and the prince, on Comtesse Schoboleska's arm, went into the gaming rooms. There he bet on the age of one of her sons. They never stayed for long; he was unable, he said, to support the odor of *those creatures*—and it was necessary to see the gesture with which he indicated the prostitutes; but if, by chance, fortune favored him, he graciously handed the banknotes to the child who had brought him luck; and it was never less than twenty or twenty-five louis, for he had a habit of playing for high stakes.

"From there we went to lunch at some Rumpelmayer's and returned to Nice in a slightly bleak silence, hearts gripped by a sort of anguish in spite of the enchantment of the dusk and the feverish gaiety of the comtesse. Her witty sallies hadn't succeeded then in cheering up the prince, and in that sadness I diagnosed one more sign of his imminent end; I've noticed that all individuals marked by death have those mute sadnesses at nightfall.

"Those sadnesses, Comtesse Vera Schoboleska remarked, as I did, with an evident anxiety. By force of circumstance, the Polish woman and I were now seeing one another every day, and had finished up being linked, if not by amity, at least by interest in Prince Wladimir's health. Following the advice of Princesse Benedetta, I had gone to visit the Pole. I had not hidden the condition of the prince, doomed according to my anticipations and those of many others, but whose life might perhaps be prolonged for three or four years by aiding him to live well. I had emphasized the word while looking Schoboleska in the eyes, recalling the princesse's instructions.

"'Anyone who has any affection for the prince ought to make every attempt to persuade him to look after himself,' I said. 'The prince can only be useful while he's alive; his friends will lose him twice over if he dies, for he won't leave them anything in his will. He's a child and he's too fearful of death to make a testament in favor of anyone. The prince is superstitious and fears summoning death by making a will. Prince Wladimir Noronsoff will die intestate; all his friends, therefore, have an interest in his staying alive. As long as he's on his feet, he's the master of the villa; he receives whomever he wants, commands and orders; laid low by illness, once he's confined to bed, it's the princesse who will resume all authority, and Princesse Benedetta Noronsoff's authority is terrible. We ought, I believe, to do everything we can to persuade the prince to take care of himself in earnest.'

"'That's also my opinion,' the comtesse replied, in the most natural tone. 'The prince has been too good to me and my children for me to forget him. Prince Wladimir is calumniated; he's one of the most generous and noblest souls I know, people are very unjust to him.'

"'That's also his mother's opinion,' I couldn't help observing. 'The princesse sets great store by Prince Wladimir.'

"'He's her son,' she replied to me, simply. 'For me, he's only a benefactor; and ingratitude would find it convenient to believe all the legends put about, but I'm not like that; I'm proud to declare that I owe everything to the Noronsoff family. In helping me to raise my sons, the prince has acquired imprescriptible rights to my gratitude. It's Princesse Benedetta who sent you, isn't it, Monsieur? Tell the princesse that I will do everything possible to get the prince to look after himself.'

"'It's a pact, then?'

"'No, I'll be your friend, if you wish, but not your ally. There's no more question of emoluments for you than gratifications for me; I'll use all my influence over the prince to persuade him to follow your prescriptions because I love Prince Wladimir . . . ally, no. I'm untrustworthy, being a Slav. For people must have prejudiced you enough against my race and my nation. I am and will be, for you, Monsieur, a solid friend; I'll do everything to help you, first for the sake of conscience, then as a matter of inclination, and also a little out of coquetry, to give the lie to Princesse Benedetta Noronsoff, who hates me and whom I forgive, because she loves her son as I love mine.'

"And with that, the comtesse rang for someone to bring her sons to her. I was dealing with a strong player. In any case, they were charming, the two little Schoboleskis, Nicolas nearly seventeen and Boris barely fourteen, both as blond as their mother, with large violet eyes fringed with long black lashes. Oh, Comtesse Vera's blue and mauve irises! They were the great charm of that narrow and delicate face, miraculously conserved in all its delicate elegance.

"Made up, certainly, that woman of thirty-eight or forty evidently was, and exquisitely, in the fashion of a pastel, the temples and plane surfaces of her pretty face were barely brushed with a rosy adherent powder, blurring the features delightfully. It was an expert and discreet make-up, which respected the vibrant nostrils, the purity of the profile, and the slightly emphasized dimple in a chin that was perhaps a little too willful, all modeled on a figure that one might have thought Greek if there hadn't been something of the Orient in the laxity of her falling eyelids and the insistent languor of her gaze.

"A Greek of the islands, a Chrysis of Alexandria under the reign of the Ptolemies, that was the type Comtesse Vera must have been at fifteen. Although Polish, she belonged above all to Asia Minor in the suppleness of her attitudes and the imperious magnetism of her entire person. A kind of caress emanated from her. Her slightly muted voice, her bright and slow eyes, the inflection of her slender neck, and her slenderness moving beneath shining fabrics, were all imploring, supplicant and caressing. I understood the empire that such a creature might exert. Only the thin lips and short teeth belied that sensual face. Comtesse Schoboleska was controlled, seemingly frivolous, flirtatious and witty, but with a serious gravity in the eyes that was becoming; she was scented by musk and lace. Her slightest movements emanated grace and heady odors. She was not a woman of that era; even in Nice, that fatherland of cosmopolitanism, she belonged to elsewhere, and, above all, to another age.

"Comtesse Schoboleska emphasized her Greek beauty further by means of the Empire fashions that she invariably adopted: the tight furs, the silk scarves and mantles with three collars; immense hoods of satin or pleated gauze refined the narrow oval of her face further, as they brightened the blue mauve eyes. In the two years that I spent almost side by side with her, I always saw her in those slight, extravagant outfits, by Muse or Malmaison, but they suited her marvelously, and nothing is truer than the expression current in Nice, in her regard: that she resembled a portrait. The fact is that the comtesse might have been signed by Ingres or Gérard.

"Noronsoff, who didn't mince words, often said: 'That dear Schoboleska must have loved a hussar in the guard and retained the fashions of her first lover.' Once, when the comtesse kept him waiting—which was rare, for she was as punctual as duty—he said: 'You'll see that she'll arrive in a kolbak. She still thinks she's at the baptism of the King of Rome.'

"And with the malicious joy of a child contentedly pulling apart a toy: 'She has had a few adventures, our friend Vera, but she hasn't kept anything of her old conquests. She conquered many, but money and men have always slipped through her fingers. Can you imagine that Prince Rokine had her served at supper one evening, stark naked on a tray—a silver tray carried by four waiters and preceded by a herald who was sounding a fanfare. Our friend was deposited on the tablecloth in the midst of a litter of lilies and roses, and everyone could appreciate the dish . . . by eye, for Rokine was as jealous as he was vain, and our friend Vera's modesty had demanded valuable pearls in all the interesting places . . . a garnished nudity, the oyster and its pearl, and oyster is, in fact, the right word. What has she kept of those jewels? The poor woman only exhibits herself in humiliating jewels, the tinsel of a schoolgirl; but her two sons are beautiful to behold and plead well for their mother.'

"And that was the tenor of Prince Wladimir's words regarding his best friend, the current woman and the only influence that Princesse Benedetta feared.

"The influence that Comtesse Schoboleska exercised over the prince was certainly real, but how fragile and how precarious it was! With that mobile and eccentric character, one could not be certain of a tomorrow; one could as easily anticipate an east wind. Noronsoff had sudden unexpected impulses and abrupt transports, in which a Cossack vulgarity sometimes burst forth, impudent and cynical, in the course of a conversation or a walk, cracking the varnish of the great lord.

"Well rewarded as she was by the prince, the comtesse lived in apprehension. Her perennial gaiety, her wit, on parade in quest of distraction, were nonetheless anguished, and confronted by that face, attentive to the slightest gesture of the despot, those tensed eyebrows and that ever-laughing mouth, I often felt sorry for that sad adventuress, whose faded beauty was now supported by her sons, and, in the frame of luxury and ruinous prodigality in which her salaried mediocrity moved, I sometimes surprised such a lassitude in her step and in her eyes, that Princesse Benedetta, had she seen it, would have felt sorry for her too.

"Two events that I witnessed will establish things more clearly. One evening, at about six o'clock, we were coming back from Monte Carlo; the prince had won a tidy sum but had not gratified young Boris Scholboleski, out of malice. In a cheerful mood because of his win and perhaps because of the comtesse's slightly disappointed face, he would not shut up making jokes about her attire and beauty. In the increasing malaise of a tense situation, the comtesse being embarrassed, the child anxious and distressed, and me more than irritated by it all, Noronsoff even dared to make a few allusions to la Schoboleska's past. 'Did you see the pearls that that prostitute was showing off in the atrium?' he said, suddenly, risking addressing her as *tu*. 'She was wearing a fortune. What pearls! Were the ones that Rokine gave you as beautiful, Comtesse?'

"This time, la Schoboleska paled at the insult. 'You're drunk, Prince,' she said. And, leaning on the appeal button she called a halt and tried to get down. Boris, in tears, had thrown himself into his mother's arms. Very annoyed, the prince apologized, claimed that it was a joke and, in order to calm the Pole down, took off a large sapphire ring that he was wearing and put it on her finger. Furious, the comtesse returned the ring. She had opened the carriage door and Noronsoff could not find any other means of placating her than forcing the child to accept the ring and begging him to intercede with his mother. As the comtesse was still hesitating, a ruby followed the sapphire, and Boris returned to Nice with his hand florid with jewels. The prince would have given all his rings; but that day, the comtesse left it there.

"The second occasion was more serious. The comtesse, the prince, Nicolas and I were traveling in a landau on the road to Venice. Noronsoff spotted a little beggar on the road, called a halt, and, seized by a sudden caprice for the child's dark eyes and rags, invited him to climb into the carriage in order to install him on the seat between him and la Schoboleska. The latter protested and wanted to get down, she and her son refusing to accept the equivocal company of that road-runner. Stubborn in his idea, the prince did not stop her. Not wanting to leave the comtesse alone on the highway, I got down with her and Nicolas.

"The prince took away the delighted and amazed young beggar, sprawling amid the silk cushions. We went back on the railway.

"The beggar, imposed on the cook that evening as a scullion, was dismissed after three days. The next day the prince went to Comtesse Schoboleska imploring her pardon, and buying it with banknotes.

"However, those excursions in carriages, journeys by road, became dangerous; there were unfortunate encounters there. The open air excited the prince and health developed maleficent instincts in him. The comtesse became pensive.

AN ASIAN COURT

"ONE DAY, the prince's landau did not come to find me. I also waited in vain the next day. What was happening? On the third day, I went to the villa.

"I found Noronsoff sitting in his miraculous bathroom. Clad in an improbable caftan in pink Turkish silk, his fingers laden with pearls and turquoises, he was hosting a full court. All the elegant rabble of Nice was there, famished Russians, English exiles and Italians in quest of adventures. There was even a renter of furnished rooms, a merchant of works of art on the ground floor who had living trinkets on the floors above, and a former coachman, now established as a hirer. A squadron of white muzjiks was guarding the doors, a living fresco applied against the painted frescoes of the walls.

"Lying amid the cushions of a divan, the prince was swooning with pleasure at the recitation of a German arrived from who knows where, a stout Bavarian whose flesh one might have thought stuffed with lard. Both serious and comical, the latter was recounting, with curt gestures, a police raid on an equivocal house: a sanitary sweep that was the scandal of the week, and which he, Meinherr Schappmann, had escaped. Arrested with the laborers and clients of the place, he had simply asked for the German consul and had been released within the hour. The police had only kept the French subjects.

"Meinherr Schappmann, his hands entangled in the opals of a Muslim chaplet, was struggling in his story as if in a pod. He was primarily concerned with exculpating himself and attacking the other clients. How had he come to be there? One of his compatriots, encountered the previous evening at *Tannhauser*, had offered to take him to an amusing place. His eyes wide behind green-tinted spectacles, the frightened Bavarian was miming modesty. Noronsoff was in the seventh heaven.

"Were there really only girls in the establishment? There was mention of complete furnitures, a large Danish dog clad in a strange costume; there was also mention of a stout gentleman surprised in a pink satin corset and running round the apartments on all fours. A married pharmacist from Cannes, a father and a churchwarden, some said, a foreigner staying at the Westminster Hotel, others claimed, unless it was Meinherr Schappmann himself, for the man had been corpulent. And with a ferocious joy, the prince harassed and bombarded the bewildered, tense and fidgeting Bavarian with questions. It was a pleasure to see the worthy German squirm at every insinuation by the prince, like a plump oyster under a jet of lemon juice.

"The audience roared with laughter at each quip from the prince, and he, with his favorite monkey curled up on his knees, was using a fork to spear iced strawberries in a bowl placed on a small side table. And I had forbidden the use of ice! Then, ten minutes later, a samovar was installed before him and he was drinking hot tea, an internal Scottish shower, the murderous effects of which on the worn-prince I deplored more than any other.

"While drinking, Noronsoff was toying with the hair of the elder Schoboleski, Nicolas, who was sitting next to him on the divan; his hand lingered in the child's dense blond curls. That boy of sixteen was listening to those conversations. What was the comtesse thinking? She was there, moreover, enthroned in the front row of the audience, her younger son standing between her knees and leaning on her affectionately; the mother and child formed a tableau, he clad in black, she in white.

"As soon as I came in I sensed that the game was lost. 'Come and listen to this, Doctor,' Noronsoff shouted to me, as soon as he saw me, 'and no scenes! Finished, the carriage rides. I coughed more when I came back from them, and then, they saddened us, didn't they, Comtesse? My friends have come back, and hurrah for the company! You should know my four-to-sevens; everything there is of the most amusing is present!'

"'What, Comtesse!' I said to la Schoboleska, evidently holding her responsible.

"'Oh, don't blame the Comtesse,' the prince interjected. 'She's had enough trouble renouncing those excursions. The landau was her triumph; men no longer look at her except in a carriage!'

"Schoboleska had turned traitor. Flattering the prince's liking for adulation and malevolence, she had brought back to the villa the equivocal little court of parasites and idlers. In counseling the prince to resume his receptions, she had suppressed at a stroke the excursions by carriage, the danger of encounters and caprices, and reestablished the special atmosphere of adoration and malicious gossip necessary to the infantile and cruel nature of the dying despot.

"All the entertainers admitted to distract the prince were, primarily, her creatures; she had made herself the dispenser of liberalities and gifts. To obey her was to be paid by Noronsoff; there was no competing with an entire complicit house. I could no nothing but withdraw—worse, there was nothing to do but let matters take their course, having become an impotent adviser.

"And the collapse commenced, in terms of health and in moral terms, if the word moral can be applied to such a milieu. I stopped my visits, and only resumed them in response to the supplications of Princesse Benedetta, who returned to the charge three times, crazed, indignant and in tears. 'The whore, the abominable Jewess—for she's a Jewess, I know—she's killing my son!'

"*And not saving her own*, I thought privately. *What will become of those two childhoods in that atmosphere of corruption?* To calm her down I said: 'Yes, la Schoboleska is dangerous, but another might be worse.'

"'Worse!' The princesse spat. 'But what do you expect? The woman has the genius of her race; she's a Jewess, I tell you. She has the instinct of destruction.'

"Out of regard for that dolor, I consented not to abandon the prince, but I made it a rule not to go to the villa unless summoned, by Noronsoff himself, requesting a consultation . . .

"Yes, in truth, I was then witness to some strange things. With the regime of iced drinks, hot beverages and late nights—there were also suppers at the villa now—the little health the invalid had was worn away rapidly, and his character became embittered too. There were now abrupt fits of wrath, quasi-epileptic crises of fury, over nothing; veritable crises that, once past, left the patient exhausted, annihilated, almost dead, his eyes revulsed and his limbs paralyzed, as if emptied of blood. And God knows how the subjects of anger multiplied in the disarray of that dwelling delivered to a haphazard staff, servants engaged on a whim, the troop of which Gregory de Gourkau strove in vain to master; a troop of freed men, favorites of an hour and masters of an evening, tyrannized, tyrannical and insolent.

"And in the mourning of an agony that one might have thought hastened by an expert and criminal hand, there were also the most comical scenes.

"One evening, for example, I was summoned in all haste; the prince had just been seized by a crisis. I found the house in an upheaval, the garden full of lanterns and errant lamps; the entire staff on the move, armed with poles, ladders and ropes. One of the prince's pet macaws had escaped. It had broken the silver chain of its perch and had reached the treetops. It was Wladimir's favorite parrot, a gray macaw with a pink breast speckled with spots of blood. The bird had escaped at one o'clock and they had been hunting it ever since. It had taken refuge in a clump of palm trees and, hidden by the drooping leaves, remained invisible, deaf to threats and prayers. Where was it?

136

"The furious prince, who had gone to bed at first, was now directing the search. Barely dressed, his bare feet in slippers, careless of the cool of the evening, he was running back and forth in the garden, fearfully thin in a flapping white silk gandoura; his hands sometimes joined and sometimes extended in a gesture of distress, he was shouting to the ingrate at the top of his voice. The most tender names pressed upon his lips: 'My darling, my love, soul of my life, my rosy jewel!'—a whole adoring litany, suddenly replaced by insults and oaths. He damned the perfidious bird, threatened it with the worst tortures, and, without wanting to hear anything, either from Gourka or his mother, poor woman, who had come running and was begging him to go back, the prince, a veritable fanatic, sent for a revolver and started firing into the trees at random.

"The frightened parrot quit its perch and flew further away, into the park of a neighboring property, which the prince wanted to invade. The concierge there opposed him and, in a virile rage, Noronsoff gave the order to wring the neck of every one of his parrots—an order that was not followed, naturally, for fear of the next day's caprices.

"The prince went back up to his bedroom, exhausted. I had to sit up with him for part of the night.

"Another time, it was something else. Someone came to fetch me for the prince at a great gallop. His monkey had bitten him and he thought it was rabid, the little monkey with the blue sex organ that the comtesse had given him.

"After the four-to-seven reception, Noronoff had gone up to his bedroom, and as he was lingering by the open window, in one of the melancholies that was customary to him at sunset, with the creature, as usual, cradled in one of his arms, the prince had been seized by a coughing fit and, in an unconscious movement, had clasped the animal too tightly; for, with plaintive little cry, the animal had turned round swiftly, climbed up to his face and bit him on the cheek.

"In pain, the prince had let go of the monkey, only to recapture it immediately and, in a fit of manic fury, had thrown it out of the window; then, screaming for help, he had fallen on his bed.

"Noronsoff had no doubt that the animal was rabid, and thought himself doomed. The villa lived in apprehension for nine days. In spite of the immediate cauterization, there was no longer any talk of anything on Mont Boron but the Institut Pasteur. For nine days that prince did not want to hear any mention of Comtesse Schoboleska; she was the author of all the evil. For nine days she was forbidden entry, and Princesse Benedetta was able to hope that the Pole's reign was at an end. On the ninth day, however, the reassured Wladimir had a fit of tenderness; he asked about his victim, learned that Taitou had been picked up, his ribs broken, by a groom and was dying slowly in the stables. Wladimir wanted to see it again; the agonizing beast was brought to him. He wanted it in his room; it received the best of care there, his own, and lived for three more days.

"It was buried in the garden in a sandalwood box, and a veritable funeral was held. Comtesse Schoboleska was there; it was her return to grace.

"What more can I tell you? It would be simpler to leaf through Suetonius, the chapters consecrated to Tiberius and Caligula. The old soul of the Caesars lived again in that Russian, bizarrely mingled with the puerile instincts of the satraps of Asia. Rages and crises succeeded one another, ever more precipitate, more frequent and also more violent, weakening the invalid and taking him another step closer to death every time.

"And the comical aspect of all that sadness was the very futility of the reasons for so much anger.

"Sometimes it was a silver tray that one of the kitchen staff had stolen; three scullions were sacked, the police called, the house searched. After a week, a gardener found the tray in a bush. Another time, a muzjik—one of the sacred battalion—had spent the night elsewhere, and Wladimir had entered into a fury that was simultaneously terrified and jealous: that vermin was going to bring back some frightful malady from the low quarters of Nice and contaminate the whole dwelling. With foam on his lips and his torso shaken by spasms, Noronsoff vociferated and railed, spitting insults and blood.

"The stupefied Princesse Benedetta looked on in anguish and fear. Comtesse Schoboleska waited.

THE FAVORITE

"THE POLE had become mistress again. Above all, to occupy the prince, not to allow him any respite, to enervate him in a fever of projects and pleasures, to encroach on the slightest minutes of an existence stimulated to white heat, not to permit the invalid to breathe or to reflect for a moment, such was the program adopted by la Schoboleska. Noronsoff must not be able to think or to get a grip on himself.

"A fury of fêtes and receptions now blew through the villa, of which the comtesse was the inspiration and Gourkau the stage-manager. In stimulating the vanity of the prince, the adroit creature had found a sure and generous seam to exploit. The morbid child that Wladimir was now wanted to dazzle the Riviera with the luxury of his dinners and the refinement of his menus. Dying, purulent in the bronchi and everywhere, he dreamed of nothing but parties and feasts worthy of Trimalchio. Like Nero, he wanted to astonish the world.

"Comtesse Vera had put it into the head of that human wreck to give himself the renown of a satrap and a prince of the Arabian Nights in that land of prodigalities and ruinous follies that is the Côte d'Azur.

"And the dance of millions commenced. Not only were the receptions from four to seven extended, open to the curiosity of all the foreigners in the big hotels and the villas, but invitations began to rain down all over the Riviera, disturbing in their winter idleness Grand Dukes on holiday in Cannes and snatching the princely punters of Monte Carlo from the gaming tables. Wladimir, allied to the greatest families in Russia, issued invitations in the name of Princesse Benedetta, and thus forced the hands even of the most recalcitrant; they came, if not for the son, at least for the mother. It is true that people were not caught out twice, for the princesse never appeared at those dinners; the comtesse presided over them; and only the men, amused although sometimes scandalized, accepted a second invitation, then escorted by a few high-class whores collected from the Trente et Quarante or the reserves of the Riviera.

"As long as they were pretty and decked with jewels, Noronsoff closed his eyes to that. It was an opportunity for him to get out his jewel-cases. He competed in the splendor of rings with the donzelles brought by the diners, and had the flair of a lapidary for winkling out and denigrating dubious diamonds. He discovered false pearls at a glance; pearls were his pride. As he said himself, with the joy of a parvenu, for pearls he feared no one.

"On those evenings the comtesse appeared as embellished as a reliquary, ornamented with Noronsoff's most beautiful jewels. The Russian lent them to her in order to do honor to himself, and you can believe that, of the number of jewels, the sly borrower sometimes forgot to return a few.

"A frantic extravagance reigned in the antechamber as in the kitchens. There was the joyful chaos, the alarming flux of a badly kept inn fallen into the hands of its service staff. The orchestra of *musicanti*, scraping and fluting, led the saraband and the disarray of millions. At four o'clock, the park filled up with waltzes and tarantellas. They did not cease until far into the night, relayed from time to time by marches and Tzigane czardas, for Noronsoff now had two troupes of musicians, one for the four o'clock receptions and one for the evening dinners.

"The prince now gave two or three dinners a week. People were invited late for nine o'clock, but the guests were often still waiting at half-past ten. The prince remained invisible and the comtesse, taking the arm of the oldest or most important indi-

141

vidual, then went into the dining room, and people took their places at table.

"With bare shoulders, frock-coats constellated with decorations, diamonds, pearls and brooches, eyes enlivened by kohl, edifices of tinted hair and nacreous necks, they elbowed one another, brushed one another or looked one another up and down as if at a table d'hôte, amid the coming and going of servants disguised as muzjiks; conversations quickly deviated amid the odor of venisons, the pepper of rare spices and the musky fragrance of vintage wines; on the tablecloth, there were avalanches of rose petals.

"Camped on a platform, as in a night restaurant, equivocal Tziganes, wearing seductive make-up, scraped waltzes and distributed winks and leers; the laughter of tickled women burst forth in corners; an odor of moist flesh and faded flowers trailed through the hall and the men, excited by the refined nudity and the delicately powdered white breasts of the intangible, distant la Schoboleska, with a fresh smile on her mauve lips, might have believed, without that reserve and haughty grace, that they were dining in a den of vice.

"The conclusions of the prince's dinners and suppers? Sometimes, toward midnight, when the overheated fête took on the appearances of an orgy, the orchestra played the Russian national anthem and all eyes turned, alarmed, toward the entrance of the room. A specter had just appeared there: the livid pallor of a man in a black suit, the quasi-macabre emaciation of Noronsoff. And, his fingers sparkling with pearls, diamonds as large as hazelnuts on the plastron of his soft shirt, Prince Wladimir advanced hesitantly, his arms on the shoulders of two servants.

"His cheeks rubbed with rouge, he was smiling painfully, his chest obstructed by rattles, shaking over his white cravat the astonished face of an old woman. A crisis had laid him low since nine o'clock; he had thought he was going to die. He was up there in his bedroom, spitting out the last of his lungs, while they swilled champagne and buttered bread with caviar; but he had wanted to shake the hands of all those good friends who were aiding him to die so joyfully; he had got dressed, no matter what the cost, and had come to bid them *bonsoir*, perhaps *adieu*—for who could tell whether he would last the night? And a strange smile, composed of scorn and sarcasm, then pulled his pale lips back and uncovered his teeth.

"Oh, the long and already loose teeth, the teeth of the dying consumptive that Noronsoff showed then, while studying with a curious eye at the discomfort of his guests! In some of them, it was even fear. He enjoyed their malaise then. Their fearful eyes repaid him for all his fatigue. He excused himself in a coaxing and hoarse jargon and saddened them with the recitation of his woes, irritating them with the sight of his decadence, and then, abruptly, started laughing, asking for iced champagne and saying that it was nothing, that in twenty-four hours he would be fine, and, facetious and mocking, he invited someone or other for dinner the night after next . . .

"But his presence had cast a chill; men asked for their hats, women their pelisses; and the prince was left alone with the Pole, laughing and choking, laughing to the point of tears. 'Did you see their mugs, comtesse? They could have seen you naked on a platter and they wouldn't have pulled such dirty faces. What a man of the theater I would have made! When they saw me, their foie gras rose up to their gullets. May they die of indigestion tonight! I have a strong desire to have the food drugged one evening. Can you see all those beautiful women writhing with the colic? Oh, their panic, their lamentable panic, if they thought they'd been poisoned! Load of parasites and schemers, may the plague choke them! How I hate them! How well they are!

"'Who was it who paid court to you his evening? Luigi Frozzi didn't take his eyes off you, it seemed to me. That one, I'll permit you; he's quite handsome. You haven't brought Boris, or Nicolas. You did well. They're too pretty for those boors. *Margaritas ante porcos*. Yes, swine, veritable pigs! All the same, what if we poisoned them one night?'

"And the comtesse, with her soft smile: 'What a fine Cesare Borgia my prince would have made!'

And Noronsoff, flattered: 'Yes, I was born too late, and three centuries earlier, perhaps the world would have seen things! But patience, we'll end up by astonishing all those people one day and making them cry out, for you hate the world too, you're a nihilist.'

"'A true Borgia,' cooed the comtesse, continuing to play her role.

"'Yes, I have Florentine blood in my veins; I also have the blood of the Romanoffs, via my great-grandfather, who was Catherine the Great's lover. Let's go and sleep, Comtesse, your carriage is here.'

"And those were the tender dialogues, after supper, between those two creatures.

"Prince Wladimir was killing himself. Fabulous sums were spent on those dinners. He was ruining more than his health now; he was dilapidating his fortune. The entire dwelling was pillaged; the business agents had received orders from Gourkau to sell villages and woods; Princesse Benedetta, informed, was irritated, but kept quiet, impotent. The Pole pursued her work, intent, one might have thought, on destruction; the nihilist appeared in the woman.

"To what order was she obedient? She seemed to me to be magnified, to have become the soul of some obscure conspiracy, incarnating in my eyes, at moments, the Spirit of Perdition, I know not what tangible Perversity. How she had played with me! With what skill she had enabled the prince to escape the tight mesh of my prescriptions and my orders. She had broken it with patience, slowness and certainty: la Schoboleska was triumphant!

"However, she nearly sank within sight of port, and, by virtue of a malicious combination of circumstances, almost left her influence in the hands of one of the thousand and one amusers she had brought to occupy the prince.

144

"The crowd of adventurers and actors picked up at the hazard of encounters in order to animate Wladimir's four-to-sevens and suppers was the *olla podrida* of all the talents and all the merited or overblown reputations of theatrical and mountebank Europe: Italian baritones performing in Monte Carlo, operetta stars of the program of the Théâtre de Nice, acrobats and jugglers from the Kursaal, ranging from singers at social matinées and salons in eternal expectation of an engagement, Muses crooning verses by Jacques Normand and Verlaine, bluestocking declaimers of their own lucubrations, to lisping and puerile perverts, evidently intended to stimulate the curiosity of old gentlemen; the bewildered curiosity of Noronsoff's guests went as far as Spanish dancers from an ill-famed bar in the vicinity of the railway station, and one evening, he even offered to our stupor the decorated and blue-tinted nudity of a tattooed man, the muscular body, as if embroidered with fairground arabesques, of a fairground wrestler picked up who knows where, at the Marché de Ponchettes.

"Among that procession of pretentions, monstrosities and affectations, the toys of a day or puppets of an evening rapidly thrown into the street by the prince's enervated caprice, it happened that Sacha conceived a keen sentiment, a sort of tender and melancholy amity, for a sailor from Aigues-Mortes—a 'navigator,' as anyone who has ever set foot on a boat entitles himself pompously in Marseille—one of those pedlars of the sea who, scarcely disembarked at La Joliette, runs to skim the Riviera in winter and the spas in summer, in quest of adventures and marks on whom to offload their stock of Japanese robes, Chinese pongees, ivory carvings and Turkish embroideries bought in the course of their landfalls in the Orient.

"Clad in blue suits with metal buttons, coiffed in yachtsmen's caps, these marine traffickers ordinarily operate in pairs and, with their bales on their shoulders, go to ring at doors in the morning. Loquacious and boastful, with joy in their shining eyes—the joy of the mariner on shore and the crafty businessman—they approach maidservants, smiling, with the air of friendly pirates. Tanned by the spindrift, their skin bronzed and robust, they have retained in their eyes the deep blue of the Mediterranean and the changing gray of the Ocean; they carry a scent of tar, liberty and the open sea; and their rowboat gait, the rhythmic sway of their seductive build, the boldness of their gestures are the amusement of the street, to the amazement of the passer-by.

"Such was Marius Rabassol.

THE REIGN OF MARIUS

"SO, Marius Rabassol was a vulgar jester. A former able seaman and mechanic aboard the *Formidable* in the Mediterranean squadron, on his release from the service he had joined the Compagnie Touache and had spent three years on the run from Marseille to Tripoli, with ports of call at Tunis, Sousse, Sfax and Gabes, and sometimes a detour from Tunis to Palermo on the way back. Then he was a mate aboard a Bastia coaster, had become familiar with the coasts of Sardinia and Sicily, and for a year he had fallen back to stoker on a China transport. That was his first voyage to the Far East; he had brought back a pack full of fabrics and small objects, which he tried to sell as dearly as possible to people wintering on the Côte d'Azur.

"A Basque from Biarritz, Pierre Etchegarry, a former navy man like Marius, encountered in some Marseille dive, accompanied him on his round. The two of them made a pair. They came to Cannes, where they had scant success, held back by the porters of sumptuous hotels and the livery of princely villas, but they hoped to do better in Nice, Beaulieu and Menton, where the less worldly life is more propitious to commercial temptations. In any case, they were determined to do everything to make a success of their business, and, as true Mediterraneans, passionate for games of chance, had formed the project, once their stock had been sold, of trying their luck in Monte Carlo and risking their profits on the number of their age. If Rabassol was twenty-eight, Etchegarry was no more than twenty-five.

"Such was the couple who crossed the path of Comtesse Schoboleska one morning in the vestibule of her hotel. The two companions had displayed their merchandise there. The Pole was coming down to breakfast with her sons. The two children paused over embroidered robes and the porcelain figurines, and the comtesse amused herself with the chatter. Lit up by the prettiness of the woman, the two mariners competed in verve and exaggerated resprect, restrained their wheedling, and, deceived by the Pole's elegance into believing in the lucky find of a rich client in that small hotel, were all smiles.

"Their youth and their gaiety appealed to the adventuress; she judged at its true value so much enthusiasm and robust health. Yes, those two pedlars would certainly amuse the bleak Wladimir, their good-humored loquacity would at least fill up one of the prince's days. She bought a trifle and gave them the address of the villa: 'After five o'clock, Villa Noronsoff, on Mont Boron. If the concierge makes difficulties, give him this card and ask for Comtesse Schoboleska. There's no need for both of you to come. You come,' she said to the Provençal, unconsciously sensible to Rabassol's sea-green eyes and Saracen face, 'and your friend can go in the meantime to place his merchandise at the neighboring properties.' And she gave him the addresses of a few villas.

"That day, Noronsoff offered to the guests at his four-to-seven the disarticulated contortions of a human serpent—a performer, I believe, at the Kursaal. The spectacle was rather meager. Molded in a leotard of silver scales, threadbare in places, the acrobat stretched out an impressive thinness, and, his belly abominably hollow and his stomach protruding over the projection of the ribs, he twisted and knotted, like scarves, two long filamentous arms and two heron-like legs devoid of calves. It was a nightmare vision, aggravated by the poor fellow's wan and sulfurous face.

"His features capsized by anguish, he coiled himself up, with a strange fixity in his eyes; then, his tangled limbs adhering to his body, reduced to the smallest volume, as if amalgamated with one another, he lay at the bottom of a glass box, and in his yellow face, emerging between his thighs, two gaping attentive eyes radiated an empty gaze of Medusa, and everyone, men and women alike, felt their hearts constricted before that tortured immobility. The emaciation of the starveling, the fearful distress of the torture victim, and the exsanguinated pallor and hypnotized eyes of the captive; all of that was in the hallucinatory spectacle, and even more of fear and fascination: the fascination of a staring octopus flattened against the green-tinted walls of an aquarium.

"The moment was rather painful. A muzjik came in on tiptoe and handed a card to the comtesse. 'Good, have him wait,' the Pole replied.

"But Noronsoff, bored by the spectacle, wanted to know. 'What's this, more secrecy?' And he questioned the comtesse.

"'It's a seller of fabrics and chinoiseries I encountered this morning at the hotel. He has some nice robes; I asked him to come.'

"'Some Jew?'

"'No, a mariner, a voyager.'

"'A mariner? Let him in!'

"And Noronsoff, suddenly interested, got up from his divan, and signaled that he had had enough of the contortionist and his ugliness. The human serpent emerged slowly from his tank, braced himself, stretched himself and, cracking his joints, bowed to the audience. Already indifferent—worse, almost forgotten—he went out backwards, sponging his moist brow.

"Marius Rabassol had just come in. It was as if his broad smile, his short beard, his round and bronzed face and the bright gleam in his green eyes, all the gaiety of his person, had illuminated the room. He had stopped on the threshold, slightly bowed down by his bundle of fabrics, brusque and cheerful, with joy in his eyes.

"'I like him,' declared Noronsoff, falling back on his cushions. 'What a stature! My compliments, Comtesse, you know what's what in men!' And on that impertinence, he told the mariner to advance.

"Encouraged by a glance from the Pole, the pedlar did so. He set his pack down in front of the prince, got down on one knee, and briskly, with a flurry of movements, displayed his stock. Boris and Nicolas Schoboleski had approached, delighted with the fabulous animals of the embroideries and the sculpted contortions of netsukis.

"Put entirely at his ease by the welcome, the Provençal started talking up his merchandise; his eyes and his patter were sparkling. It was a picturesque jargon, with invented words and unexpected metaphors. There were licentious audacities and allusions that he risked, emboldened by attitude of the prince, and a chalet of implausible tales made up to add value to his objects and explain their provenance. All the bluster of Marseille flowed from his gestures, his mouth and his eyes.

"In the general attentive silence, Wladimir listened, enigmatic and mute. 'Choose, my lads, take, my lambs.' And, touching Boris or Nicolas lightly on the shoulder, he urged the two adolescents to make purchases, directing their choice, overcoming their hesitation. He bought the robes for the comtesse, collected trivial trinkets for the other guests, and never took his eyes off the merchant. His face impassive, he studied the projection of the forehead, the profound framing of the eyelids, the abrupt nose with the motionless nostrils, the thick lips, the short teeth and the tanned complexion. The Russian gazed at the Provençal as sickness ought to gaze at health.

"Eventually, the man stood up; he had sold everything. Wladimir had Gourkau settle up with him. 'Do you have other trinkets in your hotel?' Brutally, the prince risked addressing him as *tu*.

"'Certainly, Monseigneur, or rather, I have no more myself but my friend still has some.'

"'Oh, you have a friend? You're not traveling alone?'

"'A friend, which is to say, a companion. No, I'm not traveling alone. For running around the country, that would be too sad.'

"'Are you married?'

"'Me? Married every night.' And the mariner blushed, as if having said too much.

"'That's good. Come back tomorrow with your merchandise, but don't bring your friend.'

"Marius withdrew, almost dancing with joy.

"'You have a fortunate hand, Comtesse. That man is gaiety itself; he'll deliver us from a nightmare.'

"And the reign of Marius began. He came back the next day, the day after that, and all the days after that as well. When he had exhausted his stock, and those of the shops in the Avenue de la Gare, represented as exotic objects to Wladimir's new folly, he returned in the capacity of storyteller, at a salary of forty francs a day. Gourkau settled up every evening, and every morning, at the approach of noon, the Provençal reported for duty. Wladimir was still in bed, Marius was given breakfast in the servants' parlor, and at four o'clock the prince's official storyteller began his employment.

"Sacha now imposed him on his four-to-sevens. The dismissed orchestras only played now at meal times, and, in the silence of the whole audience, the matelot, watered with lemonade—like all southerners, Marius was sober—recounted his voyages, narrating his childhood as a cabin boy, his years of service aboard the *Formidable*, and, overexcited by the stimulating sound of his own voice, invented and dared hyperboles, ever loquacious, mimicking and monologuing with the inexhaustible enthusiasm of men of his race. That descendant of Troubadours, his imagination broadened by years of adventures and distant expeditions, turned out to be a marvelous raconteur.

"With his elbows on his knees and his chin in one hand, Wladimir, with an astonishing rejuvenation of his entire face, drank the mariner's words. He also drank his eyes, his transparent and green liquid eyes, in which the reflection of so many horizons quivered; he drank, one might also have said, his health and his strength, so much did his pitiful old woman's face become animated by an intense passion at Rabassol's fanciful and spicy tales.

"The mariner talked about shipboard chores, adventures below decks and in hammocks, brawls between marine infantry and sailors while ashore, squadron pay days and watches in warm streets, nights at the Chapeau-Rouge, the drunkenness of Bretons and the practical jokes of mokos, girls in doorways and men rushing over the thresholds of closed houses, gallantries and tall stories, and dances in bars. And the hallucinated Wladimir relived with him an entire life of youth in rut—robust, healthy animal debauchery. He clenched his fists nervously and held back exclamations, thinking he was sniffing the odors of the tide and make-up. The mariner's stories reeked of garlic and musk; his slightest gestures evoked tucked-up dresses and whores swooning in the muscular arms of lads, in the flight of peignoirs; and Wladimir envied those mariners and those whores; the old prostituted soul of the princesses of his blood reawoke in him.

"Then Rabassol recounted his voyages. There was white Algiers, staging like cliffs the chalky cubes of its kasbah, the fried fish, the Moorish cafes and, by night, the violent pleasures of the Arab city. There was also Spanish Oran, the filth of the Jewish quarter and, more Oriental than the Orient, the iridescent, colored anthill, gouached with silver and gold in the semi-darkness and the artificial light, of the busy crowds of the souks of Tunis. The mariner also talked about Sousse, Monastor and Sfax, Gabes and its camp of Spahis, Gabes and its esparto loaders. He also talked about Djerba, the ancient isle of Calypso according to some, the isle of the Lotus Eaters according to others, and the red sails of coral fishers swarming over the blue Mediterranean, the red sails of fishing boats resembling at sunset a flock of pink flamingos over the sea. Finally, he talked about Tripoli, Tripoli in Barbary, the Tripoli of corsairs, Spanish expeditions and the distant princesse, and Sacha, transported elsewhere, Sacha transfigured, listened to those stories in the adoring hypnosis of a nomad listening to a camel-driver's tale in the blue shade of a caravanserai.

"The Asiatic reawoke in him; the debauchee had given way to the dreamer; all the names of the barbaric cites of the Tripolitan and the Tunisian South inebriated him like a philter; there was also the incantation of an invitation to the voyage. He saw all those cities, some in the midst of the palm trees of their oases, others encircled by high walls, all lying nonchalantly in the glare of the sands and, above all, in the mirage of leagues, leagues upon leagues, which increased, deformed and magnified the settings.

"The mariner also told tales about Sicily, the Latomies of Syracuse, the Spanish palaces of the city, the Road of Tombs and the panorama of grandiose melancholy that one discovers in the Greek theater. He talked about Messina, the lighthouse set at the end of the mole; Catania and its streets paved with hardened lava, its congealed causeways, steep and black; Naples and Vesuvius, the osterias of the Basso-Porto and crapulous nights in Portici on the edge of the sea. He knew Sorrento—he had spent two years there—the splendor of the Gulf of Salerno and the enchantment of the rocks and water of Amalfi. The Provençal had also seen Palermo, and was able to describe Monreale and the Concha d'Oro, the garden of flowering orange trees and lemon trees, enervating in odor and mildness, the elegant and pumiced crowd of the Quatro Santi, trident fishing and Mont Pellegrino.

"Marius Rabassol had also been to China.

THE DISGRACE

"THOSE décors of dream and reality, that Orient of enchantment and that Sicily of apotheosis, that Provençal populated with adventures, burnooses, silk gandouras, the embroidered
trousers of Jewesses, the transparent haiks of Fatimas, necklaces
of jasmine flowers, and jackets armored with gold, sparkled
and floated in the stories of Algiers and Tunis, pell-mell; and
here and there, the dolmens of officers rubbed shoulders with
the blue uniforms of riflemen. In the stories of Sicily, peasant
women with medallion profiles danced, sheathed in pink shawls
and heavy robes, with men as svelte and brown as Moors. For the
mariner, Naples and Sicily were lands of gypsies devoted to the
Madonna, immodest and tempestuous; the men ran naked over
the strand there, and the women, carefully wrapped up, came
and went, dirty and hypocritical, from the Duomo to the brothel
and the houses of procurers at the chapel of the Sacred Heart.
All Sicilians, Neapolitans, Spaniards and even Corsicans—for
that damned matelot had been to Barcelona and Bastia—Marius
designated with the scornful name of *macaroni*; he thus affirmed
the arrogant superiority to which the Marsellais lays claim over
all the Latin races, and the special disdain of the Phocean, the
Greek, for the races of Italy.

"Macaroni! And on his mother's side, Prince Wladimir was
Italian. He had not even shuddered, entirely held by the charm
of the voice and the gray eyes of the storyteller. The storyteller,
however, scarcely renewed himself. In similar décor, there were

always the same brawls, the same adventures in dens and dives, the same dirtiness of mariners ashore, mostly concluding in the gutter or the police station, where the consul came to reclaim them; at length, Marius's repertoire exhaled a monotonous odor of camp beds, anisette and kennels. The comtesse yawned ostentatiously, and people began to decline invitations to the dinners on which Noronsoff now imposed the pedlar.

"With his hands on the rounded napes of Nicolas and Boris, however, Wladimir did not weary of listening or of hearing. It was, above all, the settings in which he lived, transported by a strange doubling of his being to the lands the storyteller evoked; the magic of skies and seas, especially, delighted him. In depicting them, the Provençal had a veritable gift for imagery and color. Oh, the rosy gold and incandescent sulfur of the dusks in his crossings, and the blazing clouds of the dawns, poised on the horizon as if on the edge of a mirror. The matelot also had worse stories; he did not hide the fact that he had a liking for the prostitutes of all latitudes, and it was that genre of adventures that delighted Wladimir most of all. Marius seasoned them with Marseillais sayings and dirty jokes; he brought out the whole vocabulary and the special repertoire that the sailors of the old port trail though the bars of the Rues Ventomagy and de la Rose.

"Wladimir reveled in such turpitudes, rejuvenated, and, one might have thought, returned to health, as if Rabassol had infused him with new blood along with his stories. Decidedly, the invalid was not only drinking the words and the eyes of the pedlar; one might have thought that in putting him to sleep with his tales, the other had poured his youth and strength into him. The prince could no longer do without Marius; he wanted to install him in the villa, but the mariner was intent on retaining the liberty of his nights. He arrived in the morning, at midday, and he went away every evening at eleven o'clock, but he had brought his friend, his companion in trade, Pierre Etchegarry, and the Basque's exclamations—'Do you remember when . . . ! Yes, that's the way it was . . . ! No, you're forgetting . . . !'—now animated Rabassol's stories and renewed Wladimir's joys.

"For the two friends it was a perpetual party. Dressed in new clothes, delicately shod, their waistcoats clinking with gold chains, their fingers sparkling with rings, they drank lemonade and smoked Londons all day long. Both coquets, Marius as a Marsellais and Etchegarry as a Basque, they sported bright cravats and reeked of musk and fragrances.

"In the entourage, people mocked their pretentions and their gaucherie. 'They're the prince's new parrots,' said the comtesse smiling—but underneath, the Pole was seething, devoured by anxiety, and resented the increasing favor of the intruder. She had tried to intervene in the middle of Rabassol's interminable tales and had been harshly rebuked by the prince.

"One day, at one of the four-to-sevens, she interrupted the storyteller and tried to insert one of her own memories, a witty anecdote of which she had been the witness, and one appropriate to the adventure Marius was narrating. 'Don't break the flow,' the curt voice of the prince had wheezed—and, when the pretty woman pulled a face and said: 'But I've traveled too,' Noronosoff had retorted: 'Pardon me, Comtesse; Monsieur has been a navigator, you've been a tourist.' And Schoboleska had been put in her place.

"Another time, after a more than spicy anecdote, the Pole got up from the table, gestured to her sons and, suddenly recovering all her modesty, said: 'How can you support that, Prince? It's a compost heap that is being raked in front of you.'

"To which Noronsoff, playing with his pearls, retorted: 'A compost heap of wrack, which is worth as much as a hothouse compost heap. Are you comparing your past with his, Vera?'

"The insult was bloody; Schoboleska fainted; she allowed herself to be carried away by her maids. As the prince said; 'She saved herself with her exit!'

"She sulked for three days and came back; she did not find Wladimir in his bathroom. He was in the kitchens supervising a bouillabaisse that Marius was concocting for him. The Provençal now reigned by virtue of his culinary talents; with a squadron of scullions at his orders he simmered crab and garlic soups that delighted Wladimir; the prince licked his fingers over them. He spent his days in the basement now, around stoves, interested in the manipulation of saucepans, the dosage of spices and the concoction of sauces.

"In the bathroom, in the midst of the erotic frescoes, the habitués of the villa commented on Wladimir's absence; there was the usual flow of implications and disobliging allusions to the empire exerted by the new favorite. The comtesse arrived in time to hear the abominable Marseillais denigrated, and, delighted by comments dear to her rancor, she sniggered in a strident voice: 'The prince and his *hommes de joie!*'[1]

"'His *hommes de joie* and his *dame d'ennui.*' That was Noronsoff, who had just come into the room, and kissed her hand ceremoniously.

"Clad in white aprons, with chefs' smocks passed over their jackets, the Basque and the Provençal guffawed in his shadow. The entire audience felt obliged to hold their sides, for the Pole it was decidedly disgrace, retirement to the background, an atrocious fall—and she was the one who had introduced the accursed Marseillais.

"In the servants' parlor as in the kitchens, the fête continued; had the two companions not invited the prince to breakfast at a little restaurant in Ponchettes, where street porters and fishermen danced with one another in the evening, and, luring Sacha with descriptions of the dances performed at the Chapeau-Rouge, as in all the coastal fêtes, had they not persuaded the grand seigneur to go with them—prowlers of the quays—into that dive?

"Noronsoff had come back enchanted with the cuisine, delighted by the menu, and enthused, above all, by the welcome. Oh, the bonhomie of those fellows, the frankness of their laughter, the strong grip of those handshakes! How one sensed natures and characters therein. Those hearts had never lied—and it was

---

1 The French *filles de joie* is invariably used with reference to prostitutes, so the implication of the comtesse's improvisation is clear and explicit.

necessary to see the gaze with which the prince scrutinized the comtesse. But what had charmed him, and about which he never shut up, was the dancing.

"Our two friends had assembled a dozen clowns, jacks-of-all-trades, loose-limbed and bold, stevedores from the port and disembarked mariners, the scum of Genoa, Toulon and Nice, but all accomplished dancers; and, to the sound of the guitars of three expert string-pluckers, all that rabble, watered with Asti, had invaded the restaurant during dessert. All of them, taking one another by the waist or with hands on shoulders, had amazed the prince with the suppleness of their torsos, the flexibility of their ankles and the grace of their attitudes. They waltzed, looking one another in the eyes, their limbs entangled and yet free, fingers knotted over hips, with an ensemble in the movement that was truly unique, a certainty of rhythm that is only encountered in that region.

"The prince had come back from that breakfast transported, and wanted fervently to learn to dance that kind of waltz, with Rabassol and Etchegarry as teachers.

"It's implausible, but it happened as I'm telling you. We had the lamentable spectacle of Prince Noronsoff, that rag and wreck, that consumptive and neurasthenic, waltzing, swooning like a little girl, alternately, in the arms of the Basque adventurer and the Marseillais favorite.

"The dying Russian died twice over in the Midi.

"The orchestra of Tziganes accompanied the prince's first steps. A frightful fit of coughing interrupted his debut; blood spurted from his mouth, staining the plastron of his shirt. He collapsed in the arms of his dancing partner and we carried him away, soiled with red drool, his eyes revulsed, hypnotically stiff, a puppet broken by hysteria.

"That first dancing lesson kept him in bed for a week. During that week la Schoboleska had the luminous idea of asking the two mariners to teach her sons to dance; she could no longer recoil before any means of pleasing. So, Boris and Nicolas learned the mokote waltz. Like good fellows, the Basque and the Marseillais consented to the lessons; they owed too much to the comtesse to be able to refuse her, and anyway, the two darlings were truly too pretty.

"On the day of his reawakening, as he termed it himself, the prince had the spectacle of Rabassol and the Basque dancing with the young Schoboleskis. The mother had organized it with the complicity of all her friends; the two pedlars were costumed for the occasion in naval uniforms, Boris and Nicolas were dressed in the Polish style.

"Still pale after a week of hemorrhages, the invalid watched the couples twirling with a mysterious smile. 'It's a ballet,' he said, over the last chords of the Tzigane waltz, and, kissing la Schoboleska's hand, delicately: 'What a friend you are, Comtesse! You've divined my dearest desires.'

"He did not say any more.

"The comtesse remained disconcerted,[1] and did not come back into favor. The two *hommes de joie*, as she had stigmatized them, continued to reign at the villa. Health had returned to Noronsoff and the convalescent went on the spree with them; their whims and their pranks were, for him, the words of the Gospel.

"Did they not have the aplomb one evening to persuade the prince to accompany them to the *Briques*, the brothels of the Riquier quarter, the frightful blocks of old dwellings accumulated in the corner of the same small street, almost impinging on the main road that leads to the barracks.

"Marvelously placed between the Italian idleness of the Place Garibaldi and the quotidian rush of soldiers on leave, their five leprous façades constitute the red light district of Nice. Each interior is sordid; the rooms are open, whitewashed or coated

---

1 The word I have translated here as "disconcerted," *interdite*, has a double meaning in French, not only signifying disconcerted or nonplussed, but also prohibited or forbidden—both meanings are relevant to its use in this instance.

with yellow emulsion, with waxed benches sealed into the walls; men in soft felt, Alpine hunters and artillerymen from the fortress wallow there pell-mell with crewmen from yachts and stevedores; those gentlemen smoke, spit, nudge one another and loaf. Lamentable and resigned in the excessively short costumes of babies or Swiss maids, a female livestock does the rounds of its rooms, with atrociously weary faces; the seated men continue chatting among themselves, indifferent to the parade of women; they come to spend the evening there, because it's cheaper than the café; the errant meat-rack passes back and forth. Sometimes, a man makes a decision and touches a girl on the shoulder with his fingertip; it's a place of monotony and abominable sadness.

"Noronsoff came back from it revived, delighted by the disdainful attitude of the men, their evident misogyny—for the true Southerner a woman is only an egg-layer or an instrument of pleasure—flattered above all in his Russian ferocity by the brutalized air and slavish eyes of the prostitutes. 'Those are men as I understand them,' he said to the comtesse the next day. 'For them, woman is not a goal in life as she is among us, she's what she ought to be: an accessory and nothing more. Those houses have reconciled me with life; I feel avenged in watching those creatures circulate. Oh, the Midi truly has a superiority over us.' And his vitreous eyes searched the Pole with a singularly sharp gaze. La Schoboleska could no longer have any doubt; she really was in disgrace.

THE PLOT

"'WELL, DOCTOR, can you tell me what's happening here? My son is living with the cooks now; it appears that he never quits the stoves. Prince Wladimir Noronsoff peeling garlic and stirring sauces! He's under the orders of two scullions! That's the end of the world, the abomination of desolation, and you've seen that, Doctor! And you didn't warn me! I no longer have any confidence in you!'

"And Princesse Benedetta, getting up from her chair, broke the thin ivory paper knife that she was holding in her hands, with a dry click. She dominated with her full height the table before which I had just been summoned to appear. It was a veritable summons; alarmed by the way things were going, she had sent for me, to be interrogated. She wanted to know.

"I was truly very guilty. What were those two port prowlers that were now reigning at the villa? Two creatures of la Schoboleska, surely, since she was the one who had brought them,[1] and they were the Pole's two henchmen, perhaps her lovers, trained and fashioned by her to complete the ruination of the prince's reputation and health. Their installation here was a permanent scandal; a Noronsoff, with imperial blood in his veins, could not take up with two sailors; the Pole was sufficient to dishonor him. That

---

1 It is from this point on that the text of this chapter in the serial version is replaced by text from the next chapter in the book version; the order of the two muddled chapters is switched in the book version, leaving the preceding text and the equivalent section of text in the next chapter out of place.

whore wanted to kill her son, and she cited to me, as supporting evidence, the famous dancing lesson terminated in a crisis of hysteria and blood, and Wladimir's visit to the ill-famed houses of Riquier. Those two ruffians were now dragging him into dens of vice, and the death throes of a Noronsoff were being trailed through those evil places.

"'My son is playing Nero, I swear! I don't know what fate he reserves for me with that damned Jewess in his shadow, but I won't play Agrippina. I'll defend myself against my son and I'll be able to defend him against her and against himself. We're living in frightful times. One might think that the abominable charm has returned and that the frightful soul of the princesses of the race sometimes torments my Sacha!'

"She went on, telling the long rosary of her rancor. I listened silently to that mother discharging the heavy burden of her suffering. Her face pale, her eyes feverish, her tall stature and long mourning dress made her a living statue of Dolor; her eyelids were red from so much weeping, but for the sake of pride she had dried her eyes, and in the violet gleam of her irises, more than the anguish of a mother was burning: the anguish of an entire race.

"The princesse went on: 'The final straw, Doctor, the ultimate in folly or audacity, is that my son has taken it into his head to make me eat with those two vagabonds and make me sample their cuisine. He wants to bring them to my table! He never runs out of eulogies on their account, their character and their gaiety; he's infatuated with them as I've never seen him infatuated with anyone before. He's cooking dishes with them and harassing me to make me eat I know not what horror of their invention, which they call bouillabaisse . . . a sort of fish soup, it appears. It's enough to make one shiver! And Sacha wants to make me have lunch with those two specimens—me, who has always refused to see the Pole!'

"I took pity on her at the same time as an idea occurred to me. 'Comtesse Schoboleska won't be present at that lunch, I assume? She doesn't come here until four o'clock'

"'You know full well that I've signified to my son once and for all that I shall never see that Schoboleska.'

"'So, it's breakfast only with the two men?'

"'Yes. Why are you asking me that?'

"'Because it's necessary to consent to that lunch, Princesse.'

"'Me!'

"And I explained to her, in effect, the unexpected favor of Marius and the evident disgrace of the Pole. Perhaps there was something to be gained by flattering the prince's liking for the two pedlars. Perhaps it was the sole means of ending the credit of la Schoboleska permanently. Her influence was only hanging by a thread; the new favorite seemed rather good-natured; one could get around him.

"The princesse opened her eyes wide and drank in my words like those of an oracle. A new horizon had just appeared to her; she would have accepted anything in her hatred for la Schoboleska; she understood my implication. 'It's necessary to dine with these men, then?'

"'It's necessary. You can judge them for yourself at table.'

"'So be it, I'll have lunch. Thank you.'

"The lunch took place. That same evening, the princesse summoned me. 'They're not dangerous, in fact. I've seen them. Thank you.' She obliged me to sit down next to her. 'They have enthusiasm, a kind of communal gaiety and facile glibness that amuses Sacha's indolence, but not a trace of cunning. It's vulgar gossip that the least *facchino* in Naples could reel off. Their coarse and simple nature relaxes the prince, a rest from the complexities of the Pole. I know my son, he's a child. He'll rediscover himself with those two brutes . . . yes, two joyful brutes with all the health and freshness of blood that Sacha no longer has; but they're a peril nevertheless for the prince, since they're dragging him into dens of vice and bringing him back dying from expeditions where he'll end up remaining one day. What do you want to do with the two sailors? Do you have a plan, an idea? They aren't ambitious enough to be interested in the dismissal of the comtesse. For them she remains their benefactress; they're souls too new to savor the pleasure of betrayal. I sense in them a possible lever, a chance of ridding ourselves of the comtesse, but how? I've thought about it, but, thus far, I can't see anything, and haven't found anything.'

"I begged the princesse to be kind enough to listen to me. I told her in detail about Marius's entrance, the prince's sudden infatuation, the installation of the mariner as a storyteller and the kind of adoring hypnosis of Wladimir during the Provençal's tales of vice dens and crossings; the real talent of Rabassol for evoking the skies and atmospheres of countries and the transfiguration of the prince in listening to them: the prince metamorphosed, rejuvenated, almost cured, with blood in his cheeks and life in his eyes when the Provençal took him from Tunis to Gabes and from Malta to Sicily with words evocative of wide vistas and infinite horizons . . .

"And the princesse, thoughtful, her eyes elsewhere and yet attentive, sometimes interrupted. 'Yes, yes, that's it. As a small child, he loved stories. Already eccentric and rebellious, one could obtain anything from him by telling him about djinn, giants and fays; he has a poetic imagination. Oh, if Paris, Vienna and Saint Petersburg hadn't spoiled him, perhaps my Sacha would have been a Lermontov, a Dostoevsky or a Tolstoy! He had marvelous gifts!' And the pride of that mother, imaginative like her son, consoled her for present shame in the hypothesis of a future that might have been, and the deceptive mirage of memory.

"When I had established the real situation for her regarding the threatened credit of the comtesse and the unwitting favor of the mariner, and, in spite of recent follies, the villa somewhat healthier by virtue of the presence of the two men and a certain reversal of the tuberculosis, as if Marius had breathed in a lungful of sea air, she said: 'Yes, there's something to be done. I sense it; I divine it—but what?'

"Before the supplicant gesture of the mother's joined hands I forgot my visit and my first conversation with la Schoboleska.

In any case, was she not a traitor, and by putting a stop to the excursions by carriage had she not broken the treaty of alliance herself? Then too, Princesse Benedetta was wringing and stirring my heart with the intensity of her passion for her son.

"'What? There are voyages. What if the prince could be persuaded to make one, if he could be extracted from Nice and this villa?'

"'No, it's necessary not to count on that: making him quit his luxury, his ease his atmosphere; and then, the railways, long journeys, hours of departure with his nervous accidents and destroyed health. And then, what would we do with the two sailors? I don't see it; I can't imagine it.'

"'But what if all that luxury, comfort and atmosphere were transported with him? And if Etchegarry and Rabassol became necessary—better than that, if their presence were obligatory, and explicable, in the voyage I'm proposing.'

"'How?'

"'What if the Pole were suddenly eliminated from the prince's life, and if, in the voyage that I envisage, the health of your son were, on the contrary ameliorated?'

"'Tell me, then, Doctor, tell me. Save us—save him, save me!'

"'What about life on a yacht, Princesse? A luxury yacht like one of those moored at Cannes, and sometimes here, underneath the villa? Don't you have three hundred thousand francs to hand?'

"'Oh, you can be certain that I'd give twice that and more to save Sacha.'

"'A great luxury yacht, the *Wladimir*, or the *Alexander*?'

"'Oh, not the *Wladimir*—the *Alexander*! Wladimir is a name already borne, which summons misfortune.'

"'Rabassol and Etchegarry installed aboard as mates, or even cooks, and long cruises in the Mediterranean, ports of call along the Adriatic: Venice, Trieste and Ravenna. Long sojourns in the ports of Sicily, ports whose pronounced names make your son whinny and shiver. That, I've seen with my own eyes. The isles of the Archipelago and the cities of Greece; a winter in Corfu, a spring in Salerno, summer in the bay of Naples, in the cool shade of the forest of Castellamare; part of the autumn in Amalfi, the enchantment of Paestum, and then the errant course resumed in the infinity of changing horizons and their free delight; and then, afterwards, there are the Balearics and the ports of Spain: Cartagena, Malaga, Alicante; and then, Africa, and Malta, and Athens again; life with full lungs in a décor of dreams, between the sky and the sea.'

"'Yes, and you'll come with us, Doctor, won't you? While the other is here, consuming her impotence and rage?'

"She had seized my hands abruptly, and not even naming the Pole for me: *the other*, she designated her by that term, all the more eloquent in its imprecision. *The other!* An entire joy possessed her, not so much at the thought of saving her son as that of snatching him away from that woman.

"'Yes, I'll sail with you for six months, and then you can disembark me somewhere, at Reggio or Salerno, in Italian waters.'

"'Yes, that's it; out there, I fear no one. In Italy, I'm at home. Perhaps we could even take the Pole!' A bitter smile creased her pale lips, and the tip of her tongue protruded, licking avidly. Oh, with regard to detesting the comtesse, Princesse Benedetta certainly detested her. 'Yes, but how can we convince Sacha. He has a horror of the sea; he's always been sick. The longest crossing he ever made was from Naples to Palermo, and he didn't quit his cabin going or coming back.'

"'Exactly. Seasickness will cure him; it's twenty-four hours to get through. I'll answer for his health once we're in the open sea. But that's the nub: how to get him to do it.'

"'Prescribe the voyage. At the next consultation, advise the yacht and a cruise to Sicily, or Greece, wherever he wishes. Insist; convince him. I'll ask for the consultation, Doctor; I'll give you a start.'

"'Yes, but it's necessary to prepare him for it, to give him the desire to depart, a nostalgia for far horizons.'

"'You tell me that Sacha is animated merely by the story of a voyage, that he has adventure in his blood?'

"'Certainly, he has Rabassol in his head above all, and it's him that it's necessary to acquire first. Nothing can be done without him and his friend, without the two of them. We need the collaboration of those two men. It's necessary to involve them in our project, to associate them with our design.'

"'With money? Those men are needy. By giving them a large sum?'

"'Those men are, before anything else, mariners. They love the sea and are already bored after a long sojourn on land; then too, until further notice, they're with the comtesse. She still has the prestige of being their benefactress; they owe their good fortune to her, and they don't realize the extent of their power; it will be difficult to detach them from her.'

"'And yet that's necessary.'

"'Absolutely. Nothing can be accomplished without them. It's necessary to sound them out carefully, to make the command of the yacht shine in their eyes, to seduce the adventurers they are with the luxury and liberty of the cruise I outlined. Your two clowns won't resist that; but how to propose it to them without arousing suspicion?'

"'Perhaps my chaplain might be able to do it. They must be superstitious, being mariners.'

"'No, Your Père Angelo is Italian; he wouldn't have any purchase on that man from Aigues-Mortes. Let me think about it. We'll find a way, but prudence and precaution, Princesse. Three-quarters of this house, its servants and suppliers, are under la Schoboleska's orders.'

"'I'm sure of Gourkau.'

"'Yes, I know. He could negotiate the purchase of the yacht; but first he'll appeal to the *hommes de joie* for us.'

"'*Hommes de . . . ?*'

"'Pardon me, Princesse, for the term; it's la Schoboleska's.'

THE HOROSCOPE

"AND SO, with the complicity of Gourka, a plot was woven. The important thing was to have the yacht on hand when Wladimir was persuaded to make the projected cruise; it was necessary not to give him time for second thoughts. If he were brought to embark, the thing had to be done within two days, without his having a moment to reflect; anything was to be feared in that friable and mobile nature.

"A large English yacht was moored just then in Cannes, which fulfilled the desired conditions of luxury and comfort. Its owner was willing to yield it for six months, the six months necessary for the construction of the vessel that the princesse desired for her son. Gourkau, as if acting in the name of the prince, entered into negotiations with the owner of the *Edward III*; the price of the hire was agreed, and it only remained to fix the dates—which depended on Wladimir's caprice.

"No step had yet been taken in his regard; it was necessary to be suspicious of him and the comtesse. The two mariners were fully acquired. They had let go of the Pole with an unconscious facility, far more tempted by the joy of going back to sea than Gourkau's resonant arguments. They were worthy fellows, in sum, and the princesse, with her grand air and her genuine dolor had been able, in three conversations, to detach them from la Schoboleska.

"Marius, above all, had allowed himself to be caught by the chagrin of the mother in perpetual anguish for the life of her

168

son; in a corner of the Camargue, by the side of some white road, he too had a wizened old woman with stiff hands as knotty as olive branches, an old mutterer of prayers, idling in a corner of the hearth, whose voice suddenly dissolved in tears when she pronounced the name of her son Marius; that Provençal was a good son.

"Etchegarry, a natural child, had a less sensitive heart, but whatever Marius wanted, he, Pierre Etchegarry, wanted. On that one, the princesse had imposed herself, with her profile of a great race; and then, it was a good deed, in sum, that they were doing in getting that sick man out of the clutches of that slut; and they approved of being for the mother against the favorite. They were defending the family, not to mention that their good deed would have a big reward, that they would gain the liberty and joy of navigating—the greatest of all for them—and keep their situation; they would remain Wladimir's pampered friends.

"With tranquility of conscience and no risk, our two companions were making themselves new souls by betraying their benefactress.

"Their favor, however, without decreasing for that, was less marked. Sacha was beginning to weary of capsicum salads, anchovies with tomatoes and larded veal with pistachios; Marius's stories were also captivating him less. For the moment it was the Basque who held the grace note, in pelota games organized by him in a corner of the park; other Basques, found here and there, formed the teams.

"The park was on a slope, nets with tight mesh had been strung between palm trees to retain the balls; the games were played in the worst conditions, hampered by clumps off agaves and bamboo, and beds of flowering anemones; Etchegarry's partners soaked their shirts with sweat there, cursing and swearing in the hoarse patois of Saint-Jean-de-Luz and Ustaritz that pelota could not be played on such a terrain; but Noronsoff's munificence retained them. Quite incapable of judging the shots, he was only interested in the agility, the deployment of strength and the skill of the man from Biarritz and his friends. As supple and muscular as cats, their slenderness also delighted him; and, abruptly giving up his four-to-sevens, he now spent his days in the park—which put blood in his cheeks and gave him an appearance of restored vigor.

"In the meantime, an active correspondence was exchanged between Gourkau and Lord Feredith, the owner of the *Edward III*; Princesse Benedetta no longer quit Sainte Réparate, where she had mass said and burned candle after candle for the success of her project for the abduction of her son Wladimir; a hysteria of devotion possessed her. Directed by Brother Angelo Cappini, she filled all the parishes of Nice with Italian mummery. I had not been able to refuse to go with her and Gourkau to an office celebrated with the same objective at the cathedral, but I made her understand that the assiduous presence of all three of us at votive masses in the churches of Nice might be noticed and reported someday to the prince, who would surely be alarmed by it; I was able, consequently, to avoid the ennui of those ceremonies and acts of faith.

"Gourkau remained the designated companion of those pilgrimages; they took place in the mornings, during the prince's exhausted sleep, which retained him in bed until one o'clock; they maintained the princesse in the state of feverish overexcitement and desirous hope that reminded me involuntarily of the hyperesthesia of the first Christian neophytes. The prince continued to interest himself in the wicker gloves and red tayolles of the pelota players, and everything, thus far—the entire abduction project—seemed to be on the way to success.

"'The dissimulation of those Russians! The falsity above all, of that Wladimir! Can you imagine that he's in the process of buying a yacht? Yes, yes, a yacht, the *Edward III*, at Cannes, and that he hasn't told me anything? It's Gourkau who has started the negotiations. You don't know anything about it either?'

"'No, truly. Are you sure, Comtesse?'

"'Yes, I'm sure! The owner is one of my friends, Lord Feredith. He's written to me for information. He wanted to know whether the proposition was serious. I replied that it wouldn't stand, that it's a caprice of the prince, and you know how long his caprices last! You don't know anything, then?'

"The comtesse had just sat down next to me; we were on this very terrace, before the panorama of the Esterel and Mont Chauve, the mountain and the sea; under the bamboos, the children and Etchegarry's partners were playing pelota.

"I supported the interrogation of la Schoboleska's sharp eyes without flinching. 'Nothing.'

"'What a rogue that Wladimir is. It's just like him not to tell me anything. He gets that Jesuitical soul from his mother, but that Gourkau didn't tell me, that's what I can't permit. I can doom whomever I wish, here.' And her mauve eyes were still locked on mine. 'So you're in the dark too?'

"I attempted to save the situation. After all, perhaps the proposition for the sale hadn't come from the prince; Gourkau knew the entire Russian colony; he might perhaps be operating on someone else's behalf; perhaps he'd been commissioned by . . .

"'The princesse! That would be even worse. Anyway, such is the valet, such is the master; this abode is that of intrigue, and everyone here fishes in troubled waters. Bonsoir, Monsieur Rabastens and thank you.'

"And the comtesse, getting up, went to join Noronsoff, who was in the process of explaining a dubious shot to her sons.

"That same evening I informed the princesse.

"It was only an unfortunate coincidence, the bad luck of him knowing la Schoboleska and having written; nothing was lost as yet. If the Pole had the aplomb to interrogate Gourkau, he would give the name of one of the princesse's business agents in Russia; what it was necessary to know, as soon as possible, was whether the two mariners had talked, and whether their boasting in some tavern might have compromised everything. Something might have been reported to the comtesse. If she had caught wind of the hiring of the two men, the game would become dangerous, she would warn Wladimir. Who could tell whether she had not made the two pedlars come, and got them to confess everything with her indifferent air and her feline nonchalance?

"'That avaricious Polish bitch could have rolled those fools like meatballs in flour.' And Princesse Benedetta became angry; an entire vocabulary of base insults suddenly rose to her lips.

"Information was obtained; the two mariners had not said anything. The comtesse had indeed summoned them to her hotel and had proposed a very advantageous engagement to them aboard a yacht at Cannes, the *Edward III*, owner Lord Feredith, but they had not flinched, sniffing a trap, and had said no. They did not care for the discipline and the etiquette to which one is constrained aboard yachts; they preferred the casual and friendly life and unexpected windfalls of coasters. They had even informed the comtesse that the Bureau de l'Inscription Maritime in Marseille had reclaimed them, and that they were embarking at the end of the month.

"Her vigilance had therefore been deflected, but she had caught wind of something and all her police must be on the alert; it was absolutely necessary to bring forward the departure. The consultation in which I was to order the voyage was urgently necessary; we were all agreed as to that. So the princesse asked her son to be kind enough to reassure her by means of a consultation given by me in her presence; she saw, it seemed to her, her Sacha returning to health, but appearances could be misleading, and she wanted to be edified as to his condition; he could not refuse that slight inconvenience to her maternal solicitude.

"The prince replied that it was ridiculous, but that he would receive us the following day, at three o'clock.

"On the eve of that memorable consultation, in the course of one of the customary games of pelota, an incident occurred, the memory of which still intrigues me. Noronsoff was there, as always, attentive to the tactics of the two sides; that day, Rabassol was taking part; he was fond of the game and wanted to play pelota like the others; his lack of skill amused Wladimir, and he was still laughing with the comtesse at the last shot missed by the Provençal when the pelote, caught in flight by Marius's *chistera*, deviated from its trajectory, and headed straight for the prince's temple. With an instinctive gesture, Noronsoff lifted his arm to shield himself; a second later and the shot might have killed him.

"There was only an exclamation. The prince had stood up, a little pale, with his hand simply numb; the armature of rings had protected his fingers, but the bezel of one of them had been shattered. It was a mosaic from Florence depicting an erotic subject.

"Confused, redder than a lady-apple, Marius made his apologies, standing before the prince. Calmly, Wladimir removed his broken ring and passed it over the mariner's finger. 'Keep it as a souvenir of me and your clumsiness.'

"But the comtesse had taken possession of the hand. She turned it back and forth, with the curiosity of a chiromancer, studying the form of the nails and the lines of the palm, and, as she was observing, an anguish and an anxiety rose in Wladimir's eyes.

"'Well?' said the Russian, impatient at her slowness.

"'Well, you've had a narrow escape, and I still stand by what I've told you; the lines concur, there's danger for you: it's there.' And with a gesture, she embraced the entire horizon of the bay. 'It's necessary for you to beware of everything that comes from the sea.'

THE PRINCE'S GAMES

"THAT consultation! At three o'clock I was at the villa and was almost immediately received; the prince was waiting for me in the small drawing room with the trellises, where I had found him on my first visit, and, as in my first visit, Princesse Benedetta was present.

"I ausculted him; I made him walk; I palpated his joints and his kidneys; I listened attentively to his respiration and his cough; I took his temperature and, having remarked the ploy of the previous day and the anxiety of the prince when the Pole had read his hand, I lingered for a long time myself over the examination of his fingers.

"'Do you know the art?' Wladimir asked me, nonchalantly.

"'No, but we physicians are also mages of a sort. The lines don't tell us anything, but many things are revealed to us by the softness or hardness of the fingers.'

"'And what do mine tell you?'

"'Nothing you don't know: physical depression, mental depression, a state of languor and enervation.'

"'Indeed, you're no great clerk. If it's only to recount those verities that you've disturbed my poor mother, oh, my poor doctor . . . !' And the prince smiled.

"'But I also see something else, and it's your lungs that have informed me of it. They've improved; there's less rattle; the air is circulating more freely; the liver is also less swollen in spite of your Provençal's diabolical cuisine, and the circulation is better, naturally.'

"'Then I'm cured? You're happy, now, Mother!'

"'Cured, no, but you could be if you wanted to be.' And, emboldened by a glance from the princesse, I launched into a long enumeration of plausible and agreed reasons.

"'Certainly, he's doing better, thanks to the life in the open air that he's almost consented to lead now. If he's finally able to breathe it's because he wants to spend his days in the park and has resigned himself to going out. It's distraction that he needs most of all; he would return to health if he abandoned the rarefied atmosphere of his four-to-sevens and, above all, his dinners and suppers prolonged into the night. Oh, if he wanted to try the animal life, the robust and fortifying life of simple folk . . . exercise, open air and calm, a great deal of calm, physical and mental repose, far from the gossips of Nice and the intrigues of his petty court—it's that life and his circle of familiars that is anemiating him.'

"The princesse approved with a nod of the head. One hand clenched against his teeth, Wladimir was listening while biting his fingernails; his jaundiced eyes never quit mine, and, slightly oppressed, I continued: 'There might well be a means, but could the prince resign himself to abandoning the villa temporarily? Others have tried the means and all of them have found it marvelous; invalids even further advanced than him have recovered their health . . .'

"'And that means?' Wladimir's irises, from yellow, had become green. 'That means, do you know what it is, Mother?'

"And Sacha, turning toward his mother, searched her with an ardent gaze.

"'But yes, we've even talked about it with the doctor, and at length,' the princesse replied, without being disconcerted.

"'Really! Well, I'm waiting. Speak!'

"'Well, Monsieur, it would be to navigate.' And, risking everything in order to win the game, I praised the advantages of life on a big yacht, the immediate benefits that he would obtain from all points of view: recrudescence of strength, mental peace, not to mention the diversion and changing panorama of coasts, the delight of living on the open sea, the unexpectedness of ports of call, mornings never the same before towns surging forth with the dawn ahead of the boat, and gulfs fleeing behind the yacht in the golden blaze of sunsets.

"I sensed myself becoming a poet in telling him about the mirages and moving shores of the life of a yachtsman: all my Latin and Greek humanities returned to me in reminiscences, fragments of Virgil and Homer were translated of their own accord on my lips, I was Odysseus and Aeneas by turns, and I was also Rabassol. I surprised myself with the intonations of the voice of the Provençal; in order ro depict Tunis and Palermo I had the matelot's fortunate images. Like him I evoked, in an *olla podrida* of epithets, Maltas of apotheosis, Tripolis of dream, and chimerical Tangiers. A kind of folly possessed me, and, out of arguments, jabbering in the precipitation of my dithyramb, I concluded:

"'The princesse is ready to go with you, and only asks to come; the Provençal and the Basque could also be embarked; they would be two joyful companions already found.'

"'And one could disembark in Italian waters as soon as one was out of sight of the French coast.' With a thin smile, Wladimir applied his narrow shoulders to the broad back of his armchair.

"The princesse and I exchanged a rapid glance. But the prince had already resumed his lofty indolence. 'Come on, Doctor, continue.' And, a little like a somnambulist, I resumed the long chaplet of agreed arguments. Indifferent, his eyelids now lowered over his gleaming irises, Wladimir let me talk. Without the watchful glint in his eyes one might have thought he was asleep; my words were lulling him and he allowed himself to be lulled; a lassitude also seemed to be depressing him.

"A malaise was growing between us, an embarrassment aggravated by the uncomfortable silence; each of my sentences seemed to coagulate, but I continued even so. I was praising cruises and halts, the peninsulas and the archipelagoes when the wheels of a carriage stopped under the windows and the horseshoes made the gravel squeal.

"The prince got up, went to a window, and then, coming back toward us, placed his hands on the table and, leaning forward, his shoulders high, as if ready to deepen: 'And what about the sea-sickness, the sea-sickness that empties me like a bottle and shakes me like a plum-tree, the sea-sickness that disrupts my heart, my liver and my bowels, have you thought of that, Mother? If the doctor doesn't know about it, you can't be unaware of it. You've seen me on board during two crossings, the only two of my life, and you've decided to make me navigate! You're weary of seeing me live, then? For the little time that I still have to bore you with my presence, you might have let me die here.'

"'Sacha!'

"'What harm have I done you, that you want to finish it so soon? Oh, that fortune, that wretched fortune, which unleashes that pack of interests and intrigues in that house of suffering and makes you fight over the shreds of my agony! Oh, those millions, those millions as hereditary as the malady that is twisting me, those millions that stifle me in a court of hirelings and parasites, those millions that have corrupted the doctor as they madden you, Mother, since you've arrived at desiring my death.'

"'Me!'

"'Yes, you're trying to abridge my life.'

"The princesse had risen to her feet, white, with a frightful tremor in all her limbs. The prince was trembling too, but with a contained fury, a concentrated fury, slowly amassed, which was gripping him by the throat, strangling his voice and making him chew the words between his teeth. He emphasized his phrases by making pauses, like a hole-punch, and that cold rage, those slow invectives, were horrible to hear. The princesse did not say another word; she too had leaned both hands on the table and was looking Sacha in the eyes, fixedly; he fell silent then, and the silence between the mother and the son was a terrible silence.

"With a strangely shrunken face, the prince resumed slowly: 'I've been given two years, a maximum of two years, to live. Couldn't you wait two years?'

"'Sacha!'

"But Sacha pressed a bell-push; a muzjik surged through a door-curtain. 'Has the comtesse arrived?'

"'Yes, Monseigneur.'

"'Ask her to come up.'

"'Never! You won't make me meet that woman.' And the princesse, drawing herself up to her full height, sketched a movement toward the door.

"'Yes, you'll do this for me, Mother. You won't refuse this favor to your beloved Sacha. Think about it—a dying man!' And swiftly, with the agility of a cat, he went around the table and seized the princesse by the wrist; his bony fingers closed like a vice on his mother's arm, an atrocious energy was alive in his yellow eyes. With an evil smile on his lips he maintained the princesse standing against the table. 'Come in, Comtesse, come in, dearest. We're waiting for you.'

"Delectable and slim in a long coat of mauve silk, with an enormous knot of bouffant white muslin beneath her pointed chin, the Pole made her entrance. Her long eyes enlivened with kohl, her entire freshly made-up face respired a serenity of command, an indescribably cunning candor. She entered in a waft of bergamot and an eddy of silky underwear: an enormous capote of mauve tulle stamped her face with a pastel softness.

"'Comtesse Schoboleska, my mother.'

"The comtesse bowed with the gaze of a frightened hind.

"The princesse didn't flinch. 'You're hurting me, Sacha,' she murmured. 'Let go of my arm.'

"'Pardon me, mother; I have no feeling any longer—the hand of a dead man.' And, addressing the other: 'You know what state I'm in, Vera. You've heard my cough and seen the blood that I spit. I'm a doomed man, or almost, no one here is unaware of it. Well, do you know what this Monsieur'—his hand designated me—'in connivance with my mother, has found to cure me? Guess! A sea voyage, a cruise along the coasts of Sicily or Greece, no matter where; but they found that in order to make me embark, to make me navigate, me, a sick man, when, even when I was well the sea would already bring me to the brink of death. I vomit blood on land, but that's not enough for them. Me, at sea, can you see that? I wouldn't last three days; it would be immediate death, with a fixed term. When, in your solicitude, you came to warn me about the negotiations for the purchase of this yacht—for it's the comtesse who warned me—when you came to tell me that they wanted to abduct me from here and make me embark, I didn't believe you, I couldn't believe it. This consultation has taken place; I believe you now. They want my death!'

"'My son!'

"'Shut up, Mother, you can talk after the speech for the prosecution.'

"'We're on trial here, then?'

"'You're culpable.'

"'And it's Madame who charges us?'

"'No, it's Madame who convinces me. I have the evidence.'

"'It's an attempted murder, then? I, your mother, attempted to end your days.'

"'My days! Much worse, you attempted my liberty, for, once on that yacht, at your mercy, with this doctor and those complicit matelots, you'd disembark me in Italy and intern me in some lunatic asylum, for it's the sanitarium that you had planned for me. I know full well that the life I lead here horrifies you; you hate everyone who loves me; you criticize all my pleasures, and your blind maternal passion is so jealous that it's no longer anything but hatred. You've been living for years with the thought of this kidnapping and abduction; you've finally found accomplices, but fortunately, Madame was alert.'

"'It's doubtless Madame who loves you.'

"'The comtesse only loves herself and her children. She has an interest in pleasing me and giving birth to my caprices; my caprices are her living; she cultivates them, she has reason. I prefer her interested complaisance to your egotistical love, your devotion, which hinders me, and your resignation, which obsesses me like a remorse. What does it matter to me that you love me, if you do me harm by loving me?'

"'Sacha!'

"'Yes, you love me maladroitly, like all women and like all mothers; only those who obey me love me. I'm not sensitive, I'm willful; I'm a millionaire and dying. I have the right twice over to submission.'

"The princesse was leaning on my shoulder; I felt her fainting. 'For pity's sake, Prince!'

"'Oh, it's you, Monsieur le Docteur! How dare you still be here? Have you been paid well for this criminal consultation?' The invalid discovered in his anger a veritable eloquence. 'Don't you know that what you've done here is against the law? I'll let you off. Go and get yourself arrested elsewhere. I've seen enough of you—get out!'

"'Monsieur!'

"'And you too, Gourkau; you have nothing more to do here. And you too, the two imbeciles, the two idiots of bouillabaisse, the two scoundrels of peppered anchovies and tomato salad!' And he showed the door coldly to the steward and the two mariners, who had come running with the entire staff at the noise; the whole household had thought it was another of the prince's crises.

"A flabbergasted silence gave every word the weight of a judicial sentence. He looked slyly at his victims. 'I annul my endowment,' he said to Gourkau.

"'I'll maintain it,' riposted a hoarse voice, that of the princesse.

"'Naturally, you're paying for the treason. I said get out, all of you!'

"'Me too?' The poor woman's voice was strangled.

"'You too, if you wish, Mother. You're free to stay to watch me die.'

"The princesse took a step, and then tottered backwards. Madame Schoboleska sketched a step toward her. Princesse Benedetta straightened up, took my arm, and went out slowly, with an indescribable majesty.

"She did not look at her son; her fixed eyes had not let a single tear fall. The Pole had not seen her weep.

"The door curtain had scarcely fallen back when there was a burst of laughter in the boudoir.

"'Are you content with me, Comtesse?' Prince Wladimir was amused.

SACHA IS AMUSED

"I was sacked; a Swedish physician replaced me. There had been a veritable palace revolution; a third of the staff had been replaced, la Schoboleska had only conserved her own creatures; it was the complete triumph of Poland. After ten days' absence, Gourkau had returned to grace; they could not do without his services. Princesse Benedetta retired to Cimiez, to the convent of the Dames Assomptionnistes; she had been unable to support the insult of the reproaches heaped upon her in the presence of her enemy. It was the first time in seven years that the princesse had quit her son. The Pole's victory was a stab in the heart.

"The event caused a sensation in Nice; people talked about it for a week—almost an eternity in a city where the average of scandals is three a week.

"For a fortnight I had encountered Etchegarry and Rabassol hanging around the Avenue de la Gare. Scrubbed up and brand new, they did not quit the tables of the Régence and the Brasserie Alsacienne, installed from morning till evening with orangeades. They saluted me with a smile and a wink, testifying in their fashion that they didn't bear me a grudge. Our plan hadn't succeeded; that was the way of games of chance; the two mariners were good losers. Then, one day, I no longer saw them; they must have returned to Marseille.

"I sometimes crossed Gourkau's path in the vicinity of the Crédit Lyonnais, but he put a particular care into avoiding me; I must have been suspect at the villa, and the good steward feared compromising himself.

182

"The princesse had me summoned to the convent twice. I found her encamped in a whitewashed room, almost a cell, the only kind of room that the Dames Assomptionnistes put at the disposal of their inmates. She lived there amid a clutter of unpacked trunks and the alarm of three Italian chambermaids lodged at the other extremity of the building far from their mistress, whose slightest ring filled the religious silence of the corridors with a frantic gallop. It was the summary installation of a woman always on tenterhooks, whom one would have thought on the eve of some departure.

"The princesse only received Gourkau and me, waiting, in order to return to the villa, for the prince to give her a sign; but Wladimir did not budge. He had fallen back entirely under the domination of the comtesse, and that mother languished there, in the convent, eight hundred meters from the regretted villa, like a queen in disgrace whom the dauphin no longer wants to know.

"She had me summoned for cardiac troubles from which she said she was suffering, and, during my two visits, did not even pronounce Sacha's name; then she no longer asked for me. The Swedish physician had replaced me with regard to her too; she had him care for her. Through him, at least, she knew a little of what was happening at the villa. She was devoured by the desire to hear mention of her son.

"I too no longer knew anything about Noronsoff but the gossip current among the suppliers, and truly, I missed that unhinged Russian and the unexpectedness of his whims; I had ended up almost liking that singular invalid. In spite of all his follies, the Slav had a charm that forced attachment. Fallen back into my ordinary clientele of visitors and winter residents, I seemed to have had a dream. In Noronsoff's house I had lived a tale from the Arabian Nights, and down-to-earth life had reclaimed me. One always awakes from a dream painfully.

"What was Wladimir doing between Gourkau and la Schoboleska? The pace of life in the house had, it appeared, been restrained, and some of the guests of the four-to-sevens eliminated; the comtesse supervised the invitations, only brought her own creatures, and maintained a good guard; it was almost a claustration. A sister of hers or her husband's, a Baronne Narimoff, summoned from who knows where, accompanied her in her trips around the city; she was seen sitting with her in the depths of the prince's landau. She was a rather beautiful woman, taller and stronger than la Schoboleska, but who had renounced pleasing, the freshness of her complexion completely destroyed, with extinct eyes, as if tarnished by dint of weeping; she had a rather grand air and the attitude of a poor relative; the children called her 'Aunt.'

"And a sort of calm seemed to have succeeded the folly of luxury and feasting at the villa. One of the orchestras—the Italian one—had been dismissed.

"The favorites of the moment were a Piedmontese tragedian and a Venetian *jeune premier* from the Théâtre Risso, both members of an Italian troupe that gave performances in the courtyard of an inn, amid the reek of the stables and the henhouse, and with which, because of the rarity of the events, the society of Nice was infatuated for an entire winter. On the strength of an article by a passing Parisian chronicler, the All Nice of the *vegliones* and floral battles thought it ought to pile into the benches of the Risso, alongside the Neapolitans from the port and the Piedmontese from the Place Garibaldi; it was necessary to applaud la Miligenti in *Amleto, principe di Danimarca* and *Elisabetta, regina d'Inghilterra*, Faccio and Shakespeare, Shakespeare and Rossini.[1]

"La Miligenti, an enormous quadragenarian with a fine profile, unfortunately swollen by lymph, truly stirred the fibers of the public in the fifth act of *Elisabetta*. Within the gaudy rags of a fairground booth she had found gripping death-throes, and caused a frisson by the alarming realism of her coughs and gasps.

---

1 The original gives the name of the Italian composer, twice, as "Giacometti." I have substituted the actual composers and restored the Italian titles.

In *Amleto* she contrived to dissimulate her paunchy silhouette beneath a marvelous arrangement of the pleats of her mantle. Sheathed in eight meters of black cloth she provided a great somber specter, whose astonished face of a blonde and bloated angel imposed the Prince of Demark more than all the tragediennes who have incarnated him since. In her, the science of attitudes was logical and rare, and for one entire winter, the flashy and barbaric Nice of the big hotels and villas savored that artistic pleasure meekly. It was the fashion to go and applaud la Miligenti, good form to love her and understand her. From one franc fifty the best seats rose to ten francs; the rest of the troupe was irrelevant. The following year, la Miligenti, to whom the grand dames of the Italian colony had sent jewels, dresses and flowers the previous winter, played to empty benches; the tragedienne had reverted to her public of street porters and fishermen. Fashion, which had been infatuated with her, had forgotten her. Infatuations do not last long in Nice; the local climate causes women and flowers to fade rapidly.

"It was that outmoded plaything that Noronsoff had just discovered. To tell the truth, it was la Schoboleska who had found Sacha's new toy. She had proposed a matinée at the Théâtre Risso to him, assured in advance that the prince would be amused by the exuberance and the exaggeration of the Italian troupe's performance. In the bad play Waldimir had discovered in la Miligenti the mimicry of his mother; prodigiously interested in her gesticulation, he had invited her to the villa right away. The Risso troupe was now performing there three times a week, to the great joy of Wladimir, who pretended to recognize, in three scenes out of five, the attitudes and false airs of the princesse and her chaplain. A *jeune premier* whose pallor was punctuated by terrible moustaches, overly red lips and eyelids discolored as in aftermath of a spree, completed the picture. As gangling as a marionette, and as long as a day without bread, Giuseppe Fiaschi was his name, and Fiaschi had Wladimir and the entire villa in stitches; he thought he had impressed the prince and, as a good

Italian, he braced himself and adopted a languorous and fatal air in playing, his irises rising beneath his somber eyelids, only the whites of his eyes showing, all torso and leers.

"Wladimir was madly amused by him. It was also the joy of the comtesse to make fun of the young ham. The poor fellow was heaped with anonymous gifts: cravat pins and inexpensive little rings, in which Fiaschi appeared adorned at subsequent performances, to the scorn of all historical accuracy. To please Noronsoff, whose prodigality was legendary, the poor fellow spent his entire salary on costumes; he was decked out like a mummer, and each of his entrances was greeted with mad laughter.

"The performances were put on in the park, in the marvelous décor of cedars and palms. As soon as Fiaschi appeared in his carnival outfits, the prince fell about, choked by hiccups, and clapped his hands at full tilt in order to cover his vocal eruptions; beside him, la Schoboleska stifled hers with a handkerchief. Nicolas and Boris left, unable to take any more, and all the guests stamped their feet with joy. The Italian smiled, thinking that the prince had collapsed with admiration; at the end of the spectacle the actor was recalled and covered with flowers; there were avalanches of carnations, black irises and Nice violets. Fiaschi, streaming with greasepaint, asked to kiss the hand of the prince, who split his sides.

"Everything comes to an end. One day, after the performance, an enormous bouquet of tulips was sent to the actor on stage: giant tulips, ragged and mottled, in the most vivid colors, yellows and reds, the yellows splashed with blood, the reds striped with gold, splendid and violent flowers, so-called 'parrot tulips.' The ham folded himself in two, gratefully, and buried his face in the flowers. He straightened up again uttering a scream. Blood was spurting near his eye, staining the white velvet of his doublet; panicked wings ransacked the tulips. The *jeune premier* dropped the bouquet. On Sacha's order, a parrot had been hidden amid the tulips, solidly bound to the stem; furious, the bird had bitten the Italian cruelly on the cheek.

"The Venetian understood, and did not go back again; the Italian troupe had reigned for three weeks. 'Fiaschi has become a fiasco,' concluded Wladimir, and All Nice repeated the prince's quip.

"The prince had also resumed his excursions by carriage; his landau was encountered parked outside the suppliers' establishments. The comtesse occupied the rear seat beside Wladimir; Boris and Nicolas sat opposite. When the Pole was in Cannes—she often went to Cannes now—Baronne Narimoff occupied her place. Wladimir was never left alone. But they were not the long excursions of yore; they only went into town to make purchases. The landau was parked for hours outside the jewelers of the Quai Saint-Jean-Baptiste and the Quai Masséna; there were long negotiations in front of the windows of the Morgans and the Lacloches; the prince did not even get down any more; he remained sprawled on the cushions of the landau and had the display cases brought out to him.

"Standing on the sidewalk, an employee, or the jeweler himself, praised the orient of pearls, caused the strings to flow, or offered an opal or a ruby for admiration. A crowd gathered, and, delighted by the astonishment that he provoked, but seemingly indifferent, Sacha perorated, gave his opinion, consulted the comtesse, wanted to see other stones, put on a spectacle and generally did not make a decision. The landau departed again at a fast trot, leaving the jeweler and the crowd bewildered; but on the days when he did make a decision, the Russian was such a good client that the most ill-tempered tolerated his caprices.

"It was during one of those stations outside a jeweler that I encountered the prince and la Schoboleska one day. On the part of the comtesse there was the most gracious bow, and on that of Wladimir the most cordial smile, with a polite gesture of the hand, his handkerchief waved in appeal toward me. I returned the salutation and passed on.

"A strange character! And the princesse continued to languish in her convent and in her disgrace. It was then that All Nice burst out laughing one evening at the news of the prince's cystitis. During one of his long bargaining sessions outside a jeweler's, Wladimir suddenly got up, pushed away the display-cases, got down from the carriage, traversed the sidewalk, went into the shop and, pushing the employees out of the way, ran into the back room and there, taking possession of a flower-vase—the back room proved to be a little drawing room—he stood in a corner and relieved himself. Having done that, he replaced the flower-vase on a table, went back through the shop, saying; 'Excuse me, my cystitis!' climbed back into his carriage and left without buying anything.

"The insolence of a grand seigneur could hardly be taken any further.

LA MARISKA

IN the Russian colony the prince's cystitis was much appreciated. People were no less interested in the actions of the comtesse; war had been fully declared between her and Princesse Benedetta. All sympathies were, of course, with the mother, but the men were impassioned by the Pole's game—the men and the women too, the adventuress's science of intrigue forcing admiration. Who would remain the mistress of the place and the hour?

"The prolonged retreat of Princesse Noronsoff in the convent of the Dames Assomptionistes of Cimiez gave ground to the cause of the partisans of the comtesse, but she had skirted disgrace so many times and Wladimir was so unpredictable; any about-turn could be expected of him, and the battle, won as it was, continued with alarming alternatives of highs and lows.

"I only had echoes of it by way of public rumor, truncated and erroneous echoes that informed me less well than my personal memories of the villa. Perhaps less out of filial love as to disquiet the comtesse, there had first been vague attempts at rapprochement on Noronsoff's part, which the princesse had left abortive; she had signified that she would only return to the villa after the expulsion of her enemy, and the projects of reconciliation had had no consequence. I recognized Sacha's teasing character in that, the agitation always preoccupied with tormenting someone and causing them anguish.

"The Pole seemed, in any case, to have changed tactics. She did not watch over the prince as much, and left him alone with his ennui for entire days, sure, one might have thought, of having exhausted his caprices. She often absented herself, going to Cannes once or twice a week, where she had rediscovered friends, among others Lord Feredith, the owner of the *Edward III*, the yacht in the negotiations undertaken by Gourkau at the time of the projected cruise. She even stayed there for three days once, hospitalized aboard the yacht with her sons. In brief, the Pole allowed herself to be desired. It is true that, most of the time, she left Boris and Nicolas in Nice, and that Baronne Narimoff remained with Wladimir; Noronsoff was, therefore, well guarded. Nevertheless, something new had entered into la Schoboleska's existence, denounced by the relaxation of her assiduity at the villa and the frequency of her visits to Cannes. What could that cunning individual be preparing?

"It was during one of her absences that Noronsoff, doubtless aggravated by her behavior, meditated the possibility of bringing his mother back to the villa, calculating in advance the joy that he would have in seeing la Schoboleska's face when she found the princesse at Mont Boron again.

"Informed of the conditions posed by his mother, he preferred to address himself to her tenderness, and, without caring about the panic into which the news might throw her, he put himself to bed, feigned a crisis, and summoned an Orthodox priest; he was about to die and wanted to confess. He also wanted his mother's forgiveness; it was necessary that the princesse be reinstalled in her apartments, and, amid the fright of the entire staff, unaware of the comedy, he summoned Baronne Narimoff to his bedside, terrified her with his gasps and acrobatic bodily convulsions, and, in brief, brutalized the poor woman with the spectacle of a mimicry of death-throes, and sent her in all haste to the convent with the mission to bring back the princesse.

"Convinced by la Narimoff's alarm, Princesse Benedetta came running. Noronsoff's stage management had been thorough. The princess found the servants at prayer, candles lighted in the hall and the Orthodox priest in tears on the staircase; he threw himself at the knees of the princesse and wet her hands with his saliva and his tears. The prince was doomed, doomed for earth and heaven, for he had not been able to absolve him. Delirious, in the throes of death, he had made the strangest confession, confessing in Russian the usual run of peccadilloes and venial sins, but jabbering in Italian as soon as it was a matter of grave sins, and the unfortunate priest did not understand Italian. There was no religion in the world in which such a confession could be received, and the priest, prostrate at the knees of the princesse, was sweating in large drops, sobbing and lamenting.

"At that strange confession, Princesse Benedetta paused, unconsciously put on guard. She remained standing on a step, illuminated by the candelabra held up by the muzjiks; she could not explain that culpable lucidity of the moribund, deviating in the confession and suddenly switching languages in the exposition of his sins; she recognized in that the twisted mind and knavery of her son, and hesitated, as if before a trick.

"She had, however, decided to go up when a door opened on the landing and Gourkau appeared on the threshold. He ran to the princesse and begged her to go back down and return to the Assomption. 'Monseigneur is mad. In truth, I cannot let Her Excellency witness the prince's eccentricities.'

"Loud bursts of laughter, emerging from the door, which stood ajar, completed the instruction of the poor woman. She had already taken Gourkau's arm and was ready to go downstairs.

"Standing on his bed, with a green silk gandoura thrown over his shoulders, hastily turbaned with blue and gold cloth, the prince had improvised the appearance of a mamamouchi in order to greet his mother. He had counted on the masquerade to hasten the denouement and to obtain his forgiveness by surprise. He had prepared his funniest speech and his most tender pleas; but Gourkau's human respect had saved the mother from that humiliation. Gourkau had remembered that the princesse had maintained the endowment annulled by the prince; the perfect steward had a good memory; he also had flair, and had no doubt that the princesse would outlive her son.

"The princesse left the villa without having seen Sacha's carnivalesque death-throes. Noronsoff was compensated for that; the bewilderment of Baronne Narimoff, confronted by that resuscitated corpse in the folly of a disguise, consoled him for having missed his stroke.

"'You nearly found my mother here,' he said to la Schoboleska the following day. 'Yes, the princesse came here yesterday; I was dying without you, but she took fright on seeing your sister; she went back as she had come, without having seen me. Bless Heaven, Vera. My mother is a Russian of the old race; she hates the Turks, and I was dying as a Turk in order to have a right to the Paradise where I would surely find you;

> There is a Heaven that Mahomet
> Predicts for his apostles.
> But the pleasures that are promised there
> Are not worth as much as ours . . .'

"And that was the usual tone of his divagations.

"The jester in him was accentuated; a measure of ferocity also pierced his pleasures. He had always been cruel, but that cruelty became brutal. Once refined, as if veiled by irony, it now became insolent and heavy. One might have thought that the Pole was striving to develop within him the evil components of his barbaric soul.

"He retained a sly rancor against his mother, unable to bear the thought that she was able to go such a long time without seeing him. He thought her domesticated by her tenderness, and the final incident of the prolonged separation, her interrupted visit and her further retreat to the convent, irritated him as a crime of lèse-majesté toward him, as the head of the family and the bearer of the name. It was that muted animosity toward the princesse that nearly made the fortune of Mariska Zisco, a demoiselle of Monte Carlo whose eccentricities were the fable of the season that year.[1]

"A Hungarian Jewess born in Budapest, some said, a Tzigane according to others, la Mariska really was a divorced princesse, by virtue of the caprice of a Russian of high society, and perhaps even more so by the hazard of a bet. At the end of a supper she had wagered that she would be married to Zisco, had been able to refuse herself and had succeeded; the bet won, she had spent a million and bankrupted the husband.

"She was not so much a courtesan as a cosmopolitan adventuress. She drained Berlin, Vienna, Saint Petersburg, the spas of the Rhine, the Riviera and the stations of Austria, but disdained Paris. Paris lowers people's status, if it puts its mind to it. Born in the Pusta, that Bohemian had the appearance of a grand dame. In Vienna, the archduchesses copied her dresses and admired her luxury. At the cabaret she drank from a jade cup encrusted with rubies; la Mariska lived for the gallery. By means of her aplomb, her prodigality and the audacity of her repartee she dazzled, bewildering idiots and plucking them to be bone; she was a frenzied spender, a terrible devourer.

"Nothing was more deliberate than the apparent eccentricity of her conduct; la Mariska kept her public breathless, and snobbery is the soul of the public of today. Apart from not yet committing suicide, she had done everything to fill the Europe of big spenders and permanently scandalous women with her whims and bluffs. La Mariska had found a great many imbeciles; it is true that she had a particular flair for discovering them.

"She was a slender and spare woman, almost androgynous in the fortunate eurythmia of her slim legs and torso, as brown as a cigar with lips rouged with a burning redness, and long bright

---

1 Lorrain subsequently wrote a ballet-pantomime entitled "La Mariska" featuring a Hungarian gypsy dancer, which premiered in 1905 with Natalia Trouhanova in the lead.

eyes with blackened eyebrows. She was, above all, singularly mobile, restless, unable to sit still, always ready, one might have thought, to dance a czarda of her homeland.

"Those czardas and tzigane steps she sometimes danced at first light, after a long supper, in night restaurants. After the fifth bottle of champagne, to the thrusts of a bow of a Zorath or a Boldi, la Mariska got up, tucked up the tumult of her silk underwear, arched her waist and let herself go . . .

"She danced for pleasure, with a furious ardor, careless of the gallery; the soul of the Pusta possessed her entirely. It was a dance of the damned or a sibyl. She writhed, with appeals of the tongue and the extended arms, her bare heels hammering the floor; for, in order to dance, la Mariska took off her footwear, sending her satin mules and ten louis stockings flying to the four corners of the room.

"She danced, legs naked, disheveled, her heavy black tresses scattered over her face; and that moist face with dreaming eyes, pupils absent, was the charm and the great seduction of the courtesan; she danced, her hands on her temples, sustaining, one might have thought, her aching head. She danced a crucified species of dance, a tortured, lascivious, extenuated dance, and that sweating face and pallor maddened the diners at the Burghaus in Vienna as it did the feasters at Ciro and the Hôtel de Paris in Monte Carlo.

"When the dance was over, la Mariska pulled down her skirts, put up her hair, and became an exquisite socialite again. 'A few louis for the Tziganes,' la Mariska commanded, in a slightly hoarse voice, of the men who formed a circle around her. The Tziganes earned ten or twenty louis that way.

"That spring, la Mariska was playing a hellish game. It was at the roulette table that Noronsoff encountered her. He had gone in with the comtesse, Nicolas and Boris; the hazard of an excursion had brought them to Monte Carlo.

"As they entered they fell upon a troop of amused gamblers

around the dispute and cries of two women. Standing on a table, facing the public, an elegant young woman was showing her fist, in an insulting fashion, to an old lady with a chip-basket, who fell back fearfully, clutching a small bag of banknotes. As the prince came in, the croupier's rake had drawn away a wad of banknotes set before the elegant gambler.

"The young woman, clad in white lace, was la Mariska; the humble old lady was her mother, Mirka Shovani.

SACHA FINDS SOMEONE TO TALK TO

"THAT DAY, luck had betrayed the courtesan. No number had come up; it was a black run. She had just lost forty thousand francs; on top of that, she had lost her sang-froid, and was stubbornly following an illusory martingale, striving to recover her money; her aged mother, the bearer of the little bag, finally alarmed by the run of bad luck, and, as a good treasurer, frightened by the destruction of her daughter's profits and savings, had just refused her further funds. She had shut the bag and was now clasping it against her, no longer wanting to know. La Mariska, who sensed that her luck was about to turn, had insisted, and threatened; nothing had shaken the prudent miser. Obstinate in not yielding anything, she contented herself with muttering prayers or insults in Hungarian, and her clenched fingers would not let go of the bag, gripping it hard enough to scratch the leather.

"It was beautiful, the contest between the passion for gambling and avarice, those eyes of lucre and those hands of covetousness around the bag of blue bills. La Mariska had tried hard to seize it, but the old lady had leapt backwards with a brisk bound; the amused public had formed a circle, and there was now a Homeric tirade, a volley of low insults, jabbered by the old woman in a Tzigane idiom, and by la Mariska in suburban Hungarian. The courtesan vociferated them with gestures of a Fury, her face decomposed by rage, soaked with sweat, and marvelously beautiful in the fermentation of make-up. The laughter of the audience excited the two women. Extenuated, her voice hoarse by virtue of screaming, la Mariska suddenly bent down, took off her shoe and hurled it at her mother's head. The old lady sidestepped, avoiding the impact.

"The prince approached then. He had listened to the quarrel and had savored its tone, understanding the Hungarian. 'My compliments, Madame,' he said, bowing to the courtesan, 'you know how to treat mothers as they deserve.'

"But la Mariska, still trembling, snapped: 'What's got into this one? Do I know you?'

"The prince named himself: 'Wladimir Noronsoff, Madame, to admire you and serve you. No one is more tragically beautiful!' And he exaggerated the salutation.

"La Mariska had looked the interloper up and down. By the heavy rings on the fingers and the hoarse and caressant voice she had judged the man. 'Yes, I know how to treat mothers, and you, do you know how to treat women, Monseigneur?'

"Wladimir did not react to the insolence. 'Why aren't you in the theater?'

"'How do you know I'm not? I play comedy in the city.'

"'And you have the voice for it. I've just appreciated it. Do you sing?'

"'No, I dance.'

"'Yes, I know. I've been told.'

"'And I'm even more beautiful dancing than I am gambling. You've never seen me dance?'

"The impertinence was turning to affectation. 'No, I can see you, that's sufficient for me.'

"'You're wrong; it would interest you. I'll dance this evening, at Ciro's. Come.'

"'I don't eat supper away from home.'

"'You fear unfortunate encounters?'

"The prince suppressed an unkind remark. 'I no longer fear them; I have no more health; I sup at home on doctor's orders.'

"'That's true; I'd forgotten.' La Mariska remembered the legends now. 'Believe in my regrets, Monseigneur.'

"There was a silence.

"The prince stared at her, prodigiously interested by the dilapidation of the visage of passion and pallor. He was also watching Comtesse Schoboleska from the corner of his eye, who was standing to one side with her children, and slightly anxious. 'Believe that I regret it too.' And then, after a pause: 'Would you like to come and dance one evening at my house?'

"'After dinner, for your guests? There's a fee.'

"'No, I'm inviting you to dinner as well.'

"'I never dine in other people's homes.'

"'But other people are other people, and I'm me.' And with an authoritative gesture, Noronsoff took the courtesan's hand.

"'You're a despot. You have a manner that pleases me. And who would I be dining with, at your house?'

"'With whomever you wish; give me your list.'

"'With women of the world. That will change my mind; I'm only dancing here in front of whores.'

"'So be it; you'll have women of the world.'

"'From Nice?'

"'From Nice and Cannes.'

"'That's better; real women of the world? Truly, you know some?'

"'I don't know any others.'

"'How bored you must be!'

"'And I'm sad too, as you see.'

"'Very sad, in fact.'

"'And it's charitable work, distracting me. What evening would you like dinner? What about tomorrow?'

"'No.'

"'The day after? Nor then? Would you like Saturday?'

"'Saturday—agreed.'

"'Agreed. You'll preside at table, and afterwards, you'll dance.'

"'I only dance after supper.'

"'We'll have supper, then,'

"'Dinner, supper, all the joys. I play too; I'm mad about cards.'

"'We'll play, then. Order, order!'

"La Mariska's gaze had just fallen upon the two Scholboleskis. 'Will there be pretty men at your house?'

"'Bring them from here. That will be surer.'

"'Pooh! They're rare, and I prefer them unknown.'

"'That's all right; I'll provide them. You appreciate pretty boys?'

"'Almost as much as you.' And she pirouetted on her heels, with a ballerina's bow. 'Indeed, you're well-born!'

"And thus were made, in five minutes, the introduction and the invitation.

"'She's dining at the villa on Saturday,' Wladimir declared, as he installed himself in the landau. 'Afterwards, we'll see her dance. Who can we invite, of possible women?'

"'But no possible women will come,' snorted the comtesse. 'One doesn't make decent women dine with a whore.'

"'You think so? I'll make my own list. All those from Cannes will come. It's an economy to see her dance at my house. It's still ten louis gained, after the journey, and supper.'

"'At your whim. She isn't even pretty.'

"'How unjust you are. She didn't take her eyes off Boris. Nicolas is to her liking as well.'

"'She's very generous, but she'll have to do without my sons. We're dining in Cannes on Saturday.'

"'Because I have la Mariska in my house that evening?'

"'Perhaps! What if it doesn't please me to dine with that Mariska?'

"'As you please. There'll be no lack of other women.'

"'Especially if I'm not there!'

"'Especially if you're not there.'

"'And la Mariska will preside.'

"'As you say, she'll preside.'

"'You can tell me about the feast the next day; it might be funny.'

"'It will be better than funny.'

"'It will be shameless; she's a rising star.'

"'Yes, perhaps a new favorite. Mariska rhymes with Schoboleska.'

"That conversation, reported by Noronsoff, completed the joy of the Saturday dinner. Wladimir recited it like a consummate actor, imitating with a rare perfidy the slightest intonations of la Schoboleska. The Hungarian listened indifferently enough. Sitting opposite the prince, she struck poses, languidly, and then looked the other women assembled there up and down, arrogantly; there was a noisy joust of furbelows, diamonds and shoulders. La Mariska had brought out pearls almost as beautiful as Wladimir's and, a quasi-ingénue in a savant décolletage that made her chaste amid so much offered flesh, she affected a profound ennui and only deigned to smile at the prince's quips.

"In spite of the enchantment of a luminous table, ablaze with flames reflected in mirrors, and the luxury of implausible garnitures of mauve and yellow orchids linking the crystal candelabras, the dinner dragged somewhat. La Mariska had made everyone wait; invited for eight o'clock, she arrived at nine, giving as an excuse having run into an American friend in the atrium when she went back to the hotel to dress.

"The prince having authorized her to bring whomever she liked, she had brought the Yankee. He was a tall, robust fellow, clean-shaven and fresh-faced, whose strong build seemed a threat for his thin black jacket. La Mariska had scarcely introduced him, and had demanded the place next to her at table. For that, the order of places had been disturbed. Master Edmond did not speak French and the poor fellow would have been all at sea far from her. Master Edmond, installed next to his friend, devoured like an ogre and only stopped eating to parade his large, bright and empty eyes over the assembly.

"The implantation of that intruder had cast a chill; the lateness of the courtesan had already indisposed the prince. Her casual attitude, her fashion of imposing her American, authorized as she was, completed Wladimir's enervation. He had the eyes of his bad days, strange, shrunken eyes with troubled yellow gleams; he did not take those eyes off the Yankee.

"La Mariska did not depart from her hostile attitude either; she had come with a ready-made insolence and to offer herself the heads of the women invited in her honor. 'I don't see the pretty woman who was accompanying you in Monte Carlo the other day,' she suddenly said to the prince.

"'The comtesse? She's in Cannes. All Cannes is here this evening; she's gone to see a few friends in Cannes.' Wladimir immolated the absentee.

"After a pause, the Hungarian went on: 'How pretty her sons are! I'm told that you've adopted them, Prince.'

"'Oh, at the most I have the affection of a relative, an old uncle, for the Schoboleskis, like you for this monsieur here.' And Wladimir indicated the colossus next to the courtesan.

"La Mariska was all of thirty-five; the thrust carried; she paled slightly beneath her make-up.

"They got up from the table and went on to the terrace; coffee was served there. It was an admirable evening: an enchantment of rocks, clouds and frissons of the distant water, staged in a sky tinted with turquoise. Riddled with stars above the mountains, striped with gleams over the sea, it was a unique sky, which one might have thought ordered for an apotheosis; the odor of mock-oranges, the sugary scent of lilacs and Judas trees made the atmosphere languid; the night was as sweet as honey.

"La Mariska let herself yield to the charm of the hour and the landscape. 'An incomparable property,' she said to Wladimir. 'I don't know anything similar, even in Austria, on our Adriatic.'

"'*Alla disposición della señora,*' cooed the Russian, gallantly.

"'Oh, if I took you at your word, there wouldn't be enough bailiffs to throw me out; I know these Spanish fashions; one offers everything and gives nothing. By the way, the specimens of Nice and Cannes that you've brought out are rather ugly. You promised me pretty men. It's very naughty of you, prince, to hide your friends from me like this. Are you afraid that I'll take them from you?'

"Noronsoff's yellow eyes blazed like topazes; he offered his arm to the Hungarian. Everyone went back into the drawing rooms; they were already humming with Tzigane waltzes. Women surrounded la Mariska, begging her to dance.

"The courtesan defended herself. 'After supper! After supper! I said after supper. Prince, you promised to enable me to gamble.'

"A baccarat table was set up; la Mariska took the bank. She played an infernal game, losing and winning as she wished. The prince succeeded her as banker; la Mariska doubled and tripled her stakes, carried away by gambling fever; wads of banknotes accumulated in front of her. When she had no more of them, she demanded that the American stand behind her, and when the American sat down in her stead, she was the one who directed his play; and, the Yankee having lost, she was the one who pulled out a little white leather sack and passed him the banknotes.

"The waltzing couples had stopped dancing. A circle formed around the enraged punter; the prince, visibly aggravated, sweating large beads, was pale and enervated; the interminable game was extenuating him. 'You're making a common purse,' he sniggered at a third transfer of blue bills between the Hungarian and her partner. 'Has it a trade mark?'

"'Exactly, prince, an Unlimited Company. I've never been salaried. I'm not Polish.'

"The prince got up. He excused himself; he had to give a few orders. He summoned Gourka, and took him into a corner. 'Are the three men here?'

"'Yes, Monseigneur.'

"'Well, do as I said.'

"'Is Monseigneur serious?'

"'Do it.'

"'But has Monseigneur thought . . . ?'

"'Do it, I tell you.'

"Gourkau retired.

"La Mariska had also stood up. To a phrase of the waltz that was more tender and more insistent, she had sketched a long glissade, tucked up her dress under her skirts, and in a stir of silk and lace, got ready to dance. Already, people were grouping around her; la Mariska was going to dance.

"It was then that the prince intervened. 'After supper,' Wladimir purred. 'You said after supper.' And, affectionate and playful, he slid his arm under the courtesan's. 'You are served, Madame. Let's refresh ourselves first.'

"The supper was set out in the bathroom.

TRIMALCHIO'S SUPPER

"THE PRINCE had done things well. Everyone, as they came in, had difficulty repressing a cry of admiration. An enormous round table occupied the center of the room of frescos, in the very place of the hexagonal swimming bath. An improvised parquet covered it, raising the table up slightly, as if on a platform; sheaves of white irises, narcissi and roses were placed in their monsters' mouths; the eight malachite frogs were standing sentinel around it; rose petals were scattered on the paving stones, and the illusion of a supper in the home of Nero was perpetuated by the rounds of satyrs, nymphs and goddesses painted on the walls: friezes of ancient idylls animated around batrachians spitting jets of flowers. A perforated Venetian guipure tablecloth was also strewn with petals; silver candlesticks sported pink candles, and while the women and the black jackets marveled, the prince took his place, with la Mariska to his right this time and some grand duchess to his left.

"A delightful little she-monkey in a Turkish costume was opposite, and presided over the supper, supervised by two muzjiks. Slightly bewildered, she turned her anxious little head continually toward the doors, and got up abruptly from her armchair, but the muzjiks sat her down again by force and kept her prisoner there. Smiles relaxed all physiognomies; they were about to be amused—but a malaise was almost immediately painted on all faces.

"A strange, enormous centerpiece occupied the whole table, the form and proportions of which could not fail to be intriguing. Dotted with magnolia flowers, white roses and mauve carnations, it was a kind of dust-cover of golden gauze, like a great luminous veil, bizarrely hump-backed and lifted up in places, and one sensed that beneath that gauze was something alive. It was breathing and stretching with a visible effort to retain its breath, and that mysterious life froze more than one smile and made more than one eyebrow frown; people were only eating gingerly. That flowery Zaimph was a threat for everyone, a threat to the modesty of the women and a threat to the dignity of the men; anything could be expected from Noronsoff. From him, everything was to be feared.

"'Perhaps there are snakes swarming under that gauze?'

"'Or bullfrogs, as in the zoo!'

"'Or perhaps a roe deer.'

"'A living roe deer, whose throat is going to be cut before our eyes.'

"'What horror! I'd rather leave right away.'

"'Or perhaps rats.'

"'You're being sinister!'

"'Shut up.'

"'No, it's a wild boar.'

"'Domestic.'

"'I feel ill.'

"'Let it go; it's his parrots, which are going to invade the table-cloth suddenly and spread out over our knees.'

"'But I can't bear them.'

"'As long as the supper isn't poisoned.'

"'No?'

"'Oh, with him, I don't say arsenic, but perhaps rhubarb.'

"'No, cantharides.'

"'But that's the Marquis de Sade.'

"'What do you think it is, then?'

"'Oh, Baron, where have you brought me?'

"That was the tone of the asides; everyone wanted to laugh, and they were only talking in monosyllables. Fortunately, czardas and Hungarian marches animated the silence, played by the Tziganes installed alongside.

"Only la Mariska was showing enthusiasm; she had finally cheered up and, her lips in flower and a sparkle in her eye, was leaning toward the prince, laughing with all her teeth and allowing her glass to be filled over and over. Wladimir's words seemed to excite her, and she allowed herself to get drunk on champagne, going full tilt, like a playful filly.

"The waiters had just removed the third course and placed enormous fruits in silver baskets filled with crushed ice between the candlesticks. Four muzjiks had appeared at the two extremities of the table. Prince Noronsoff rose to his feet.

"'I would have liked to offer you Comtesse Schoboleska and her sons. I was obliged to fall back on other specimens of humanity; but your modesty will be saved, Mesdames, my specimens are tattooed.'

"And with a wink, he signaled to the muzjiks to uncover the centerpiece. The removal of the flowers and the gauze laid the entire table bare. Lying on an immense mirror, three stark naked men displayed their hard torsos there, caught, one might have thought, like fish in the tight mesh of a net. There was a cry throughout the room. The unkempt hair, the rude fingernails, the calluses of the feet, the suntan of the hands and the napes spoke clearly of fishermen or street-porters. It was too much. Women withdrew, asking for their mantles and their carriages indignantly; men, very pale, exchanged brief comments; was it necessary to slap the prince, to hand him their cards? Other women intervened: 'He's mad! Or ill!'

"In the disarray of the tumult, the three naked men remained motionless and the Tziganes continued playing.

"La Mariska had also stood up, but she stayed where she was; she had picked up her lorgnette and was leaning over the strange centerpiece, studying it curiously, like an interested connoisseur.

"They were three solidly built fellows, three Riviera mokos, whose brown flesh was strangely tattooed. One, lying on his belly, offered the famous tattoo known as the 'fox-hunt,' which Pierre Loti has described in his *Mon frère Yves*: drawn in blue ink, the dogs and the horses, the pack and the riders, wound around the shoulders, the chest and the torso in pursuit of the fox, disappearing into its earth; it is a classic tattoo. Another, lying on his back, his hands crossed over his face, was displaying, from his shoulders to his knees, the effigy of a vulture with its wings partly furled; the bird's beak occupied the middle of the chest; the last plumes of the wings extended over the kneecaps; the claws were clutching a strange perch. The third, lying on his side, enriched his dermis with architectural details; an Arc de Triomphe surmounted his kidneys, one of the fountains of the Concorde spread over his abdomen; lewd captions underlined the designs.

"The room had almost emptied; only a few curious and one or two blasé individuals had stayed. A joy in his yellow eyes, the prince enjoyed the universal panic and the alarm; he also observed la Mariska, intrigued by her calm and perhaps seized by an anxiety. La Mariska was still examining.

"'Interesting tattoos,' she said, finally, 'but Monsieur's are better.' She indicated the Yankee. She had let go of her lorgnette and taken the prince's arm.

"The few remaining guests followed them into the drawing room. All the others had departed without taking their leave. Only five people remained, and the Tziganes on their platform.

"'Shall I dance for you now?' asked la Mariska.

"'No, that would be cruelty, there's no one left. Those imbeciles aren't able to appreciate their good fortune. It was an unexpected stroke of luck for them, though. Personally, I have nothing to ask of you, and I remain your debtor. You've played marvelously for me, and I thank you.'

"'I've even won.'

"'I'm not talking about the baccarat; you're an accomplished actress; I suspected as much. I've won my wager with myself; that's the greatest joy anyone can give me: that of not having let me down, and you haven't disappointed me.'

"'So we've both won the game,' replied the courtesan, with a half-smile.

"'I'll offer you a return match, if you wish.'

"'No, the sides aren't equal; you're playing the same game as me.'

"'We'll leave it there, then.'

"'Yes, and without rancor. I don't have time to waste. With you, it's fencing for sport; the thrusts don't carry, you're armored; you've understood me?'

"'Adieu, Madame.'

"'Adieu, Monsieur. Ask for my carriage, Sir Edmond.'

"And that was the extent of the skirmishes between Noronsoff and la Mariska. If she had wanted to, the courtesan would have been able to play a large part in the prince's life. She had impertinence, arrogance and even rudeness, a kind of spitting grace of which Wladimir would have ended up loving the dolorous smart. He had found a sort of sensual pleasure in her stinging repartee, and throughout that night of Neronian farce, the courtesan's curt tone and the persistence of her long, sharp eyes had made him shudder softly more than once, but as the Hungarian had said, she had no time to waste. She had better things to do than provoke and suffer the caprices of a maniac.

"On returning to Monte Carlo, she told the story of the dinner and the supper on Mont Boron in terms that made a fortune all the way to Menton; with regard to Noronsoff, his physique, his tics and his neurosis she found images and epithets that ran all over the Principality; la Mariska's vogue increased in consequence. There were people who took her to supper in order to hear her play and see her mime a fête at the prince's house; all the men were grateful to her for having stood up to and reckoned with that stingy Russian filth. The Hungarian's stories were highly appreciated; the coastal newspapers took possession of them; la Mariska's remarks returned to Nice, amplified and sharpened; they were reported to the prince, who was upset this time, and pulled a face.

"The scandal of the centerpiece had caused comment; the audacity was too new, and this time, public opinion, indulgent to Sacha's pranks, rebelled; the invention was too Asiatic.

"The p.p.cs[1] rained down on the villa after the night of the famous supper; visitors became rare there, and even the parasites absented themselves. The base rabble of familiars did not like the police, and the police were disturbed by that supper. And but for the Russian consul . . .

"In brief, Noronsoff would do well to absent himself. Those, naturally, were the words of the most compromised of the band; only the guilty seek to disculpate themselves. In sum, Noronsoff found himself rather isolated. Abandoned by his mother, abandoned by Comtesse Schoboleska, who stayed in Cannes with her two sons. He supported that abandonment poorly and discharged his ill humor in terrible scenes, sometimes on Gourkau, sometimes on poor Narimoff; his health also deteriorated, his tuberculosis aggravated by enteritis. With his cystitis, his congestion of the liver and his neurasthenia, it was a complete set of maladies; his Swedish physician, frightened by so many symptoms and various accidents, even came to consult me.

"Life was no longer tenable with that hysteric. The crises of fury were followed by frightful prostrations, lethargies of three or four hours, from which the invalid only emerged in order to spit insults and blood. Princesse Benedetta had not even been informed. What welcome would that dangerous madman have reserved for her? And in the absence of la Schoboleska, Baronne Narimoff became his victim.

"What was the Pole doing in Cannes? From time to time, a telegram gave news of her sons and asked about the health of the prince. She was living aboard the *Edward III*, Lord Ferelith's yacht, and spent her days in excursions at sea; there was even question of a cruise to the coasts of Corsica. The hypothesis of that voyage put the unhappy Sacha in a rage.

---

1 A "p.p.c." [*prendre pour congé*] was a message scrawled on a visiting card left or sent by someone about to depart of a voyage—effectively, an apology for absence, often used as a polite way of refusing an invitation.

"He was nurturing a ferocious rancor with regard to the Pole, and meditating atrocious projects of vengeance against her; his morbid imagination was ingenious in refining affronts and tortures; he would have her thrown out of the door when she presented herself at the villa, or have her sequestered in the bathroom, plunged forcibly into the swimming bath, have her given the knout, what do I know? He would strangle her with his own hands. And, the gestures of a harpy punctuated his divagations. Claws extended toward his victim, he became delirious, and finished up choking, foaming at the mouth and with blood in his eyes. The terrified Baronne Narimoff watched.

"When a telegram from Cannes announced the departure of the *Edward III* for Nice, Wladimir, suddenly calming down, was exultant; and when, preceded in the morning by an enormous basket of pansies and narcissi, the Pole presented herself at the villa, at four o'clock, the prince, suddenly cured, did not have enough eyes or smiles for her; it was the return of the prodigal child. He took possession of the comtesse's hands, took the gloves off, kissed them, bit them slightly, and kept them in his own, with tender words and *cara, carissima Veras*.

"The Pole appeared rejuvenated too. 'Wasn't I right not to attend that supper, the feast you gave that whore?' she said, patting Wladimir's cheeks. 'Horrors happened there, it appears; I'm told that it was an orgy. I was wise to be absent that day. You wouldn't have wanted to see my Boris and my Nicolas at table with that Mariska.'

ENVY

"A ND LORD FEREDITH became Wladimir's obsession.

"La Schoboleska never ran out of eulogies on the equipment of the yacht, the comfort of its cabins, veritable apartments installed on board; then there were dithyrambs about the obliging crew and their efficiency, the owner's receptions and the legendary courtesy, even temper and munificence of Lord Feredith. On the *Edward III* one only saw the most choice society; Lord Feredith had held a few parties there whose program had revolutionized Cannes; the English colony and the Russian colony disputed the invitations, and that in spite of the presence on board of the poet Algernon Filde, the English laureate, whose recent divorce had been the talk of London: Algernon Filde, the author of *Venus and Adonis* and *Bathsheba's Masque*, played on all the stages of the three kingdoms and the United States, the quasi-scandalous and yet illustrious writer of *Hadrian on the Bank of the Cydnus*.

"That Algenon Filde had just had a quarrel with the law of his country, and, condemned by contumacy, was traveling for the love of independence, far from the English coast, where the authorities might seize him. He was an audacious man, but prudent. His success in the theater and his contracts with major publishers assured him of a good living. Algernon Filde was traveling in foreign lands in quest of sensations and adventures, preceded everywhere by a rather bad reputation, which had worked to his advantage thus far.

211

"While returning from a cruise in the Adriatic, Lord Feredith had found him in Naples, installed in a villa in Posilippo, and, being a great admirer of the poet and his work, had initially invited him on an excursion to the Gulf of Salerno, Reggio, Paestum and Amalfi, and then had convinced him to accompany him to Cannes.

"Lord Feredith had got it into his head to impose the compromised writer on English society. Cannes is nowadays a suburb of London, and to have the poet of *Hadrian* accepted by the winterers of Great Britain was almost to win his lawsuit before the peerage and ensure his return in triumph, if not for the imminent season, at least for the Cowes regatta during the first fortnight in August. For that imposition it would be sufficient to interest Lady Saymoor and the Princesse de Troie, née Epsom, then on holiday from California. Intimate friends of the Princess of Wales and very fond of the Prince, they directed the elegant movement of Cannes and had already been ruling the colony there for three winters. Last spring, the Princesse de Troie had traveled the Spanish coast aboard the *Edward III*, and it was on her that Lord Feredith was counting.

"With Anglo-Saxon obstinacy and the stubborn will of a man with a square jaw he had harnessed himself body and soul to the task of having the eccentric Algernon Filde received in Cannes. For what could he be reproached, in sum? Peccadillos, slightly repetitive fits of tenderness for minors—but does one ever know the exact age of those Irish barmaids whose pullulation encumbers the City? Who in London is unaware of the effrontery of young maidservants, the cynicism of horseguards and the license of park benches?

"Without that adventure of a vicar's daughter the police would never have intervened. The sacred character of the victim's father had spoiled everything. It was outraged religion and the religion of the State that had avenged it by pursuing Filde; this time his excessively tender heart had gone astray and chosen badly. The respectability of the clergyman had determined a pursuit. That altercation apart, the Englishman's conduct was the current conduct of other men. The Englishman is, by nature, fond of early fruit; divorces could no longer be counted in London if, for love of the family and also out of modesty, honorable ladies did not close their eyes to the exploits of their brothers and husbands.

"That cause, with its attenuating circumstances, Lord Feredith had pleaded so well with the Princesse de Troie that he had also won it with Lady Saymoor. The two women had agreed to come aboard and dine with Filde; they had even brought the men of their company; grand dukes had been invited. During dinner, the yacht had put out to sea, and, on the deck, illuminated by moonlight that one might have thought ordered for the occasion, sailors costumed and rehearsed by Filde had mimed miraculously a sequence of tableaux from Hogarth, comical scenes deftly chosen from among the series of *Marriage à la Mode, The Punch Drinkers* and *The Card Game*.[1]

"Decked out in enormous wigs, clad in immense Basque jackets ornamented with large buttons of strass and marcasite, bespectacled, and with huge bouffant knots of muslin beneath the shaven faces of pirates, they had made the beautiful ladies laugh until they wept; it was, unmistakably, the ill-tempered self-importance and the crippled majesty of the painter's sheriffs and aldermen. His hips stuffed with padding under swathes of brocade with shiny seams, and his waist pinched in tight whalebone corsets of flowery satin, a cabin boy had mimed the simpering of a demoiselle of quality with an instinctive debauchery. Filde had made him up personally, and beneath the beribborned batiste of his eye-shade, the child had pursed his lips, maneuvered his fan and fluttered his eyelashes with such a sincere pretention and such a natural conviction that the game had been won. One could not hold in rigor a man capable of organizing such entertainments. The poet's delicate verses underlined each reconstitution of the tableau with irony; it was animate and vocal painting. The

---

1 The latter two titles are improvised, although some of William Hogarth's satirical drawings do include scenes of card games and drinking.

moonlight was an element of the fête; the masts, yardarms and rigging entered into the décor; it was an artificial and precious spectacle whose value was brought out by the sea, the night and the solitude. The soirée was an ovation for Filde.

"The Princesse de Troie and Lady Saymoor returned to Cannes delighted; the next day the story of the fête was recounted, amplified, at every five o'clock tea in the villas and the grand hotels, and all curiosities ignited.

"The stiffest and most puritanical women of the English colony were in despair at not having seen the Hogarth series organized by Filde; the extravagances of his private life were forgotten, and nothing was any longer remembered but his talent. His talent! The author of *Venus and Adonis* was a genius. In brief, fashion got involved, Lord Feredith was solicited to put on a second performance on board, requests for invitations rained down on the yacht, and Lord Feredith, after having made them beg a little, was about to consent when Lady Saymoor did better. She offered the marvelous garden of her villa in order to put on the second act of the poet's Biblical drama *Bathsheba's Masque* there.

"To the great emotion of the entire society, the spectacle was organized, and this time it was not humble sailors who filled the roles but the most notable personalities in the colony. The Princesse de Troie was eager to incarnate the royal concubine, and on the day of the performance All Cannes, assembled under the palm trees of the Villa Marpha, was able to admire, lying on thick furs, with her elbow on Asian cushions, the near-naked beauty of Georgina Epsom, Princesse de Corinthe et de Troie.

"With the immodesty of a true grand dame, the princesse had consented almost to undress. Sheathed in a narrow robe of yellow gauze embroidered with large flowers of red pearls at the place of the breasts, she inclined the dream of a grave and pure profile under a heavy diadem of opals and sardonyxes; an embassy secretary with a fluvial beard played the role of King David. As for the prophet Nathan, that was Algernon Filde himself, with his ascetic thinness, the grim gleam of his large hollow eyes, the

214

entire face of fever and passion that made the poet a sort of consumptive Lord Byron. As soon as he made his entrance he moved the entire audience to terror, and forced them almost to tears with the impetuosity of his gestures and his imprecations. Young women chosen among the season's professional beauties played the legendary courtesans of the Apparition scene.

"*Bathsheba's Masque* was a triumph. Another performance was put on a week later, and other fêtes followed, as many aboard the *Edward III* as in the homes of Lord Feredith's beautiful friends. Grand Duchess Paul, who was in Cannes that winter, was absolutely determined to have the poet at her table and to make her debut in one of his works. These Russians are mad about acting. With the most defective pronunciation and quasi-vulgar gestures due to a maladroit imitation of Granier, she appeared in *Fear of Scandal*, an early work by Filde and one of the less perfect, and nearly caused the play to flop. It was a terrible soirée. Only the presence of the Grand Duke prevented bursts of laughter, and women withdrew shaken by nervous tremors. The Princesse de Troie was in bed for a week, ill, she said, with repressed laughter. In brief, there was no fête without Filde; the poet was the lion of the season.

"And it was that man, acclaimed and adulated, wanted by everyone, who was moored in the port of Nice, directly beneath the villa; the *Edward III*, in which Noronsoff's mother had wanted to abduct him, was three minutes away from his terrace as a bird flies. Without even leaning over, Noronsoff could see the yardarms and the high mast, and by leaning over, the bulwarks at the level of the quay.

"Lord Feredith's yacht caused a sensation. From morning to nightfall there was a curious crowd assembled at the stern. A continual flow of visitors besieged the gangplank, a flow for the most part turned back by the sailor on watch; one only penetrated the *Edward III* equipped with a card from the captain.

"With his binoculars aimed at the yacht, Wladimir now spent his days watching the comings and goings of the crew and the guests on the deck.

"The yacht obsessed him; it was an attraction, a bewitchment. It was like a weight on his chest all the time when he had it before his eyes, and like an atrocious emptiness, a kind of hunger, when he ceased to see it. He also felt full of anger and hatred; he detested that Lord Feredith, whose fêtes had stirred Cannes and made the joy of the spring; he detested him and envied him for the success of his receptions, the luxury of his yacht and his reputation as a magnificent host. Schoboleska's stories, adroitly mixed with reticences, had inflated him with a muted hatred, a morbid and ferocious hatred, the hatred of the invalid and the déclassé for health and consideration.

"He also detested la Schoboleska for her unwelcome eulogies and her admiring remarks; her perpetual dithyrambs on Feredith and the *Edward III* had envenomed his soul. Lord Feredith was rich, Lord Feredith was healthy. Solid and young, he lived at sea all year; Lord Feredith was an oracle of good taste, his word was law in London, the ladies of the aristocracy fought over his invitations; Lord Feredith was the friend of princes, Lord Feredith hosted parties like no one else; Lord Feredith imposed his friends on society, even flawed—and Lord Feredith only had twenty millions, while he, Wladimir had more than forty. But, déclassé, expelled from Russia in spite of being related to the Tsar, sick and worn out, rotten to be bone, he was stranded there in a life of distress and isolation, in the enervating mildness of the climate of Nice.

"An object of curiosity at first, and horror thereafter, people were intrigued to meet him, and then to avoid him; worse than that, he was abandoned like a man infected with the plague. His pranks had put him in the pillory of public opinion. Even his mother had quit him. He remained alone, almost moribund, with a casual physician and a Slav adventuress, in the power of hired help.

"Oh, how he hated her, that Pole! However, he could not do without her, now more than ever, since she too had abandoned him, invited aboard that accursed yacht almost every day, and departing on excursions at sea at least three times a week. He would have liked to lash out at her, to reach her via her children, but Boris and Nicolas hardly ever came to the villa; Lord Feredith had taken the two Schoboleskis into affection, and kept them with him for days. When they came up Mont Boron they were accompanied by their mother, and the Pole almost always came alone. Yes, it really was execration that he was nurturing against her. When she was absent, it was as if a hunger were hollowing out his stomach and abdomen, at the same time as a kind of bolus rising to his gullet was strangling him; when she was present he felt his fingers clenching instinctively and wanted to put them around her fragile blonde neck like claws. Was she not humiliating him now? Yes, she dared to do that, the whore, who would be dead of hunger without him, whom he was still maintaining, the eternal kept woman!

"Should she not have brought him that Lord Feredith and that Filde? Her first duty was to introduce him to the owner of the *Edward III*; he might have hired it, after all, and that Englishman owed him a visit. He had been waiting for that visit for a week with a sly joy, impatient to dazzle the yachtsman with the luxury of his park and the staff of his villa; no one could compete with the installation of Mont Boron, and Noronsoff knew that.

"Then he had made an advance; he had manifested to the Pole the desire to receive Feredith and Filde at a dinner at his house; but negligently, in an affected manner, the comtesse had replied that Lord Feredith never allowed himself to be introduced to anyone, but had people introduced to him; in any case, Lord Feredith had enough relations, he did not want to extend them. Lord Feredith was not an ordinary winterer and did not care for compromising friends.

"'What about his poet condemned for offending morality?' Wladimir had almost howled, foaming at the mouth—but he had contained himself, meditating a surer vengeance.

"That Schoboleska was torturing his agony. At all costs, at no matter what price, by no matter what means, he would have the guests of the *Edward III* at his table, in his home, in the gardens of Mont Boron.

ABOARD THE *EDWARD III*

"AND NORONSOFF decided to visit the *Edward III*.

"'Since the sea will not come to the mountain, it's the mountain that will descend to the sea,' he declared one day to the Pole. 'It's necessary to resign myself to it; your friends are pretending to ignore me, and I'm curious about that yacht. But for you, perhaps I would have sailed on it! Would you care to facilitate that visit for me, to obtain from the commandant the card necessary to go aboard? You can't refuse that to your old friend, Vera.'

"The prince made himself mild and conciliatory. It was toward the end of May and a rain of clematis was embalming the terraces.

"'Nothing simpler,' replied the Pole. 'Why didn't you say something sooner? Lord Feredith will be glad to receive you. Fix the day yourself.'

"'Oh, I don't demand that he be aboard; you've told me that he doesn't care for new acquaintances. I would have been delighted, for my part, but it's only a caprice of a sick man, the desire to see that perfect installation at close range. The fault is yours, Comtesse, you've praised the yacht so much to me.'

"The Pole made herself caressant too. 'Don't be childish, Wladi; you're burning to meet Lord Feredith. There's a misunderstanding between us; I said that Lord Feredith doesn't make visits, but I didn't say that he doesn't return them; he's the best brought up man in the three kingdoms. What day do you want to come on board?'

"'No, let's leave the choice to him; I don't want to disrupt a party at sea; the sooner the better, but I can wait another week.'

"'As you wish, Prince. Lord Feredith will write to you.'

"The comtesse had risen to her feet. Noronsoff took possession of her hand and kept it in his own. Noronsoff had rarely seen her thus; la Schoboleska was especially pretty that day, as if aureoled with light, transfigured by an unknown joy: florid eyes, a bright expression, and a mischievous seduction in her gestures and her voice. Involuntarily, Wladimir was subject to the charm. 'How beautiful you are today, Vera!'

"'I'm happy.'

"'May one know why?'

"'Because we're going to see you on board and I love you very much, you and Lord Feredith. Adieu, I'll go and take him the good news. By the way, do you have blue clematis in flower? These have a pleasant scent, but the color is a trifle insipid.'

"'I'll send someone to ask the gardener.'

"'It's for my hair. There's a dinner this evening and white doesn't suit me.'

"'You're calumniating yourself, Comtesse.'

"'Pfft!' She modulated a little expostulation while pursing her lips. 'Thank you.'

"The gardener returned with a sheaf of large blue clematis: stars. The comtesse shredded one in Sacha's face. 'See you soon then, perhaps tomorrow, but remember my prediction: beware of everything that comes from the sea.' And she withdrew, blowing a kiss from her fingertips.

"*What a coquette she is*, thought the invalid. *What marvelous youth, what a second crop of youth! She has the air of a bride*. And until nightfall, the prince remained absorbed and pensive.

"The next day, a very amiable note from Lord Feredith invited Prince Noronsoff to lunch on board; the invitation was for two days hence, at five o'clock.

"I was informed by Dr. Filsen of events and actions at the villa. Not a day passed when the Swedish physician did not come to consult me, confused by the astonishing Sacha's disconcerting illnesses and alternating crises of improvement and relapse; the poor fellow could not understand his patient's condition at all. He died only to be reborn, abruptly resuscitated only to fall flat again. The prince's existence was a series of frightful agonies, and the Swede was even more stupefied by the energy and strength of that destroyed health than the frightful attacks that shook him almost every day.

"After a fortnight of prostration during which the invalid had not quit his long Japanese silk dressing-gowns, reduced to being carried down the steps of the perron in an armchair and spending all day collapsed on a wicker chaise longue, the placement of which was changed as the sun rose, now he was talking about going out, demanding stimulants and fortifying potions in order to be able to go to this lunch. He wanted health from one day to the next, talked about organizing fêtes, even emitting the hypothesis of an excursion, and imperiously demanding from his physician a suppressant that would settle his stomach and permit him to spend a few days at sea . . .

"With enteritis, dyspepsia, neurasthenia and liver disease! Filsen was in despair.

"'Give him bromide the night before and strychnine arsenate on the morning of the day when he's going out. Begin at ten o'clock. By four o'clock he'll be on his feet.'

"On the Wednesday, at half-past four, the prince's daumont went down the slope of Mont Boron at a fast trot, with the postillion's bells jingling, went around the quays and, in the tumult of four horses beribboned and pompommed like mules, joined the wagons, carts and tumbrils of the port, to come to a halt in front of the mooring of the yachts. There was a great stir among the coal-heavers and caulkers engaged in daubing two Corsican cargo vessels, and also aboard the other yachts. A curious crowd was already gathering on the quay, where other carriages were stationed in front of the *Edward III*.

"Delighted by the effect produced, Wladimir got down, stuffed with cola and rejuvenated for the occasion. Scarcely made up, but with his hair bulging in an expert undulation, he no longer had the face of an old woman and was only wearing his forty years. He stiffened his torso, strapped into a narrow jacket, and only sported three jewels: a black pearl in his cravat and two rings on his right hand, although the sapphire of one of them was worth nothing less than a hundred thousand roubles, a hereditary sapphire celebrated throughout Russia. Gourkau and Filsen accompanied him. The crowd interrogated the muzjiks behind the vehicle; bright dresses and garish umbrellas circulated aboard the yacht, and with his eyelids creased, Wladimir was triumphant.

"But his joy was of short duration. As he was about to step on to the gangplank, he was obliged to stop and give way to two women in mourning who were descending to the shore. Cap in hand, Lord Feredith was escorting them; the two women passed before Sacha and climbed into a coupé, which departed, and Lord Feredith, standing before Wladimir, extended his hand to him.

"The prince had recognized his mother.

"Had the princesse recognized him? Certainly, but she had pretended not to see him. Wladimir did not like the coincidence of their double presence aboard the *Edward III*. Nothing was more natural than the princesse having had the curiosity to visit the yacht on which she had been dreaming of abducting her son; it was the same sentiment that had brought him aboard—but that Lord Feredith had assigned the same day and almost the same hour to the mother and the son . . . there was more than chance in that, there was la Schoboleska, and Wladimir only offered his host a darkened expression.

"He cheered up on board. The bright dresses and the gaudy umbrellas were those of Lady Saymoor and the Princesse de Troie; Grand Duchess Paul had also been invited, and among those women with bright eyes and young complexions, undulating and elegant, the Pole, sitting in the shade of a coral silk awning, appeared even younger and fresher. What fountain of youth had that Schoboleska found, then? She attached large candid eyes to the prince and made the introductions. Noronsoff being of imperial blood, the women were introduced to him, he was not introduced; only Grand Duchess Paul had the right to treat him as an equal.

"Lunch was set up at the front of the boat and served by sailors. There was a simple and comfortable luxury, all of the refinement of which was in the silverware and a Minturne service with amusing decorations; pink geraniums ornamented the table. It was neat, bright and discreet; the silk awning, set off by the blue of the sky, gave the flesh of the women a flowery transparency; gazes were enlivened, as if bathed by the azure, by the ambience of the Mediterranean; a slight breeze inflated the pleats of the awning gently, and Wladimir could not take his eyes off the mauve irises of the Pole.

"Her two sons had the same eyes of candor and light, for Nicolas and Boris were there, singularly suntanned, seemingly developed in strength, like two fine fruits. Wladimir scarcely recognized them, so assured in manner did they seem and so broad in the chest; something had changed his two Schoboleskis; their violet irises were shining like the water in their full bronzed faces. 'How healthy they look,' Wladimir could not help remarking.

"'It's the sea air,' said Lord Feredith, smiling. 'A fortnight of excursions at sea has made two Hercules; and yet we return to Cannes every evening.'

"'Hercules! I'll stop you there,' sniggered the thin lips of Algernon Filde. 'That one, perhaps, but this one'—and the poet pointed at Boris—'is entirely Adonis, the Adonis that I see, and whom I would like, if I ever put my poem into the theater.' And, bowing to the comtesse: 'My compliments, Madame, you succeed with sons.'

"*A little better than my mother*, the prince thought, privately, and his gaze, fallen on to his emaciated hands, rose again to the calm and round forehead of the younger of the Schoboleskis, aureoled by fine blond hair.

In the depths of an obscure wood with old branches,
Adonis, the handsome shepherd, the son of the gods,
Listens to the sonorous murmurs of the forest,
And his flute with seven holes beneath his thumb,
Repeats them in echoes, in deep pure notes.
In the sixteen years that he has been roaming the woods,
His mouth has acquired the bitter taste of mulberries
And his heavy russet tresses the living gold of the sun.

"It was Algernon Filde who, noticing the prince's attention, underlined it with those verses whispered in his ear; and Noronsoff did not like having been divined by the poet. Instinctively, he detested that thin and clean-shaven Englishman with the cunning face of an old priest. With his prominent chin, his hollow cheeks and his bitter smile, and his eyes above all—his gray eyes simultaneously piercing and troubled, profoundly sunk beneath the brow of the ample forehead of a thinker—Filde evoked a certain resemblance to Dante, but a Dante who had lingered and delighted in the circles of an equivocal Inferno. There was mystery in that emaciated profile of the Florentine school, but there was more sarcasm; and beneath the nobility of the forehead the eyes were ardent with wicked desire. There was a cruelty in the irony of those mobile pupils, and the impression was even more disconcerting when the pupils remained fixed. Wladimir felt that he was being examined by the poet, and did not like it.

"Lord Feredith, his face tanned and blond, a thickset benevolent giant, muscular and cheerful, offered two puerile eyes in the baked face of a pirate. A great drinker and ardent lover of all sports, he was dressed like a sailor in blue serge, and combined the forthrightness of a mariner with the exquisite urbanity of a great lord.

"Him, Wladimir liked right away, and the excursion aboard the *Edward III* would have passed off quite well, in sum, in spite of the encounter with the princesse and the excessively perspicacious poetry of Filde, if an annoying ovation had not awaited Noronsoff on his return to land.

"The news of his presence aboard had brought out the entire quarter; alerted by their friends, all the idlers of the Place Garibaldi had come running. Wladimir's escapades were as popular in Riquier as in Ponchettes; his crazy expenditure in houses of ill-repute and his generosity in the dives to which Etchegarry and Rabassol had taken him had made him famous among the rabble of the port. The story of the three tattooed men, offered as a centerpiece, had ignited all covetousness; their performance had been richly rewarded, and it was in the midst of a joyful crowd of mocking beggars and soliciting friends that Wladimir went back to his carriage.

"Scarcely had he appeared on the gangplank than his advent was greeted with jeers and cries. '*Evviva el Russo! La salute a nostro principe!*' All Wladimir's friends jostled one another trying to reach him, imploring him for a glance, and above all for money. '*Per mangiare?*' coaxed the Italians, while the Niçois louts wheedled for a twenty-franc piece. The boldest tugged on the tails of his coat. Such must have been the welcome of the Duc de Beaufort in Les Halles under the Fronde.

"Disconcerted, Wladimir could scarcely move forward; grouped at the stern of the yacht, the bright dresses and the gaudy umbrellas were watching. It was a scandal, and Noronsoff, foaming with rage, pale with fear and shame, felt sweat dissolving his make-up.

"The two muzjiks descended from their seat and liberated him; a handful of coins thrown to the crowd produced an eddy that allowed him free passage. A battle now broke out at the edge of the quay, of mobile rags and hand-to-hand combats; and Noronsoff finally escaped in the midst of laughter, cries and insults, *carogna tantas* and *figlio di puttanas* vociferated by hilarious mouths, escorted by rounds of unsteady gamins and the anger of brandished fists.

"Comtesse Schoboleska watched her friend's departure standing between Lord Feredith and Algernon Filde.

FROM HOGARTH TO FRAGONARD

"'I told you to beware of the sea. You had to come aboard. Could I foresee that ovation? You're too generous. Those people were translating their gratitude to you in a slightly ill-timed fashion.'

"'The wretches! There wouldn't have been enough knouts for them in Russia.'

"'But we're in Nice, under the Republican regime, involved with immortal principles; it's necessary to put up with the rabble here, or to have stayed in Saint Petersburg.'

"'You're not generous, Vera.'

"'But you're also exaggerating, Wladi. Those people love you, in their fashion, but they're a trifle familiar.'

"'But what did Lord Feredith say? What must his guests, Lady Saymoor and the Princesse de Troie, have thought?'

"'You're preoccupied with the opinion of women now! But, my dear, you're lowering yourself.'

"'And the English poet with the sour face and the shaven lips, what did he say? I'm sure that Filde sniggered. I don't like that man. He has the air of a culpable bath attendant.'

"'Oh, charming! I'll tell him that. He'll be delighted. Your altercation with all those people, my dear Wladi, amused them greatly. Lord Feredith declared that the Latins should always be kept at a distance, and that you were very good to distribute your money to them. A Saxon wouldn't have flinched, but we Slavs have the souls of children; your satrap side wanted to be generous. Generosity is a hard métier to continue.'

"'When they're not exploiting you, they're insulting you.'

"'But those beggars haven't insulted you.'

"'Do you think so? There's nevertheless been a scandal, and the coastal newspapers have got hold of it.'

"'And you're worried about the newspapers? You really are very ill.'

"'It doesn't alter the fact that neither Lord Feredith not Algernon Filde has returned my visit.'

"'What? What about the two cards?'

"'Yes, two cards, but they didn't come in.'

"'You were asleep, you weren't receiving. They couldn't force an entry.'

"'All right, but they came in an automobile; they didn't even get out.'

"'That's a matter for the footman.'

"'They came at two o'clock.'

"'To see you.'

"'No, because I was on their route. They were going to Monte Carlo. I can see clearly, Vera, even though I'm ill. I'm a man that no one sees any longer; I'm invited once, but no one comes to my house. I'm Noronsoff the tainted, a fallen prince. It's truly very kind of you still to come here'

- "'But Wladi, this is silly, you're delirious! They returned your visit within three days. What more do you want?'

"'All right, but why the p.p.cs with the cards?'

"'But they're putting to sea this evening. The yacht is going to Corsica.'

"'Are Boris and Nicolas aboard?'

"'Yes; they wanted to see Ajaccio.'

"'And are they coming back?'

"'In ten days.'

"'And Lord Feredith and Sir Algernon, will I see them again?'

"'Naturally. Without a doubt.'

"'Without a doubt, or naturally?'

"'I don't know. It's certain that you'll see them again.'

"Wladimir had fallen back under the empire of la Schoboleska; he put his forehead in his pale hands and closed his eyes momentarily; then he opened them again, and after a silence: 'Come on, in all sincerity, if I invited Lord Feredith and Sir Algernon to dinner, do you think they'd come?'

"'Why not?'

"'You're avoiding the question. I want an affirmation, not a doubt. Will the people of the *Edward III* accept an invitation to dinner from me?'

"'I'm sure of it. You've come aboard. You're torturing your mind, my poor Wladi. Certainly they'll accept; but wait until they return.'

"'I want to invite them right away. Where shall I send my telegram?'

"'You're inviting them by telegram?'

"'Oh, a telegram drafted like a letter, with all the desired ceremonial forms.'

"'Telegraph them at the port of Ajaccio, then; but they won't get there until tomorrow, at midday.'

"'It doesn't matter. My telegram will be waiting for them there.'

"The next day, at half-past three, Sacha's landau stopped outside the comtesse's hotel; the prince had an urgent communication to make to her and begged her to come instantly. La Schoboleska put a last cloud of veloutine over her face, moistened the silk of her long eyelashes with kohl, passed her lipstick over her lips and climbed into the carriage.

"Wladimir was waiting for her on the terrace. Already on his feet, he extended the livid thinness of two long bare arms toward her, protruding from excessively long sleeves—the prince was in a dressing-gown—and brandished the blue paper of a telegram joyfully. 'I have the response! Come quickly!' he shouted to the comtesse from a distance. 'They've accepted! They've accepted! Read this—I received it two hours ago.'

"The prince was exultant. It was the mad, quasi-frenetic joy of a nervous child who has just been given a coveted toy. He read and reread the slip of paper. The telegram was laconic—*We accept for 30 May*—but Sacha could not take his eyes off it. The comtesse observed him silently.

"'They accept. What are we going to offer these Englishmen? Come on, Comtesse, advise me. It's necessary to dazzle Albion: something to astonish them, amaze them, that they've never seen before.'

"'Remember that they've been to India,'

"'I know, but something exquisite and refined, French artistry at its purest. They're mad about the eighteenth century in London. Oh, nothing Asiatic, I assure you.'

"'So much the better, for Lord Feredith has the most reliable taste and Algernon Filde is erudite. Be prudent, my dear Wladi. I don't want to know your plans, in order to savor the surprise fully. But above all, no tattooed men. They'd take that poorly; and then, as regards tattoos, they have all that could be desired on board. Adieu—I don't want to know anything.'

"And the program for the famous dinner was elaborated. Gourkau was consulted and, taking inspiration from the scenes from Hogarth staged aboard the *Edward III*, Noronsoff settled his choice on three living tableaux imitating Fragonard. The invisible collection in Grasse made Fragonard the subject of all conversations.[1] The American of Grasse, the maniac possessor of the most beautiful specimens of the French school, who was stubborn in not allowing anyone to see them, was the bête noire of all the winter visitors. Grand Dukes had groveled in the hope

---

1 The painter Jean-Honoré Fragonard was born in Grasse. His reputation suffered a long eclipse in the nineteenth century, when he was virtually forgotten until undergoing a spectacular rehabilitation in the *fin-de-siècle*. His works were not inaccessible in 1901, but the most famous of them, *The Swing*, also known as *Les hasards heureux de l'escarpolette*, was (and still is) in the Wallace Collection in London. *Le Verrou* [*The Lock*] is now in the Louvre. The third painting described is not easily identifiable and is probably fictitious.

of being admitted to contemplate the *Escarpolette mystérieuse* and the *Amant heureux*, which were only known through prints hawked on the quays. Fragonard was in the air of the locale, and it was a charming attention to offer living facsimiles to art-lovers unjustly weaned from the originals.

"Noronsoff sent to Paris for the collection of prints, asked for a painter of mock-ups, costumes and sets, had research carried out at the archives of the École des Beaux-Arts on the exactitude of the colors. The thing cost what it cost, but in order to perfect the three chosen tableaux, Wladimir ransacked shops and libraries. Everything was ordered by telegram; Sacha was passionate about his work. The three paintings were the *Heureuse illusion*, the *Escarpolette mystérieuse* and the *Verrou*. Then it was necessary to find actors. Gourkau had to make enquiry after enquiry of directors of the Opéra and the municipal theater. For the pretty, petulant and mannered men of Fragonard he had to settle for travesties, but when it was necessary to find female models, Noronsoff could not find any minor players who were sufficiently lissom and delicate. It was necessary to address leading actresses. The comediennes and singers approached pulled faces. It was too thin an employment. What would become of their talent in that exhibition? Were they whores, of whom nothing was demanded but beauty? It was necessary to vanquish their scruples one by one; jewels softened them initially, and then the prince's munificence convinced them. The costumes were ordered chez Landolff.

> *Fragonard! Duchesses, marquises,*
> *Nymphs wandering old parks*
> *At whom, amid exquisite poses*
> *The gods take aim with large bows.*

> *With what petulant ardor*
> *Would the divine prowler be able*
> *To rummage with a gallant hand*
> *In the jewel-case of your modesty?*

At the foot of beeches that grow
In the blueness of the evening.
Those swings that glide,
Mysteriously in the dark . . .

What sophisticate can surprise them
Above a loquacious pond
In the shadow observed by Leander?
Say, nymphs of Fragonard . . .

Under the chemise that he tucks up,
What can on the edge of clear streams,
In the dark green freshness of moss
Ignite the rose of flesh?

And those enterprising male hands
Those tenderly languid eyes.
And on the quivering throats,
Long kisses stolen by surprise!

Those glazes of changing fabric.
Those arms cast like a net
Around fluttering waists
In the hollow of rebellious breasts.

Those confessions in amber napes
And beneath the blue rain of lilac,
Far from lackeys and hajduks,
Those falls in great furbelows!

Those pirouettes, as if winged,
Of lovers, and God knows where,
Among the flying skirts
The gallant pushes the bolt!

Flesh of satined shoulders
Blazing in the depths of lawns,
The squeals of tickled women
Fading at the sound of tambourines.

Fragonard! The inebriations
Of a century of amber and satin,
Of graces and coquetries
Light, godless and libertine,

Suddenly reappears, a feather
In the cap, the magnetic gaze,
At that name full of a secret
And delirious voluptuousness:
            Fragonard!

"And, with a curtsey, her skirt pinched in her fingertips, the reciter, a made-up child-like face dotted with beauty-spots, inclined the edifice of her powdered hair, and swiftly slipped away, in a pirouette and a rustle of furbelows; the living tableaux commenced.

"First, in a décor of osiers, reeds and willows, there was the mischievous glide of the mysterious swing, the elaboration of the celebrated print with the girl tipped back on the swing and the bare knees appearing amid the flying skirts; the watchful covetousness of the lout crouching in the grass, in front, underlining the lewd aspect.

"The other scene was even more lively, the curves of the robust fellow emphasized by cotton trousers, the gallant of the *Verrou* maintaining a half-swooning beauty in a vigorous embrace, out of reach of the latch; the shot bolt determined the victory; the beauty was the gallant's, in the intimacy of the untidy bedroom, the detail of the unmade bed, close by, aggravated the amorous disarray of the young woman, her passionate emotion and her bewildered modesty, all effort futile.

"The *Heureuse illusion* showed the same bedroom and the young woman, extenuated by fatigue, sliding over the edge of the bed in the solitary alcove, the amorous woman smiling at her dream, holding the bolster against her with one arm and the other arm gripping the leg of a stool tipped over in the struggle.

"The spectacle had been put on in the dining room. They had sat down at table at nine o'clock. The prologue had been recited over dessert and Noronsoff's guests digested the implications of the reconstituted scenes at the same time as the liqueurs. The orchestra of the Opéra—a night when there was no performance had been chosen—played Rameau, Haydn and Mozart softly. In honor of Lord Feredith, the muzjik servants had traded in their white silk blouses for crimson foulard blouses, red being the color of England.

"Unfortunately, the fête only had a restricted audience. The prince presided there between the Pole and Baronne Narimoff; Lord Feredith was opposite, flanked by the two Schoboleskis; Algernon Filde sat to the left of the comtesse. Gourkau and Dr. Filsen had taken places to make up the numbers; the other guests were absent. Lady Saymoor and the Princesse de Troie had sent their excuses the day before, having been summoned to Florence; Grand Duchess Paul had not come.

"Wladimir dissimulated his ill humor poorly. Everyone withdrew at midnight.

THE FÊTES OF ADONIS

"AND the news spread through Nice that the villa on Mont Boron was going to be the theater of an unusual and unique fête, a fête that was going to eclipse all those so far offered by the Russian, the splendor of which would efface the memory of all the analogous spectacles provided in the last twenty years by the extravagant and prodigal residents of the Riviera. The fêtes were to be held in the gardens, before the horizon of mountains and the sea that the terrace commanded; they would begin at dusk and would be prolonged into the night by torchlight. It would be an antique reconstitution in the vein of those that had once got Sacha banished from Saint Petersburg: lupercalia, bacchanals or Orphic celebrations of a sort, the corteges of which would be compose of at least three hundred actors.

"A search was already being mounted for pretty young women and handsome men for the composition of the groups; beaters were scouring Nice and the surrounding area; the fête being only a pretext for an exhibition of nudities, they searched above all for impeccable physiques. A considerable number of port laborers and Italians from the new quarters had already been enrolled; even a few fishermen from Pointe Saint-Jean had been conscripted. Attempts at enlistment had even been made with regard to the tenth Artillery of Nice and the sixth Alpine of Villefranche, but the colonels of the solicited regiments had put a stop to them. The officers had no desire to see their men figuring in the masquerades of that madman Noronsoff, and the most severe orders had been given in the barracks.

"Gourkau, the prince's usual stage manager, had been forced to fall back on the chorists of the Théâtre de Monte Carlo, for there would naturally be choirs and songs during the parades; Vurabourg gladly put his troupe, both men and women, at the disposal of the prince, for it was necessary not to count any longer on the theaters of Nice, closed after the thirtieth of May. For dancers—for the fête also included dances—he was obliged to address himself to La Scala in Milan.

"All that represented an enormous expense, between thirty and forty thousand francs; indeed, the men of the figuration, street porters, Italians, laborers and fishermen collected at hazard, received, for their part, a louis a day for the fête and ten francs for the rehearsals, and the prince also bore all the expenses for the costumes. Everything had to be new; Landolff had received the order; in addition, there were a thousand and one accessories— but what would they be? To what epoch, to what people, would the action be attached? That was a secret; at any rate, nudity would be displayed there triumphantly, for, once the subjects had been chosen, first Gourkau and then the prince made them pass a veritable examination.

"Before being inscribed on the lists, every figurant, male or female, had to undress and submit, for at least twenty minutes, to the investigative gaze of Noronsoff and his steward. The prince was in permanent session, from four to five, in the hall of the villa; the aspirants of the cortege, sent for a preliminary bath in the morning, undressed in a neighboring room and filed, as Antinous or Phryne, before the Areopagus; Wladimir decided the admissions: a singular fashion of employing his leisure, which now entertained the entire city. The refused figurants came back laughing, and the tallest stories ran around the poor quarters regarding the strange competition. In spite of the precautions imposed, a permanent odor of sweat and dirt plagued the examination hall; there was now the appearance and atmosphere of a quotidian draft board at the villa.

"But what would the fête be and for whom would it be given? That was the obscure point that impassioned the whole city. The season was advancing and all the important winter visitors had left; Nice and the Riviera, returned to calm, were becoming drowsy in the enervating warmth of their spring. The *Edward III* was no longer in the port; Lord Feredith, it was said, was traveling the Ligurian Riviera, the enchanting coast between Livorno and Genoa, and the preparations for the fête were continuing feverishly in the sunlit torpor of an abandoned Nice.

"To what Grand Duke or mysterious sovereign was that mysterious staging dedicated? The date had been fixed for the thirtieth of June, and several rehearsals had already taken place. Human voices could be heard from the road, intoning and repeating ensembles interrupted by the recriminations of an orchestra leader; a former sergeant major in the hussars was having other movements executed. Established in two rows or disposed in groups, men and women were moving as if on a drill field; they processed along pathways and retraced their steps, or arranged themselves on terraces at commands of *halt*, with regulated movements as in a ballet; an Italian dancing master indicated the poses and corrected the attitudes.

"The figurants had been interrogated in vain; as none of them had yet tried on their costumes, none could deduce anything therefrom, and God knows how overexcited curiosities were. People went as far as waiting at the exit of the rehearsals. People were collected still warm as they came through the gates, and brothers and friends took them away to refresh them in the taverns of the port and the Rue Cassini, but without obtaining anything. All of that rabble, brutalized by orders and commands, only knew one thing, which was that one was to hold a staff, another was to walk with a basket balanced on the head and a third was to throw flowers while walking; that was the whole of their indiscretions.

"Comtesse Schoboleska and her sons witnessed the final rehearsals.

"Comtesse Schoboleska was the instigator. She was the one who had put into Wladimir's head this new extravagance of the fêtes of Adonis, for it was to be the funeral and resurrection of the Ephebe of Asia that the files and corteges rehearsing on Mont Boron were to represent.

"Dr. Filsen, escaping from the villa one evening, finally satisfied my curiosity and gave me the details. He no longer had a minute to himself. To begin with, the prince had demanded his presence at the beauty contest over which he presided every day. It was not only physical examinations that the figurants underwent but veritable health checks: a further demand of la Schoboleska, justly alarmed by all these promiscuities on behalf of her dear Boris, for the younger Schoboleska was to take part in the fête; he was even to be the king, the demigod, by turns acclaimed and mourned, Adonis himself; and the vigilance of the Pole, alerted regarding all the chance figuration raked from the depths of old Nice and the wings of Milan and Monte Carlo, had been able to communicate her anxiety to Wladimir.

"As long as all that Italian rabble and Niçois scum didn't bring smallpox to Mont Boron, or any of the other filthy diseases that the poor people of the Riviera always trail after them! The Slav had been able to terrorize Noronsoff for himself and for her son; he might be infected, and the god of the fête along with him. She did not have any great difficulty in scaring Wladimir; the mania for precautions had become a malady in him; after the veritable draft boards installed in the villa he had now established a surveillance committee. All the figuration, men and women, had to submit to the examination of the doctor, assisted by Gourkau, once a week. Anyone who tried to avoid it was immediately scratched from the lists; the rehearsals were conducted militarily. In confrontation with all these formalities, thirty men withdrew. They were no longer in the service; did the prince think they were in barracks? What had commenced in laughter threatened to end in inconvenience and annoyance. The desertions continued; six dancers and singers left; it was very difficult to replace them, and the prince continued to live in apprehension.

"Would the fête ever take place? The costumes had not arrived, figurants were slipping away every day. What if Boris were to fall ill? Precautions were redoubled; the prince's neurosis was exasperated; his demands became intolerable; Gourkau could not take any more; Dr. Filsen was at the end of his tether.

"Only la Schoboleska came and went, fresh, supple and radiant, in the midst of all that turmoil, anguish and disarray.

"And the unhappy Swede mopped his brow, shrugged his shoulders and put his fists to his temples. What infernal idea had that Schoboleska had, and what was she scheming underneath it all? He too was beginning to fear the Pole. Her smiling calm scared him.

"I listened to him without understanding. In the chopped speech, denatured by his Swedish accent, I could not grasp either the motive for or the objective of the fête. What was this new fantasy of Noronsoff's? I knew that he was as proud as a peacock, but I could not see his interest in dazzling with his prodigalities a Nice that was already half abandoned, and would certainly be empty by the end of the month.

"Filsen was kind enough to inform me. He finally told me what must have started it off.

"It was in honor of the people of the *Edward III* that he was taking all that trouble, in order to bring to repentance and force to admiration Lord Feredith and Sir Algernon, who had remained rather cold on the Fragonard evening. They were coming back from Italy on the day fixed and bringing with them Lady Saymoor and the Princesse de Troie, presently in Florence. A royal prince of the house of Savoy and his entire retinue would also witness the fêtes; the Princesse de Troie had written to la Schoboleska and had formally promised the presence of His Highness. All of Wladimir's vanity was at stake, and God knows, it was immense; I remembered a remark by the Pole: 'As immense as a steppe; he's lost there.'

"So the fête was to be royal, a fête offered by a satrap to a poet and the son of a king. It was Prince Emmanuele who was announced, and when I mentioned the figure of forty thousand francs already cited by the city, Filsen cried: 'Forty thousand francs! But it's by the thousand roubles that it's necessary to count. Forty thouand francs! The figuration alone eats that much in the rehearsals. Remember that the corps de ballet comes from Milan; we've had the expenses of the voyage—and then people know the prince, and they increase the prices for him. Oh, that one can boast of being treated as a great lord! I've seen the mock-ups for the costumes: fifty francs each . . . designs after Alma-Tadema.'

"'For the funeral of Adonis? That's very Roman for a Greek celebration.'

"'It's the Comtesse who wanted it. It's necessary above all to please those Englishmen, and in London, that Alma-Tadema is their painter. The prince only dreams and only wants one thing: to astonish Lord Feredith, to obtain the approval of the poet. Oh, he's taken the lack of success of his last dinner to heart. I know that he can afford it; the millions are there; but he can't renew this kind of amusement often. For these funeral celebrations of Adonis, I wouldn't be able to pay the expenses with a check for a hundred and fifty thousand.'

"'Damn!' And involuntarily, I bit my lip. I hadn't thought Wladimir so generous.

"A hundred and fifty thousand! And to retract them from the prince's wallet it had only required a casual remark—what am I saying? a wave of the fan—from la Schoboleska.

"It was after a visit from the Pole, two days after the Fragonard dinner, that Wladimir had made the great decision. What could she have said to him? But Gourkau had been summoned to the boudoir, and scarcely had he gone in than the curt voice of the prince had wheezed: 'It appears that we've taken a false route. Lord Feredith and Sir Algernon didn't care for our Fragonards; the spectacle was too delicate for them, and it was a copy. Without meaning to, we were inspired by their fête on board—you know, the Hogarths? It's an error for which half the responsibility reverts to you, but I wasn't able to contradict you. We need a revenge on these Englishmen.

"'Madame'—and he indicated the Pole—'has been kind enough to inform me as to the taste of these fellows. Lord Feredith and Sir Algernon only like the antique. Naturally, the author of *Hadrian on the Cydnus*! The Museum of Naples, the excavations and frescoes of Pompeii, that's what these English need. Telegraph London to send us colored reproductions of five Alma-Tademas immediately, of which Madame will give you the list, and you, my dear Gourkau, are going to organize for me, in accordance with those paintings, the funeral celebrations of Adonis.

'I won't have any difficulty with you; you're the foremost scene-setter in Russia, and if your place wasn't with me, it would be at the Théâtre Michel. We'll go, if necessary, as far as a figuration of three hundred persons; the fête will take place in the gardens; these Englishmen are open air people, they adore nature. Madame's younger son, Boris, will play the role of Adonis; his mother consents to that. No need to recommend his costume to you: a god of Asia and loved by Venus! It's Sir Algernon Filde who designated him for that role, for everything we do is to please that poet. Yes, we're groveling, we're licking the hand that has been refused to us, in order to cut it off afterwards, isn't that right, Comtesse? From today onwards we're domestics at the orders of Lord Feredith, and we're putting on these fêtes of Adonis because Algernon Filde is the author of the famous poem *Adonis and Venus*, not *Venus and Adonis*! What a Venus you would have made, Comtesse! Thank you anyway, you're lending me Boris.' And he kissed her hand for a long time.

"'For the expense, my dear Gourkau, carte blanche; you'll spend whatever is necessary.' And he emphasized his words: 'I want to dazzle these Englishmen.'

TOWARD THE IDOL

"AND the day of the fête arrived; the preparations had been made in an effervescence of fever that had ended up infecting the entire population. The overexcited city finally knew what it was all about. The final dress rehearsals had informed intelligences; but the curiosity was only more ardent. According to the figurants, the luxury of the corteges surpassed anything that had ever been seen in previous carnivals. It would be more beautiful than at the Opéra! For three days already the entire crowd of the idlers of Nice had been laying siege to the surroundings of the villa, massed on the heights of Mont Boron, trying to glimpse through the foliage the maneuvers of the figuration. The country was struck by a sort of admiring stupor, and, overheated by the indiscretions of the men of the corteges, the rumors grew from hour to hour, exaggerating and magnifying the sumptuousness deployed by Wladimir; and the entire hypnotized city had eyes glued to the Villa Noronsoff.

"In the few hotels that were still open, people were desolate that the prince was giving his fête so late in the season; the porters and the interpreters would have made a fortune from foreigners. No matter what the cost, they would have obtained from the prince's staff a few entries to the spectacle, and at the Municipal Council the question had been raised as to whether Noronsoff ought to be requested to put on a second performance for the benefit of the city's poor. In any case, the deputy mayor, who was the president of the festival committee that year, was of the opinion that the Russian ought to be approached with an offer to acquire all his costumes, in anticipation of the next carnival. The administration of Monte Carlo, it was said, also made overtures, with a view to productions of *Messaline* that it was to put on next winter. Financiers were going mad; their rabble abounds on the Riviera, and a fury of speculation unknown in the summer months shook the Côte d'Azur out of its torpor; Sacha's prodigalities had set all covetousness ablaze.

"The fête fell on the thirtieth of June. Two days before, the *Edward III* moored in the bay, Lord Feredith preferring the coolness of the open water to the dusty vicinity of the harbor; a steam launch came every morning to pick up Comtesse Schoboleska and her sons from the shore; they left the port at ten o'clock and returned at one thirty in order to assist in the last rehearsals. The *Edward III* would only come to the quay on the day of the fête; no one wanted to disturb the prince during the turmoil of the final hours. Lady Saymoor and the Princesse de Troie were on the yacht; the presence of His Royal Italian Highness had also been signaled.

"At the villa, Wladimir could no longer contain his joy. It was as if his satisfied vanity, the success of his continuing project, the incomparable splendor of the fête, the effect of which he had been able to judge in recent days, and the certainty of astonishing his guests this time had regenerated, reestablished and cured him. Filsen could not believe his eyes; his invalid had been changed for him. By virtue of an incredible effort of will, health had returned to him. Transformed and transfigured, Wladimir came and went, giving orders, occupying himself with the slightest details, rectifying costumes and mistreating Gourkau. He seemed to have worn away his illness in vertiginous activity. Sacha had rediscovered in the organization of the fête the kind of rejuvenation that I had observed in him during the sojourn at the villa of Etchegarry and Rabassol, especially in the early days of Marius's favor.

"'Bah! he reserves many others for you,' I said to Filsen, who came to see me on the morning of the famous day. 'He's the most astonishing invalid that I've cared for during my long career, and I've been a navy physician; I've known opium smokers and hashish eaters. But beware of the collapse after the fête. I've witnessed his returns from the drinking dens and brothels of Riquier; arm yourself with courage and patience for tomorrow, if he doesn't slip through your fingers this evening.'

"'This evening! Oh, that would be too unjust, for that man truly has genius! His fête will be unprecedented, unique—and to think that you won't see it! Oh, if you had seen it yesterday, in the gardens, by torchlight: those bronzed nudities under those antique garments, the flow of peplums and the flutter of fabrics of the Pompeiian and dancer, and hues such as one only ever sees in frescoes—I maintain the word, in frescoes—saffrons, crocus yellows, glaucous blues and lacquer reds, the tones of the mosaics of Herculaneum . . . and the prodigious beauty of types under the eurythmia of helmets or headbands, all the profiles brought back to the classic, the brutality of certain heavy jaws, become Roman, and the divine bestiality of certain narrow foreheads crowned with poppies and lotus flowers! In truth, it was an evening in Greece, an evening of Thesmophoria in Ionia or Sicily, and in the gardens that you know; and we had the moon, an implausibly golden enormous moon, and the sparkle of a pale nacreous sea under the nocturnal blue of a sapphire sky . . . Oh, the moonlight! And we'll have one even more beautiful this evening.'

"Dr. Filsen was delirious. His Swedish coldness had melted, unfrozen by contact with the prince's dancers and figurants. The Russian's folly had infected him, unleashing an enthusiastic Hellenist within him. He never shut up about the twelve Italian women of the corps de ballet from Milan, the breasts captive in golden mesh, while the skin of loins, haunches and bellies shone with pearly light through the smoke of long violet gauzes weighed down in places by coral darts. Brandishing lighted resin torches in one hand, agitating thyrsi bloodied with roses in the other, dangling like the torches, twelve ephebes followed, in green silk breeches; and an orgy of roses bled in the gardens, red roses, sulfur roses, white roses and more red roses: two thousand francs' worth of roses, the booty of surrounding cultivations devastated by order of the prince, all the surrounding countryside pillaged, an inebriating harvest with the peppery scent of shredded roses, execcsively open, as if extenuated by living: all the ardor of Venus radiating in an efflorescence of stupor over the adored body of Adonis; all the sap of Cythera and all the incense of Lesbos, the falling of petals and enlacements of groups, an orgy of Mytilene and a reminiscence of Paestum.

"Filsen, the grave and mild Filsen, waxed lyrical about the prince and his fête in prose that one might have thought translated from Theocritus; I no longer recognized my Swede; all his University memories had gone to his head; he was living in full antique idyll, drunk on eclogues and oaristys, like a new wine.

"'And Boris?' I said, interrupting his panegyric.

"'Schoboleski, Adonis: an idol!' And Filsen, completely beside himself, blew a kiss at the ceiling.

"'But Doctor, I no longer recognize you.'

"'More beautiful than a god, he justifies the scandal of the fête, he's the living excuse for it. In any case, you'll see his portrait this winter at Georges Petit's; the prince has commissioned it from Garino, the painter of the Avenue Notre-Dame. When he appeared, yesterday, lying on his litter, in the midst of the pontiffs and priestesses of Venus, there was a cry of amazement in the crowd. Imagine Heliogabalus, the childhood of Domitian, the triumph of Bacchus. You have no suspicion of the splendor of that made-up face and large starry eyes beneath the diadem! What a pity you can't be there! But I must run; I have to be at the villa by midday.'

"'And his costume?' I said, retaining Filsen by the arm. My curiosity had been ignited by the recitation of all those extravagances. 'In what state of undress is he offering la Schoboleska's son to his guests? The Mother was once served naked on a platter—at least, that's the legend.'

"'His costume? Oh, I don't know! It's as indescribable and as crazy as that of Salammbô in Gustave Flaubert or Heliogabalus in Jean Lombard's *L'Agonie*; Gustave Moreau also painted like that. It's as if he were clad in ash, but ash in which reflections of water and gems palpitate; the entire fabric of the robe is woven from moonstones, opals and sardonyxes; a pectoral of amethysts grips the torso and an enormous crown is made of large violet-tinted poppies: poppies of darkness with ruby pistils, something monstrous and mad, but adorable, an emperor's dream, a poet's invention, the apotheosis of a god.

> *In perfumes and ambrosia,*
> *Forehead circled with light,*
> *The young gods, sons of Asia,*
> *Appear, proud and charming!'*

"And with that quotation, Filsen ran away, as if he had said too much.

"It was an endemic fever. Wladimir was contagious; his madness had infected the doctor. As Nero had once depraved the Augustans, Noronsoff was contaminating his entourage; he had even converted Dr. Filsen to the cult of Adonis.

> *One single man is sufficient to corrupt an empire.*

"Nice was also contaminated, the entire city prey to the erotic and sumptuous mania of the prince. From two o'clock onwards all the streets were empty, the shops closed, life suspended, the entire population emigrated to Mont Boron to try to glimpse fragments of the spectacle, corners of the Russian's fête.

"That day, extended all the way to the Avenue de la Gare, there was the aspect of death and abandonment offered on carnival Sundays on the heights of Saint-Sylvestre, Saint-Barthéleny and Saint-Maurice when the file of masks swarms and bawls from the old quarter to the Place Masséna and the accumulated crowd rushes before the carts from the Quai Saint-Jean-Baptiste along the Promenade des Anglais. On those days, a pneumatic pump seems to suck the population toward the sea. In the abandoned high city there is the silence left by a panic; the fury of pleasure has emptied the streets like a plague.

"Now, on that thirtieth of June, from two o'clock onwards, Noronsoff's fête had made Nice a desert. An implacable azure reigned over the sky and the sea; and, a refugee in my study, behind my closed shutters, I counted the hours, regretting, involuntarily, that I was unable to witness all those splendors, unconsciously attentive to the artillery salvos that, it seemed to me, ought to have announced the fête.

"Four o'clock. The guests ought to have arrived; the cortege was setting forth; I ought to be hearing the cries of the crowd and the music of the orchestras. And, incapable of thinking about anything else, I lived minute by minute the phases of the spectacle of Mont Boron, my eyes on the hands of the clock, hypnotized to the point of malaise by the details learned that morning, evoking the groups and the costumes in a quasi-dolorous hallucination. That accursed Noronsoff had bewitched me in my turn; I too was subject to the obsession of Adonis. Then, as the afternoon advanced, the slats of the shutters filtered a daylight that was less raw; I changed the placement of a vase full of roses, the odorant agony of which was inebriating me; I opened the shutters and, leaning on my windowsill, I cocked an ear in the direction of Mont Boron, on the alert for clamors and voices.

"Then the air freshened; a gust of wind from the sea caused a current of air and plucked the petals from the sheaf of roses placed between two open windows. I beg your pardon for citing all these details, but in truth, I have rarely lived moments so intense: a sort of presentiment told me that something unusual was happening out there.

"A splendid sunset heaped up a mass of clouds on the horizon; the Pointe d'Antibes turned violet behind a screen of gigantic golden arabesques, and I thought that, out there, on the heights of Cimiez, in the retreat of the Dames Assomptionistes, a woman was surely sharing my anguish and suffering, perhaps also leaning on her windowsill, attentive to the rumors coming from Mont Boron, her eyes staring at the sea, also trying to distract herself with the changing play of the light and the hour.

"And then the sky darkened, the street turned the color of ash, the room dark. My housekeeper appeared on the threshold and announced that dinner was served.

"I went to table. I had scarcely finished my soup when the roll of a carriage stopped outside my windows. Someone ran up the stairs precipitately, and the maid entered like a gust of wind, carrying a letter. 'Monsieur! Monsieur! It's on the part of the prince. They're waiting for a response.'

"Noronsoff. I had divined that it was to do with him. I unfolded the note; it was from the princesse: *Come, come quickly, not a minute to lose. You are my only hope; my son is dying.*

SLAVIC VENGEANCE

"I arrived at the villa at nightfall. A veritable mob occupied the gardens. In the blue shadow of the most beautiful June evening, there were the imprecations, demands and mocking insults of an army of figurants; three hundred men and women, half-naked under brightly colored garments, were shouting and swearing in all the idioms of the Riviera: Piedmontese patois, the jargon of the Basso-Porto of Naples, the picturesque argot of the old quarters of Nice. Women were squealing with shrill cries that cut through the mass of the hoarse and whiny male voices like fifes. Here and there, blazing torches illuminated tragic faces, irradiating the gold of a diadem, slapping with red the nudity of a torso jutting from a peplum. There was a sickening odor of dirt and sweat; the heat was suffocating, aggravated by the reek of resin and so many roses heaped up in every corner of the park.

"Bloody strips mingled with tresses, vivid crimson floods fell from high foliage, an entire orgy of roses, the one denounced the day before by Filsen, was bleeding, streaming, shining and stagnating, like a river of wine, in the pathways and over moist flesh. The enervated and strident laughter of tickled women overlapped the growling threats and gross gaiety of men. '*Paga mi, m'en an ail!*'—pay me so I can go—clamored the echoes of the garden.

"It was simultaneously the atmosphere of the rut of a festival evening—the popular festivals of Nice and the surrounding area are only held in summer—and that of a popular insurrection. Gesticulating hands were agitating; a frenzy of mimes was twisting arms, shifting fabrics, and the reek of musk and armpit hair was troubling. It was mingled with the incense of roses; the night was languid with insipid odors.

"And standing on the perron, dominating with his tall stature all those threats and grimaces, gemmed foreheads and extended fists, Gourkau was trying in vain to obtain silence. The tide of solicitors jostled him, and Gourkau, in the light of torches, took a step backwards and went up a step, like some shipwreck victim stranded on an islet invaded by the waves, while the wind carries away his voice. For Gourkau was speaking; his lips opened and closed, to open again, but not a word was audible.

"'*Paga mi, paga mi, m'en an ail!*' And the frantic tumult of laughter and cries grew; there was also anger. Submerged by the crowd, the steward stood firm in spite of everything, but he was hard-pressed and was about to weaken and be defeated.

"The prince and his guests must have retired before the storm, because, above the dark ground floor the first-floor windows were flamboyant in the night.

"And the rising fury was unleashed.

"I had not been able to get anything out of the muzjik sitting beside me on the way; laughing groups encountered on the way, the cries and gibes of overexcited people, had told me that something had happened up above, but I was far from suspecting a popular movement, and we fell into the midst of an insurrection.

"As we passed through the gate the muzjik prudently raised the screens; the crowd parted before the horses; we were greeted by jeers, brandished torches and sweaty faces; lighted resin torches hurled by strong arms were extinguished against the carriage doors; strings of roses whipped the windows; semi-naked women attempted to hang on to the wheels; it really was a riot.

"Gourkau saw us and sketched a gesture: finally! An order was murmured and ten muzjiks ran to help us to get down, escorted us and defended us against the mob; the cries of '*Paga mi! Paga mi!*' redoubled. Gourkau had grabbed hold of me and dragged me into the villa; the doors closed behind us. '*Paga mi! Paga mi!*' the hysterical crowd howled and laughed; blows of fists shook the shutters; on the first floor, a broken window shattered into smithereens.

"'The brutes!' Gourkau hissed, in a hoarse voice.

"'And the prince?'

"'The prince! Ah! Have you arrived in time? May it please God! He's bad, the prince! Oh, that Pole!'

"In the bedroom, flooded with light, thrown fully dressed across a bed cluttered with pillow, cushions, the turquoise-blue brocade quilt not even drawn back, was the large, collapsed and inert body of Sacha. He must have been carried there in the disarray of an attack. A muzjik was finishing removing his stockings, another was trying to disengage two stiff legs from his trousers. Panic filled the entire room with mute comings and goings and fearful gestures.

"Next to the bed, two men watched by a woman clad in black were busy; there was a sickening odor of ether. The two men were Dr. Filsen and the prince's valet de chambre. The woman turned round when I came in and showed me, distraught with anguish, the face and hallucinated eyes of Princesse Benedetta.

"'Doctor! Doctor! It's you! Finally!' And the princesse launched herself toward me, seizing my hands feverishly. 'Can you save him? See what she's done to him! Oh, that Schoboleska!' And she dragged me toward the bed.

"Lips tumefied, eyelids blue, all of his bad blood risen to his cheeks, simultaneously violet-tinted and livid, Prince Wladimir, felled by a congestion, offered the atrocious aspect of a drowned man. He was green-tinted under the blinding light of candles and lamps, like living carrion—for his pulse was still beating, and a horrible rasp, less a breath than a rattle, was still lifting, at intervals, that commenced decomposition. A horrible detail: in the violence of the crisis the prince's false teeth had come unfastened, and the tip of a rough violet tongue was dangling, bitten, between the springs.

"'Can you save him? Do something! What can you do?'

"I wiped away a little red saliva oozing at the corners of the lips, asked Filsen to send for hot water and to wash and pad that clenched mouth. The heart was functioning but the feet were already cold; the legs and thighs were cold, and also the hips; all the lower parts of the body were already dead; by contrast, the temples and the cheeks were hot. I demanded a footbath of hot water, flour and mustard, coarse salt and sinapisms. Princesse Benedetta repeated my orders in a cutting voice. Then, in spite of the fear of the Swede, I demanded his medical kit and, rolling up the sleeve of my patient, I ordered that his torso be maintained while I attempted to bleed him.

"The moribund body was sat up on the edge of the bed. Two muzjiks and Filsen supported him by the armpits; his feet were plunged into the steaming water of the bath, and sinapisms were applied to the thighs. The princesse held ice applied to the temples. I was attempting, I knew, an impossible reaction; however, the discolored flesh reddened somewhat, its lividity became animated; the pallor of the arms, still bloodless at the first thrust of the lancet, were tinted pink at the second; for a third time I dug the steel point into the thinness of the arm, a little higher up; blood finally pearled.

"What blood! Rather a serosity, a blood resembling pink oil, the slow droplets of which stained the silver of the bowl with the creamy pus of an abscess. Then a redder and more vivid blood spurted, and the drops could be heard tinkling. The rigidity of the arm relaxed, redness also appeared in the thighs, the toes were reanimated and clenched in the bath; and with a slight sigh, the cadaver that was Sacha tipped his head back; the neck had also lost its rigidity. I unbound the arm and left Filsen to do the bandaging.

"Two large tears now ran down Sacha's cheeks; the marbling of the faces had almost faded. The valet de chambre had removed the dentures delicately from the soft lips and had put them in a glass; the toothless mouth was now gaping like a hole; we laid the prince down in his bed.

"'He's saved again for this time, Madame.'

"'Thank you.' The princesse had taken my hand and inclined her head as if to raise it to her lips. I stopped the gesture.

"The clamors of the crowd were continuing; the laughter and threats of a figuration overexcited by cupidity and wine were rising up, howling, under the window. 'Since two o'clock in the afternoon they've been getting them drunk to persuade them to be patient,' muttered Filsen.

"That crowd! In the fever of giving first aid to the prince I had completely forgotten them; but they were intent on affirming their presence; obscenities and insults reached us distinctly, mingled with the obstinate *paga mi*. The name of the prince was no longer being respected; mouths were vociferating it, attached to the strangest epithets, and to Italian dirty words that the princesse understood. She listened to them, white and stiff, in a dolorous stupor, with only one gesture, the gesture of someone wounded compressing the lurches of her heart with her hand. There were songs too, sniggered by the voices of drunken men, the refrains of which were taken up in chorus; the crowd clapped hands; the light of the torches made the windows rosy; handfuls of flowers—for the crowd was, in sum, amusing itself—came to splatter on the windows. One might have thought it an evening battle between the Greens and the Blues under the terraces of the Hebdomon in the splendid and crapulous centuries of Byzantium.

"Byzantium! The door opened before the entrance, in a gust of wind, of Gourkau. The princesse baulked before the irreverence. 'What is it?'

"'I can't hold them back. They're going to break down the doors. I've sent word to the gendarmerie, but between now and then I can't make myself understood. That Italian jargon! Will you try, Doctor? You speak Niçois.'

"'Hmm! A singular service you're asking of me; they'll boo me.'

"'They all know you.'

"'One reason more—I won't have any authority.'

"'*Paga mi! Paga mi!*' And the cries redoubled.

"'I beg you, Doctor,' the princesse insisted.

"'All right, I'll try. Have a window opened.'

"Scarcely had I leaned out over that confused mass of ruddy heads, however, than invectives and gibes greeted me: '*Il papa Rabastens, il papa des pagagai.*' And, like a firework display against the somber blue of the night, a flock of dazzling birds rose up. Out of malice, the rioters had opened the aviary and liberated the parrots. Blinded and frightened, the prince's favorite creatures were flying madly around the park. Two magnificent macaws, their eyes rounded by fear, came to alight on my shoulder, where-upon the nickname sprang from all mouths: '*Il papa des papagai.*' I withdrew, to an immense burst of laughter.

"I had only succeeded in being grotesque.

"'*La principessa! La principessa!*' the voices were now demanding; the silhouette of the princesse had been recognized. The princesse was adored in the low quarters of Nice; she distributed abundant alms there, perhaps in the secret hope of redeeming Sacha's escapades, Cries were now demanding *la buona donna*, the good lady.

"'You speak Italian, Madame,' Gourkau implored. 'They'll listen to you.'

"And, having had the two battens of the large door-window of the balcony opened, the princesse presented herself to the crowd; and there, in the midst of a sudden silence, she spoke in a broken voice, in the purest Florentine idiom.

"'Gentlemen, my son is dying. He needs the greatest calm, and I, his mother, have come to beg you, in the name of Christ and the Madonna, to let him die in peace.'

"'*Eviva la donna! Eviva la principessa!*' the crowd acclaimed.

"'Thank you, my friends,' the poor woman had the courage to find, 'thank you. Now, would you like to withdraw, and come to the villa tomorrow at midday; you'll all be paid; that which is due is due.' Already, however, there was a stir in the crowd; the hoofbeats of horses and the rattle of sabers and spurs announced the arrival of the gendarmerie. The mutinous figurants withdrew almost peacefully into the night.

"The princesse had sat down, overwhelmed, next to the bed.

"The two fugitive macaws had perched on the back of a chair next to the prince's bedhead; the larger one was grooming its feathers, its eyes anxious, still frightened by the alert, while the other, a white and pink macaw,[1] was gazing at us with a pensive expression. The comicality of their presence was one sadness more in the gravity of the hour. Like us, the two extravagant animals seemed to be watching over the prince, meditatively.

"Sacha had not opened his eyes. He continued to sleep silently, his breast raised from time to time by profound sighs, the sighs of the great chagrin of a child that sleep cannot console. Suddenly, he sat up, and in a changed voice, hoarse and hateful, he stammered a few words in Russian that caused his mother to raise her head; then he fell back into his torpor.

"'Daughter of a bitch, bastard Jewess, prostituted larva,' the princesse translated into French. 'He's thinking about la Schoboleska; it's her memory that's obsessing him. But that's true, you don't know anything, it's necessary to tell you everything, Doctor. Do you know where the comtesse is at this moment? She's headed for the coast of Sicily, in company with Lord Feredith, aboard the *Edward III*. This is the letter that she had delivered to my son at seven o'clock in the evening, after five hours of interminable waiting. She was supposed to be at the villa at two o'clock for that abominable fête.'

"I smoothed out a crumpled piece of paper, torn in places.

"*Dear Prince,*

"*You have given me a taste for adventures, cruises and sea voyages. I am allowing myself to be taken to Sicily by Lord Feredith. I have listened with you to too many of the stories of your friends Etchegarry and Marius. When you receive this letter the* Edward III *will already be in sight of Cap Corse.*

---

1 I have translated the French *ara* literally, although the bird in question is presumably a cockatoo.

"*Don't hold it against me too much for taking Boris away from you and not attending your fête. We regret it, the poor child and I, but Lord Feredith does not care to see his future son-in-law figuring in masquerades. The era of follies is over; in a month's time there will no longer be a Comtesse Schoboleska; Lady Feredith will inform you of her marriage as soon as it has been celebrated in Palermo. I have had the caprice to be married in the Palatine Chapel.*

"*Why could you not support the sea better? My son and I would have loved to visit Sicily with you; this time we would have done you the honors of the yacht; you have done us those of your villa for such a long time. Perhaps we should have put more discretion and tenderness into it, but one cannot remake the Russian character.*

"*Shall we ever see you again, Prince? I don't believe so, for Lord Feredith is a trifle jealous—how mistakenly, you know! Yes, jealous of you. He does you that honor. Personally, I am making you my adieux here, the adieux of your Vera. I dare not hope that you will regret us. If, by chance, you find a tear, remember my horoscope. Today, as tomorrow, beware of everything that comes from the sea.*

"'The wretch!' I cried, at the signature.

"'A Jewess and a Slav,' sighed the princesse. 'She is avenging herself like those of her race and those of her country, at a distance and surely, but she is killing my son.'

THE RUSSIAN SOUL

"**B**UT SACHA did not die. There was such an energy in that destroyed organism; such an intensity of life galvanized that cadaver that he escaped death once again. The ordeal, however, had been terrible. For ten days we worked in shifts, Filsen and I, beside the invalid, convinced every evening that he would die during the night, and convinced every morning that the day would be his last. He deceived all our fears. There were ten days of lethargy, two hundred hours of unconsciousness from which the moribund only emerged to stammer vague words and dissolve in tears. We sustained him by means of artificial alimentation; it was exactly that semi-slumber that saved him; the shaken nerves of that undermined constitution could not have survived another crisis. The princesse watched over him with us, admirable in her silence.

"That strange prostration had something of enchantment; I rediscovered next to the dormant individual the unreal atmosphere of the tale that I had already lived next to Sacha. During the long hours spent at his bedside I obtained from Filsen the details of the unforgettable day, the slow and progressive exasperation of the prince brought to its paroxysm by a culpable combination of circumstances meditated and planned by la Schoboleska. The Pole was worthy of Russia; she had returned, in a single day, a hundredfold, all the affronts received and all the humiliations suffered. Her plan had been made for a long time; she had dissimulated it with a strength of mind extraordinary in a woman, allowing nothing of her future triumph to show; and yet, she was certain of success, Lord Feredith having asked for her hand two months before.

"It was only when she was certain of being married, and having fixed the date of her marriage, that she had harnessed herself to the task of stimulating in Wladimir the thirst for consideration, the need for receptions and visits, that folly for ruinous fêtes, and the extravagant desire to dazzle his guests that had brought about the catastrophe of the thirtieth.

"She had labored on a terrain prepared by the Russian's immeasurable vanity. Wladimir had always had a love of ostentation, but to whip it up she had given him the lesson of Lord Feredith; the perversity of Algernon Filde had provided an accomplice. Everything had been organized and planned to madden Sacha, to exasperate his hysterical vanity: the lunch aboard the *Edward III*, the indifference of the Englishmen to the Fragonard fête, and their polite coldness in response to advances from the villa.

"It was by means of a slow work of crystallization that she had put into his head the Neronian fantasy of the fêtes of Adonis; and, once the fête was prepared, the roubles dispensed without being counted, the figuration styled, the choirs too, still present on the eve of the final rehearsal, she had had the cruelty, when the great day arrived, to leave the wretched Sacha in uncertainty and expectation for sixteen hours, the ferocity to enervate him, minute by minute, to refrain from telling him the truth until the very last minute, to devastate him with the final catastrophe.

"Oh, that day of the thirtieth of June! I relived it, hour by hour, with Filsen, who now gave me the details: the prince risen at ten o'clock, almost young in the joy of the success; the arrival of the figuration at one o'clock, the dressing of the three hundred Italians and Niçois of the corteges—and than an alert. The news that the *Edward III* was no longer in the port. Nor was it visible at sea, and Gourkau and Filsen had, at the same second, the suspicion of a treason. The prince was anxious too, but would only believe that it was an excursion at sea, an unfortunate idea on the part of Lord Feredith, who wanted to make Boris late; for they learned from a figurant that the comtesse and her son were aboard; the steam launch had come to pick them up, as it did every morning, at ten o'clock. And Wladimir became impatient, and the horizon remained empty. No yacht at sea; were they going to miss the fête? And Sacha muttered Russian insults addressed to la Schoboleska.

"The figurants were ready; all eyes were fixed on the sea, the sea of which the Pole had told Sacha to beware; and, troubled involuntarily, the Russian remembered the horoscope. The implacable azure of the Mediterranean was dazzling—the sea rubbed with garlic, as they say in Nice—under the ardent June sun, but there was no sail, not even a fishing boat, the silhouette of which might have provided a momentary hopeful illusion. The costumed figuration was also giving signs of enervation; the park was buzzing like an immense beehive; the rumor of the crowd enveloped the villa. And Sacha decomposed beneath his make-up. His hallucinated eyes no longer quit the sea; it was a joke that la Schoboleska was playing; they were going to arrive from Villefranche; they wanted to amuse themselves with his anguish.

"Then it was four o'clock, the time announced for the opening of the fête, when the corteges were supposed to set forth. And Boris had not arrived, nor the others, detained God knows where, by that accursed Schoboleska. And the prince was no longer alive. They sensed that he was ready to fall apart, his heart ready to break, his voice already changed when he gave an order.

"He had the figurants given asti to calm their impatience; the rabble grumbled. What were they waiting for? And the sun was setting in a magnificence that was a regret for the failed fête, for everyone sensed now that the guests were not coming. Sacha had himself injected with morphine and went up to his bedroom; he had thrown himself on the bed and given the order that he was to be woken up when the people from the *Edward III* arrived. But he did not sleep, his eyes alert beneath his lowered eyelids, and

257

his silence was more alarming than the insults muttered a little while before, addressed to the comtesse.

"And there were three mortal hours of uncertainty, of terror and suspense, with the mutiny commencing in the midst of the costumed, enervated and intoxicated crowd, the men excited by the contact of the women, the women amused by the nudity, their own and that of the men. *Paga mi*s were heard.

"It was then that, in the warm shadow of all those promiscuities, a courier from the Hôtel de Hollande had come to deliver la Schoboleska's letter.

"Sacha had got up and read it at the window, by the light of a hastily lit candle, for he had demanded darkness during his repose. Oh, the strange play of the prince's physiognomy while he deciphered the Pole's prose! Filsen said that he would always remember it; it had been a terrifying thing: the Russian's entire face as if shrunken, the eyes singularly narrowed, only allowing a golden gleam to filter through, the features contorted and furrowed like those of a very old face, in which all the wrinkles had been hollowed out simultaneously.

"The prince had read in silence; then the astonishing face of a mummy had suddenly darkened; from wine-lees it had become violet, then aubergine; then it had been the head of a negro with eyes revulsed and white. The prince had not uttered a cry; he had spun around and his valet de chambre had received him in his arms. It was a serious apoplexy. Someone had run to Cimiez immediately to inform the princesse.

"I knew the rest; I had arrived in the midst of the riot of the figuration, I had witnessed all the scenes of that memorable evening, the Machiavellian work of la Schoboleska.

"She had planned her denouement well; and the death of the prince, struck down by rage in the midst of the ruined fête, would have closed the series of her former affronts tragically; the Slav was a woman of all the refinements.

"Hazard undid her plans; in life, only the unexpected happens.

"Wladimir got himself out of trouble. After ten days of apprehension, he came round in a crisis of tears, and attached a singularly puerile gaze to us, child-like eyes, one might have thought, resurgent from the depths of his soul, an unknown soul, or at least rediscovered, in dolor . . .

"He looked at me for a long time, and held out his hand to me. The emaciated Christs of Cosmè Tura and Holbein have those exsanguinated and delicate hands, in which all the bones are apparent: Christs with protruding ribs and livid flesh, of whom Sacha ended up having the appearance with his sparse beard, already ten days long, his excessively bright eyes and his hollow face. He also looked at his mother, standing at his bedside, a dolorous Pieta of a bad Christ, whose vices had put him on the cross . . . and an infinite tenderness relaxed all of Sacha's features.

"The blow struck by la Schoboleska had made another man of him.

> *The horseman Woe who rides in silence,*
> *The horseman Woe has pierced me with his lance.*[1]

"No regrets, no recriminations, not a word about the terrible event of the thirtieth, not even an allusion to the Pole. Had Lord Feredith, Boris, the Schoboleskis, ever existed? Wladimir seemed to have forgotten the two years he had just lived. Had ten days of prostration extinguished the memory of them? No, for the sadness of his smile revealed clearly enough the humiliation he retained in his heart, and the disappointments of which his suffering was primarily made; but Noronsoff's finally reawakened pride did not know because it did not want to know, and we respected its silence.

---

1 The lines are derived from an untitled poem by Paul Verlaine, whose first two lines actually read "Bon chevalier masqué qui chevauche en silence/Le Malheur a percé mon vieux coeur de a lance." [Good masked horseman who rides in silence/Woe has pierced my old heart with his lance.]

"It was a new era that began, an unprecedented era of mildness and tender lassitude. He emerged from the crisis exhausted, and seemed to enter into a slow and quiet convalescence; weak to the point of being unable to sit up by himself, he now stayed in bed for long days but, strangely enough, was no longer suffering. The physical torture of so many maladies also seemed to have called a truce. The end was nigh, we could not doubt it, but it promised to be calm and reconciled; the prince was fading away without a start or a shock, with a soul already liberated from his flesh, emerged alive from its past.

"The orchestra of tziganes had been dismissed; it had been silent for a fortnight. One evening, the princesse, disturbed by Sacha's mutism and large drowned eyes, had given the orchestra leader an order to play, quietly, the tunes that had once been her son's favorites, but at the first bars Wladi had raised his hand and begged, with a gesture, to make them stop. He no longer wanted to hear them.

"The next day, Gourkau settled up with them; but two muzjiks were sent up from the kitchens, one young and one old, both born in the Crimea and both good singers of popular songs, which the older of the two, Iakov, accompanied on the balalaika. That is the Russian guitar. Gut or horsehair form the strings stretched over a triangular box. Very popular with the people of all the regions of Russia, the balalaika serves primarily to accompany songs or mark the rhythm of dances.

"Relegated to the basements, the poor Crimeans were frightened by the prince's new caprice. One evening, Iakov, thinking the entire villa was asleep, sang with his friend Vassili the famous Russian song of the Volga boatmen. The plaintive rhythm of the old melody had reached as far as Sacha. He was not asleep because of the heat, and Vassili's voice, a plaintive adolescent voice, had entered through the wide open windows into the master's bedroom, along with the heady scent of the tuberoses of the park. They were then in full bloom, and their waxy thyrses were exhaling their deleterious incense like as many cassolettes. The song and the perfume made the air languid, and the entire night was overwhelming and intoxicating, buzzing with mosquitoes and full of vegetal scents; close by was the imperceptible frisson of the sea, and Wladimir, suddenly invaded by nostalgia, had wanted to hear the two voices at closer range. The singers had been summoned upstairs.

"He had kept them all night.

"They sang, responding to one another, and when Iakov had intoned in his deep and sonorous voice:

> *The man is fortunate,*
> *Who has no worries.*
> *Nor love in his heart.*

"Vassili replied in his tortured voice:

> *And I, a poor girl, feel*
> *That my heart is as arid as a stone.*

"And Sacha had burst into sobs, his soul moved to tears by the intolerable suffering exhaled by the song. It was his own suffering that translated those bitter plaints, sometimes similar to a prayer of repentance, sometimes sad and soft like a child's dolor; and after that song, Sacha had wanted others; and all night long, the two singers had sung, hypnotized themselves by the anguished dolor of their voices, and Sacha had not wearied of listening to them. It was the very chagrin of his destroyed life that those popular melodies distilled, all filled with despair, like every beautiful Russian song.

"And in listening to them, he had rediscovered his soul and his homeland.

"The two muzjiks quit the kitchens and remained all day outside the bedroom door, at the invalid's orders; and an era of new favorites commenced.

THE ANCESTORS

"THE TWO SINGER-MUSICIANS no longer quit the prince's apartment. During the interminable hours of the torrid Niçois summer, their voices alternated or confounded in the same imploring anguish, rising into the semi-darkness of large rooms with closed shutters.

"An infinite distress, and all the dolors that can be contained in a human soul crushed in the grip of the forces of nature and implacable necessity were to be found in the naïve words of the songs, as in the plaintive monotony of the melodies. Sacha listened to them, his throat contracted by nervous tremors and his eyes wide, as if brightened by tears. He found a bitter enjoyment in sensing his nerves torn by those lamentations; the sadness of the notes and words entered into his breast like a jet of flame; the voices of the two muzjiks squeezed his heart to the point of spasm, but Sacha loved that pain. He brought to it a sort of pride, at the same time as an unhealthy curiosity, and I found in that new attitude all of the simultaneously lax and passionate soul of Wladimir, the mania for duplication and the voluptuous egotism whetted by analysis that are characteristic of the Russian soul.

"The princesse did not like the new caprice. As an Italian fervent for Cimarosa, Palestrina and the old masters of her homeland, she treated those popular melodies as the music of savages, and she deplored their depressive effect on her son's anemic organism; the jealous mother feared all influences. For her, there were only bad ones, since they were exercised on an invalid and counterbalanced her authority. She was unable to dissimulate her hostility to the singers, and the poor fellows, terrified by the Italian's black looks, lost all their composure in her presence; their voices choked, they forgot the words, and Wladimir, alerted by their disturbance to his mother's sentiments, now looked at her with hatred.

"The tenderness of the first days of convalescence had been succeeded by a singular reserve. It was with coldness that he greeted the princesse's visits. His mother embarrassed him. He only responded curtly to her questions. Nor did he pardon her for her redoubtable clairvoyance; he had not forgotten that she alone had seen clearly into the Pole's dangerous game, whereas he had allowed himself to be rolled over like a child. That inferiority humiliated him; the invalid returned to his former bad habits. Before repeated signs of impatience, I was obliged to beg the princesse to space out her visits, and above all to cut them short, in Noronsoff's own interest.

"'It was only a pause, then,' the poor woman replied. 'I see that it's necessary for me to resume my calvary. Oh, that Cossack blood, the barbaric blood of the son who has nothing of me! It's all of his atavism that arms him against my tenderness. I'm obliged to love him at a distance; it's necessary to resign myself to it; one can't struggle against the ancestors.'

> *Alas, the hour has come for me to quit everything,*
> *To quit all those I love*
> *And to go into a foreign land.*

"It was Vassili who was singing.

"Sacha was listening to him with the astonishing expression of the crucified, his head tipped backwards and his eyelids lowered over the heavy liquid of two large tears. I had entered on tiptoe, but the invalid had keen ears. He opened his eyes slightly, with a vague smile, and held his hand out to me.

"'Enough for today,' he said to the two muzjiks. 'Go, my friends, take a walk on the mountain, breathe well. I have no need of you before evening.' The two singers withdrew.

"Wladimir told me to sit beside him. 'What voices those wretches have! They no longer sing, they weep. They weep for my life, they weep for their own, all of Russia weeps in its songs. We're Russians, the other peoples don't understand us. How can my mother comprehend? I'm a foreigner for her; for Europe, we're barbarians. You, Doctor, at least I sense that you're a little closer to me. Have you read Gorky, Doctor? He's one of our novelists, a former vagabond, who wrote his life and that of his companions: street porters, tramps and wanderers like him. He understood us better than Dostoyevsky, or even Tolstoy. Immense Russia suffers from ennui, and the manifestations of that malady Gorky has annotated like no one before him. Ennui! A strange malady, a nervous disarray, a chronic spleen that penetrates us all the way to the profound depths of society, afflicting the vital forces of the humblest and most needy. For ennui, Doctor, doesn't always result from subtle education and the fatigue of luxury; all human creatures prey to the disease of living are prey to ennui. Thus, myself, I'm a being apart from life; but it isn't only me, there are many others who are similar. There are thousands and thousands like me in Russia, a whole army of men apart, who don't enter into the established order. Whose fault is it? Are we responsible toward life because we have no joy in living? Personally, my mother gave birth to me at a bad time and I bear within me a heap of ancestors who return. But who among us doesn't have ancestors? The least of vagabonds carries within him all the faults of his forebears.

"'Thus, myself, I've never been able to know what I want; I've always desired something, but what? I don't know. Am I, then, impotent to live? No, but life can't contain me, because it's too narrow and my desires are immense. No one knows me, no one can know me. Can my mother ever know? My mother is so far away from me, so Italian. So, Doctor, there are days when I'd like to go far away over the sea, far, far away, and never come back; at other times, I'd like all men to be my slaves, men and women; I'd like to see them spin like tops whipped by my desire. Then again, on other days, I pity everybody, most of all myself; I'd like to give my fortune to the poor, to despoil myself, to be poor and to suffer. On those days, I feel capable of dying for others; but on other days, I'd like to kill everyone, and then myself, horribly, to fill the whole world with terror . . . and that's the way it is.'

"And I listened with an infinite heart-sickness to the puerile confessions of that vagabond soul. Sometimes, an operetta Russian reappears in a Cossack illuminate. It was 1898, the same year as his death, since he expired on the twelfth of December, the same year as the Kaiser's embarkation for Venice. A particularly torrid summer lingered until October, and all the newspapers in Europe were full of the details of all the fêtes given in honor of Wilhelm and the King of Italy in the city of the Doges; and those articles, Wladimir read.

"'Venice!' he said to me, one night when I was keeping vigil. 'Would you like to go to Venice? There's a service you can render me; I'll pay for your voyage, and you might be doing a good deed—who knows? Perhaps I have a son or a daughter n Venice—a child, at any rate, if not mine, nearly mine. That astonishes you? Oh, nights spent in a gondola in the moonlight on the Zudecca canal! It was twenty years ago. Venice was less English than it is today and I was living in the Veniere palace, a palace in ruins, or, rather, unfinished, with a dream-like garden overlooking the Grand Canal. In the morning I went to visit a church, the Frari, the Scalzi or San Zaccharia; I had breakfast at Quadri's. In the day I had a siesta and in the evening I dined at the Lido, or sometimes San Nicolò, and the gondola brought me back at night across the lagoon.

"'I had a gondolier who seemed painted by Carpaccio, a gondola with a *felze* of sculpted and gilded wood that dated from the time of the Doges, and for a mistress I had a lace-maker who resembled Santa Barbara. She was from Chioggia, where all the women are beautiful, and my gondolier from Burano, but they both lived in Venice, the man at San Moisè, the girl at the Arsenal. I endowed the girl when I left Venice and married her to the gondolier. If they've had children—by the dozen, I'll wager—I have every reason to believe that the eldest resembles me. Oh, my gondolier and my lace-maker! Their names were Antonio and Zulia; they were the enchantment of my twenty years, for I was twenty, and in Venice! But where to find them? Those are people to whom I'd leave a good few of my millions, if their eldest had my eyes, my mouth, or anything of me at all.'

"The prince was drowsy, dreaming his folly aloud.

"He had others, more sinister; and the ancestors feared by the princesse reappeared in rather macabre circumstances, and like good self-respecting specters, the frightful antecedents of Noronsoff naturally revealed themselves by night, a night when Filsen was on guard duty beside the prince; we took turns to watch over him, assisted from eleven till one by the princesse, who took advantage of her son's drowsiness to come and watch him sleep.

"For some time, the prince had been more taciturn; the songs of the muzjiks found him less attentive. As if haunted by an obsession, the prince remained buried within himself, his eyes alert beneath lowered eyelids; and the golden gleam of the fêtes and orgies of the era of the Pole had reappeared in his irises, the evil gaze of the days of old.

"Of the gondolier and the lace-maker, evoked one night of tender reminiscence, there had been no more mention. Over that, as over Marius and Etchegarry, and more recently over la Schoboleska, Wladimir had passed the astonishing sponge which he seemed to have at his disposal with regard to any troubling memory. That marvelous gift of forgetfulness made him truly a prince; that faculty of suppressing people from his memory with the same ease with which he suppressed them from his life, if he had only lived a century sooner, he would have penetrated me with respect and amazement, for I knew that voluntary forgetfulness and I found Sacha all the more admirable for it.

"One Friday, during the raw heat of the day, Vassili, the younger of the two muzjiks whom Sacha had made to sing all night, felt drowsy. The poor devil had not been able to resist fatigue, and his own must have been great for him to fall asleep in his master's presence, in the princely bedroom. Sacha was also asleep—I think so, at least, for one was never sure of anything with that hysterical Slav. I was reading, installed next to a window—a work by Gorky, in fact, recommended by the prince, *Thomas Gordeyev*,[1] and slightly somnolent, affected, in spite of the powerful interest of the book, but the torpor of the room of siesta. Suddenly, a voice rose up in the silence; Sacha had propped himself up on his elbow and was watching the muzjik sleep, attentively.

"'How young he is! See, Doctor, how healthy and robust he is, and what young blood is quivering under his young flesh. Strength is circulating within him like sap in a beautiful tree. It's that blood that I need in my veins! I'd pay him whatever was necessary. Oh, to have the health of that boy! It's done, blood transfusion! Can't you try it on me with Vassili? I sense that I'd be cured if I had the youth of that man under my skin!'

"He was speaking with an increasing excitement, almost upright in his bed of misery, and his eyes were shining like carbuncles; tremors were agitating his fingers. I sensed the fever rising; I did my best to calm Wladimir down. It was a dangerous utopia that he was caressing there! In his sick and vitiated organism, even the blood of a healthy individual, like the muzjik, would have been nothing but one more ferment of corruption; it would have been precipitating the end of the invalid to activate the strength of his illness. I repaid him with bad reasons, telling him that the matter merited thought. The prince's hallucinated eyes never quit Vassili. He drank him with his gaze; thirsty eyes in the desert drink the water of mirages in the same way; the tenacity of his contemplation was such that the muzjik woke up. He put

1 In fact, the doctor could not have been reading *Foma Gordeyev* (1899), known in English as *The Man Who was Afraid*, in 1898.

his hands together, caught at fault, frightened and confused by having gone to sleep; the prince excused him with a gesture and, lowering his eyelids, extinguished his frightening pupils.

"But it was a hyena that was unleashed within him the following night. It was Filsen who was on guard, and when I arrived at Mont Boron in the morning, I found the whole villa on foot, the staff muttering and fearful; Gourkau was wearing his grave circumstances face. Filsen ran toward me, distraught.

"Wladimir had acted on his own. Who could ever have expected the events of the night on the part of such a feeble man? Worn out as he was by the malady, he had found the means to drag himself out of bed, and, crawling across the room on his hands, he had profited from the doctor's slumber to reach the divan where Vassili was lying, and there, with a clasp-knife that he used as a paper-knife, he had attempted to cut the muzjik's throat 'in order to drink his young blood, his blood fresh with strength and health,' as he cried, with sobbing bursts of laughter and an atrociously wild gaze.

"The poor boy had had to be dragged from his hands, more dead than alive; the wound was insignificant, because the thrust had been delivered poorly, but the entire villa was up to date with the story and nursing a quivering indignation. At the cries of the victim, who had not dared defend himself out of respect for the master, Filsen had uttered fearful clamors; the entire staff had come running, and the princesse herself had had the atrocious spectacle of the young man bleeding between the maniac's hands and the horror of her son's strident and frightful bursts of laughter.

"The sight of his mother, instead of calming him down, had exasperated the hysteric; a flood of insults vomited against her in the presence of the domestics had obliged her to withdraw; now Sacha was asleep, exhausted. The princesse had had Gourkau count out a sum of three thousand roubles for Vassili and had dismissed him. As soon as the poor fellow, still shaken by a nervous tremor, had recovered from his emotions, he was taken to the railway station and embarked for a village in the Crimea; his master's madness had made him rich.

"The princesse's door remained closed.

"I listened to that nightmare story, astounded. 'It's the ancestors returning, Ibsen's *Ghosts*,' the Swede said to me, 'the terrible ancestor who had the pretty girls of the steppe violated in the forest and whipped jealous fiancés until they bled: the first Wladimir of the name.'

"And I stammered, as if in a dream: 'If specters are appearing, it's because the prince is about to die.'

THE END OF A RACE

"AND the death arrived, precipitated or delayed—could one ever know with that deceptive Russian?—by the most unexpected and comical events: an entire series of circumstances piled, one might have thought, one on top of another in order to hasten the most singular denouement. And the end of the man, in the image of his life, was tragic and grotesque.

"The era of mildness created, it had seemed, by the treason of la Schoboleska, was succeeded by a period of fever and tremulous overexcitement; the softening of Wladimir by hearing the songs of the muzjiks had only led him, in the end, to vampirism, and since that frightful scene, which had put an end to the favor of the musicians, a wind of madness blew over the villa. The worst extravagances and fantasies were rife there, hazardous and frightening, as if Wladimir, odious and cynical, wanted to exhaust all the ridicule that a human life can contain. As if the princesse had not already suffered all martyrdoms, the prince still reserved other cups of sorrow for his mother.

"It was hatred that he now had for her, a hatred envenomed by old rancors, and which, catching fire, burst forth in terrible scenes. At every hour of the day there were atrocious altercations, insults and recriminations, whose violence filled the villa with cries and stupor. Wladimir brought all his bad faith to them and all the demonic imagination of a Slav and a degenerate. He arrived at reproaching his mother for his maladies and his flaws; he had the audacity to render her responsible for his vices. It was her

Italian blood that had polluted that of the Noronsoffs; she had brought into the race all the old crimes of Florence. What had got into his father's head to go take a wife in a family allied to the Strozzi and the Medici? It was him, Sacha, who was bearing the consequences. One could not introduce with impunity into a young and vigorous blood, like Russian blood, the ferment of corruption of a line that had furnished courtesans and catamites to the Vatican; and his lucid memory cited names and dates.

"The princesse listened, livid and frozen; then, her patience exhausted, she too cited ancestors; the Wladimir, first of the name, the violator of girls and the tormentor of serfs, the accredited legend and the terrible atavism. Then Sacha, choking with fury, accused her of having substituted herself for the malediction cast upon the race; it was her stupid virtue that had brought down on his own head the bohemian's spell. If she had been a whore—Wladimir risked the word—like the other princesses of the family, he would not have been the creature of folly and lust that he had become; by escaping the fatality of the blood, it was upon him that she had drawn the vengeance, and a fine advantage that she had remained honest, if she had transmitted the infamous legacy to him!

"It was him that had been sacrificed, but she had been well punished in her pride. She had given birth to a monster. But he had had enough, and it was necessary to finish with it. He had had enough of her presence and her surveillance, enough of her frightful egotism, which made her love him more when he was ill than when he was well, because illness delivered him more to her. As in all women, personality penetrated her tenderness, and took precedence over everything else. But he had had enough of that tyrannical devotion and those invasive cares, enough of that domination and that jealous authority, which set aside all affection and all amity; she had chased away all his favorites one by one, and if she supported his escapades, it was in order to supervise him more closely, to subjugate him more surely—but it was finished; he no longer wanted any spy, male or female, in his house, and he would sweep them all away: mother, steward and physicians.

"And as the princesse, contracted by stupor before that hate-filled face, murmured the name of Nero, the prince cried: 'Nero! Nero! So be it—but you're not even Agrippina! Agrippina loved her son blindly.'

"'And I see mine all too clearly,' the imprudent mother risked.

"'Too clearly! And I'm dying of your clairvoyance! It's your pitiless eyes attached to all my actions that have drunk my life, exhausted my strength. Yes, it's your eyes, your vigilant eyes, your hard, perspicacious eyes, that have poisoned my existence; it's because of them that I bless death. But your tenderness is the *in pace* of a victim of the Inquisition. I'm dying to escape a jail, the jail that your egotism had built around me, and I hate you and curse you for your honesty and your frightful love.' And, concluding with the argument of all the fallen and all bad sons: 'Anyway, did I ask to be born?' he went back to his apartment, slamming the door, demanding a revolver or poison with grand gestures.

"To acquit our conscience we hid the phials of morphine and chloroform, convinced deep down that all that play-acting would not go as far as drama. Sacha was too cowardly to make a serious attempt on his life. 'Comedy, not tragedy,' as the unfortunate princesse sighed, shaking her head in the midst of her tears.

"On the same evenings as those odious scenes, the prince summoned to Mont Boron the musicians of the Régence or the acrobats of some troupe performing at the circus in the Rue Pastorielli, and interested himself, as if nothing had happened, in the exhibitions and the music; the familiars of other winters, all the procurers, second-hand dealers and equivocal suppliers, had resumed the road to Mont Boron.

"In the meantime, the prince's condition was getting worse; his neurosis was only equaled by his weakness; the accidents and their sufferings had reappeared, and the princess wanted to attribute Sacha's odious conduct to the physical tortures. She lived in retreat on the second floor, voluntarily eclipsed before the rising tide of old clients returned, but determined to struggle until the end and dispute until the last minute the execrable and excessively loved Sacha with his maladies as well as his vices.

"It was the end of November. A letter of notification arrived from Constantinople; la Schoboleska announced her marriage therein, celebrated in Palermo on the fifteenth of July last. The Pole had waited more than four months to inform Wladimir of her triumph; one could not be more impertinent. On reading the note the prince entered into a fury.

"The name of Schoboleska, which he had not pronounced since the night of the thirtieth of June, he cried out, vociferated, and finally spat out, and with what a flood of mud! A flood of mud, filth and bile slowly accumulated in the cloaca of his rancor. I had never heard such insults. Their cosmopolitanism was frightful. In what dives of the Bosphorus, Moscow and Vienna, in what underworlds of London, Naples, Algiers and Cadiz had Wladimir been able to collect those epithets? One might have thought that his entire past had risen to his lips, perhaps at the same time as la Schoboleska's, for the couple were worth as much as one another, and with a superb unconsciousness, Wladimir howled in the volleys of invectives addressed to the absentee as many addressed to himself.

"By virtue of shouting, his voice had become hoarse; he finally sat down at a table, snatched up a pen, crumpled pieces of paper, scrawled on them, splashed them with ink, and, his hands feverish, incapable of tracing a line, tried to write to Lord Feredith in order to inform him of the infamy of his wife, reveal to him the slut's past.

"Why had he waited so long? But he would avenge himself; he also owed the truth to that imbecile, and the truth for a woman like the comtesse—what a charge sheet! Demonic and epileptic, he continued to ruin and break pens on the paper, prey to a veritable crisis.

"The princesse had come running at the noise. Filsen, Gourkau and I tried to calm the prince down. Singularly energetic that day, the princesse waited impassively for the first fit of fury to calm down; then in a blank voice, she represented to her son the futility of that letter. Signed with his name, it had no value. Lord Feredith would only see it as a base vengeance, and the ignominy of his revelations would turn to his own confusion and Scholobelska's triumph.

"'You'd be playing her game,' the princesse concluded. 'Your accusations will absolve her; she must even desire that letter. Suppose that Lord Feredith learns something, sooner or later; informed first by you, Lord Feredith will only see more calumnies, and it's you that will have put them out of account. Your resentment would only serve your enemy. Think. You're ill, in the impossibility of fighting. Lord and Lady Feredith would shrug their shoulders, but believe that she would applaud herself for it.'

"'I'll write anonymously, then,' said the prince, struck by his mother's argument.

"'Anonymously, like a domestic's denunciation! A Noronsoff does not write anonymous letters. That's a whore's vengeance.'

"'A whore! But I have the soul of a whore!' the wretch clamored, 'as you know very well, Mother.'

"'Yes, I know; but while I'm alive the world will not know it. I've been able to close my eyes to deviations of conduct, but I will not tolerate villainy.' The princesse emphasized her words, stiffened that day by a singular energy. 'You won't be suspected, as long as I'm here, of an anonymous letter. I'd rather supervise your correspondence. First of all, to whom would you dictate it? You can't write, and it isn't these messieurs, or me . . .'

"The prince listened, dazed, choked and confounded by that unexpected resistance; the mother and the son measured one another with their gaze: two champions in the arena.

"'A whore! The soul of a whore!' he contrived, finally. 'But then, it was necessary to stifle me in the cradle, to suppress at my birth that old prostituted soul of the princesses of the race before it became . . .'

"'A monster!'

"'Yes, a monster, since I assume within me all the instincts of two lines of crime, that of the Noronsoffs and yours! I'm a victim, a result of evolution. Is that my fault? If you were afraid of the future, it was necessary to dare to do for me what my father and my uncle did for Princesse Hélène. But your egotism feared the dolor of losing me. You loved yourself too much in your son to risk the chagrin of a necessary execution. You claim to love me. Get away! You've only ever loved yourself, and it's you that you have spared in me. What suffering you could have avoided if you had killed me, Princesse!'

"'Perhaps your father would have done it if he had lived. I had the misfortune to lose him young. In my family we have a respect for males. Among us, mothers don't kill their children.'

"'They rot them.'

"'Sacha!'

"And that was the ordinary tone of arguments between the mother and the son.

DOCTOR YTROFF

"THOSE perpetual recriminations of atavism, those ancestors continually evoked and thrown at the head of the mother by the son and the head of the son by the mother had ended up populating the villa with phantoms; it was in an atmosphere of nightmare that Sacha's agony was now dragging on. Anguished by terror of the unknown, the wretch no longer wanted to die. After so many threats of suicide, he clung on desperately to life, begging us to prolong his suffering and insulting us by turns; his cowardice before death was such that it became grandiose within him. It was the terror of an Augustus tracked in the latrines, the latrines to which his disrupted entrails nailed him almost night and day.

"There were, alternately, exhaustion and lugubrious silence, and demonic crises and the howls of a wild beast; the thirst for life burned so intensely in that ruined being that it made him roar with rage at death. Only his prostrations saved him. It was during those periods of lethargy that he repaired a little of the strength expended in his fits of fury. The dwelling became tragic.

"The princesse, invaded in her turn by the ambient terror, moved about there with hallucinated eyes and the gait of a somnambulist; a wind of madness—Wladimir's endemic madness—also possessed her. Among all those ghosts of criminal ancestries, the old Italian superstitions of the Florentine had also awakened. She now had an obsession for macabre adventures and tales of bewitchment: old Tuscan legends, peasant traditions of Petty

Russia, an entire ferment of equivocal and terrible tales had ended up persuading the poor woman that she too was ensorcelled. It was not the bohemian's malediction that she was expiating in her son but the vengeance of a dismissed rival.

"It was the resentment of a cousin of her husband, who had cast a spell on her wedding night: the bones of a newborn child had been deposited under the nuptial bed, she was certain of it, and it was the deleterious influence of the little corpse that had weighed upon Wladimir's conception. The seed had been corrupted within her by the errant larva associated with those bones, and Wladimir's vampirism, his frightful instincts of cruelty and lust, were explained by the horrible charm: the soul of a corpse was within him. Conceived outside of life, he was born outside of nature. And it was necessary for Filsen and me to listen to those odious confidences, from the pale lips of a bewildered old woman, while Sacha was gasping painfully in his sleep in the next room.

"Oh, the vigils of that final month of November in the apartments of Mont Boron! There were minutes when I sensed myself foundering in the unknown. One does not keep close company with hysteria and terror with impunity. That Russian disrupted everything around him, and between the demoniac son and the possessed mother, we would have gone mad if—necessarily, with that man of all surprises and all fantasies—the operetta element had not suddenly reappeared.

"The comical reentered the villa with a character of *opera bouffe*, Doctor Ytroff, a Hungarian physician, some said, Rumanian according to others, whom the caprice of Princesse Alexianeff, an aged Russian afflicted by millions and dropsy, had imposed on the snobbery of the winter visitors the previous season. The Russian colony was infatuated with the handsome Doctor Gregory; the women, especially, celebrated his merits. A triumphant moustache curled like those of an Italian tenor and insistent dark eyes were not unconnected with his charm. That accomplished ruffian had conquered absolutely the sixty-five springs of Princesse Nadeje Alexianeff.

"Dr. Ytroff was more than a physician; he was a mage. He had visited India and the Extreme Orient, had lived in the intimacy of Brahmins and fakirs, had penetrated the mysteries of forests and temples. He had brought back marvelous secrets therefrom; the invisible world was at his orders. He consulted tables on the condition of his patients and employed in his cures the collaboration of spirits; in ten sessions he had removed Alexianeff's swelling without punctures. The other physicians had abandoned her. To achieve that miracle, twenty passes had been sufficient. Evil tongues said of those passes that they were a little more than magnetic, and that it was perhaps as well that the princesse was sixty-five; thirty years younger and the swelling would have increased. The handsome doctor's treatments only succeeded on diminished organisms; he was the physician of all declines. Was it in that capacity that Sacha summoned him?

"The previous winter, he had not had sufficient jokes with which to ridicule the occultism of the handsome Hungarian and his association of a master embalmer with that old royal mummy. Before running aground in Nice, where all his flaws had naturally flourished, Gregory Ytroff, ex-physician of the Peninsular Company established in Marseille, had had a few unfortunate incidents in the port quarter. Implicated in three affairs of abortion for having cured young women in embarrassment by the application of precious stones, sacred gems brought back from India, he had been obliged to quit his cabinet in the Rue Colbert in a hurry and come to install himself in Cannes.

"His qualities as a thaumaturge had had scant success in spite of the presence beside him of a young sister, Mademoiselle Alexandra Ytroff, a Hungarian poetess of puerile and lisping diction familiar in young Revues for adroit pastiches of the *Chansons de Bilitis*.

"Strong in their exoticism, the brother and sister had laid siege to the English colony. The handsome Gregory soothed old ladies with rare gems and suspect fetishes in the form of phalluses. Collected in the abolished sanctuaries of Singapore and Benares, the rarest were encrusted with turquoises and cured spasms, cardiac pains and all nervous troubles; they were priceless talismans. Ytroff did not sell them, but he ceded them temporarily to people, always very rich; the spirits forbade him to let go of them, they would have lost all their virtue in becoming objects of commerce; once cured, the patient returned them to the doctor.

"Young Alexandra, sheathed in straight dresses in extinct hues, reminiscent of Dante Gabriel Rossetti's Damsel Elect[1] descended from her frame, delighted the five o'clocks of the great hotels with the science of her diction and the eurythmia of her attitudes. In a stammering voice flexed by strange caresses, opening her large candid eyes wide, she recited lesbian verses and sapphic idylls to which the attentive ladies listened without flinching, and nothing equaled the innocence offered by her smile. They were Hindu poems brought back by Gregory at the same time as his precious amulets. Americans and, among them, Muses mad about football, lawn tennis and automobile records, were infatuated with Mademoiselle Ytroff; the young poetess was always escorted by sportswomen strapped up in suits and shod in sturdy boots; her slenderness was further refined in the midst of the cloth caps and tailored jackets of those beautiful amazons. Old gentlemen were also taken with the puerile diction and pliant grace of the blonde Alexandra.

"The couple had reigned for an entire winter over Piccadilly and Fifth Avenue in displacement to Cannes; but the arrival of a globetrotter, a former officer in the English army returned from Cairo, had compromised the credit of the association. That damned Lord Berett had taken it into his head to recognize the Hungarian doctor's talismans as vulgar ex-votos from the altar of Priapus, coarse terra cotta facsimiles, whose sale encumbered the quays of Aden and Alexandria; Dr. Ytroff's rare fetishes were worth four shillings; that was the price at which the fellahs and caulkers of Egypt sold them to passengers on steamers calling in at ports. As for the healing stones, they were simple sapphires from Ceylon, of which the rarest, the white and the yellow, were worth four or five pounds in that country.

---

1 Presumably the painting better known as *The Damsel of the Sanct Grael.*

"The revelation, piquant as it was, nevertheless afflicted the credit of the couple. British arrogance was mortified; the more pragmatic Americans would have pardoned the hoax if it had been less vulgar. From one day to the next the doctor's prescriptions were greeted with smiles. The clan of sportswomen fervent for Alexandra still held firm, the brother and sister might perhaps have resisted but a calumny completed their ruination. Malevolent gossips remarked that the blonde mademoiselle bore no resemblance to her brother and that their relationship, like the much vaunted magic stones and talismans, might perhaps be questionable. There were eloquent silences. Dr. Ytroff magnetized his sister; she was a marvelous somnambulist in his hands, she struck inspired poses in her sleep. The names of Donato and Lucile were pronounced;[1] Cagliostro was recalled, and the term 'low adventurer' was risked. The suspect couple took refuge in Nice; the reputation that preceded them there did them no harm. Nice is curious in regard to scandal and avid for novelties; half the population lives at the expense of the other, and audacity goes a long way there.

"In every country in the world, that is called 'living at the expense of the princess,' and the princess for the Ytroffs turned out to be Nadeje Alexanieff; she was smitten with the brother and the sister, liking the care of the one and the poetry of the other; Gregory magnetized her, Alexandra chanted verses to her in her soft and lisping voice. The couple summarized all the caresses; Alexianeff attached them to her person; the sister became her reader, the brother her physician. Alexianeff was very rich and imposed her favorites on the Russian colony. Their favor had lasted a year; she had taken them away all summer and a part of the autumn to Switzerland and the Italian lakes, and had only just returned with them to Nice. That was the couple that came to descend upon Sacha's agony.

---

1 The best-known account of the experiments of the Parisian magnetizer Donato with his medium Lucile in the 1870s is a second-hand one by Helena Blavatsky, the original report having been compiled by the Russian diplomat Alexander Aksakof.

THE COLLAPSE

"NORONSOFF was not unaware of any of the Ytroffs' past. The previous winter he had laughed loudly at the intimacy of Alexianeff with the brother and the sister; now he wanted that at Mont Boron.

"A caprice of a dying man, to which it was necessary for us to subscribe! Filsen and I did not even withdraw before the newcomers. The prince was doomed. Whatever the Hungarian attempted, he could not save the patient. He might perhaps palliate his suffering, but he could only abridge a condemned life, and with the long patience learned at Sacha's bedside, we resigned ourselves to witnessing the experiments of the new favorite.

"Wladimir would have belied his own imaginative and Asiatic nature if, from the moment that he welcomed Ytroff, he had not been immediately impassioned by the staginess of the prestidigitation of the master adventurer. Dr. Gregory's charlatanism had excited his contempt throughout the previous winter; the same charlatanism now enchanted him. That was not unusual; with an individual as illogical as Sacha, inconsequence was the norm of all events.

"We had persuaded Princesse Benedetta not to say anything and to let things take their course. Wladimir was dying; let him at least die in accordance with his last desire.

"The Ytroffs exploited the Russian at high prices. It was not so much the three louis fee for visits as the exorbitant cost of necklaces, bracelets and magic belts that the doctor brought to the invalid. The Hungarian demanded that the prince kept them on day and night. Dr. Ytroff knew that the prince was far too knowledgeable about precious stones to risk the Ceylon sapphires and other gems in his medical kit on him. The amulets imposed on the patient were metal plaques. They were, expertly alternated, squares and diamonds of red copper, tin, silver, nickel and aluminum, all engraved with cabalistic signs to which the doctor attached occult virtues. The credulity of invalids sometimes rendered them efficacious. The prince had to wear them directly against his skin and change them three times a day. There were some for digestion, some for sleep and others, finally, in the form of half-moons, to facilitate natural functions, rather sluggish in Wladimir.

"Those chinoiseries delighted the invalid. They occupied his time, fragmented his days, distracted his ennui. As all those metal plaques inconvenienced Wladimir somewhat, Dr. Ytroff had decided to let him wear them over very fine tunics of transparent sink gauze, byssus thread tunics brought back by him, naturally, from the depths of India and which he ceded, because it was the prince, for relatively modest sums. A power was in them, and that was where the genius of the thaumaturge burst forth. Those miraculous tunics, before being put on, had to be incanted by a virgin, and it was Mademoiselle Ytroff who would fulfill that employment. She did not fulfill it for nothing.

"Three times a week we had the spectacle of Mademoiselle Alexandra Ytroff incanting the tunics of Wladimir's underwear. Those mummeries took place in the invalid's bedroom at nightfall. A savant illumination of green candles—they had to be green—placed three by three on the furniture, accumulated rather bizarre shadows in the corners. Sheathed in a long robe of green silk—the color of nature—the virgin stood at the foot of the bed, the tunics being laid out thereon. Odiferous powders and sachets of aromatic herbs burned in three braziers, the entire room was decked with woven vapors; blue smoke condensed there and, in that impressive stage setting, young Alexandra, slowly raising her bare arms, intoned the verses of the incantation in a dreamy voice. They were quatrains of a vague pantheism, of this ilk:

I bear within me the foamy drama of the sea!
I sense a cliff there where, in the bitter wind
Of the sea, the tall red grass of meadows
Bristles and writhes like the fur of a furious beast.

"Then she was a forest and tresses of trees, a tranquil lake in the depths of a valley, and her charming gaze mirrored nenuphars!

"Wladimir listened to that nonsense with an evident joy; he took a passionate interest in all that jiggery-pokery. Its Byzantism responded to all his puerile and barbaric instincts, and nothing was more comical than his elongated and fervent expression, under all the scrap metal with which the brother had decked him out, while the sister officiated.

"He listened, with his arms crossed over his breast, in a hieratic pose.

"Armed with a magic sword, Ytroff fenced in the shadow and, with the gestures of a bricklayer plying a trowel, he pursued the larvae hiding in the dark corners; the scene was exceedingly comical. The suggestion of it was such that at every thrust by the Hungarian, Wladimir started in his bed, with a sigh of satisfaction, as if delivered from a pain. Those exorcisms and incantations cost an average of fifteen louis a session; they made the princesse indignant; she had withdrawn, outraged, on the first evening. Wladimir had fallen back into infancy; his credulity was the fable of the city; all of Nice was entertained by the cure undertaken by Dr. Ytroff.

"To what extent did Sacha add faith to the empiric's phantasmagorias? There resides the enigma. In the absence of the Mage he sometimes took off his bracelets and necklaces and put them on his monkey and his dog. Then he laughed to see those poor animals struggling, impeded by his physician's jewelry. He was, however, terrified by the performance, gripped involuntarily by the mysterious charm of the ceremonial and the rites. Those sessions amused him, and when he was amused, Sacha suffered less.

"The powders and potions with which the Hungarian stuffed him were less inoffensive. With a perfect ignorance or a culpable insouciance, Ytroff crammed that damaged arthritic with arsenic, coca and cola; he even put alcohol into it. How would the prince's enteritis and various accidents cope with that regime of stimulants that would have killed a horse? That was the least of the Hungarian's concerns. He was caring for the prince, and that won him an enormous renown; he had attained his goal.

"The strangest thing is that that criminal treatment brought about an apparent improvement. The prince recovered strength. Stiffened and electrified by all those stimulants, his painful parts rendered insensible by stupefying agents, he had quit his bed and was able to resume his excursions by carriage. The entire city was amazed; in Alexianeff's entourage, people were proclaiming a miracle; even Princesse Noronsoff had to yield to the evidence. Wladimir was resuscitated. It was Ytroff's triumph.

"To tell the truth, the handsome Hungarian had not so much resuscitated a dead man as galvanized a cadaver; for it was a true cadaver, varnished, powdered and painted, that the villa's closed landau carried through the streets.

"Oh, the lamentable and sinister human debris that appeared at the windows, the driveways of the château or on the edge of the sea, between the Pont Magnan and the Jetée-Promenade. The prince was paraded at a trot, between one and three o'clock, in sunlit places, for preference on the Quai de Midi, whose beach was particularly sheltered.

"In the course of one of those excursions, in front of the terraces of Ponchettes, the invalid spotted a fellow in a group of fishermen busy around the net of a boat whose sturdy silhouette reminded him of that of Marius. Wladimir called a halt; the man was summoned to the carriage door. He was a Neapolitan from old Nice. He did, indeed, have the Provençal pedlar's sea-green eyes shaded by long black lashes, and the expressive mobility of the features typical of his race.

"There was an immediate senile caprice on the part of the invalid. Wladimir wanted to attach the man to his presence immediately; his resemblance awoke so many memories in him.

"The Neapolitan, bare-legged, with his trousers rolled up high on his brown thighs, listened without understanding and smiled with all his teeth; displayed gold convinced him, and he climbed up on the seat beside the coachman. The landau pulled away in the midst of the gibes of the other fishermen; Noronsoff had been recognized.

"That same evening, Tito Biffi put on the red leather boots and the white silk blouse of the princely livery. But Biffi had a girl-friend, a Neapolitan like him, the daughter of fisher folk; she was jealous and resolute, and that evening, when she learned of the abduction of her boy-friend, she could not contain her fury. She went straight up to the villa, negotiated at the gate for a long time without succeeding in having it opened, and was obliged to return to her lodgings alone—but her decision was made.

"The next morning she introduced herself into the kitchens on the pretext of having fish to sell, encountered Tito, heaped him with reproaches, soothed him with caresses and, in brief, reclaimed her man, who slipped away the same day, before noon.

"The prince learned of his flight at three o'clock. There was an explosion of anger such as we had rarely seen. In the blink of an eye, the entire villa was on foot. Gourkau, Filsen and the Hungarian himself were dispatched in search of the fugitive. Wladimir was foaming with rage; he wanted his Tito, dead or alive; he demanded him with the howls of a she-wolf. He wanted to make a complaint to the police; the scoundrel had robbed him, the Neapolitan had received an advance of two hundred francs. It was delirium. He welcomed Mademoiselle Ytroff with a volley of insults when she arrived for her esoteric session, and only calmed down when brutalized by opium and bromide, mastered by the emphatic gaze of the Hungarian.

"The next day, however, in spite of all remonstrations, he gave the order to harness the carriage, had himself corseted, dressed and made up, and went down to the port. He searched the quays without encountering the Italian; interrogated boatmen assured him that he would certainly find him at the Fish Market, and Noronsoff raced there.

"He got down at Ponchettes, strode feverishly through the anemones and mimosas of the flower market, between the piles of tomatoes, lettuces and artichokes of the greengrocers. Gourkau had difficulty keeping up with him, and, searching ardently, Noronsoff finally discovered the fisherman hiding ineptly behind a beautiful girl standing at one of the marble tables of the Fish Market.

"It was the first time Wladimir had risked himself in such a milieu. He did not know who he was dealing with; he only saw his Tito. He went straight toward him and said to him in a reproachful tone: 'Why did you leave yesterday? Aren't you content with me, wasn't the payment sufficiently generous?'

"A mighty slap was his response, a weighty and sticky slap that stunned the prince and flattened him, folded in two like a puppet, in the midst of the whitings, crayfish, skates and calamari of the stall. The fish-merchant, taking hold of a sole by the tail, had slapped him with it. The macabre and made-up doll that was Wladimir collapsed instantly, the Russian laid out full length on the paving-stones among the scales and guts, saluted with the jeers of the entire market.

"The Fish Market acclaimed Zulietta; the beautiful girl had defended her man.

"Gourkau and the two muzjiks who came running only had time to carry the unconscious Sacha to the landau; he returned to the villa without having regained consciousness. He was only reanimated in the evening to enter into death throes, vomiting the most abominable insults. This time, it was a serious apoplexy, one from which one does not recover.

"The death throes of Prince Noronsoff were an outflow of filth from an emptying sewer, the jets of pus and sanies of an old, deep-seated and purulent hatred, which finally burst like an abscess. He poured invective on his mother, the priest, Gourkau and all of us. He summoned ruination and conflagration upon the city that had mocked him, conflagration and ruination with the fire of Heaven and that of the Barbarians on the Old Europe that had corrupted him; and that furious agony had something grandiose about it.

"Hallucinated, convulsed by spasms and terror, he summoned the Asiatics and their future invasion, their vengeful whirlwind, upon the decomposition of the Old World. He condemned Nice, Florence and London to death; it was Paris, Vienna and Saint Petersburg that had rendered him gangrenous and purulent; his barbaric instincts, finally reawakened, invited the Barbarians to the chastisement. He demanded Attila's Huns and Genghis Khan's Tartars, all the hordes of the yellow races, to kill, plunder, steal and massacre the Niçois, the physicians, and Gourkau, and himself, and his mother.

"'Yes, let them come. Will they finally come? Let them burn everything here, let them pillage this villa, let them empty my jewel-cases, let them crush my pearls, let hem crucify Gourkau, let them torture Filsen, let them impale Ytroff and let them rape my mother!'

"And with a supreme hiccup, he finally spat out the old soul of Byzantium that had lingered within him for too long.

"Thus the prophecy of la Schoboleska was accomplished; Prince Wladimir died because of a fisherman, slapped by a sole in the hand of a fishwife, and, on three separate occasions, the Pole had said to Wladimir: 'Beware of everything that comes from the sea.'"

At that point, Monsieur Rabastens fell silent.

Night had fallen, and drowned the pathways of the garden with blue shadows. How many hours had we been there? At our feet, the terraces were staged, all white in the light of the moon, which had just risen over Mont Chauve and the escarpments of the Var; at the height of Antibes the Mediterranean was shining as if clad in a silver coat of mail, and in the nocturnal landscape magnified by silence there was the mild and lubricant flow of I know not what luminous poison.

Down below, one divined the masts of the port, the port where Noronsoff had so often aimed his binoculars at Lord Feredith's yacht. In that park, the witness to so much intrigue, anger, despair and folly, there was the silence of an Oriental cemetery, overwhelmed by perfumes and charged with muted fermentations of life. Strange floral vigils populated it, roses shedding their petals one by one. The marble of our bench was strewn with them, as were our shoulders and the ground. It was a kind of slow death that was descending upon us, leaves detaching themselves, creaking on the branches; saps palpitated, saps and stems. One might have thought that invisible hands were parting the foliage and stems of the plants.

We rose to our feet without saying a word. The concierge had locked the gate; we had to get him to open it, and we only recovered our assurance once we were out of those pathways full of impalpable frictions.

Printed in the USA
CPSIA information can be obtained
at www.ICGtesting.com
LVHW091324150923
758079LV00005B/1079